THE BLOODY CHORUS

JOHN MARCO

ISBN: 979-8-9873676-0-5

Cover art by Felix Ortiz

Cover design by STK Kreations

This book is dedicated with deep gratitude to the many loyal readers who waited for it for so long. Thank you, all.

TABLE OF CONTENTS

1. BLOOD AND ASHES   1

2. THE SUMMONING   12

3. BLACK LIGHT   27

4. A ROOMFUL OF LANTERNS   36

5. A GIFT OF KNIVES   47

6. CALLING THE MOONLIGHT   62

7. THE HOLY SERPENT   71

8. THE TALE OF THE REVEN   76

9. CLOSE QUARTERS   82

10. THE MERCY OF TAAN   89

11. ORKORLIS   96

12. THE WHITE   104

13. SANCTUARY   111

14. CHANSOOR MALO'N   120

15. GOLGIN   131

16. FATHER OF BEES   137

17. THE SQUARE   142

18. MOAJE   147

19. BORN TO KILL   159

20. DEAD WATER   166

21. MENDING   171

22. THE FEAST OF AMA'AGA 177

23. SLAVE HILL 185

24. DOUBTS 196

25. THE OLD MAGICS 203

26. THE SHADOW BOYS 212

27. PRISONER 219

28. PLAYING WITH FOOD 223

29. ASSASSINS 230

30. THE TEMPLE OF TYRANTS 242

31. THE VOICE 248

32. THE ROAD TO AGON 255

33. SESSIONS 264

34. REVELATIONS 276

35. AMONG THE GODS 284

36. CARCAZEN 293

37. HOWL 299

38. ADRIFT 302

39. THE MOUNTAIN 308

40. ASANA 316

41. THE HAMMER AND THE KNIFE 326

42. HOR'RORON'S BEAST 331

43. PORCELAIN 339

44. ALIVE 344

45. MIDNIGHT MEETING 348

46. THE LAUGHING GOD 356

47. ESCAPE FROM AGON 360

48. LINBETH 376

49. THE VIRTUOUS TIGER 381

50. NAGANA AND VAUS   386

51. OF THE BLOOD   391

52. INTO THE FIRE   398

53. THE RETURN   406

54. ONE MORE MISSION   415

55. RECKONING   417

56. SCARS   423

57. BROTHERS   424

58. DRIFTING   430

59. LEVIATHAN   432

60. ON THE BEACH   439

61. THE ORDINARY DAY   444

Chapter One

BLOOD AND ASHES

The sea raged for days after the old Tain's death.

No one told the goddess of his passing. He was part of the sacred waters, as she was, and just as she could feel the births and deaths of the dragon-whales, so too had she sensed his murder. Her mourning churned the seas of Nesenor, piling broken shells high on the shores and up-rooting kelp from the crystalline depths. The goddess held no dominion over the air, and so the heavens remained still while the seas boiled. Yet beneath the serene sky, in the waters that surrounded her beloved islands, the goddess Clionet made known her misery.

Haru barely noticed the goddess' rage. Like Clionet, he grieved too. He spoke no prayers to the goddess, made no offerings of camellia blooms or egret feathers like the mariners and Venerants had. His father's death had been so sudden, so violent, that he could scarcely recall the last few days at all. He remembered the flash and the blood and the way his father disappeared in fire. He remembered Liadin's comforting arms. But his ascension to the throne was a blur, a hurried ceremony in the aftermath of tragedy. Today, even surrounded by thousands, Haru felt friendless and alone.

Within his hands rested a jeweled and golden chest, barely larger than a loaf of bread. Sixteen-year-old Haru stared at it blankly, trying to comprehend the strangeness of its contents. The sea slumbered now. Clionet at last was calm, waiting for Haru out beyond the shore. Beneath his feet crunched the sugar white sands of Dragon's

Tongue, a spit of land on the windward side of Nesenor, the very place where the first Cryori had met the goddess a thousand years before. Haru could trace his bloodline back to Hiaran directly. And that was the only reason—that random act of fate—why he was standing at the shore with the golden box.

A breeze stirred Haru's cerulean hair. Half a dozen beast-ships patrolled in the distance, protecting the islanders gathered on shore. Blue were the people, like the ocean they worshipped, with shining eyes and lips that matched their sea-toned skin. Some had come with shinogin, the pear-shaped Cryori lute, playing mournful dirges while children sang and danced in bright dresses. A trio of barefoot boys waded into the water until their mothers angrily called them back. Haru remained detached in the commotion, vacant and broken. Only the golden box held his interest. It seemed so small, far too small to hold the remnants of such an imposing man. There had been so little left of his father after the burning...

Just ashes, thought Haru darkly. Blood and ashes.

To Haru's right stood Shadur, nervously flexing his crystal hand. To his left waited the feline Elsifor. Of the Chorus, only the two of them were in attendance for the ceremony. No one had expected the introverted Valivan to come—the presence of so many people would have shattered his fragile mind—but Haru had hoped Siva would show. She hadn't even acknowledged his message.

Haru shrugged off his disappointment. He didn't really need Siva—two of the Chorus was enough to protect him. Behind him stood Liadin and his fellow Venerants, arrow-straight in their silvery robes. Their sukatai—the curved spears of their holy order—rose up upon their backs. Liadin stood ahead of the rest, closer than either Shadur or Elsifor, near enough to whisper encouragement into young Haru's ear.

"Look at them," urged Liadin. "Do not look down."

Haru straightened at the advice, meeting the gazes of the gathered Cryori, an ocean of azure faces with sapphire eyes, no two significantly different. They had come from across Nesenor, men and women and shoeless children, old mariners, pretty young girls, decedents of the royal blood and nameless fisher-folk, all to mourn their dead Tain and to glimpse his son, their new ruler.

They had come, too, for the spectacle of Clionet.

At the edge of the shore an ornate raft swayed with the tide, beached but eager for the sea. Festooned with flowers and ribbons and hand-written notes, the raft would take Tain Sh'an's remains to the goddess.

First though, words were required. Haru cleared his throat, and the throng fell quiet. The shinogin players silenced their instruments. Attention gripped the crowd. The sharp exhalation of a dragon-whale pierced the waves with a cone of steam and fire. Clionet herself had called the creatures from their watery caves near Jinja. Except for her, only the Tains of Nesenor could summon the beasts. Today the dragon-whales were Clionet's heralds, and though their numbers had dwindled over the centuries, they were still an astonishing sight.

In the days when Nesenor dominated the waves, the *shenen-ra*—the dragon-whales—numbered in the hundreds. Together with the beast-ships they were the terrors of the continent, spreading Cryori terror to the barbarous east to bring back riches and slaves. Some recalled those days as glorious and lamented their loss. Others thought the past well buried. Haru had little opinion about these things. Until just a few days ago, he thought only about girls and sailing.

"Speak now," said Liadin. The Arch-Disciple touched his shoulder. "And remember who your father was."

Haru raised the golden chest high above his head. There hadn't been time to fully rehearse the charm, so he'd memorized just enough of it to please the goddess, spending hours the night before with Liadin as the old priest taught him the ancient phrases. At first he'd stumbled badly, the words impossible to recite. But gradually he improved, until at last Liadin declared him ready. Haru took one breath...then spoke the charm.

"Eyi-hrawl, U'uulia Tat yuonn. Eyi-hrawel, Clionet, Gaj-Kwyoan Midia!"

They were simple words really, difficult to speak but clear in meaning. And all the gathered Cryori, even the youngest ones, understood their significance.

To water return us, bound by blood. To water return us, Clionet, immortal mother.

"Louder," urged Liadin. "You are Tain now. Demand that she come!"

Haru had never called the sea goddess before. Like most Cryori, he had never even seen her. But his father had called her upon the death of his own father, and so it had been since Hiaran, Haru's long-dead ancestor. Liadin had summoned her too, because he was Arch-Disciple and knew the charm to bring her forth. Yet it was a rare thing indeed to summon Clionet, and it seemed to Haru that all of Nesenor had come to witness it. So he did as Liadin urged, repeating the words with authority, imagining how his dead father would speak them, loud enough so the men on the distant beast-ships might hear.

"Clionet! Gaj-Midia! I am Haru, Tain of Nesenor, son of Sh'an! U'uulia Sh'an! Come, Blessed Clionet! U'uulia! Take him!"

The thousands gathered on Dragon's Tongue stared seaward. Except for the ripple of the submerged shenenra, the waves remained still. Haru froze, his face hot with embarrassment. Had he mangled the charm? Surely Clionet was out there—she had summoned the dragon-whales. He turned toward the clerics behind him, all of whom wore the same troubled expression.

Except for Liadin.

Ever confident, Haru's old tutor allowed a tiny smile to crack his bearded face. "Capricious," he jested.

"She won't come," said Haru. "What should I do?"

"Seduce her," replied Liadin. "Pretend she is one of your giggling girls."

"What?"

"Clionet is full of vices," said Liadin. "You think because she is immortal, she is so different from the rest of us? Make her come to you the way you get the girls to kiss you, Haru. You are new to her. Make her trust you."

Haru's panic grew. He leaned closer and whispered, "Liadin, I don't know how. Everyone's watching..."

Liadin radiated calm. "You are her new lover, Haru. Her chosen. She will obey you because that's her promise. I've taught you the words; the rest is up to you."

None of it made sense to Haru. None of it was how it was supposed to be. He felt stupid with all of Nesenor watching, wondering why their new Tain couldn't do what all other Tains before him had managed. He looked helplessly at Liadin, then at Shadur and Elsifor, his bodyguards. They too had patron gods, but their gods paid attention. Their gods didn't leave them looking like fools. Angered by Clionet's disregard, Haru broke away from the others and trudged down the beach with the golden chest. He reached the raft, refusing to place the chest upon it as planned. Instead, he splashed into the water beside it, wading in up to his knees.

"Clionet!" he shouted. "I know you can hear me! I know you're powerful and I know you're angry, but he was my father! What was he too you but another Tain? You weep for him? I weep for him! I..."

The emotion came over him so fast he couldn't quell it. Suddenly all the tears he had restrained for days came gushing down his cheeks to stain his satin blouse. Furious, he lifted the golden chest over his head, barely able to check himself from hurling it into the sea.

"This is all that's left of him!" he bellowed. "Not enough to fill a box! You want him? Take him!"

The sea stayed silent. Haru tossed the box onto the raft and cursed his tears, wishing a wave would come and drown him. Better that than face his people, he decided. Better than being the failure his father had predicted.

"Come. Don't come." Haru shrugged. "He's dead. And you can't bring him back, Clionet. No one can."

Up on the shore he caught a glimpse of Liadin. There was no reassurance on the old man's face. Only pity. The mystic Shadur stared at him. Elsifor shifted his cat-shaped eyes down the shore. A small boy at the front of the crowd asked his mother what was happening, but the woman didn't answer. Confusion had been all Haru could feel since his father's murder. Confusion overrode everything, even his grief. He began trudging up the beach, ready to offer apologies to Liadin and the other Venerants. They would be polite, he knew, but they would think his father was right—he was a silly boy who'd never be Tain.

He had taken only a few steps when he felt the water dragging him back. The receding tide grabbed his ankles, nearly pulling him off his feet, but when he looked back the water wasn't leaving the shore. It *was* moving though, suddenly alive, as though great invisible ropes were swishing beneath the surface.

Not ropes, thought Haru. *Arms.*

He peered into the water and watched as the liquid appendages drew themselves around the raft, churning up the sea and snatching the raft from the beach. A gasp went through the crowd, then a roar of approval. Instead of retreating Haru trudged deeper into the water, following the raft until the water was at his waist.

"Come out, goddess!" he cried, and swept an arm toward the thousands on-shore. "Let us see you!"

The water roiled and the little raft pitched as the magical current drew it further and further from shore. Then, when it was some hundred yards away, the sea opened beneath it like a maw, swallowing it up in a waterfall before snapping shut. It was simply gone. The waves becalmed. Haru waited, wondering if it was done. Before he could turn or utter a word, a purple tentacle whipped from the water, wrapping itself around him and snatching him off his feet. He fell face-first, smashing against the water and feeling himself being pulled across the surface. He heard the shocked cries of the crowd dying away behind him as water filled his ears.

Deeper and deeper he went, dragged into the inky cold. The powerful tentacle tightened around him but he didn't struggle. It was the sea goddess, he knew, and there was no way he could break her hold. He held his breath as the sunlight faded above him, growing ever paler as he fell down, down through the depths. Panic rose up in him; his insolence had doomed him. She would drown him, and that would be the end of his brief rule. He let out the last of his breath in a bitter curse.

Then, he saw her...

Clionet.

She was monstrous, beautiful, a luminous blue being as large as a dragon-whale and as insubstantial as a jellyfish, floating naked near the sea bottom. Beneath her torso squirmed a mass of tentacles, but above that she was woman-like, with breasts that bobbed in the current and strands of seaweed circling her arms. Her hair shined golden, her eyes a grassy green. She parted her lips, birthing an enormous bubble from her mouth that grew larger and larger until she herself was inside it. The tentacle ensnaring Haru drew him into the bubble. Suddenly he could breathe again. He gasped, staring into Clionet's enormous face a hundred feet beneath the surface.

"Goddess!" he sputtered. He dug his fingers into her tentacle, terrified but not wanting to show it. "Take me back up!"

Clionet drew him closer, then pursed her lips to gently blow on him the way a mother would a crying child. Haru jerked back, making her laugh. Even through his shock Haru noticed her unnatural beauty. She astonished him.

"Speak, please," he implored. "Say something!"

"Do you want me to release you?"

"Yes!"

"If I release you, you will surely die."

"Then take me back to the beach!"

Clionet smiled with white coral teeth. Her skin shifted colors as she spoke. "Your father knew how to speak to me," she said. "Why didn't he teach you? He was Tain long enough to instruct you."

Haru groped for an answer. "Liadin tutored me. My father..." He stopped himself. "My father's death was sudden."

"Yes," sighed Clionet. The tentacle around Haru slackened. For a moment he thought he might fall, right through the bubble to drown. "Your father was my beloved. He knew all the words. You know none. Your tutor has failed you."

"I spoke the words the way Liadin taught me," said Haru. "I spoke them properly, I'm sure of it."

Clionet nodded. "The words, yes," she granted. "But I knew your father's heart, while your heart is a mystery to me. Even your mother accepted the love I shared with Sh'an. But you—he kept you from me. His only child." She considered him curiously. "Why?"

Haru couldn't bear to tell her. "My father loved me," he answered. "Till the day he died, I never doubted it. Tell me what you want of me, goddess. Tell me and I will serve you as well as he did. No! Better. Tell me and I will prove it to you."

"Prove it to me? Or to someone else?" probed Clionet. Her lips glistened, wet with sea water. Her smile enchanted Haru. "I wonder why you are so eager to please. But oh, you are a beautiful boy." She lifted him closer, turning him a bit to see his profile. "Handsome. Do you have many lovers?"

Haru hated blushing but couldn't help himself. "I have...girls," he said, though in truth he'd only been with one the way Clionet meant, and she hadn't meant anything to him. He had always been a favorite of the girls in the castle, though. But those girls were people, and he had no idea what the goddess was hinting at. "You and my father...were you...lovers?"

"I have been the mistress of every Tain since Hiaran," purred Clionet. She reached out a giant, glowing finger and smoothed down his blue hair. "Each has pleased me in different ways. Now it is your turn...*Haru*."

There was heartbreak in the way she spoke his name. Haru looked into her sparkling eyes, wondering how to ease her pain. She retracted her blue finger and leaned back in the giant bubble. A school of minnows circled outside the magical chamber. Clionet's tentacles shifted to a luminous silver, mimicking them. Haru had a thousand questions for her, but asked only one.

"Do you know who killed my father?"

"If I knew that, I would lock the villain in the dungeons beneath Jinja Castle and feast on his marrow. But I do not know. Whoever took Sh'an away from us is far away from here. Somewhere in the Alliance."

"You're sure of that? How do you know?"

"The Alliance," repeated the goddess.

The Alliance was what the people of J'hora—the continent—called themselves now. For centuries they had warred against each other, leaving Nesenor the only real power in the world. The rise of the madman Reius and his new religion had changed all that.

"It was old magic that killed him," said Haru. "That's what Liadin says."

"Some in the Alliance remember the old gods," said Clionet. "Not many, but J'hora is too vast to find them. I would discover these plotters but away from these waters, I am weak."

"The Venerants think Reius himself gave the order to kill my father. I'll find them, whoever it is. Even if it is Reius."

"If you were older, you would know how ridiculous you sound," said Clionet. "You think too much of yourself. It is not just me and my family that are weak. Nesenor is weak. The dragon-whales, the beast-ships—they are too few to make war on J'hora. Your father was wise enough to know that. Are you?"

Haru bristled at the question. "Maybe I'm stronger than you think. You want a lover, you want a leader...but you think I'm weak? I won't just sit back and weep, Clionet. I was there, remember. If you'd seen how they killed him, maybe you'd be hungrier for revenge."

The long, silvery appendage tightened around Haru. "I do hunger, boy," she hissed. "I rage like a storm! Any J'horan ship that dares sail my waters will be brought down for the eels to consume. If I could reach that recreant Reius I would suck out his eyes and feed him his own bowels. But I *cannot* reach him. And neither can you."

"I *will* avenge my father, Clionet."

"How?" asked the goddess pointedly. "How will you avenge my beloved Sh'an?"

"I'll figure it out," argued Haru. "I've only been Tain a few days."

"Which means you don't know anything yet. Your head is empty, but your advisors will try to fill it. Men like Liadin who think they know everything. Men who are cowards and men who crave war. They will crawl over you like insects. They will want favors of you. They'll offer you fealty. But who will you listen to, Haru?"

"I trust Liadin," said Haru. "As my father did. As you always have."

"And what about the Chorus? Two of them have already abandoned you."

Haru writhed in her grasp. "Why are you taunting me? I have said I'll avenge my father and I will!"

"How?"

"I don't know yet!"

Haru slumped, unable to break her grip and knowing he couldn't survive without her anyway. "I need time." He looked up at her. "Will you give me time? Will you accept me as Tain? Come when I call you? Give me power over the dragon-whales?"

"How will those things help you make revenge?"

"Answer me, Goddess—Am I your Tain or not? No one else will follow me if you don't believe in me. My father never did. Will you?"

"I promised my loyalty to your family a thousand years ago," said Clionet. "Some Tains were wise, some evil, but all had my devotion because I had theirs."

"You have mine. I swear you do." Haru placed a kiss upon his palm and held it up for the goddess. She tilted forward to accept it, letting Haru touch her cheek.

"Then we are one," said Clionet softly.

"One," Haru agreed, "until the day you take my own remains." He looked curiously at her. "What will you do with my father now? I've always wondered. Some say you eat the bodies of the Tains. Is that true?"

Clionet made a disgusted face. "If you believe that, you truly are too young to be Tain. I return their bodies to the sea. Your family belongs in the sea. I found Hiaran in the sea, remember."

"I remember," nodded Haru. Every Cryori knew the story.

"Your bloodline is uncommon, Haru. Let others bury their dead in the dirt. Let them be worm food." Clionet smiled with satisfaction. "Every Tain since Hiaran has been returned to my sacred waters. The promise has never been broken."

"But where's the box?" asked Haru. He glanced around their magical bubble but saw nothing but himself and the goddess. "Did you already open it? We had to cremate him," he added. "You must have seen that."

Clionet had so many tentacles, and Haru had barely paid attention to them. Now one of the appendages emerged from beneath her, expertly gripping the golden box in its pink suckers. The sea goddess said nothing. She simply stared at the box—at the remains of the man she called beloved—for a very long moment. The look of grief returned to her face, and then one of sad acceptance. Then, she stretched out the tentacle, slipping it through the wall of air so that the box was once again in the water. Miraculously, the bubble didn't puncture. Haru watched as the tentacle squeezed open the chest, popping the lid. As water rushed inside, the dark plume of his father's ashes floated into the sea. The school of minnows darted through them. The current caught them like a breeze. Quickly, they vanished into the vastness.

Haru realized his father was gone forever.

"I'm ready, Clionet," he said. "Please... take me back now."

Chapter Two

THE SUMMONING

On his twentieth day of being Tain, Haru awoke in the bed his father had shared with his long-dead mother. Just as he had for the past three weeks, he breakfasted alone on a balcony overlooking Jinja province while his manservant Calix readied his clothes. The day was calm and, as always, a beast-ship patrolled the harbor just beyond the castle. Down at the bottom of the mountain, shop keepers opened their doors and rolled carts into the street. A mockingbird sang in the cherry blossom sprouting over the balcony. It was all beautifully ordinary, as if nothing had happened to shake Haru's world.

Jinja Castle had been constructed nearly two-hundred years ago, built into the side of a mountain overlooking a province of farmers. Farmland still encircled much of the mountain, though the province had changed dramatically over the decades, becoming the seat of Cryori power and the permanent home of Haru's family. Haru had spent his entire life in Jinja Castle. The keep, where his family and closest attendants resided, was a seven-storied structure of wood and white stone, with a view of the province only birds could match. Besides the Tain and his family—of which Haru had none now—the castle and its grounds were home to clerics, servants, accountants, cooks, fighting men, and, until very recently, a quartet of divine-ly-touched individuals known as the Chorus.

Haru sipped his tea, listened to the mockingbird, and tried to forget what had happened. The Chorus had failed to protect his father, and that failure had driven them apart. Some said they were never really a team anyway, not like the Choruses of old. Now, only Elsifor and Shadur remained in Jinja Castle. Valivan had returned to living with his mother. And Siva...

Haru hadn't seen Siva in weeks. She, most of all, perplexed him.

It was Siva who'd reinstituted the Chorus. Haru's father had never wanted bodyguards, and so declined to form a new Chorus when the old one finally died away. He was always like that—breaking traditions—and soon the world forgot the Chorus...

Until Siva came. She saw the rise of J'hora, convinced Sh'an he needed protection, and found three others just like herself, all of them kissed by the gods. But she had no teacher, and no way of knowing how to bring a team together. Haru missed his old friend, but he pitied her too. His father's death had hurt them all, but Siva it had crushed.

He chose a square of dried fish from his plate, staring at it with little appetite. Since becoming Tain, there'd been very little to occupy his time. Running a country should have been enormously difficult, but Liadin and the other Venerants had taken over all those mundane duties, giving Haru time to mourn and adjust to his new position. He was already excruciatingly bored.

But not today.

Today Haru had a plan, and as he ate his breakfast, he watched Calix in the other room as the old man chose a traveling jacket from the wardrobe. Next a pair of sandals appeared, the tatty ones Haru wore nearly every day. Calix set these down close to Haru's bed. He hadn't asked Haru where he was going but a tiny smile of anticipation revealed his curiosity. Haru beckoned his manservant to the balcony.

"No sandals today, Calix," he said while the old man refilled his cup from an alabaster teapot. "Boots."

Calix raised an eyebrow. "Will you be going far? Shall I pack some food for you?"

Haru set down his cup without taking another sip. "I need you to keep a secret for me," he said. "I'm going to Ama'aga's temple. But you can't tell anyone. Don't even say I'm gone, alright? I don't want anyone following me."

Calix scowled down at him. "Elsifor will follow you, you know that. And Liadin will come to get you for your lessons."

"I'm tired of lessons. I'm Tain now. I don't need to be tutored like a child."

"You are a child," corrected Calix mildly.

"I'm sixteen."

Calix hovered over him. He was a tall man, taller even than Liadin, with gnarled hands and grooves in his forehead that deepened when he frowned. And just like Liadin, he had been close to Haru since childhood. But Calix was a human, the product of slaves stolen from the continent back before he was born. He had lived his whole life in Nesenor, but no one could ever mistake him for Cryori. Or any of the other slaves who survived. Hundreds of them still called Nesenor their home, though hundreds had fled. Worse, many, many had been murdered in the massacre. Calix, born of castle slaves, had been spared that horror. Even after so many years, his brown eyes and pink skin still fascinated Haru.

"Sixteen is old for some, young for others," observed Calix. "You must *learn* to be Tain."

"I am trying. It's a lot."

"You won't be able to sneak away without Elsifor noticing." Calix placed a bit more food on Haru's plate. "He's got a nose for sniffing out secrets."

Haru leaned back and picked up a pickled radish with his fingers. Elsifor would indeed be a challenge, but he had another, too. "There is one thing," he said, lowering his voice. "My father's betrothal ring."

Calix pretended not to understand. "Ring?"

Haru looked earnest as he chewed up the radish. "I'm going to the temple to find it, but I'm not sure where he buried it. Do you know?"

Calix's expression went from amused to troubled. "Why do you want his ring?"

"I need it for something special. A promise I made," said Haru. "It's hard to explain. Please tell me, Calix—do you know where he hid it?"

"I do not," said Calix. "Nor would I tell you if I did."

Haru grimaced. "The temple isn't that big. If I look long enough, I'll figure it out."

"Ama'aga's temple is a holy place. You can't just go digging it up."

"Don't worry, I'll be careful. Promise. It doesn't matter any-way—no one's seen Ama'aga for years, not even the Venerants. Be-sides..." Haru pushed aside his plate and stood. "You're not Cryori. Ama'aga won't blame you."

Haru managed to leave the castle without confronting Elsifor. In his blue jacket and knee-high boots, he looked like any other young man leaving for a hunt, and no one paid any attention as he exited the main gate and sauntered out into the streets of town. Although he was Tain, most of the occupants of Jinja Castle still saw him merely as Sh'an's callow son. They bowed respectfully, offered po-lite greetings, and let him go his way without suspicion. By the time Haru reached the periphery of the village, even he was surprised by the ease of his escape. He brought no weapons with him, and needed no map to find his way. The temple of Ama'aga was on the other side of the forest, right at the ledge of the seashore, and he had been there many times.

The day had only just begun, and the road east through the province was nearly deserted. Haru passed a handful of travelers on his way, mostly farmers taking ox-drawn carts into town. Not surprisingly, the peasants barely noticed him. When he came to the forest, he glanced around to make sure no one was watching, then ducked onto the foot path. Instantly the forest swallowed him, the tree limbs knitting over his head. White-faced monkeys jumped between the branches, watching him with curious, yellow eyes. Behind him the road quickly fell away, and in the quiet of the forest the castle became a memory. He snapped off a tree branch, quickly pruned its leaves, and with the makeshift walking stick began his hike to the shore.

The path to Ama'aga's temple had grown narrow and weedy. Haru tried to remember when he'd last seen it. Like Clionet, Ama'aga had his worshipers, mostly mariners aboard the beast-ships. Ama'aga was their patron, but he'd abandoned the Cryori once Nesenor turned peaceful, and in the decades that followed his temple had fallen into ruin, like the little forest path. As one of Clionet's many offspring, Ama'aga was immortal, but Haru had no fear of him. It would take more than digging up his old temple to rouse the bitter god, he knew. Besides that, he was Clionet's favorite. He was sure he was in no danger from Ama'aga.

He began to whistle as he walked, then abruptly stopped himself. Who would worry about him? Not his father. Not anymore. Not his mother. Haru barely remembered her. Liadin? The old man was too busy to pay him much attention these days. Haru's good mood shriveled. He had no one to worry about him, he realized. For the first time in his life, he was truly alone.

"Like an orphan," he mused.

His pace slowed as the realization sunk in deeper. Being a Tain meant being lonely. He let the tip of his stick drag in the dirt as he walked, his thoughts glazing over. He had a promise to keep to Clionet, but the task seemed impossible without allies. He needed the Chorus.

Then, as if summoned by Haru's thoughts, Elsifor dropped out of the trees. Haru jumped back, his heart bursting with surprise. "Mother goddess!" he laughed. "You frightened me!"

Elsifor, who had landed on both hands and feet, remained in that feline pose. "You should have known I'd follow you, Haru."

"Sorry, Elsifor," said Haru sheepishly.

"I have but one duty in life, Tain Haru—to protect you. Others may have forgotten that duty, but not me."

"And I'm glad for that," said Haru.

"You're going to the temple. Why?"

"Really, I can't tell you."

"I'll ask Valivan. He'll tell me."

"Valivan doesn't know," said Haru, wishing Elsifor would simply step aside.

"But he could find out! Make it easy on both of us and tell me, alright? Your father wouldn't want you going out alone."

"I used to go out alone all the time before he died."

"Before he died, yes," Elsifor pointed out. "From now on that's how we'll be talking about things—there'll be things that happened before he died, and everything after. This is after. Sorry, Haru."

Elsifor sprung up to face Haru. He had the features of a Cryori, mostly, but enough hints of his patron goddess to make him oddly beautiful. His eyes were sapphire, like all Cryori, but his pupils were gray slivers. His ears were pointed, his hair thick, and his fingers terminated in knife-like talons.

Of all the Chorus, Elsifor was the only one gifted in the womb. And only the goddess Paiax could perform such a miracle. Just as Clionet was goddess of the sea, her daughter Paiax claimed the creatures of the land as her domain—that and the lust of men. It was Paiax who made the wombs of women fertile and gave men the desire to fill those wombs with seed. In Elsifor she had created the perfect vessel to fill with her power, a shape-shifting man-creature eager for her love. Each in the Chorus could do amazing things, but only Elsifor could transform himself, becoming even more like a leopard, the favorite guise of his patron goddess. And though Elsifor seemed mild, he became a killer when the bloodlust overcame him.

"I'll compromise with you, Haru," said Elsifor. "I'll go back into the trees if you prefer, but I won't let you travel alone."

Haru pushed past Elsifor and continued down the path. "Go home, Elsifor, please. I don't need you."

Elsifor didn't follow Haru, but rather let him keep on walking. "I'll find out the truth of what you're doing quicker than you think," he said. "You're my responsibility."

"My father was your responsibility," said Haru without turning around, "and look what happened to him."

The words slipped out before he could stop them. Haru stopped walking and turned slowly back to Elsifor, whose cat-like eyes narrowed in offense.

"That was wrong of me," said Haru. "I'm sorry."

Elsifor remained stiff. If he'd had a tail, it would have stuck straight up. "We're all angry, Haru. We all blame ourselves for what happened. Siva most of all."

"Have you seen her?" he asked.

Elsifor shook his head. "Not since Sh'an died. She's on Tojira, I've heard. I could find her if you want me to, but Tojira is Jaiakrin's island..."

"No," said Haru. "Leave her alone for now." He hesitated, wondering how badly his friendship with her had fractured. "She'll come back to us when she's ready. I hope. Now let me go, alright?"

Elsifor looked imploringly at Haru. "We have already lost a Tain to murder. I'm begging you—think what it would do to Nesenor to lose another. Keep your secrets if you like. I don't need to know why you're going to the temple. But you must be guarded. How do you know there isn't another assassin waiting for you when you get there?"

"Because no one knows where I'm going," Haru lied. "Just you. And if you'd let me be on my way..."

"No," said Elsifor sharply. "I'm going with you. For your father's sake if not for your own."

"This is for my father!" Haru tossed down his stick. "What? You think I'm going to the temple to meet a girl? To skip stones? If you honor my father the way you claim, then show me the same respect. Don't question everything I do. And don't follow me. I hate it. I hate being treated like a child."

Elsifor seemed genuinely surprised by his outburst. "My lord, it's the Chorus' duty to keep you safe."

"You've said that already. You keep saying it, Elsifor, all of you. You've finally decided to take your vows seriously. Great! But not today. Take a sniff—what does that nose of yours tell you? Be honest. Do you smell danger?"

With a tilt of his head, Elsifor turned his beastly senses on their surroundings. His ears twitched. He closed his eyes to listen. After a deep inhalation, he shrugged. "Nothing. But that doesn't mean there isn't danger."

"I'm safe, Elsifor," Haru insisted. "Now listen to me—do you honor my father's memory?"

Elsifor quickly nodded. "Of course I do."

"Am I your Tain?"

"You are my Tain," he said without flinching.

"Then please—just let me go. If it goes as planned, I'll tell you all about it, but I can't risk anything going wrong."

Elsifor frowned. "You can trust me. You should know that."

In truth Haru didn't know who to trust anymore. He replied, "You can't follow me to the temple. Not this time. For the sake of that trust—for the sake of my father—please...go back to the castle."

Frustration blazed in Elsifor's strange eyes. He flexed his clawed fingers and grit his fanged teeth and said, "Don't be too long. If you've not returned by suppertime, I'm coming back for you."

He bowed his head, letting his long hair fall around his face. Then, he sprang up into the trees, catching the branches with his claws and propelling himself into the canopy. A shower of leaves fell to the path as Elsifor bounded unseen across the high branches, disappearing amongst the birds and monkeys. Soon the noise of his departure died away, and Haru was alone again. He waited a moment, retrieved his walking stick, and started off again toward the temple of Ama'aga.

As a boy Haru had made the trip to the temple many times. He had no brothers or sisters, but the children of the castle's servants had sometimes been his friends, and together with Valivan they'd played war games in the forest and around the ruins of the temple, hiding from their chores and parents until the sun went down. Haru remembered those days, happily recalling all the times he had sat on the granite slabs of the temple overlooking the bay, watching the distant beast-ships and dreaming of the time he'd captain one himself. In those days the responsibilities of his bloodline barely entered his mind. The son of a Tain never served aboard ship, but Haru hadn't cared. He was a boy with dreams, and that was all that mattered.

Those friends were gone now, mostly, off to other lives and duties, and those that remained in the castle saw him differently these days. Some had even gone to sea, taking Haru's dream for their own. Even Valivan had changed, driven ever-deeper inside himself by his so-called "gift." Haru had nothing but attendants now, and though he loved Liadin and knew the cleric felt the same, Liadin was an old man who had forgotten what being young was like.

Haru swatted at a crab apple dangling from a branch above the path. "Young," he scoffed, laughing at himself. He'd been young for years. Too long, probably. And then suddenly he wasn't young anymore. Suddenly his father died and just like that he was a man.

As the path began sloping upward, Haru saw a bit of the temple above the trees. He trudged up the narrow path toward the cliff. The sounds of the ocean reached him through the foliage. A flock of blackbirds rested on the temple's broken roof. The muscles in his thighs burned as the incline steepened. Gradually the trees thinned, revealing the ruins of the holy place. The statue of Ama'aga, with his shattered spear and missing arm, stood guard at the edge of the cliff, a few good storms from tumbling into the sea. Ravaged pillars strained to keep the remnants of the roof aloft, strangled by vines. Haru grunted up the path, glad to see the ugly place, but as he neared the plateau a strange noise emerged. He paused at the sound.

Like singing, he thought, cocking a puzzled ear. The temple wasn't forbidden. Anyone who wished could visit it, but no one ever did. Haru eased toward the voice, unafraid and curious. *No, not singing*, he realized. *Chanting.*

He crossed the rock-strewn grounds and spied a figure near Ama'aga's statue, looking out over the water as he chanted. At once he recognized the long silver garb of a Venerant, but with the man's back turned toward him...

Haru froze, then laughed with relief.

"Liadin!"

The old man whirled around angrily, fixing on Haru before realizing who had called him. All the ire blew out of him instantly, replaced by simple surprise.

"Haru? Boy, what are you doing here?" The old cleric looked around. "Are you alone? You shouldn't be alone..."

Haru flung his walking stick over his shoulder and went toward Liadin. "I'm fine, Liadin, don't worry. What about you? I thought you were back home. What was that singing?"

"You heard that?" Liadin seemed embarrassed. He hesitated, then shrugged, then said, "That was the Charm of Summoning."

Haru looked at his tutor. "Oh," he said stupidly. The Charm of Summoning was for calling the dragon-whales. Only Tains ever spoke it. "Why?" asked Haru. He glanced out over the sea, remembering suddenly that this was a gathering place for the shenenra, who favored the warm waters of the bay. "Are you trying to call them?"

Liadin laughed. "Only a Tain can call them. I came here to practice. So I could teach you, Haru. The Charm is sacred. You must learn it."

"I know," Haru nodded. His father had taught him none of the holy Charms; he'd learned them all from Liadin. "But why come here to practice, so far from the castle?"

Liadin took the sukatai from the harness on his back. It had two blades, like the forked tongue of a serpent, and Liadin was never without it. But wearing the weapon made sitting difficult, and as Liadin removed it he summoned Haru closer, lowering himself down on one of the giant slabs of stone that sat at the edge of the temple. "I come here precisely *because* it's far from the castle," he sighed, "because I'm usually alone here." He patted the spot beside him, bidding Haru to sit. "I don't want others hearing me. No one else should learn the Charm. Only you."

"I'm sorry," said Haru. He sat down beside Liadin. "If you want me to go..."

"Ridiculous," croaked Liadin. He had his spear planted between his feet and leaned on it with both fists, smiling and looking out over the calm water. Despite the Charm, not a single shenenra had appeared. He surprised Haru by not asking him why he'd come to the temple. Instead, old Liadin seemed troubled.

"What are you thinking?" probed Haru. It was an old game; they'd played it hundreds of times, but it only worked if they were honest. Liadin was always honest. Even when it pained him.

"About your father," he said. His voice was low, confessional. "Lately all I can think about is Sh'an. No one even came from J'hora to see his death rite. Not one ship. Not one friend. Not even Whistler."

"There wasn't time," said Haru. "I doubt Count Whistler even knows he's dead."

"He knows. Surely by now he knows. It's been weeks! Where is he? Not a word." Liadin lifted his spear and stamped the ground with it, staring down at his feet. "There was a time when the death of a Tain would set the world weeping. When your grandfather died they came. Fleets of them, from every nation on the continent. The Vizier of Carcazen sent a dozen slaves to sacrifice to Clionet. They tied stones around their necks and threw themselves into the ocean. *That* was loyalty. Your father and I were just children then, but I remember."

Haru put his hand on Liadin's shoulder. He knew he needed to tread carefully. "That was a long time ago. Things are different now. I wouldn't want anyone sending slaves."

"No," agreed Liadin, "I suppose not. I lived through the Massacre of Chains. It broke your father, you know."

Haru didn't like to think of his father as broken. "He freed them. He should have been a hero."

"It's hard for people to change. Even I argued against freeing the humans. I told your father to send them back to the continent. We started dumping them there like trash. Most of them had forgotten their homelands. I think leaving them on shore was worse than killing them." Liadin stared blankly into the distance. "I don't like change. We turned our back on the humans and found out they were carrying knives. One by one all our old friends have left us. They've all fallen under Reius' spell."

"Not all," said Haru reassuringly. "There're still countries the Alliance hasn't conquered yet. Like Agon. And Ghan. And us. Never us, Liadin."

"No, not us. But the others—they'll fall in time. Ghan is too weak and Agon too small. They'll have no choice. Joining the Alliance will let them survive. Whistler knows that. Soon Agon will be like all the others—a puppet dancing on Reius' strings."

"I don't believe that," said Haru. "Whistler will never give Agon over to Reius."

"Why do you think that? Because he gave you treats when you were a boy? When Reius comes with his hordes, Whistler will succumb. When his people are starved enough and tortured enough, he'll give Reius whatever he must to survive. That's politics, Haru."

"Politics? What about friendship?"

Liadin looked seriously at Haru. "If you want to be a Tain, you'd better understand something—Nesenor has no friends. Not even Agon."

They were difficult words for Haru. Count Whistler had been a friend to his father nearly as long as Liadin had. His father hadn't trusted many outsiders, but he'd trusted Whistler. Agon was the one country all Cryori believed would never fall to Reius and his false god.

"Then we'll stand alone if we have to," said Haru.

Liadin smiled, but it was the kind of smile parents give small children, meant to humor them. "Why'd you come here, Haru? You haven't told me yet."

Haru grimaced. "You'll think it's stupid. I'm here to find my father's betrothal ring. I know he buried it here when my mother died. I need to find it..." He glanced around. "But I don't know where to start."

"Start by learning to breathe underwater," said Liadin. He pointed toward the sea. "He tossed it in there."

"What?" Haru got to his feet. "No! He buried it somewhere here at the temple. That's what he told me."

"That's what he told everyone. I was with him when he tossed it away. We were standing right here by the statue. That ring is gone."

"Why? Why would he do that? He loved my mother!"

Liadin put out a hand and pulled Haru back down beside him. "Of course he did," he said. "You don't even know yet what that kind of love is like. He was fitful when Airi died. He cursed Clionet, cursed Ama'aga... He would have thrown himself off this cliff if I hadn't stopped him."

The news stung Haru. His eyes danced between the cliff and the waves, imagining his father's grief. "Why'd he lie to me? He could have told me the truth."

"Who knows?" shrugged Liadin. "Sometimes a lie is easier to take. You were so young, Haru. You'd just lost your mother. Sh'an was being strong for you. Try to remember that, eh?"

"I know," said Haru despondently. "But...I need that ring."

Liadin nudged him with an elbow. "Tell me why."

Haru didn't want to tell. He'd kept his secret from Calix and Elsifor, and had planned to lie to Liadin about his reasons too. Now, though, none of that seemed to matter. "Liadin, when I was under the water with Clionet I made a promise to her. I told her I was going to find out who killed my father. I told her I was going to have revenge on whoever did it."

"You promised that? To the sea goddess?"

"I did. And I meant it. I'm going to find out who killed him. I just don't know how."

"Reius killed him," said Liadin. "Only Reius could have given that order. I told you that, Haru."

"Maybe," said Haru. "But I need to know for certain. Then I can figure out what to do next."

"And how would the ring help you do that?"

"Shadur. If he had the ring, he could use his sight. My father once told me Shadur can see things from a person's past. But he needs something to spark the magic, something dear. Something that's a part of the person."

"Shadur's gifts are the strangest of all," said Liadin. "It's true his sight brings visions, but he needs to touch a person to make it happen. A ring? I don't know..."

"But it's not just a ring. My father cherished it. Or I thought he did." Haru's mood blackened. "His chamber's full of old junk, but nothing important enough. I need something that was precious to him. I need that ring!"

He got up again and looked despairingly around the temple ruins. The weathered statue of Ama'aga looked past him, uncaring. Certainly, there was nothing amid the ruins worth taking back to Shadur. If the ring was gone, his plans were pointless.

"Did Shadur tell you he would do this thing?" asked Liadin.

Haru shook his head. "I didn't ask him. I wanted to get the ring first."

Liadin stood and set his sukatai against the slab. "Maybe you don't need the ring after all," he said. "Your father and I loved secrets. He knew more about me than any man alive." He opened his robes and slipped his hand toward his belt. "You see this knife?" he said, pulling the thin dagger from its black sheath.

"Yeah..." Haru had glimpsed the knife at Liadin's side many times.

"Your father gave me this knife before you were born. Before he met your mother, even. It belonged to his father. He was supposed to pass it along to his own son someday, but he gave it to me when I became Arch-Disciple."

"Liadin, this story isn't making me feel better."

The old man laughed. "It's just a knife, boy, not an heirloom. But I know Sh'an loved it, and that's why he gave it to me. Here, look at this..." Liadin put out his hand, showing Haru his open palm. See that scar? Your father had its twin. Made with this very knife. We were blood sworn."

Haru still wasn't understanding. "I know you were friends, Liadin."

"No, not just that," said Liadin. He handed the dagger to Haru. "It means your father's blood touched that blade. Maybe that will be enough for Shadur to work his visions."

Haru took the dagger, holding it flat in his palm and studying it. The blade was spotless, bright silver without a nick. But if his father's blood had stained it, even once...

"Yes," thought Haru. "Maybe..." He glanced up into Liadin's hopeful face. Just an hour ago he thought he had no friends, no one he could trust. Now, that notion shamed him. "Thank you, Liadin. But if I take it I can't give it back. Shadur's sight will ruin it."

"It should have been yours anyway," said Liadin. He turned back to the sea, but his gaze drifted to something further than the horizon, something deep in his memory. "I know it pains you, what your father thought of you. But he loved you, Haru. He always loved you. He just never thought you were suited to be a Tain. Day-dreaming and pranks...those things don't suit a Tain. Do you see that?"

Haru gave a small, silent nod. It had always been enough for him to know his father loved him. He hadn't expected the need to prove himself so soon.

"You becoming Tain—it's a terrible time for it," Liadin went on. "The J'horans want to frighten us. If you don't bend a knee to Reius, he'll try to kill you just as he did Sh'an. Oh, but there was a time when we were the terror of the world, Haru! When the men of the continent turned white at the mere sight of a beast-ship! They were right to fear us back then. We could have enslaved them all. Not just a few thousand to work the nets and pull radishes out of the ground. We should have governed their cities and installed regents."

Liadin's tone unnerved Haru. "That's not what my father wanted."

"And now he's dead." Liadin closed his eyes. "And I can't sleep a night without seeing him in my dreams, or say a prayer without weeping."

"Liadin, we're still strong. We won't fall to the Alliance."

"Even you don't believe that. I can hear it in your voice."

"I know I have a lot to learn," said Haru, "but if we stand together..."

Liadin said nothing, but Haru could see him struggling with his thoughts. The old man reached for his sukatai when a strange noise crested over the waves. They both turned toward the water, unable to locate the sound. Then it came again, louder, a plaintive wail coming closer to the shore. Liadin forgot his spear and walked to the very edge of the cliff. Haru realized what they were hearing and hurried to join him. Just as he looked down, a great geyser of fire and steam jetted up from the sea surface.

"Shenenra!" Haru shouted.

The scalding spray rained down on them. Below, the dragon-whale breached the waves, its spiky head emerging from the foam, its finned tail whipping the air. The creature was enormous, bigger than any shenenra Haru had seen, all alone in the bay. It turned its yellow eyes up to them, and once more let out its mournful sounding.

"Liadin, the Charm!" cried Haru. "You summoned a dragon-whale!"

Liadin watched the creature with a peculiar glare. "No," he said softly. "It came because you're here, Haru. It heard my voice but ignored me until it sensed you. You are Tain now, Haru. Truly.

"I am?" Haru took a deep breath as he watched the powerful beast spin through the water. "Yes, I am," he said with a grin. All it had taken was a fire-breathing giant to convince him.

Chapter Three

BLACK LIGHT

S hadur's grim little house stood in the shadow of the northern wall, far from the main keep and the activity of the yards, near the cemetery where the dead of Jinja Castle lay buried beneath moss-covered markers. Like the cemetery itself the house was in disrepair, neglected by its occupant but favored for its quietude. Dark ivy and mildew climbed up the walls and insects feasted on the beams. Rust caked the door's hinges, leaving streaks of decayed iron down the wooden jamb. The house had few windows, all of them shuttered, and the bricks of the chimney had begun to crumble. As Haru and Liadin approached the place, lantern in hand, a cat skittered across the roof.

Just hours earlier, Shadur had greeted them with a scowl, angry at the intrusion to his privacy and not impressed at all that Nesenor's new Tain was paying him a visit. Haru had not even been invited inside, an unspeakable violation of courtesy. The insult riled Haru, but it was Liadin who calmed him, asking the moody mystic when they could return and explaining to Haru that Shadur wasn't like his other subjects.

"His patron is Skorthoros," Liadin urged Haru to remember as they returned to the shabby house. "Shadur has forgotten what it's like to deal with people."

As an immortal, Skorthoros wasn't a person at all. In fact, no one even knew if Skorthoros had a gender. He—or she—appeared mostly as a shadow, neither male nor female, with no voice that could be heard by normal ears. Some considered Skorthoros the god of night, others the goddess of death. In truth, Liadin liked to say, Skorthoros was nothingness, like the twilight place separating life and death. The explanation had never made sense to Haru, but it had turned Shadur into a recluse, not unlike Haru's boyhood friend Valivan. Still, it unnerved Haru that Shadur had asked him to return at midnight, when the sane of the castle were asleep.

Haru paused at the threshold. He held up his lantern to see Liadin's face. The old man looked untroubled, as if Shadur's oddness was to be expected. The cat leapt from the roof and scrambled through the unkempt grass toward the graveyard. For the tenth time, Haru checked his pocket for the knife.

"Go on and knock," bid Liadin.

Light flickered from beneath the door. Haru supposed Shadur was waiting for them. With his free hand he knocked thrice. This time, he would not let Shadur turn him away.

The door opened and there stood Shadur, awash in the yellow gleam. He was the oldest of the Chorus but younger than Liadin, with luminous cerulean skin a shade bluer than most Cryori. He wore simple clothes, the way a peasant might dress, and had doffed his usual black tunic. His eyes were emotionless, almost sleepy. But most remarkable of all was his crystal hand. Haru couldn't stop his gaze from darting toward it. As a boy he had been fascinated by it. The hand was totally transparent, almost invisible, with fingers that moved as naturally as his own. It had no blood vessels, nothing at all to animate it, just the waviness of glass. When it moved it made a peculiar tinkling sound, as if about to fracture.

"Tain Haru," said Shadur.

"Shadur, good evening."

The mystic looked at Liadin. "Arch-Disciple, please leave us."

"What?" said Haru. "Why?"

Liadin said calmly, "I am here to protect the Tain, Shadur. Not to steal any of your secrets."

"I have spoken with Skorthoros over this," said Shadur. "Skorthoros asks that it be only Tain Haru."

Liadin looked disappointed, but nodded. As a Venerant he served all of Clionet's family, even the mysterious Skorthoros. He made no attempt to challenge Shadur's claim. He turned and considered the darkness, then said, "Haru, the lantern, please. Shadur can give you another for your return."

"Liadin, I want you to stay. That's why I asked you to come."

The old cleric held out his hand. "Be grateful Skorthoros agreed to help you. The lantern, please."

Reluctantly, Haru gave up the lantern and watched Liadin depart. Shadur bid him to enter with a wave of his crystal hand, then closed the door behind them. The home was typical of Cryori houses, mostly one big room with sliding doors leading to a hidden kitchen and sleep chamber. In the center of the main room sat a low, black table of polished lacquer, and upon that sat a forked candelabra with two dancing flames that tossed shadows onto the bare white walls. There were no flowers, no pottery on display, no artwork of any kind. It was, Haru supposed, the barest home he'd ever seen, but remarkably clean considering the shabbiness of its outside. Shadur offered no tea or refreshments. He seemed preoccupied as he sat down cross-legged before the table, staring up at Haru.

"Sit," he said simply.

Haru took Liadin's knife from his pocket, placing it on the table before him as he sat across from Shadur. Unsure what to say, he waited for Shadur to speak. Shadur rested his crystal hand on the table, not unnaturally, and took Haru's measure.

"How does this work?" Haru asked. He slid the dagger closer to Shadur. "You need this, right? This is the knife I told you about."

Shadur didn't reply, not even with a nod. He didn't even seem to be listening, at least not to Haru.

"Is Skorthoros speaking to you now?" probed Haru. He glanced around for any sign of the genderless god. "Why doesn't Skorthoros want Liadin here? Do you know?"

At last Shadur said, "You don't know much about me, Tain Haru, do you? You've never shown much interest in the Chorus. Now you're full of questions."

"I admit that," said Haru. "I never paid you much attention. But I need you now, Shadur. You said you'd help me. Will you?"

"I'm curious about your opinion."

"About what?"

"About the Chorus."

"I don't really have one. I hardly know you or Elsifor."

"But you know Valivan. You know Siva."

"They're my friends."

"Do you blame us for letting Sh'an die?"

"I blame a lot of people, Shadur. I even blame myself."

The mystic seemed surprised by his answer. "We're a mess, you know. The Chorus, I mean. We always were. We thought we were special because the gods gave us talents."

"Siva tried to bring you together. I know she did."

"She did," granted Shadur. "For that first year, at least. We followed your father everywhere, until we realized he never actually went anywhere. He never wanted us around. He was secretive, your father."

"Yes," said Haru sadly. "He was."

"Eventually we just melted away from him. We were his Chorus only in name. That's why your father's dead. Because we failed him."

"And because someone murdered him," said Haru. "Don't forget that."

"You're being kind," said Shadur. "Maybe you have grown up."

"Let's just agree that we don't really know each other."

"Tain Haru, I have done all I can so far to discover who murdered your father. The spell that killed him was chosen carefully so that no trace of him would be left for me to follow. That's why he was burned so completely. And so quickly."

"But I have a trace of him—on the knife."

"You miss my point. It is the strength of the magic we're up against that matters."

"So? Who could cast a spell like that? If you know..."

"Of course I don't know," snapped Shadur. "What I do isn't easy. It's not like looking in a mirror. If that were so I'd know all the secrets of the world."

"Shadur, I'm sorry, but you're confusing me."

"Did you know," said Shadur, "that every Tain before your father had a Chorus? Even Hiaran. Do you know what we were called before the peace? We were known as the Bloody Chorus! We served the Tains and the gods. There are centuries of history for you to learn and no time to teach it to you." Shadur held out his crystal hand. "Look at it," he said. He flexed the transparent fingers. "I've seen you staring at it. It's alright—it's good to be curious. Do you know how I got this hand?"

"I think so," said Haru. He leaned forward and studied the appendage, fascinated by it. "But I wouldn't mind hearing you tell the story."

"Once this hand was flesh, just like the other," said Shadur. "But Skorthoros is a demanding patron. Not like Paiax or Clionet. It took more than a month to burn away the skin and bone. Drip by drip of molten glass. Agonizing. No food. Just water and prayer. I was quite demented when it was over."

"I'm sure that's true."

"I barely survived it! But when it was done Skorthoros had his sacrifice, and I had the sight."

"But it's alive," said Haru. He peered deeply into the living crystal. "How's that possible?"

"The life within it belongs to Skorthoros, not me," said Shadur. "Otherwise, it would be as dead as stone." He held the hand up to his face. "When I look through it, I see things no mortal should ever see. The past. The dead. But I only see what Skorthoros allows. Which is why what you've asked of me is so difficult."

"But it is *your* hand, Shadur, isn't it? Can't you command Skorthoros?"

"Command Skorthoros?" Shadur smiled with real amusement. "Like you command the shenenra, you mean? Skorthoros isn't an animal, Tain Haru."

"But it's your gift," argued Haru. "Like Elsifor's powers, or Valivan's. Their patrons don't give and take their gifts away. Why should yours?"

"Now you're asking the right questions! So let me answer you with one of my own. Imagine for a moment what the world would be like if you could know anything you wished—what people were thinking about you, the answer to any mystery, even the day you were going to die. The past or the future—it wouldn't matter. If you could know all those things, what would your life be like?"

"I don't know," said Haru honestly. "Difficult?"

"You're just guessing to please me. But you're right—it *would* be difficult. More than difficult. It would be chaos. No one could live with that kind of knowledge. There would be no point to life. That's why Skorthoros doesn't always grant me the sight. Sometimes, I have to beg for it."

"Did you beg for me?"

Shadur looked humbled. "You are my Tain. Believe it or not, I would do anything for you."

"And did Skorthoros agree?"

"Yes."

"Because I'm Tain?"

"No," said Shadur. "Because Skorthoros trusts me. Because I've given my life to using the sight well. Remember what I told you—Skorthoros isn't like other gods. There's no love or vengeance in the heart of that one. No heart at all, really. The only thing within Skorthoros is reason and balance. And balance is fragile. What we do here tonight will tip it."

Haru thought a moment, biting his lip. "I know that should probably frighten me. To be honest it does. But I have to do this. Let the gods worry about balance. Let them damn me if they want to."

"Gods don't damn people, Haru. People damn themselves." Shadur twirled the dagger between his crystal fingers. "Are you ready for that?"

Haru shrugged. "I don't think I can be ready for that," he said. "So let's just go ahead."

Shadur nodded, took a breath, then took a longer, deeper breath. He laid his crystal hand down flat on the table, palm side up with the knife resting on his outstretched fingers. Then, he leaned forward and surprised Haru by blowing out the twin candles. Haru froze, his eyes adjusting to the darkness, spying the silhouette of Shadur in the feeble light from the window. Suddenly he was conscious of every sound—the slight breeze stirring through the tombstones, the far-off cry of the cat, even his own nervous swallowing. The bright sapphire of Shadur's eyes pierced the blackness, but there was no movement from him, not even to blink. Haru grabbed the edge of the table. Slowly his vision improved, revealing the metal blade before them. The fingers holding them swirled with inner light. Dark sparks flashed within them. Haru leaned in for a closer look, just as the black flames erupted.

He jerked back, startled and dumbstruck, as the heatless flames danced up from Shadur's fingers, licking the ceiling and bathing the room in...

Light? Haru didn't know what to call it.

Like a mist of darkness, it somehow illuminated the chamber, nearly blinding Haru with its intensity. He put his hand up to touch it, piercing its core with his fingers and watching as it stripped the meat from them. Haru jerked back his hand, then realized there was no pain at all. His fingers were whole again. He gazed at Shadur through the veil and saw a skeleton sitting there instead. Shadur's fleshless face looked back at him with empty eye sockets. The bones of his jaws began moving, speaking words in a secret language as the dark flames spat up from his crystal digits.

Haru wanted to speak but didn't. Surely this was what Shadur intended. He convinced himself of that even as the skull's chanting grew louder and the black flames licked the ceiling. Movements formed inside the mist, faint at first, then gradually swirling into smoky figures. What looked like a woman held what looked like a baby in her arms.

Haru peered closer. *Not a baby*, he realized. *Two babies*. Two wretched, misshapen infants. Somehow their cries reached through the darkness, a tortured, heart-breaking wail of helplessness. Haru sat transfixed and horrified. He watched as flames engulfed the woman, as her own screams rose above the babies' cries. In a whoosh of smoke, she vanished.

For a moment, there was blessed silence.

Then Shadur's voice rose up again, singing now the dead language, his skeletal frame shaking with effort as he wrenched the black light from his unmoving hand and summoned images from the flames. The sound was unbearable now. Haru flinched against it but did not look away. Two more figures emerged, larger than the first ones, their skin white and ghostly even in the black and magic light. Human men, Haru decided, but with bleached flesh and gangly arms, hunched over in robes that revealed their crimson eyes.

Haru could hold his tongue no longer. "Is that them?" he shouted. "Is that who killed my father?"

But across the table Shadur did not answer him. The mystic's whole body was shaking now, even his once still hand. His skull-head tipped back in a scream. The white figures in the smoke turned as if to look at him, and the dark light vanished, smothering the room in darkness. Suddenly blind, Haru got to his feet to search for Shadur. The mystic's scream trailed off, the flesh returned to his face, and his head hit the table with a thud.

"Shadur!" cried Haru. He picked his way around the table, finding Shadur in the darkness and touching his shoulder. He was breathing but unconscious. "Shadur? Wake up!"

The candelabra flashed suddenly to life. Haru felt a chill rake his skin. He exhaled and saw his breath curdle into mist. Shadur's crystal hand lay unmoving on the table, once again translucent. Haru stood up slowly. The magical light was gone, replaced by the dim illumination of the candles. Shadows returned to the wall, then started moving.

"Shadur..."

A single shadow broke free of the others, creeping along the white wall. It moved slowly, like a pile of leaves, tumbling and growing until it nearly touched the ceiling. It had no shape, yet it moved like a creature, bits of it breaking off into appendages that stretched out and disappeared. Haru knew he wasn't seeing the beings from the flame. The coldness of the room, the blackness of shadows—these things revealed what he was seeing. He stepped cautiously toward the shadow.

"Skorthoros?" he whispered. "Is it you?"

The thing gave no response, hovering against the wall, watching Haru with non-existent eyes. Another tendril broke from its body, this one shaped like an arm. It stretched out to the other shadows, one long finger growing out of the shifting hand. Haru watched in awe as the finger drew more shadows on the wall, spinning them to life so that one by one they encircled the chamber. Images of men and women, of battles and death, of children, of thrones, of war beasts and soldiers on the march—all these things came alive on the walls of Shadur's home. Haru held his breath. The living shadows danced around him, begging his attention. He spun to see them all, overwhelmed.

"What are you showing me?" he asked. "Who's the boy? What's this war? What am I seeing, Skorthoros?"

The god of balance remained bleakly silent. The great black finger retracted, and slowly the shadows dissolved away, replaced by the prosaic silhouettes of Haru and the furnishings. Skorthoros, however, remained. The immortal patron of Shadur shifted its form into something like a thundercloud, full of tumult, and formed a pair of blinking eyes that stared at Haru questioningly.

"Skorthoros, I don't understand," Haru pleaded. "I don't know what any of this means. You have to tell me."

If Skorthoros had a head, it would have shaken in denial. Haru sighed, frustrated and confused.

"Alright," he agreed reluctantly. "Thank you, Skorthoros. Thank you for helping me."

Skorthoros lingered a long, emotionless moment, then went the way of the other shadows, slipping like black sand down the wall.

As normalcy returned, so did Haru's senses. He looked at Shadur, still unconscious, then hurried from the house to fetch some water for his fallen friend.

Chapter Four

A ROOMFUL OF LANTERNS

An hour after midnight, Haru finally left Shadur's shabby house. He had managed to awaken the unconscious mystic by splashing water on his face, gently shaking him until Shadur's stupor abated. Summoning Skorthoros had drained Shadur completely. His skin had turned ashen and his eyes struggled to stay open as Haru helped him into bed. Haru had countless questions about what he'd seen, but Shadur was no help answering them. The mystic merely babbled about the mysteries of the gods and insisted Haru let him sleep. No sooner had Shadur hit the pillow than he was unconscious.

With only moonlight to guide him, Haru made his way back to the keep through the grounds of the castle, minding the folks already asleep in the homes along the lane. He was exhausted but too baffled to sleep, and the visions Skorthoros had shared haunted him as he made his way up the road. Two figures—both deformed—and all those faces and events; Haru recognized none of them. He looked up at the slumbering castle. Liadin's precious knife was gone, and all he had to show for it was riddles.

"Tain Haru!"

Elsifor sprang from the top of a nearby wall, landing before the startled Haru.

"Elsifor! What...?"

"I've been waiting for you," said Elsifor, hopping up to meet him. "You must come."

"Come where?" asked Haru, catching his breath. "I'm going to bed."

"No, you're not. Count Whistler is here."

"Count Whistler?" parroted Haru. He looked around, confused by the emptiness of the street. "Whistler's here?"

"He's with the Arch-Disciple. He arrived an hour ago. Look—his ship sits at anchor."

Elsifor stretched a talon toward the dark horizon. Haru followed the finger and saw it, nearly invisible in the churning fog—the Agoni sloop of Count Whistler, sitting quietly in the harbor.

"Why's he here?" asked Haru. "Do you know? Is he alone?"

"He's alone, but I don't know why he's come. Liadin asked me to keep watch and fetch you."

Haru couldn't believe it. He hadn't seen the Count in years, not since his last visit to Nesenor, and that had been in far better times. He felt ill-prepared, as though he should first change his clothes or meet with his advisors...

"Tain Haru?" Elsifor gestured toward the gate. "We should go."

In the center of the castle complex stood the keep, the most ornate and least fortified of Castle Jinja's structures. It was also the residence of the Tain, and that made it the perfect place to host visitors. As he stepped inside the keep Haru noticed servants, roused from sleep and buzzing with activity. They bowed as he entered, offering their usual greetings, but they all knew Haru was in a hurry, staying well clear as he made his way down the corridor toward the only chamber suitable for greeting important guests.

The lantern room was on the eastern side of the keep, so-called because of the hundreds of hexagonal lanterns hung in perfect rows from the ceiling. Lighting them all was a monumental task, the effect of which was stunning. In truth the lantern room was merely a large dining hall, with polished wooden floors that glowed in the yellow light and depictions of shenenra and Cryori deities, water-colored along the pearly walls. It took the castle's servants hours to light all the lanterns, but as Haru expected there hadn't been time to welcome Count Whistler so grandly. In fact, only a single festive lantern had been lit, illuminating the very center of the gargantuan table, where Liadin sat with Count Whistler, speaking softly with tea cups in their hands.

Haru paused just shy of the threshold. Before the speakers could notice him, he smoothed down his hair and shirt, fixed a smile on his face, and entered the lantern room.

"Arch-Disciple?" said Elsifor softly, careful to keep behind his Tain. "I found him."

Liadin stood up at once. "Haru...look who's come."

Count Whistler rose slowly. His eyes got big as he took in Haru. He lifted his face in surprise, clearly shocked by Haru's appearance.

"Haru?" The count gasped as he got to his feet. "Taan's death, look at you! You're all a man now!"

"Count Whistler, it's good to see you," said Haru, surprised by how much he meant it. All his wariness disappeared at the sight of the gentle count, replaced by a powerful memory of better times. "I'm sorry we're so unprepared to welcome you...we didn't know. You should have told us, sent word you were coming."

Count Whistler stretched out both arms, bidding Haru closer. He looked as regal as Haru remembered, his thin body draped in a crimson coat with golden stitching, his eyes twinkling like the rings he wore on every finger. His silver hair—not grey—bobbed at his shoulders. Haru went to him without hesitation, though behind him Elsifor stiffened.

"I shouldn't call you Haru," said Whistler jokingly as they embraced. "And I certainly can't call you a boy! You are Tain, truly you are!" He stepped back and admired Haru. "You are your father's son. Handsome. Strong like him, too. I can see it in you!"

Haru loved the flattery, but knew Whistler was famous for his charms. The Agoni was a diplomat above all else, a gift that had enabled his tiny country to thrive among its larger, stronger neighbors. But he was also an honest man, a rare thing among humans. It was why so many on the continent valued his counsel, and why Reius hungered for his fealty.

"Sit please, Count," said Haru. He looked at the table's offerings, wondering if they were enough. "We can bring you anything you like. Have you come alone? No retainers?"

"He's alone," Elsifor piped in. His cattish face grimaced. "I thought it best after what had happened."

"I sent Venerants to the dock to escort him here," explained Liadin.

"And don't apologize for it," said Whistler before Haru could speak. "What happened to your father..." The Count's words tripped with emotion. "A tragedy."

"A horror," said Haru. "It happened right here in this room. There were so many people. My father was greeting them. He was happy. And then—"

Emotion stopped him from saying more. Liadin quickly rescued him.

"I've told it all already, Haru. All that we know, at least." The old priest guided them all to sit. Haru ignored formality and, instead of sitting in the center of the table across from his guest, sat directly beside him. Whistler made himself as comfortable as he could, sitting back on his knees rather than the traditional, cross-legged Cryori manner.

"I knew you'd come," said Haru with a smile. "I was just saying so to Liadin—I knew you'd come once you heard. Did it take so long for the news to reach the continent? We must be more isolated here now than I thought."

Liadin and the Count shared a knowing look. "Haru," said Liadin, "Count Whistler—"

"No," interrupted Whistler, "let me." He turned his twinkling eyes on Haru. "I'm heartbroken by Sh'an's death. You should know that, Haru. Your father was a great Tain, but he was my friend, and friendship is a rare thing. You may not know that because you're still so young, but when you get older, you'll cherish your friends."

"Yes," nodded Haru.

"I'm not here just to pay my respects," said Whistler. "I've been to J'hora." The charming smile all but vanished. "I'm here to bring news."

Haru's insides clenched. "Bad news?"

"Necessary news," said the count. "We of Agon—we have joined the Alliance. We're part of J'hora now."

Haru felt wobbly. Behind him, Elsifor barely suppressed a gasp. The servants looked at the floor, pretending not to hear.

"You joined J'hora?" asked Haru in disbelief. "You've joined *Reius?*"

"We did," said Whistler without flinching. "We did the prudent thing. The only thing we could do."

"No, you could have resisted," said Haru sharply. "As we've resisted! Count Whistler, Reius killed my father! How could you join J'hora and call yourself his friend?"

"Temperance, Haru," counseled Liadin.

Haru half rose to his feet. "You knew this, Liadin? And sit there so easily? This is a disaster!" His voice climbed an octave. "What friends does Nesenor have left? If Agon goes so goes all others; you've said so a hundred times."

Liadin silenced Haru with a glare. "Is that how you show strength? This disaster has already befallen us. Let us manage it."

Haru struggled to control his anger. "Count Whistler, I need to understand this," he pleaded. "Because I can barely believe you'd become a slave so willingly."

The count turned his best, plaintive expression on Haru. "Haru, you're a ruler now. You can't afford to be so childish any longer. You've lost the luxury of being boastful. Soon you will understand what hard choices really mean, of bending a knee or watching your people starve. People need bread first—they cannot eat virtue. You think me a coward for bowing to J'hora—I can see it in your eyes. But you have no idea of J'hora's strength. Reius and his movement—they're not a band of fanatics anymore. They have an army, a fleet—the old ways cannot stand up to them, or their god."

"God," spat Haru. "Taan is no more a god than this teacup," he said, picking up a cup and slamming it down. "Taan is a myth, a story made up by the deluded and believed by madmen like Reius."

"There are only old gods," agreed Liadin. "They can be forsaken, but they cannot be exchanged for new ones."

"But they have been, my friend," said Whistler. "In Agon we gave up your gods the moment your beast-ships left out shores. But we remained a friend to you."

"Because it suited you," said Haru. "Forgive me, but you needed our protection from Ghan and Carcazen and the others."

"And did it not suit Nesenor as well?" argued Whistler. "To have a voice on the continent that wasn't always calling you demons and blaming you for years of thievery? Let us say it plainly—we used each other, but that doesn't mean there wasn't friendship." He turned to Liadin and said, "Arch-Disciple, you see my point. You must! You're wise enough to know that Agon cannot survive alone, with only Nesenor for an ally. We would be outcasts, as you are. We are of the continent. And the continent belongs to J'hora now."

"I understand that you were in a terrible predicament," said Liadin, "but do you understand that you remain in one? The Lord Guardians of J'hora are dogs. No matter what deal you struck with Reius, you will still be on his leash. You had a choice between death or slavitude. You chose slavitude. You haven't earned my anger, my friend. Just my pity."

"What did Reius promise you, Count?" asked Haru. "Your throne and survival, or something more? And what of my father? Please don't tell me he gloated over his murder. If you listened to him brag about it..."

"Haru, you break my heart," said Whistler, tilting down his silver head. "How could you think I would ever stand for a thing like that? I have not even spoken to Reius myself. No one sees him—all our dealings were done through underlings. And Reius did not kill your father. I have been assured of it by the same J'horans that dealt with me in Agon."

Liadin leaned intently closer. "Say this again—Reius has denied a hand in Sh'an's death?"

"He has, and done it publicly," said Whistler. "It was magic that killed Sh'an, you've said so yourselves. And no one practices those arts in J'hora, not unless they want a tour of Reius' dungeons."

"I don't believe that," said Haru. "You surprise me, Count."

"I believe it because it is so," insisted Whistler. His face contorted in the lantern light. "Reius serves Taan. He hates the Cryori because he hates the old gods and magics you brought to us. He would never ally himself with them."

"He hated my father, too," Haru pointed out.

"Yes, but do not misunderstand me—Reius and his acolytes shed no tears for Sh'an. They would have murdered him gladly. Given the chance, Reius might have sent a priest or ranger to kill him, but he would never have sent a sorcerer."

Haru considered Whistler's words. His father had thought Whistler an honest man, but that didn't mean the count was always right. Perhaps the old man was just too affable to see the truth. And then there was Skorthoros. Haru didn't know what the strange god had shown him, but the powerful visions remained fresh in his mind.

"At least you came yourself to tell us your news," said Haru sadly. "I'm glad for that, Count Whistler. "But what happens next? Who's left to stand with us? Ghan has never been an ally. Nor has Lumeszia."

"Or have they given their fealty to Reius as well?" probed Liadin.

Whistler looked uncomfortable, the way a man who's hiding something looks. "Ghan already joined the Alliance," he said, "two months ago. Lumeszia will soon. All will soon, my friends. It's the way the world is turning."

"Like day to night," said Elsifor.

Haru looked at him and grinned. "Our world is shrinking fast, Elsifor. Who'll be our friend now that we've lost Whistler?"

"Haru, I'll always be your friend," sighed Whistler. "But you're right to be afraid. Reius doesn't need to send assassins to kill you. He has his seabreakers, remember."

"And we have a sea goddess who'd love for him to send them here," said Haru. "The next time you're in J'hora, tell Reius we're not afraid of his seabreakers. Tell him that our goddess will shred his crewmen into shark food if he dares cross his fleet into Cryori waters. We can still defend our island."

Whistler put up a hand to rub the frustration from his forehead. "Haru, you can't win a war against the Alliance. I've just spent the last hour trying to convince Liadin of that!" He let out a mirthless laugh. "Gods, you are a stubborn people! The whole world thinks you've gone soft, but you know what? You're as warlike and stupid as ever! You're stuck in the past. You need to open your eyes and see the future."

"A future with false gods and mad kings?" quipped Liadin. "Never."

"No?" pressed Whistler. "Is a future where Nesenor is broken and starved out of existence more to your liking?"

Liadin snorted at the notion. "You underestimate us."

"And you underestimate J'hora! I've been to their city, Liadin. I've seen their armies, their sciences—they aren't barbarians. They're the strongest force the world has ever seen. Stronger even than Nesenor in its day. Imagine all the old nations under one leader, all of them obeying and pledging their armies to him. That's what J'hora is now. Reius calls it the 'Alliance,' but it's not. It's an empire."

Count Whistler paused to study their worried faces. The servants both glanced toward the exit, wishing desperately to be gone. Liadin said nothing, knowing it was Haru's place to speak. Yet Haru was speechless. For all his bold talk of war, he'd never seen battle in his life. In truth, the prospect terrified him.

"We could win if we had allies," he said. "You should have stood with us, Count Whistler."

Whistler looked remorseful but said, "There's another way to skin this harpy." He leaned in close to Haru. "Every two years Reius holds his Guardian Council. Every Lord Guardian and governor in the Alliance comes to J'hora for the meeting. It's the only time anyone sees Reius but his acolytes. This year's Council is three weeks away." The count smiled encouragingly. "Reius wants you to attend."

"What?" said Haru.

"What?" Liadin barked. "Reius wants Haru? To go to *J'hora*?"

Elsifor leapt in. "Absolutely not. I forbid it."

"As do I!" said Liadin.

"Wait," said Haru. He looked sharply at Whistler. "Say this again, please—Reius wants me at this council meeting? His men told you this?"

"I've been sent here to invite you, and to offer you Reius' assurance that no harm will come to you in J'hora. It's a peace offering, probably the only one you'll ever get."

Liadin got to his feet and scowled down at Whistler. "Is Reius out of sorcerers? Has he no one else he can send to kill Haru on our own soil?"

Whistler rose at once, leaving Haru sitting and confused. "This is not a trap! I swear I would never lead Haru into danger!"

"Swear to who? To Taan?" growled Liadin contemptuously.

"Please stop," bid Haru, rising to get between them. He turned calmly to the servants and dismissed them both. As they scurried away, Haru looked back at Whistler. The count's face was flush with anger. "Count Whistler, you know I trust you. My father trusted you and that man trusted no one! But how can I do as you ask? Cryori are despised on the continent, and in J'hora most of all. To go there willingly? I might as well slit my own throat."

Whistler was unrelenting. "The only ones who might die are those who'd dare lift a finger against you, Haru. Reius has pledged your safety. He's given his word on it. No one in J'hora would dare defy him on this. He has torture chambers your grand-fathers could only dream of."

"But why Haru?" asked Liadin. "Why now?"

"I confess I do not know," said Whistler. "For a chance at peace—that's all I was told. Reius intends to meet with you directly, Haru. No go-betweens, no advisors. Have you any idea what a rare thing that is? The people of J'hora consider Reius as holy as they do Taan. Almost no one is granted a private audience with him."

"Should I feel honored?" smirked Haru. "Because you seem quite enamored with Reius, Count Whistler, and it pains me to see that."

"I wouldn't have delivered Reius' message if I didn't think it the best chance your people have, Haru. The troubles your beast-ships have had with the White Fleet are just the start. The seabreakers will keep on coming, pushing you into a war you can't win. Even your goddess won't be able to stop them all. At least think on it, please! Don't send me away until you are sure you'd rather die than try for peace."

Behind him Haru could feel Liadin readying a spiteful answer. Haru said quickly, "I will think on it, Count Whistler. For the sake of my father's friendship with you, I will. Give me a day at least. Stay with us here in the castle. Bring your men ashore if you wish.

We'll make all of you comfortable, resupply your ship, whatever you need." He turned to Elsifor. "Elsifor, see to whatever he needs. Let me speak alone with Liadin."

Elsifor agreed, leaving with Count Whistler while Liadin sat back down with a grumble. The old cleric pushed aside the tea kettle, reaching instead for a decanter of wine the servants had set out. He filled his tea cup with the ruby liquor, cursing before taking a drink.

"That man is a traitor," he said blackly. "Did I tell you? No one from the continent can be trusted—the men of those lands are worthless, every one of them. Even Whistler. He has damned himself by siding with Reius, damned himself and all his people." Liadin drained the tiny cup, then called Haru closer as he poured himself another. "Come—tell me what happened with Shadur."

Haru's head spun from the night's events. He sat down again across from Liadin, glad they were finally alone. "I saw Skorthoros, Liadin," he whispered intently. "It made the shadows come to life! It showed me things; I don't even know what they were... And Shadur fainted! Collapsed right there at his table. I practically had to drown him to get him awake!"

Liadin lowered his cup. "Is he alright?"

"I think so. He's sleeping now. He couldn't stay awake. The effort really drained him."

"What did you see, Haru?" pressed Liadin. "Tell me everything."

Haru fought hard to remember, recounting every detail possible for Liadin. He told of the strange figures he'd seen, the gangly, stooped twins and how they had been infants first, growing up before him in the strange, black light. He spoke of the fire and how he'd put his hand through it and of seeing Shadur's flesh-stripped skull, and how Shadur how collapsed.

"That's when Skorthoros came," said Haru. By now Liadin was frozen, holding his cup halfway between the table and his lips. "The candles lit up and the room got cold, and Skorthoros just grew out of the floor. It was like ink spreading across the walls. Skorthoros just put out a finger and started drawing."

"Drawing? Drawing what?"

Haru shrugged. "Things. Ships, soldiers, children. I saw a battle, I saw a city—but I didn't recognize any of it. And then it was gone! I tried to ask Skorthoros what I was seeing but he...or she, it, I don't know...wouldn't speak to me."

"And that was it?"

"Yes. Then I went to get Shadur some water. I woke him, made sure he was alright and put him to bed."

"And then came back to the castle to hear Whistler's bad news," said Liadin. His rheumy eyes darted across the lines of dead lanterns, then back to the single, glowing one above him. "That's us," he said softly.

Haru looked at the lantern and got his meaning immediately. "Alone."

The word hung between them, frightening Haru and making Liadin wistful. Both of them wished Sh'an was alive, but neither dared say it.

"You've had quite a night," said Liadin finally. "You look tired. You should sleep. We'll talk in the morning, figure out how best to deliver your refusal to Whistler." He got up and headed for the door. "And if you're not tired, well I certainly am. Goodnight, Haru."

"Liadin...wait," said Haru. He looked up at his old mentor, the best idea he ever had hatching in his mind. "I'm going to J'hora. I'm going to meet with Reius."

Liadin reared back. His face went ashen. "Are you mad, boy?"

"Maybe," said Haru. Fractured bits of a plan began knitting together. "Maybe... But first I need to find Siva."

Chapter Five

A GIFT OF KNIVES

On the island of Tojira the rains had come, falling in giant teardrops from the sky and swelling the lagoon where the silk-oysters nested. The rain came each noon on a carpet of thunderclouds, shrouding the sun and leaving behind a cool oasis, a paradise of birds and flowers refreshed by the life-giving waters. The lagoon was Tojira's beating heart, the place where the white deer came to drink and the enormous eel-fish spawned deep within submerged caves. A twenty-foot waterfall fed the lagoon, spouting down from a cliff of volcanic rock, gradually spreading out into the peaceful lagoon to lap at its muddy, grassy shores.

Siva looked down from her place on the cliff, her naked body warmed by the sun. She had waited for the clouds to pass, watching them release the sunlight upon the island. Beside her sat her empty diving basket, soon to be filled with silk-oysters. She was weak and tired from fasting. Her blue skin clung like shrunken fabric to her ribcage. She would need to end her punishment soon, she knew, or risk Jaiakrin's anger. If she had been Valivan or Shadur or any other Cryori, he would have slain her for stepping foot on his holy island. But for Siva, Jaiakrin's love was boundless. He could forgive her anything.

Except her suicide.

Love has conditions, he had told her.

She could fast, she could flog herself, but she could not end her life. It seemed an odd punishment to Siva. Cruel, even.

I will eat tonight, she told herself as she spied the blue-green waters. The silk-oysters were deep, far too deep for her to see, but she liked to stare down into the lagoon and imagine herself a bird. Like the black loons she would dive and come up with her treasures, the way her sisters always had. She would spin clothing from the oyster's silk, as her aunt had taught her all those years ago. She had come to Tojira wearing only her sahi and kusu, the traditional skirt and top-cloth of Cryori diving girls, leaving behind her leathers and armors and her array of metal blades. She had forgotten how good it felt to dress like a woman again, a real woman like her sisters.

If Jaiakrin insisted she live, she would live like a villager.

But to dive meant to be naked, and on Tojira she was wonderfully shameless. Here there were no men to covet her. There was only Jaiakrin, her beautiful, lustrous patron. It was said that Jaiakrin had fathered many children in the bellies of Cryori girls, yet Siva had no fear of him. She walked like a child on his island, naked and confident, for unlike mortal men Jaiakrin had no lust for her. He was, she supposed, what a father should be like.

Today Siva had an empty basket and a sky free of clouds. The water beckoned her. She took one tiny step to the rim of the cliff, curling her toes at the edge of the rocks, filling her lungs with breath. A moment later she was falling, head-first into the lagoon. Her hands split the surface and down she plummeted, first quickly then slowly, spreading out her arms and legs and propelling herself into the depths. Fish darted past her. Strands of sunlight touched her path. She felt the burn inside her chest, the slow, desperate seep of air. Her powerful strokes drove her down, down, toward the bed where the silk-oysters waited.

Siva reached the nest and laid down her mesh bucket, letting its weight hold it down. Slowly she let the air from her lungs, timing the exhalation to a stream of little bubbles. She let her body sink, her knees just kissing the mossy bottom, then went to work, digging her fingers through the sea grass to find the best prizes. Silk-oysters lived long but grew slowly, and she could only pick the largest ones if she expected the bed to survive. They would die once taken, living only long enough to expel the soft, silk pearl that made the amazing thread. Siva had no spinning wheel, but had learned from her aunt how to carve a spindle from a stone. It made no difference to her that it would take her years to spin enough thread to barely cover herself. She was an outcast now.

Her fingers searched the bed carefully. This time, she found only three silk-oysters large enough to take. Frustrated, she continued working while the pressure built inside her lungs. The voice in her head told her to head up. Siva pushed it aside.

One more, she told herself.

The beds covered the lagoon bottom, but she had so far confined herself to those close to the waterfall. It made no sense to spread out her search too quickly. Once a bed was harvested, moving on would give it time to grow back. But she had learned from her aunt not to be wasteful, and her aunt's voice shoved aside her better judgment. Siva dug as deeply as she could, ignoring the burning in her breast until finally it crept into her brain.

Enough!

Clutching her bucket, she darted for the surface. Suddenly the lagoon seemed far deeper than before. The last of the air left her lungs, replaced by a shriveling pain. She mustered her strength, charging hard for the distant sunlight, refusing to release her bucket.

Stupid...

She was too weak to dive so long. Lack of food and lack of air strained her senses. The overwhelming urge to take a breath screamed in her brain. Her pace slowed as her consciousness dimmed...

And then she was up, breaking the surface with a gasping scream. Barely able to swim, she bobbed for air and clutched her bucket, suddenly terrified of what she'd done.

"Stupid!"

The shore was merely yards away. Siva fought to catch her breath, to clutch her stupored mind and swim. Beneath her the water gave way to soft earth. She clawed across a rocky shoal, tossed her bucket ashore, and rolled onto her back upon the stones, gasping and staring into the sky.

"Siva," she whispered to herself, mimicking her mother's voice. "What are you doing?"

She had exiled herself to this life, driven by the guilt of Sh'an's death, leaving behind every familiar face to punish herself in paradise. The thousand pains she'd inflicted on herself pricked her body, and she wondered if she truly wanted to die.

"Not want," she told herself. "Must."

She closed her eyes, not bothering to drag herself fully ashore, and let the water lap against her legs. She seldom slept at night; dreams were a plague. But exhaustion overtook her quickly, and soon her mind drifted away, lulled by birdsongs and falling water.

Siva slept, deep and dreamless.

Then, a sudden cry knifed her sleeping brain.

Her eyes snapped open. She jerked upright, following the noise down the shore where a panicked struggle shook the water. For a long, confused moment Siva stared, making out a white mound and flailing, hooved legs.

A white deer.

Siva sprang across the shore, bounding over the rocks and grass. The deer let out a frantic peel as a tentacle snared its neck. A fanged snout breached the water, opening wide for its struggling prey. The thing stayed mostly beneath the surface, letting its twin tentacles ensnare the captured deer. Siva hammered toward it, then dove straight at the creature as the deer lost its footing. Together they collided, the impact rolling the beast and exposing its scaled belly. Siva clawed it madly, searching for a soft spot. The thing released the deer at once, whipping back its tentacles toward Siva. Water sprayed, hooves kicked, blinding Siva in the foam. She worked her legs around the creature, squeezing with all her strength. A tentacle coiled across her belly. The sting of suckers punctured her skin. Siva reared up out of the water.

"Jaiakrin! Help me! Strengthen me!"

The beast's green jaws hissed open and its eyes rolled backwards. Siva plunged her fingers down like daggers, stabbing the grotesque, grey orbs. The left one punctured, firing a stream of ooze. The creature gave a gargling roar, rolling and dunking Siva beneath the waves. She held on, then felt the other tentacle around her throat. A whiff of panic pricked her. With a wordless scream she summoned her patron.

Jaiakrin! I need you!

In an instant it was on her, the great glamour of the hunter-god, flooding her limbs and quickening her blood. It came like a wind, sudden and painful, making her scream out beneath the water. Siva's body trembled with the power, barely able to contain it. Quickly she righted herself, jerking the unseen monster up to the surface. Her fists balled into hammers, pummeling the hard reptilian head. The tentacles slipped, then tightened again around her belly and neck. Siva spit wildly for air.

"You'll not have me," she sputtered. "You will *not!*"

She grabbed the tentacle circling her neck, prying her fingers beneath the slimy cord. Precious air reached her lungs. She released her leg-hold and pulled for shore, hauling the creature up where the stricken deer still lay, wounded and kicking. Siva towed the beast like an ox-drawn cart, grunting and cursing, hacking at the tentacles with her hands until finally, when she was knee deep in foam, the glint of a weapon caught her eye. Just beneath the surface lay a rock, volcanic, sharp, and perfect. With the creature pulling her toward its snapping face, Siva reached down and snatched the stone, cutting her hands on its jagged surface and streaming blood into the water. She hefted the thing above her, held her ground for one more moment, then let the tentacles whip her forward.

The great snout opened. Siva flew toward it, weapon in hand. She brought down the stone and drove it into the one good eye, bursting it wide. The creature gurgled, the tentacles slackened, and Siva continued, blow after vicious blow, pulverizing the reptilian head, spraying black blood and ooze. She roared like a wild-woman, filling every shot with rage, feeling the skull crack beneath her. Finally, the two appendages uncoiled from her body. The beast's unseen legs paddled madly, trying to escape. Siva snatched the tentacle around her belly and yanked the thing toward her.

"No, no, no, monster!" she bellowed. "You won't get away!"

Jaiakrin's power surged inside her. Mercilessly she brought the stone down a final time, shattering it against the pulverized head, then used her bloodied fists, beating the creature until it shuddered.

She staggered backward, the limp tentacle still in hand. She stared at the thing, its strange body deflating and spreading out along the top of the water. Her own body burned in agony as the glamour left her. Scars from the suckers rose up on her neck and belly. Blood sluiced from the cuts in her hands. Panting, she pulled the creature ashore where the wounded deer lay, twisted and wailing. The madness of the scene enraged Siva. She fell to her knees between the creatures, one beautiful but cruelly dying, the other a freakish, nightmare-thing. She had spent her life in the waters of her homeland and never seen anything like it.

"J'horan filth."

Probably brought to their shores by Alliance ships, she decided. Her world was changing, and this abomination was a sign. She hugged her arms around herself, cold and nauseous from her wounds. Blood and grime soiled her skin and hair. She thought of going to the waterfall, but felt too weak to move. Jaiakrin's glamour was powerful, but always took its toll.

Sleep, she told herself. *And food*. That's what she needed. She shuffled on her knees to the once fabulous white deer, running a trembling hand over its wounded belly and seeing the marks in its snowy fur, the same marks pocking her own skin. Those might heal, she knew, but the legs looked broken. And if the deer couldn't walk, it couldn't possibly survive. Siva laid her head against the animal, feeling its pitched breath. Even on Tojira, life was pitiless.

The deer's suffering was unbearable. She lifted her head to find another rock, then saw the glorious figure of Jaiakrin emerge from the trees along the beach. Siva sat up, awestruck as she saw the dread on his bronzed face.

Jaiakrin, lord of the hunt and master of the holy island, looked at his slaughtered deer. He walked slowly, clearly appalled by the bloody sight marring his beach, his sandaled feet leaving no impression at all in the sand. He appeared in his most mortal of forms, that of a golden man, with a mane of sunlight and a hairless, muscular chest, laid partially bare by his loose-fitting tunic. Tongues of flame leapt from his fingertips and his eyes shined like emeralds, but a pall dimmed his beauty and his face hung with sadness. He glanced sorrowfully at Siva, still kneeling in the grassy mud, then at the strange beast she'd slain. Beside her the deer bucked and wailed.

"Jaiakrin," said Siva plaintively, "do something."

The hunter-god floated closer, eight feet tall but silent as a breeze. Drops of flame fell like tears from his sun-fired hair. He knelt beside the suffering stag, running his enormous hand along its velvet antlers, his skin untouched by the mud that soiled Siva. Slowly his fingers crossed to the beast's breast, resting above its racing heart. The deer's breathing stilled and its cries grew mercifully silent. Calm befell its anxious eyes. Then, as if time itself had frozen, the breathing stopped. The lush white breast stilled. And the last spark of life vanished from it gaze.

Jaiakrin drew back his hand. Misery washed his golden face. He stood, towering over the kneeling Siva, and she realized he still hadn't looked at her.

"I tried, Jaiakrin," she said. "I was too late."

His youthful eyes went to her at last. "Let me look at you," he said, offering down his hand.

Siva reached up and let her patron help her to her feet. She wobbled unsteadily for a moment, feeling no shame in her nakedness as she stood before him. Jaiakrin examined her wounds, looking perplexed.

"I'm sorry, Jaiakrin," she offered. "I was resting by the water. If I hadn't fallen asleep..." She slipped her hand out of his. "I'm no protector at all. Not of men, nor of any creatures."

There was no anger in Jaiakrin, just resignation. "You're hurt."

Siva shook her head. "It's nothing."

Jaiakrin looked at the beast Siva had slain, going toward it and kicking at it with his golden toe. He was said to be Clionet's favorite child, an understandable choice given his beauty.

"I've never seen a creature like that," said Siva. "I'm sure no one in my family has either. It's J'horan. It must be."

Since anyone could recall—from the very time of Hiaran maybe—Cryori waters had been protected from the continent's atrocities. The shenenra had seen to that, devouring the strange creatures that strayed too close to Nesenor. But like every other protection from J'hora, that too was crumbling. Even the gods couldn't stop it.

"Whatever these nameless things are," said Jaiakrin, "they're dangerous. You're in danger too." He looked at Siva. "Is that why you were so keen to fight it?"

The accusation surprised Siva. "I only fought to protect the stag. Not to test myself."

"Or to harm yourself?" Jaiakrin barely hid his frustration. Except for the sound of the waterfall, the lagoon was hush. "I have watched you torment yourself since you came here. I have tried to give you time to heal, but you seem no better at all."

"It's true," Siva admitted. "My soul is...gone."

"Only misplaced," said Jaiakrin. "But you will rediscover it. Tojira is magical that way."

"It is," said Siva. Even the island's mud felt good on her.

"If you'd been anyone else, I would have killed you for stepping foot here. But your grief was so great..." When Jaiakrin shrugged, embers jumped from his shoulders. "I have wondered how you have endured it. So, I've decided something—you will mourn for Sh'an no longer."

Siva sank to her knees. "Lord Jaiakrin, my grief is all I have..."

"Grief is poison. You're drunk on it." He stooped to meet her eyes. "My Siva. You came here to beg me to let you die. Did I not refuse you?"

Siva nodded, mute from embarrassment. She tried to look away, but Jaiakrin's golden hand took her chin and turned back her gaze.

"When you defile yourself, you defy me," he said. "And you break my heart. You will keep your vow to serve me, Siva, and you will live. You will mourn no more. For your sake and mine." Jaiakrin rose to tower over her. "Now go."

The order startled Siva. "Why? Are you sending me away?"

"Never. You may stay on Tojira as long as you wish. It's been joyous having you here. But you have a visitor."

"A visitor? Here?" said Siva, astonished. "Who?"

"Who?" chortled Jaiakrin. "The only one young and stupid enough to task me, Siva. Can you guess, or do you need another hint?"

There was only one person like that, Siva knew, and the answer made her grin.

The white sands of Tojira had been visible for more than a mile. Haru steered the keth into the waters lapping at the beach, ordering Elsifor to lever-up the retractable keel. Half a day ago, a fair breeze had blown them out of Jinja's harbor, past the ancient ring monuments and along the coast of Nesenor to the quiet waters of Naga province. They had watched the water change from blue to crystal, feeling their old lives slip behind them as the keth bore them away. Neither of them had eaten, though they had brought provisions for the trip. The excitement of their destination had quashed their appetites.

Haru went to the keth's single mast and reefed the sail with the wooden winch, so that a whisper of wind piloted them into the shallow water. He had never sailed so close to the holy island. The sight of it mesmerized him. Just beyond the ribbon of beach stood a wall of ancient trees, their roots erupting from the sand. Bright colored birds and monkeys darted between the branches. Crabs and gulls picked at shells along the shore. The untouched quietude silenced Haru's fears. He was the Tain of Nesenor; Jaiakrin wouldn't dare harm him.

Elsifor, however, was less confident. The animal-man spied the island of the hunter-god, his sharp eyes searching for the island's golden master. He had agreed to join the voyage to protect his Tain, but he feared Jaiakrin's magic arrows and knew that setting foot upon Tojira would be fatal for him. Liadin had made a point of warning them both about the hunter-god's privacy. Though he had given his blessing to Haru's voyage, he made no pretense of the danger, and refused to go along or disturb Jaiakrin on the soil of his forbidden home.

"If you go," Liadin had told him, "you go as Tain. Only your blood will protect you."

So Haru had done precisely that. He said his good-byes to Count Whistler, promised the Agoni he'd see him in J'hora, and set off the next morning with Elsifor for Tojira. And he'd done it all with smile on his face, sure for the first time since his father died that his life might have some purpose. As the keth drifted silently toward the beach, Haru went to the prow and waited for the familiar bump of sand on boat-bottom. The keth heeled to a stop. Elsifor stood up but did not venture from the center of the craft.

"I'd go with you if I could," he said. He tilted back his head and filled his nostrils with the island's lush scent. A puzzled frown crossed his face. "She's close," he said with surprise. "She already knows we're here."

"Jaiakrin told her," said Haru. He stooped down to pick up the unwieldy package at the bow of the boat, carefully wrapped in cloth and tied with rope. Tucking the bundle under his arm, he cradled it as he tossed one leg over the side of the vessel.

"Does touching the water count?" he asked Elsifor, "Or do I have to make it all the way to the beach before Jaiakrin can kill me?"

"Don't joke," chided Elsifor. "Just find Siva and bring her back. I'd like to leave here with my pelt on my back."

Haru swung his other leg over the side of the keth, straddled it for a moment, then splashed down into the blue water. A few startled birds on the beach took flight, but the waves stayed calm and no lightning struck him down. Haru looked back at Elsifor with a shrug.

"Go on," urged Elsifor. "Be quick."

In truth Haru wasn't afraid, at least not for himself. He was Clionet's favorite, after all.

"Watch out for water dragons," he said. "Ama'aga might be after us too."

"Go!" barked Elsifor.

Haru gave a wave and trudged toward the beach. Just as his foot touched dry land, he called out to the god of the island.

"Jaiakrin, I am Haru!" he shouted. "I've come for Siva!"

An unimpressed crab crossed in front of him. He looked up in the sky, cocked his head for any sound, but the beautiful silence of the island continued. He took a few more steps, then turned back to the keth. Elsifor waved him onward.

"Jaiakrin," cried Haru, "we only want to see our friend. We'll leave as soon as we speak to her. But we're not leaving until we do."

The god's apathy made Haru bristle. Just weeks ago, Clionet herself had ignored him at his father's funeral.

"Alright," he sighed. "Maybe you just don't care. Either way, I'm coming ashore."

He headed straight for the trees, almost reaching the grove when he saw the leaves begin to rustle. Startled, Haru stopped and braced himself, then saw Siva.

She stepped out from the trees, her expression despairing.

"Siva...?"

She was wraith-like, gaunt and pale. Scarlet battle marks crossed her neck and belly. After years of seeing her in tunics and armor, Haru was shocked by her dress. The simple sahi and kusu left more of Siva exposed then he'd ever seen before.

"Siva...what happened to you?"

He took another cautious step. She inched closer. Gone was the muscled physique of the fighter. The woman he'd once seen outrun a hunting dog now could barely stay upright. Dead grass had replaced her splendid, sky-bright hair. Haru blinked in amazement.

"Siva..."

"Haru." Siva smiled sadly, stepping fully out of the trees. "I shouldn't be surprised. You've always been insane."

Haru smiled too. Once they'd been the best of friends. Now he barely recognized her. "You look terrible."

"I know." Her laugh was miserable. "You have to go. This is Jaiakrin's island."

"Normally that would be a problem but I'm the Tain now. Jaiakrin had no right to let you stay here, Siva. You don't belong here."

"I made a vow to him."

"And to *me*," said Haru. "You remember that, don't you?"

"Hey!" cried Elsifor from out on the boat. He waved his arms frantically at the couple. "Stop the reunion! Siva, just come aboard! I want to get out of here!"

Siva took Haru's arm and dragged him down the beach. "What were you thinking? You brought Elsifor? *Here?*"

"Who else could I have brought here? I needed someone loyal, Siva."

The word struck her. Despite being emaciated she remained inches taller than him and could shrivel him with a look. "Is that your plan? To shame me?"

"You left," said Haru. "You just left. Why?"

Siva looked at him. Haru studied her face, looking for an answer.

"You're the only one that left, Siva. Even Valivan stayed. We were friends and you left when I needed you most."

"It isn't always about what you need, Haru," said Siva. She shrugged. "I can't explain it. You came here for something I can't give you."

"Siva, I came because I need you," said Haru. This wasn't at all how he wanted their reunion to go. "Look at you! You don't belong here."

"I do," snapped Siva. "This is precisely where I belong."

From out on the boat Elsifor cried, "Shut up, both of you! We have to go—*now*!"

Haru smirked, wondering if he should give her the package. Siva stood there in her bare feet, cool and unmoved. She said, "You think I ran away from you, Haru? I did. I ran away from you and Elsifor and Valivan and everyone. But I didn't break my vow. That vow was to your father, and it broke the moment he died." She didn't look angry suddenly, just profoundly tired. "You can't be here. You need to go."

She turned and walked off down the beach. Stunned, Haru stood mutely on the shore, watching her leave. Behind him he heard a loud groan.

"Oh, heart of the mother!" said Elsifor. "Go after her, Haru!"

He clung to the mast of the ketch like a cat afraid of water, waving Haru to hurry. His furry eyebrows arched with frustration. Haru turned and dashed down the beach after Siva.

"Wait!" he called. "Siva, stop!"

Siva shook her head without turning around. Her steps grew faster. "Go home, Haru. Just leave me be."

"Be what?" shouted Haru. "An oyster diver?" By now Elsifor was almost out of sight. "You're not a peasant anymore, Siva—you're a guardian. My guardian. You're the head of the Chorus."

"I'm not, not anymore. Don't ever say I am, Haru."

"You *are*," Haru shot back. He shifted his gift to the other armpit. "The Chorus can't go on without you. You're the one that found them. You're their leader."

"They don't want to be led, Haru. They never did."

"Because my father never wanted a Chorus. But I do. I need a Chorus and I need you, Siva. No one else can do it. Just you."

"The Chorus is a lie." She looked at him plaintively. "We were never like the old ones. We're all just misfits. We were supposed to protect Sh'an, but we let him die. I let him die. "

She turned away again, slowly this time, and continued down the beach, kicking at the sand as she walked. Haru followed a step behind her. He let the gentle noise of the tide unknot the tension, staring at the trail made by her feet. Finally, they rounded an outcropping that hid them from Elsifor's sight. A collection of giant stones jutted out into the sea. Siva climbed atop one, unperturbed by the slippery green algae and encrusted mollusks, and lowered herself cross-legged upon the stone, looking down at Haru.

"It used to be so easy for us to talk," she said. "I miss that."

"We can have it back," said Haru. "You just need to stop running away."

"I can't, Haru. I'm broken."

"No way. Siva can't be broken. Siva's made of steel."

She laughed. "Maybe once!"

"My father died because we weren't paying attention," said Haru. "Not just you, all of us. I was his *son*. I know you're feeling responsible. I know you cared about him but you weren't his son, Siva. If I can live with the guilt, so can you."

"Haru, look around. Look how beautiful it is here. You know what it is here? It's peaceful."

"Oh yeah? What happened to your stomach?"

Siva waved off the question. "A little wrestling—with the ugliest monster I've ever seen!" She laughed and Haru laughed too. "Oh, but I like it here. I need to stay."

Haru smiled but shook his head. "Sorry. You don't get to walk away. Your vow, remember? I'm holding you to it."

"That's done. No more vows for me."

"Oh really?" Haru climbed one stone closer to her. "What about your vow to Jaiakrin? I see you didn't break that one."

"That's different."

"Why?"

"He's a god."

"I know you came here to die, Siva. Did you beg Jaiakrin to kill you?"

Siva nodded. "I did."

"Let me guess—he said no."

"Yup."

"And so you're going to starve yourself to death?"

"I'm thinking of eating soon," mused Siva. "Jaiakrin will let me live here on Tojira. The way I lived when I was a village girl. That's what I want."

"I don't believe you," said Haru. "Jaiakrin turned you into a fighter, not some peasant who sits around feeling sorry for herself. Look at you—you've already been fighting. That's what you really want, isn't it?"

Haru set the package down on a stone near Siva's feet. The familiar sound of clinking metal made her grimace.

"Tell me that's not what I think it is," she said.

With one pull of the string the fabric slid open, revealing the gleaming contents.

Five silver knives, mirror-bright, fanned out on the stone, leather-wrapped hilts lovingly worn, points and edges ground sharp. Siva's eyes rounded longingly.

"My sword?" she asked.

"Back at the castle where you left it. You always liked the knives better."

"You're an imp."

She slid down to where her blades waited. She had made them each herself, taught by her patron Jaiakrin how to fold the metal and balance the blades so that they cut the air like arrows. No one could throw a knife truer than Siva, or with greater speed. With one casual toss she could pick an apple off a tree. Her fingers hovered over the blades, hesitating to touch them.

"Don't you want to know?" asked Haru. "You're aching to ask; I can see it."

"You won't leave till you tell me, so speak."

"Alright. We're going to J'hora. Me and the rest of the Chorus. We're going after Reius. We're going to kill him."

He expected her to laugh, or maybe roll her eyes. Siva's hand froze over the knives. "How?" she whispered.

"I've been invited. Reius wants me in J'hora to talk. Peace, he says. Count Whistler told me last night." Haru climbed up another stone. "He says he didn't kill my father, Siva, but I know he did. I *know* it. And now he's going to pay for it."

Her eyes flared. "Kill Reius," she said deliciously. "For that I can almost forgive you for coming here, Haru. But I still have the same question—how?"

"Reius wants to talk to me," Haru repeated. "Face to face, that's what Whistler said. Once I'm close enough I can kill him."

"*You'll* kill him? You've never killed anyone in your life."

"I know that. But if anyone ever deserved dying, it's Reius."

"He'll have guards. He'll have you searched. And this could all be a trap. Have you thought of that?"

"I'm not stupid, Siva. Whistler might be, but I'm not. I know it's a trap. Reius wants me dead just like my father. But it's a chance. Just yesterday Reius was unreachable. Now he's invited me right into his home! If I can get close to him, I can kill him."

Siva frowned. "You won't be shooting Reius with an arrow. You'll have to get right up to him and gut him like a fish."

Haru made his expression hard. "I promised Clionet revenge, Siva. I promised myself revenge. I don't care who kills Reius as long as he's dead. It'll be whoever gets to him first and has the best chance."

"That's not a plan at all," carped Siva. Finally, she hopped down from her stony perch. "If you four imbeciles are going to have any chance at all, you're going to need a leader."

"We will," nodded Haru. "But a strong one. A fighter. Not a fishing girl."

Siva picked up one of her knives, sneering at her reflection in the blade. "What fishing girl?"

Chapter Six

CALLING THE MOONLIGHT

S iva did not return with Haru to Jinja. With only two days before leaving for J'hora, there were good-byes she needed to say on Tojira. She watched Haru depart on his boat with Elsifor, nodding at them from the shore as they waved farewell. They would return for her soon, Haru promised, with a beast-ship instead of a lowly keth. Until then, Siva had her knives again. More importantly, she had a purpose.

On Tojira there were no secrets from Jaiakrin. The golden god had known her decision the moment she made it. Yet somehow it was impossible to tell him. He had been so kind to her, so welcoming, that to leave him seemed an insult. Siva wasted her afternoon by the lagoon, until the sun fell away and the moon soared overhead. She needed strength for the coming battle, and so she gathered all the food she could from the nearby trees and water, stuffing herself full of fish and berries and cursing herself for letting her muscles atrophy. At first she ate quickly, almost to the point of vomiting, and when she could hold no more, she laid down near the waterfall and looked up at the moon and remembered how much she loved Sh'an.

The moon looked peculiar to her, swollen and red. She wondered if the human moon looked the same, or if the people of the continent named the stars the way Cryori did. She knew nothing of the continent, only myths and stories, but she was not afraid to face the outside world. Like Haru, she burned with vengeance, and knew that would sustain her.

But Haru—he had changed. Vengeance didn't suit him. He was bold now. Stupidly courageous. He had conceived his mad mission in a fit, somehow convincing Elsifor to join him. Shadur too.

And me, she thought darkly.

And Valivan? Siva's eyes narrowed on the moon. They needed Valivan, perhaps more than anyone else.

"It doesn't matter," Siva whispered. "I would go myself. I *should* have gone myself." She sat up suddenly. "Damn me!"

The monkeys in the trees fell silent at her cry. The stars winked peacefully above her. And then, as though her cry excised a demon, she felt contented. Her pain was easing, and she had Haru's crazy, reckless plot to thank for it.

Siva rose slowly to her feet, her packed belly aching. She stretched up toward the moonlit sky as fireflies flashed over the lagoon. Tojira was a paradise and she would miss it. Most of all, she would miss Jaiakrin. She turned to go in search of him, surprised to see his golden presence walking toward her, his sandaled feet soundless on the beach. Siva clamped down on her yawn. A flutter of nervousness chilled her. But as usual, Jaiakrin's face was unperturbed.

She prepared to greet him, then noticed the strange object in his hand. About the size of her forearm, it looked like a club or maybe a short spear. Curious, Siva hurried to meet him, reaching him just as he came to the edge of the lagoon. A sad smile curved his lips as he regarded her belly.

"Siva, you look...fed."

"I've eaten," sighed Siva. She stuck out her gut as though she was pregnant. "Too much. But you were right, Jaiakrin—I shouldn't starve myself."

"Because you need strength."

Siva nodded, chagrined. "I should have come to tell you. I'm sorry."

"Jaiakrin does not lay about waiting," he said, not unkindly. He raised the item in his hand. "I have been busy making this for you."

Siva spied the unknown object. A weapon, she supposed, and mostly straight, made of antler and elk sinew, with a spur that stuck out of one end like a hooked finger. It seemed too awkward to be a club, and too short for a spear. Baffled, Siva looked up at the towering god.

"What is it?"

"Come," said Jaiakrin, moving away from the water. With Siva following close behind, he told her, "This is an atlatl. A hunting weapon."

"Oh. Hunting? My lord, you know that I am leaving Tojira, yes?"

"To hunt a man," said Jaiakrin. "You have your knives and your sword, but you have nothing like this. Here..." He put his arm around her to draw her close. "Open your hand."

"Atlatl..." Siva let the god place the odd weapon in her fingers. "I've never heard of such a thing."

"It is a spear thrower," said Jaiakrin. He moved to stand behind her, closing her hand around the weapon so that she held the end opposite the hooked side. "Like that," he directed. "Good." He slowly drew back her arm. "Now imagine you are throwing a spear with it. Back and over, behind your head."

Siva let him pose her. "Like this?"

Jaiakrin stepped back to inspect her form. "The atlatl is like a sling. It will let you throw the spear farther and faster than even you could, Siva."

Siva held her pose. "Uh-huh. But where's the spear?"

"Are you ready to throw? You have to be ready."

"I'm ready, Jaiakrin, but throw...what?"

"Just a bit more..."

Determined, Siva drew back another inch...

...and in the cradle of the weapon grew a scintillating spear.

"Mother goddess!"

Like a living flame, the spear stretched from the spur of the atlatl to well beyond its end, as long as any hunting spear Siva had ever seen. Its dazzling light blinded her, blazing in the darkness of the lagoon and sending up crackling wisps of flame. Siva held the weapon, afraid to disturb the miracle. Her eyes flicked wildly toward Jaiakrin.

"How?" Then she noticed the god's hands, and the same fire leaping from his very fingers. "It's you! Are you making the spear?"

"Throw it," ordered Jaiakrin. "Across the water."

Like pitching a rock, Siva let the spear fly. It exploded out of the atlatl, the force of it numbing her arm, shooting over the lagoon like a lightning bolt and crashing through the trees in a sparkling shower. Branches fell and flames spat, but the magical spear was gone, leaving only char and smoke behind. Jaiakrin smiled with satisfaction.

"Whenever you call upon me, I will be there," he said. "You will be far from me. My powers will be limited, but this weapon can summon me. I have placed all that I am into its making. It will serve you, Siva, as you have served me."

Siva couldn't believe such a gift could be created, much less given to a mortal. She thought of refusing it, but only for a moment. She looked up at Jaiakrin, but could find no words to express her gratitude. The noise of the lagoon enshrouded them.

"You have been my father," said Siva at last. "I called upon you when I was a child, but I've never known why you answered."

"Because I am Jaiakrin," said the god coyly. "Because you called for help."

His answer left her empty. "Children always call for help," said Siva. "Why did you answer *me*?"

Jaiakrin stooped to face her, putting his big, fiery hands on her shoulders. "Gods sometimes choose favorites. We shouldn't, but we do. You needed me. And I needed your devotion. When you use the atlatl, remember me and know how much I love you."

"I will. I will always remember, Jaiakrin. But do not be sad—I will be home soon. Once Reius is dead I'll return to see you."

Knowing Siva would follow, Jaiakrin turned and started walking along the moonlit shore. His pace was slow, thoughtful, his face troubled. Siva hurried up alongside him.

"I know I failed to protect Sh'an, but I won't fail again. I'll kill Reius. I swear it! And with this weapon you've given me...how can I fail? Please, don't be afraid for me."

When Jaiakrin sighed, all the flames on his fabulous body flared. "You are fast. You are strong. Your heart is pure and good."

"But?"

"You are young. I made you a warrior when there was no war for you to fight."

"There's war now, Jaiakrin. Or soon will be."

"Yes," he agreed sadly. "Horrible things are coming."

Siva took his hand to stop him from walking, making him face her. "What are you seeing? Tell me."

"I'm not Skorthoros. I cannot prophesize. But I know when the seasons change. We've had years of summer..." He shrugged, almost like a child. "Now comes the cold."

"You mean Reius? Jaiakrin, he'll be dead soon..." Siva studied his face. "Unless you mean something else?"

The glow of his fire dimmed a bit. "It is not only Cryori who war, Siva. Immortals war, too." He took her hands and closed them around the atlatl. "Take what I can give you. Make yourself ready for your Tain."

His vague words terrified her. "No," she insisted. "Tell me what you mean. What are you afraid of?"

He smiled, and Siva knew he would not answer. He bent down and kissed her forehead with his burning lips. "Keep yourself safe," he said.

"I will," promised Siva. "You'll see. I'll have Reius' head with me when I return."

"A true hunter's trophy," pronounced Jaiakrin proudly.

Then, without another word, the hunter-god of Tojira turned and walked away on his fiery feet, leaving Siva in the suddenly dark lagoon.

Elsifor looked up at the moon and howled.

High in a towering tree, with the sinew of a jaguar dangling from his talons, he studied the moon and wondered at its power. All his life he had craved its light, baying at the distant orb, fascinated by its pull. Blood stained his teeth and matted his fur. He had hunted, filling his belly with the meat of the jaguar. The sweet, sticky smell of its innards clung to his face. The bloodlust had passed, yet the moon still haunted him. If he listened hard enough, he could hear it whispering. Tonight, Elsifor longed for its stories.

The moon saw everything. Nothing could hide from it. It already knew what they'd find in the human world. Elsifor envied its precognition. Were there creatures like him among the humans? He supposed not, for even he didn't know what he was precisely. Born with fangs and knives for fingers, he had won the love of his patron goddess, but on nights like this even her adoration was not enough.

Elsifor climbed higher, leaving the carcass of the jaguar hanging over a branch and clawing up the ever-narrowing tree trunk. In the distance slept Jinja, peaceful and safe, its far-off windows winking with candlelight, its children protected from the beasts of the outside world.

For now.

Elsifor had pledged himself to Haru. He would follow the young Tain anywhere, even to his own death, but he still had so many questions, and the thought of dying without answers troubled him. He was drunk on blood, his emotions spinning. But he could not weep tears, and so could only cry as animals cried.

With howls.

And when finally his throat was dry and aching, he scaled even farther up the tree, until at last he reached its peak. There he hung like a monkey, the treetop bending with his weight, the black earth far beneath him. The wind pulled his fur. The tree groaned, threatening to snap.

I am higher than anyone, he thought. *Tonight, I am as good as any man.*

Climbing down would only diminish him. In the trees he was more than either man or beast.

In the morning, he vowed.

He would wait until the sun rose. Then, he would relinquish his place at the top of the world. He would board Haru's ship and sail to the continent, and never see his home again.

From his place on the balcony, Haru could see the *Gonkin* in Jinja's harbor, asleep but ready for its long voyage to J'hora, its white sails reefed like the wings of a butterfly, its crew dormant beneath its deck. The tips of her silver ramming claws glowed in the powerful moonlight, jutting out from her prow. The *Gonkin* was the largest of the beast-ships. Ancient and storied, she had carried the old Tains to the shores of the continent, bringing rule and terror to the human world. She had a crew of fifty men, twenty-two sails, and could carry over three-hundred Cryori into battle. But tomorrow her cargo would be just five bitter misfits.

Haru knew there wasn't much time. He had said his good-byes to his manservant, Calix, and had packed everything he thought he would need for the trip, mostly clothes and a few personal items he hoped would comfort him. But he had been given so little time to plan, and he supposed that was part of Reius' design. Now, with the meeting in J'hora so close at hand, putting together any sort of reasonable plot was nearly impossible.

It was far past midnight and the silence of the courtyard below comforted Haru. Finally, he was alone. With nothing left to do but board the *Gonkin* in the morning, he could finally think.

But when he tried, he simply couldn't. It was all too much suddenly, and he sunk into his chair on the balcony, collapsing in the moonlight until his chin touched his chest and his eyes drooped from exhaustion. In two days, he had managed to convince everyone to join him, even Siva. She would wait for them on Tojira, she'd decided, and from there they would sail to J'hora and kill Reius.

Somehow.

The details of his plan had yet to be worked out, but Haru didn't care. Just a chance, that's all he really wanted. If he could get close enough, if Siva and the others could protect him long enough, he would kill Reius.

On the boat, he groaned to himself. That's when he'd prepare. With nothing else to do but wait and talk, they'd come up with the perfect plan. Or at least one good enough. He'd gotten Siva. He'd convinced Liadin. Even Valivan...

His eyes shut before he could stop them. In less than a moment, he was sleeping.

And when he awoke Liadin was standing over him, a gentle smile on his face. Haru drew a deep, slow breath to rouse himself, blinking up at the Arch-Disciple.

"Liadin...oh...I must have fallen asleep..." He stretched but did not get out of his chair. "How long have you been here?"

"Long enough to remember looking at you when you were a little boy sleeping. Children never sit still. When they're sleeping—that's the only chance parents ever get to really look at them."

"Why?" croaked Haru.

"Because children are meant to be adored."

None of it made sense to Haru. He arched his back with a giant yawn, glad but confused to see his mentor. "Liadin?" he probed. "You need me?"

"I came to ask you the same thing. I've spoken to Captain Nuara—he'll be ready to sail as soon as you're all aboard. I've had your things taken down already. Shadur and Valivan are asleep. I don't know where Elsifor is, but I'm sure he'll meet you at the ship. Anything else?"

Haru shook his head. With Shadur and Valivan already in the castle, everything was ready. "I don't think so. Just sleep." He started getting out of his chair then stopped himself. Liadin was still watching him. "Liadin?"

"Haru, I came to say goodbye to you. Tomorrow when you leave, they'll be others around. I wanted to say goodbye alone."

"Yeah," said Haru sadly. He gestured to the closest other chair on the enormous balcony. "Will you sit with me? There's no hurry."

Liadin pulled the chair right up to Haru, sitting down to face him. Clearly, something particular was on his mind. And Haru knew exactly what it was.

"So, when you say good-bye, you mean *good-bye*. Is that it?"

Liadin smirked. "Discovered."

"No, Liadin," said Haru. "I'll be back. We're all coming back after we kill Reius. I'm going to bring all of them back alive."

"I've always loved your confidence, boy."

"Ah," sighed Haru. "You don't believe me. That's alright—I don't expect you to."

"I believe you'll kill Reius. I don't think anything can stop you from that. All that matters to you now is vengeance, Haru. I'm sorry to see such hatred in you."

His words surprised Haru. "Everyone's always wanted to me change, Liadin. To get serious about life. Well, I'm serious now. I thought you'd be pleased."

Liadin put up his hands. "Stop. I promise I didn't come to lecture you."

"No," said Haru quickly. "I know." He looked right into Liadin's eyes. "This would all be a lot easier if I had your blessing. I'm sure I can do this, Liadin."

Liadin's face hardened. "I think you'll die trying, Haru. There's no way out of J'hora. Once you even attempt to harm Reius, that whole city will close around you like a noose. You need to know that, Haru."

"I do, Liadin." Haru tried to comfort the old man. "Really."

"You know what your eyes are telling me? That you're not listening. That no matter how much I talk, you won't hear me. That's why I'm not trying to stop you."

"Liadin, I made a promise to Clionet."

"Yes, you did. *You* made a promise to her. But you're not going into this alone, Haru. The others need to know how dangerous it is, too."

Haru refused to look away. "They know that. But they trust me. That's why I need to believe we'll succeed. So they believe it too."

Liadin cocked an eyebrow. "You *have* changed."

The old man stood up, smiling sadly and spreading out his arms. Surprised by the gesture, Haru rose to meet him, melting as the big arms encircled him.

"Remember something, Haru," Liadin whispered. "I love you. No matter what happens, remember that I love you."

Haru closed his eyes. In that moment, he had a father again. "I will, Liadin," he said. "I'll remember."

Chapter Seven

THE HOLY SERPENT

L iadin should have expected to see the skeleton, but the revelation froze him. It lay there in its cell, an iron collar circling
its neck, a stout chain fixing it to the wall, rusted from the moisture
of the canal rushing through the catacombs. In life the thing might
have been a man or a woman; Liadin could not tell. The dungeon
had housed both genders in its history, and time had stripped the
skeleton's flesh. Tattered rags hung from its shoulders, eaten by
vermin. Its eye sockets gaped from behind the metal bars.

The catacombs had been sealed by the time Liadin was ten, and
he had always assumed no unlucky inmates had been left behind.
But the blank stare of the forgotten prisoner reminded him of the
place's ghastly past, of the souls who'd been tortured and turned
into slaves within its tunnels, and the Arch-Disciple could not stop
a prayer from springing to his lips.

He had waited until midnight to unlock the gates, breaking the
decades-old locks that sealed off the catacombs from the castle
above. He had said his good-byes to Haru and the others, had
watched them sail away on the *Gonkin*, and then had buried himself
in the mundane work of his office, working diligently until the sun
went down, when he could finally attend to other matters. As Sh'an's
closest advisor, he had been given the keys to the catacombs long
ago, and had not expected the ancient locks to still tumble. But they
had, remarkably easily, and when he opened the door the stench
of death and ocean slime climbed up the stairway to greet him.
Two-hundred and five steps, and he had taken them all with a torch

in one hand and a heavy sack in the other, and he did not stop until he saw the skeleton, when he froze in its accusing stare.

Liadin held up his torch, peering through the gloom. The dungeon was a maze, and he knew he could easily get lose within its twists. Built into the base of the mountain, the ocean itself ran through its stone corridors, branching out into rivers. He could see the derelict hulk of a boat floating ahead of him, moored to the stone walk that lined the waterway. Once, dozens of boats like it had plied the same waters, ferrying prisoners to the cells and torture halls. They were captives from the continent, mostly, stolen during coastal raids to become slaves in the homes of Cryori nobles, to work themselves to death on fishing boats and in the fields, or to serve the lust of rich merchants. The dungeon had countless cells, and so a staggering number of prisoners had suffered in its dank walls.

Liadin steeled himself and carefully stepped along the walkway, shuffling through the rats and insects. Following the subterranean river would lead him to the sea. Even now he could hear the ocean as its waters flooded the catacombs. Iron gates partitioned the rivers, leaving the walkways unobstructed, and occasional bridges spanned the sides, allowing jailors to cross without boats. Liadin clutched his torch and sack tightly as he moved, afraid to lose either to the water. The slime covered bricks made walking treacherous. The smell of rotting sea-life and decay assailed his nostrils. He moved with purpose, passing the cells and gates and ignoring the bits of bone and teeth crunching beneath his feet. In time he passed his first gate, then another, and as the river widened beside him the sound of the ocean grew louder.

At last, he could smell the sea.

He hurried, quickened by his own nervous thoughts. What he'd done tonight had not been easy. Guilt would come, he knew, and he would suffer its torments mightily, but he refused to do so yet. Now—this night—he needed to be keen.

His Cryori fathers had been cruel. The torture devices in the cells testified to their peculiar pleasures. But they had been formidable, bringing the humans under their yoke and spreading the glory of Clionet's clan. True, there was no good reason for a dungeon so vast.

Only sadism could explain such a thing. But the old ways had taught the humans fear, a lesson Reius and his false god needed dreadfully.

His torch blazed a path along the underground river as Liadin walked on. Now he could feel the breath of the sea, brining his lips. A great, dark maw yawned up ahead, fettered by an enormous gate. Liadin moved toward it, quickly first then slowly as his apprehension grew. The stabbing light of his torch gave way to the gentle blush of moonlight. He approached the towering gate, the huge iron structure guarding the sea entrance to the cave in which he stood, water pouring past its bars. The walkway was wider now, spreading out into a platform with mooring posts and dried out lengths of rope. The rusted wheel of the gate stood before him, tall and wrapped by rusted chains. It had taken three men to raise the gate in the past, but time had ruined the wheel and sealed the gate with rock and barnacles. Liadin was sure no man could open it.

And so, he did not try.

He calmed himself. He set his torch into a crooked holder on the wall. He clutched the sack in both hands and slowly approached the gate. With the tang of seawater on his tongue, he prayed.

"First born of the goddess—I feel you! Conqueror of the seas—I implore you!"

He kept his eyes wide as he spoke, calling out to the presence in the water in the ancient tongue of his religion.

"Pity my petition. Accept my offering!"

All his life Liadin had studied the gods. He knew when they heard his prayers and when they were near. Tonight, the holy serpent was very close. His hand trembled as he reached into the sack. His fingers clenched around a tuft of hair. As he pulled the sack away, Liadin held up his grisly prize.

"My devotion!" he cried.

Calix's head dangled from Liadin's fist, his eyes staring lifelessly out to see. A wave of nausea inundated Liadin as he stuck the severed head through the bars of the gate.

"For Nesenor!" he lamented. "Clionet forgive me!"

Emotion overwhelmed him suddenly. The warrior-god was a blood-hungry patron, who loved the blood of humans most of all. With a tortured cry, Liadin tossed Calix's head into the waiting ocean, collapsing to his knees as the sea rushed in to snatch it. The bloodied sukatai still rested on his back, the very weapon he had used to slay the docile manservant. A knot tied itself in his stomach. He started to wretch, then saw the ocean swirling just beyond the gate. Slowly he raised his miserable face. A vortex formed outside the dungeon, foaming and circling in the moonlight, pulling the ocean into itself.

Liadin staggered to his feet, peering through the gate into the watery funnel. A terrible din like the barking of dogs spat up from its depths. The vortex swelled, spreading out and flattening, driving something toward the surface. Liadin lifted himself to his feet. He would not run or cower from this god—not after what he'd done for him.

A pair of enormous, green-scaled hands reached out of the roiling waters, grabbing hold of the gate. The dungeon shivered. Rust and chips of stone flaked from the ceiling and iron bars. Twisting, groaning metal bent and the wheel slipped its chains, turning for the first time in decades. The two hands rose, becoming forearms as they wrenched against the giant gate. Liadin could see their spiky armor, like the skin of a brightly colored crustacean. Slowly, slowly, the frozen relic began to rise.

Liadin looked on, astonished, as the being he'd summoned hefted the ancient gate, growing out of the waters, forcing up the age-old iron. An armored head and shoulders emerged, dark-eyed and green-skinned, crusted with crab-like spikes. A great, bare torso thrust outward, the muscled arms wrenched, and the gate crested upward, shattering coral and barnacles. The whirlpool sputtered then becalmed, and the waves crashed against his finned back. Just below the giant's navel, the smooth tail of a serpent began.

Ama'aga, warrior-god and first born of Clionet, floated on the edge of the ocean, regarding the man who'd summoned him. The painful din died away, replaced by the reassuring tide. He was an enormous being, fierce-faced and beautiful, his crab-armor purple and orange, his black hair braided with seaweed. A smear of blood crossed his mouth, as if he'd consumed Liadin's ghastly gift. The god's dark eyes tilted up toward the lifted gate, then back down at Liadin.

"That will not hold her," he pronounced.

Liadin refused to kneel. He had summoned Ama'aga for a purpose. He had done as the holy serpent asked. Now was the time for reciprocity.

"Great Ama'aga," he said without fear. "Welcome home."

Chapter Eight

THE TALE OF THE REVEN

O n board the *Gonkin*, the ocean simply had no end. It was
forever, infinite in all directions, cradling the beast-ship in
its waves. There were no islands on the horizon; Nesenor was a
memory. In all his life Haru had never felt so isolated. Or so free.

For two days they sailed east, watching the sun stroll across the
sky and porpoises race alongside. The birds and insects had vanished with the land, and behind them stretched a mile-long tail of
foam, a fading arrow pointing toward their distant home. The crew
of the *Gonkin* worked the sails and pulleys and ropes. Navigators
manipulated their gleaming instruments, reading the heavens like
a map and peeking through their brass spyglasses. Captain Nuara
strode confidently across the deck, the bare bits of his arms peppered with tattoos. Beneath the waves the *Gonkin's* keel shifted with
the currents, its mysterious armatures extending and retracting,
speeding the beast-ship through the water.

Haru had only been aboard beast-ships a few times in his life.
All his visits had been too short, but he was sure he could help the
crew—if only they'd let him. He spent the whole first day topside
and the entire night as well, plying the crew with questions. There
were forty-five beast-ships in the fleet, and Haru knew each one by
name. They were more than a hundred years old, each one built to
resemble a different Cryori creature. Being the speediest vessel in

the fleet, the *Gonkin* was a leopard, its prow shaped like a hunting cat's muzzle, its wooden hull contoured with sprinting legs. The beast-ships had been constructed in the days of conquest, inspired by the goddess Paiax and built with the help of her divine son, Hor'roron, whose secret techniques died along with the men who slaved to bring the crafts to life. Yet the *Gonkin* and her sisters survived, fascinating boys like Haru and filling their heads with dreams.

Responsibilities had already supplanted most of Haru's dreams. In a week he would be in J'hora. Then, if all went well, he'd be a murderer. The grisly future haunted him, but for not now he was glad to be a traveler instead of a Tain, and he relished the long trip ahead.

Noon brought the change of watch. As the larboard watch went below for midday meal and rest, the refreshed starboard watch took their place. The thought of food set Haru's stomach rumbling, but he was too fascinated by the happenings topside to go below. Besides that, there was always the chance that Siva or Shadur would corner him, looking for answers. Already Siva was complaining about their lack of a plan. And Valivan still hadn't adjusted to all the new voices on-board. Only Val had managed to score a private place to sleep, taking the tiny quarters of the *Gonkin's* Sailing Master as his own. The rest of them slept on hammocks with the crew, even Haru, who quickly discovered the one thing he hated about life aboard ship—the utter lack of privacy. Despite his rank as Tain, the *Gonkin* had no servants to mother him.

He headed amidships, curious for a another look at the *Gonkin's* brass windlasses. There he paused, watching them slowly spooling and unspooling, the bright white sheets taut on the towering masts. The sails fanned out from the sides of the ship like the wings of a butterfly, spreading out wide or folding back upon themselves. Just as the keel detected the water's currents, the unusual sails somehow read the winds, trimming themselves to best catch the air's fickle eddies. Haru bent in for a closer look. Seawater shimmered on the lines. Tempted, he reached out a finger...

"Not the sheets," snapped a voice.

Startled, Haru bolted upright, turning to see Captain Nuara hovering over him.

"Sorry," he stuttered.

"You've no gloves," the captain remarked. "The wrong kind of wind comes? Cut your fingers right off. Less you don't mind playing with yourself left-handed."

"I wasn't going to touch it," said Haru. "I know about ships."

"Tain Haru, you can touch anything you like on the *Gonkin*...with my permission."

"Alright," agreed Haru. Until now he'd managed to stay out of Nuara's way. "I was only looking."

"Look with your eyes, not your fingers. I had a steward got his sleeve caught in a windlass once. Chewed off his arm right up to the elbow. When Hor'roron designed these contraptions, he didn't consider stupidity."

"I said I'd stay clear," replied Haru.

Nuara cocked his head at Haru's icy tone. "One-armed men aren't much use aboard ships. I've seen you asking a lot of questions. It's good to be curious but it's better to be careful. People die at sea. If that happens to you, we can throw you overboard if you like. Or we can bring you back to Jinja for a landsman's burial. Maybe your servants could bury you in the garden, get some big roses next year."

Haru couldn't tell if Nuara was joking or not. His wicked smile made him different from the other Cryori captains Haru had met. He wore a thick brown scarf that covered his entire neck and his uniform consisted mostly of worn leather and buckles. And like most seafarers, Nuara liked to tease.

"I was aboard the *Hakar* once," said Haru. "Do you know Captain Ora? He let me spend a day aboard when he came to visit my father last year. We didn't put out to sea but it was grand."

"A good ship," corrected Nuara. "Not grand."

"Big, though. Bigger than the *Gonkin*."

"Slower too."

"Because she's a lion," said Haru. "She really looks like one, too. She's got forepaws made of iron and a mane, even. She's the only other cat in the fleet." Haru returned Nuara's odd smile. "Must be hard to be aboard her little sister."

"Captain Ora likes to politic," said Nuara. "I'm surprised he didn't kiss you when you became Tain." Then, he let his smile melt away. "My condolences to you. Your father was a good man." He shrugged. "Not a great Tain, but an honest one at least."

Nuara's candor surprised Haru. "Did you know my father?"

"I met him," said Nuara, "Once. But you miss my meaning. He was a Tain. Tains make decisions the rest of us live by. Sh'an held us back. He never let us do what we train to do. That's how he'll be remembered."

"Oh," said Haru a bit too sharply. "You're one of those who prefers war."

Nuara smirked and turned away. He crooked a finger for Haru to follow.

"Walk with me."

Haru caught up quickly, striding with Nuara toward the *Gonkin's* forecastle. Ariyo, the ship's Sailing Master, took one look at his captain's determined face before dismissing himself. So far, the forecastle was the only part of the vessel Haru had yet to explore. Nuara went to the ship's wheel. Haru sidled up beside him and tried to hide his excitement. The forecastle was only a step higher than the rest of the deck, yet somehow felt like a tower to Haru.

"It was a frosty morning on deck when my father died," said Nuara after a time. "Winter on the continent. Before the White Fleet set afloat. Before Reius." The captain spoke softly so none but Haru could hear him. "The *Reven* was on patrol near the coast of Lumeszia. Orders from Tain Karesis."

"My grandfather," said Haru.

"Karesis toyed around with peace too, but he still wanted to show the flag. He knew Lumeszia had put a new warship to sea." Nuara sighed as he worked the wheel. "But you have to be committed to peace. You can't offer a gift with one hand while holding a dagger in the other."

"Uh-huh," nodded Haru, waiting for the captain to go on.

"At dawn the *Reven* sailed close enough for the Lumeszians to see from shore. Their ship was waiting in the fog, like a snake under a rock. The *Reven* cracked like an egg when she was rammed. Most of the crew went into the water. The only land they could swim for was Lumeszia, of course. So they did. All those men went into the water. Water filled with chunks of ice. Water the Lumeszians had chummed to bring the sharks."

"Oh."

"My father wasn't anything special," said Nuara. His voice got strangely quiet. "Just a crewman. Loyal, though. He went to Lumeszia because his Tain told him to go. I was ten years old." His smile got tight and grim. He stared straight ahead. "Ten years old."

"I'm sorry," said Haru.

"Why? You didn't kill him. I tell that story because no one remembers the *Reven*. She wasn't a beast-ship so she didn't much matter. But stories are sacred to mariners. It's what we have instead of homes." Nuara stepped aside. "Here," he offered. "Take the wheel."

Haru hesitated at the honor, but only for a moment. He slid into position behind the wheel, then slowly wrapped his fingers around the polished wood, getting the feel of the massive ship beneath him. Unlike most other vessels, beast-ships were steered from the bow, where the captain could see clearly—and be seen by his enemies. The *Gonkin* kept course, confidently cutting through the waves. Haru's eyes flicked toward Captain Nuara. A tattoo of Ama'aga flexed on his bicep.

"I'm proud to be making this journey with you, Tain Haru," said Nuara. "Peace is the only treasure worth hunting."

Haru tried not to grimace. Except for him and the Chorus, no one aboard knew the truth about their journey. Suddenly the deception felt shameful.

"Some people think it's a foolish idea," Haru said. "Reius has already ended the peace. Maybe my trip is just a trap."

"Then that makes you all the braver."

Haru bit his lip. "But you serve the Holy Serpent," he argued. "You're a warrior."

"Tain Haru, if you want to me to attack, I'll attack. If you want me to defend, I'll defend. If you want me to sail you to J'hora, even for the chance at peace, then that is my mission."

"But you don't trust Reius, do you?"

"Of course not," spat Nuara. "He hates us. He hates our gods, our children...he hates everything about us. But we are here and we are not going anywhere, and if Reius is as smart as they say, then perhaps he has realized that now."

"And if it's a trap?" pressed Haru. "What then?"

"Then you'll be killed. And my crew will be killed and my ship will be taken, and our names will be forever tainted in Nesenor."

"Oh," groaned Haru. "If you really think that, why are you helping me?"

Captain Nuara replied simply, "Because I might be wrong."

Chapter Nine

CLOSE QUARTERS

"**W**e need a plan!"

Haru's announcement boomed in the belly of the ship as he bounded down the stairs. Amongst the swinging hammocks and sleeping crewmen Siva was doing pushups, her nose hovering just above the planking. Shadur looked up from his gaming tiles. From the slump of his bed sling, Elsifor opened a single, drowsy eye. Haru stopped in the threshold, surprised at how loudly his voice had carried. A mariner who was preparing to nap after his long watch pretended not to hear as he slid off his boots, while another moved to the back of their quarters. Siva grimaced at Haru as she finished her exercise.

"Softer, I think."

Haru nodded, angry with himself. Their hammocks were all bunched together near the front of the lower deck, but that didn't mean they had any privacy. It was part of the reason they still hadn't discussed their plans. He pretended to smile at the mariners as he moved toward his own hammock. Siva rose to join him and Elsifor turned to face him from his bed. Shadur flipped a few more tiles, frowning at his bad luck before pushing them aside, his crystal hand obscured by the crimson gloves he wore. Unlike the others, Shadur had already donned the garb of an advocate, a pretense suited to their mission. The loose and bulky robes would make hiding weapons easy. So far, no one aboard had questioned his costume, though Haru did wonder how the humans would react to seeing Elsifor.

"We need a plan," repeated Haru as they gathered around.

"I've been saying that," whispered Siva. Her eyes darted toward the resting mariners. "We're wasting time. *You've* been wasting time, Haru."

Shadur shot her a poisonous look. "Not here."

"I've been thinking," retorted Haru.

"Tell us," said Siva.

"No," rumbled Shadur. "Not without Valivan."

Haru struggled to keep his voice low. "Valivan isn't ready and we can't wait."

"Why the hurry?" asked Elsifor. "I asked you this morning and you said..."

Haru put up a hand. "I needed time to think." He didn't even try explaining how Nuara's ghastly story had made him feel. "In a week we'll be in J'hora. It's time to talk."

"We should wait for Val," repeated Shadur.

"He's not ready," said Haru.

But I am, Haru. I'm ready.

The ethereal voice was instantly familiar, yet the sound of it in their heads startled them all. Shadur smiled. Elsifor scratched his furry ear.

"Valivan?" Haru spoke so softly he could barely hear himself.

Haru...I mean, Tain. Tain Haru. Sorry. The voice was shaky. *Hello?* it whispered in their brains. *You can talk. The mariners won't hear you.*

His voice was clear and free of stutters. Val never stammered when he used his gift. Siva concentrated, saying to them all, *Valivan, we thought you were resting.*

I have rested.

Can we come to your cabin? Haru asked. *There are things to talk about.*

Come, then.

Val, injected Shadur, *don't invite us if you're not ready.*

I can't hide forever, Shadur. I'm fine. I've closed out the voices.

We're coming, decided Haru. He looked at the others. "Right now."

Valivan had taken the Sailing Master's tiny quarters because they were dark and quiet and away from everyone else aboard the *Gonkin*. Of all the Chorus, only Valivan could reach into another person's mind, a gift he had once described to Haru as an unending siege of voices. At just eighteen years old his odd ability had already worn him down to a shy and jittery nub, at once powerful beyond imagining and terrified to venture from his protective home. He had few friends, a mother who adored and shielded him, and a patron god who reveled in his misery. Yet Valivan had not hesitated to join Haru's mission. He had taken Sh'an's death harder than any of them, Shadur claimed, because only he could have seen it coming.

Haru and the others squeezed into the narrow companionway running through the ship. As Sailing Master, Ariyo was the only crewman except for the captain to have a cabin of his own, a rectangular chamber barely bigger than a closet. Before Haru could rap on the door, he heard Valivan's reply.

Come in.

With Siva hovering over his shoulder, Haru slowly opened the rounded hatch. A stab of candlelight poked them from the darkness. There on the wooden bunk sat Valivan, blinking through strands of chalky blue hair. Plates of half-eaten food littered the floor. Papers and books lay on the built-in desk. Valivan's shirt hung open over his hairless chest, wrinkled and stained with sweat. He put up a pale hand as if to shield himself from the corridor's fresh air.

"Val?" Haru squeezed past the threshold. "You look worse than normal. You sure you're ready to talk?"

Valivan's bloodshot eyes betrayed his sea-sickness. He kicked a plate aside then sidled over to the head of his bunk. "Sit," he bade.

They each found a spot in the cramped chamber. Siva squeezed up next to Haru, while Elsifor climbed atop the desk. Shadur struggled to close the hatch behind him, leaning against it for support. The motion of the ship and the stench of their closeness revolted Haru.

"At least we're alone," cracked Siva.

Shadur rubbed his gloved, crystal hand. "All of us this time."

Siva bristled. "Haru, you should start. Your plan?"

Haru looked at each of them. He had no plan yet, but admitting that seemed dangerous. He wondered if Valivan had read his empty mind.

"Well, I've been considering things," he began. "None of us have been to J'hora. We don't know what it looks like, the layout of Reius' palace, or even what he wants from me. We don't know anything, really. But we can't wait until we get there. We need some idea of how to kill him. And how to get out of there once we do."

The last part surprised them all.

"Haru, none of us expect to get out of there," said Elsifor.

Siva shifted on the bunk. "I promised Jaiakrin I'd come home," she said, "but I think he knew I was lying."

Shadur said, "Haru, killing Reius is enough of a feat. Just tell us how to do it. Don't worry about getting us home."

"You sound like Liadin," said Haru. He elbowed Siva and Valivan as he struggled to his feet. "Everyone is coming back from this. It isn't good enough to die trying. We're going to kill Reius and then we're going home. All of us."

Valivan squinted at the statement. Elsifor smiled. Shadur sighed as if he'd heard the impossible. Haru looked at Siva.

"If you don't believe it, it won't work," he said.

"I believe," said Siva. "It just takes me a little longer than you."

Haru gestured to the weapon at her belt. "Tell me again about that thing."

Siva patted the atlatl proudly. "It won't miss. All I need is a clear shot. I can kill him, Haru. But what happens then?"

"We make our way back to the *Gonkin*," said Haru.

"You mean fight our way back," said Siva.

"Yes, fight. You're all fighters," said Haru.

"Uh, no," said Valivan. "I'm not."

"Alright, no," agreed Haru. "But we'll get you there. We just have to get back aboard the *Gonkin*. Once we do, there's not a ship in the White Fleet that can catch her."

"So, we kill Reius in his palace, then?" asked Shadur.

Haru nodded. "He never leaves it. We just need the right chance."

"But no one ever sees Reius," Elsifor reminded. "How will we find him?"

"We'll see him," said Haru. "Remember what Whistler told me? This meeting of his—it's the only time he comes out of hiding."

"Fanatic," spat Shadur.

Valivan rubbed his temples. "S-s-so...who kills him?"

"Haru," said Elsifor. "He'll have the best chance." From atop the desk, he looked like a wild pet. "You're the only one who'll get that close to him, Haru."

"Haru's not a killer," argued Siva. "With my atlatl—"

"They won't let you near Reius with that thing," said Shadur.

"It will be under my robes, Shadur."

The mystic rolled his eyes. "They'll search you. They'll find it. And your knives." He said to Haru, "It needs to be you, by yourself. You'll have to get close to Reius, Haru. Alone."

"What about me?" asked Elsifor. "I can wear the robes, but I can't hide what I look like. They'll see my face."

"Doesn't matter," said Haru. "We're Cryori. Humans think we're all demons anyway. Especially Reius and his followers. We're not going to hide you, Elsifor."

The answer pleased Elsifor, but irritated Shadur. "Again, it should be Haru."

"It can't be Haru, Shadur," snapped Siva. "He doesn't know how to kill anyone. He's just a Tain!"

"What?"

"Sorry Haru," said Siva. "I'm saying it shouldn't be you alone. It should be all of us. We're a team."

"This Chorus isn't a team," scoffed Shadur.

"We were, once," said Siva. "When we first came together."

"That's was a long time ago." Shadur clenched his crystal hand. "Then Sh'an died and you left us."

Siva reared back. Shadur didn't look away. Haru slid between them.

"Alright, bad blood," said Haru. "I have it, too. We have to get rid of it. And if you can't, you've got to hide it, Shadur. You're mad because Siva left, I'm mad because my father died..." He looked into the mystic's eyes. "This Chorus *is* a team now. Just like all the ones from the old times. The Bloody Chorus! Remember you told me that?"

"I remember," nodded Shadur.

"Stop," gasped Valivan. He closed his eyes and collapsed backwards on his bunk. "Haru, you need to d-d-decide."

"I have," said Haru. "I'm not going to kill Reius in secret. I'm not going to poison him or stab him while no one's looking. My father died with all of Nesenor watching. Maybe Reius did that to horrify us. Well, it worked. I'm still horrified." He climbed up onto the bunk between Siva and Valivan, standing as tall as the shallow overhead allowed. "So that's what we're going to do," he declared. "We're going to kill Reius publically. We're going to kill him with everyone watching!"

"No," pleaded Shadur.

"Yes!" exclaimed Siva.

"Reius will speak to the crowds," Haru said. "It might be in the palace or it might be outside. And if I can get to him, I will. But if I can't, then Siva, you'll get a chance to use that weapon."

"I won't miss, Haru." Siva took the atlatl from her belt. "I know what this can do."

"Val, you'll be the one letting us talk to each other," said Haru. He tapped the side of his skull. "In here. That way we'll be able to know exactly where everyone else is, what's going on, everything. Can you do that?"

"You know I can," said Valivan, though he could barely keep his eyes open.

"Elsifor," said Haru, "You're going to clear our way out. You know what I mean by clear?"

"I understand," replied Elsifor.

"You've got the bloody job. Siva, you'll have to help him."

"I'll be helping you escape," said Siva. "If you're close to Reius, you'll have the toughest time getting out."

Haru knew she was right. "It'll be a fight all the way back to the *Gonkin*, and we're going to need the help of the men aboard, too. Soon I'm going to have to tell Nuara about our plan."

"What about me?" asked Shadur. "I can fight."

"You do better than fight, Shadur," said Haru. "When I went to your house—that light, remember? That black light? We need something like that. A distraction. Something to get attention. Can you do that again?"

Shadur blanched at the request. "Tain Haru, you saw what that did to me..."

"I don't want you fainting, Shadur. But that hand! The J'horans have never seen anything like it. If you can't make that light, can you make that fire?"

"I can...do *something*," agreed Shadur. Then he smiled as an idea bloomed in his head. "Yes."

Haru regarded them from atop the bunk. "It's a start," he said. "A good enough start."

"It's madness," said Siva. Then she laughed. "Madness! And precisely what Reius deserves."

Haru stepped down off the bunk, relieved when Shadur opened the door. One by one they departed Valivan's tiny chamber—except for Haru, who lingered a moment in the threshold. Valivan opened his eyes to consider his Tain.

"Val?" asked Haru. "Are you inside my mind right now?"

Valivan shook his head. "No."

"Well, if you were, you'd know how worried I am."

"About me?"

Haru kept his voice low. "It took you two days to get used to the voices on this ship. How will you manage a city full of strangers?"

"I can do it," replied Valivan.

"You sure? Your hands are already shaking."

The young mind-reader leaned over to blow out the candle on his desk. From the darkness he replied, *I've been building walls all my life, Haru. You can't see them, but I have. By the time we reach J'hora they'll be higher and stronger than ever.* His white teeth gleamed as he smiled. *If the galley has anything worth eating tonight, will you bring me something?*

"I will, Val," answered Haru, then closed the door as softly as he could.

Chapter Ten

THE MERCY OF TAAN

Haru was asleep in his hammock when he heard the shout. It reached into his slumbering mind, summoning him from a troubling dream. He tried to ignore it, desperate to stay in his fantasy—until he realized what was happening.

"Ship ahead!"

In five days of sailing the *Gonkin* had yet to encounter a single vessel. Now the deck above Haru's head thumped with anxious footfalls. He shook the sleep from his brain as his shipmates sprang for the ladder, chasing after them as they abandoned the lower deck. It had been just past noon when he'd gone below, and now sunlight stabbed his eyes as he emerged on deck. Captain Nuara stood on his forecastle, focused keenly on the horizon. Haru pushed his way toward the front of the vessel, surprised to find three of his comrades already there.

"Haru, look," pointed Elsifor.

Haru followed the taloned finger to the horizon. Three white ships sparkled there like distant stars. Over the portside rail loomed the darkish haze of land.

The Horn of Agon.

They hadn't been so close to land since leaving Nesenor. Haru jostled passed the mariners for a closer look. The three ships were certainly J'horan, but too far away to see clearly. Siva peered over Haru's shoulder.

"Seabreakers," she said drearily.

Shadur and Elsifor joined her. "Valivan's down below," said Shadur. "We should get him."

Haru's mind raced. Three J'horan seabreakers— too many for a single beast-ship to battle. Up on the forecastle, Captain Nuara spoke to his Sailing Master and Pilot, looking commendably calm. Haru, however, felt a pang of panic. He looked at Siva and the others, then back at the approaching ships.

"We need to get ready," he said. "Siva, get dressed. You too, Elsifor."

Siva and Elsifor shared a confused glance.

"He means like me," said Shadur. "Your robes."

"You're supposed to be my advisors, remember?" said Haru. "If they come aboard, they can't see you like this."

Unlike Shadur, who had kept his robes immaculate, Siva and Elsifor had both made themselves comfortable onboard, wearing the same worn-out, stained clothes since leaving Nesenor. And neither looked anything like a Tain's advisor.

"I'll get Valivan ready," said Shadur. He shooed the others away. "You two get changed. And don't forget your things—take anything you need that'll fit under your clothes."

As the trio headed below, Haru heard Nuara's summons.

"Tain Haru, come up!" said the captain. He tempted Haru with a spyglass. "You should see this."

The men parted as Haru climbed the forecastle, some of them heading amidships to help the crew. Captain Nuara slapped the heavy spyglass into Haru's palm.

"They can't match our speed," said the captain. "But if you want to outrun them you need to say so now."

Haru lifted the glass to his eye. Like most Cryori he had never seen a real J'horan seabreaker. Everything he knew of them had come from stories and—as he quickly realized—horribly mistaken drawings. His jaw slackened as the stunning vessels filled his vision. They were three-masted, like the *Gonkin*, with multiple blue, triangular sails and sharply pointed prows that peeled the water from their hulls. Ominous ports peppered their hulls, each one revealing the unblinking eye of a bronze long-gun. The white wood of their brawny sides shimmered in the sun, blinding Haru through the spyglass.

"They're definitely coming for us," mused Haru. "They'll chase us all the way to J'hora if we try to outrun them."

"Unless we turn around," suggested Nuara half-heartedly. "If that's what you want."

"I'm going to J'hora, Captain. What are they after?"

"Not a fight," Nuara surmised. "That's not a battle formation. They mean to stop us. Board us, probably."

"And then what?"

Nuara flashed a cynical smile. "That's up to you."

"But Reius asked me to come to J'hora! Don't these idiots know that?" Haru studied the calm water, realizing how easy it would be for the seabreakers to come alongside. "Slow us down."

Nuara gave the order without hesitation. His crew went to work, easing back the sails and gradually turning the ship broadside to their pursuers. The men at the weapon stations tilted down the hinged crossbows. Up ahead, the seabreakers continued their relentless trek. Beneath the waterline, Haru felt the metallic keel retract with a shudder. Suddenly, the *Gonkin* was adrift.

He could have given the order to man the weapons or stand by the sails, but he didn't. Instead, he waited atop the forecastle, silently feigning confidence as the white ships approached. Compared to the *Gonkin* their speed was unremarkable, but as they drew nearer Haru could see their anxious crews, as curious as he was about the coming encounter. By the time Siva and the others returned, all dressed like Shadur in capacious scarlet robes, the lead ship had broken off from its sisters, finally slowing as it prepared to meet the Cryori. Valivan climbed onto the forecastle without asking, his eyes wild, his blue skin insipid. Nuara gave him a withering glance, which Valivan ignored completely.

"Haru, you're g-g-going to let them b-b-board?" asked Val.

Annoyed, Haru took Valivan's arm and led him to the opposite rail. "Val, Nuara doesn't know," he whispered. "Now tell the others—warn them to get ready."

Valivan didn't nod or even blink, effortlessly sending the message with his miraculous mind. As soon as she received it Siva reached out and pulled the hood of Shadur's robe over his head. She then smoothed down her own garments, standing regally to face the J'horans. Elsifor shifted nervously on his clawed feet. Together they watched as the lead ship loomed closer, its sharp prow bobbing as the water broke its speed. By stopping broadside, the *Gonkin* had sent an unmistakable signal—she was ready to talk. The seabreaker drew up alongside, perilously close. Haru and Valivan followed as the captain made his way down to the starboard gunnel. On board the J'horan ship, a man in a uniform of blue and gold tilted up his odd-shaped hat.

Not just a man, thought Haru. *A human. The captain.*

Around him swelled his varied crew, men with pink skin like Whistler and others with skin as brown as bark. A sailor with shocking red hair stood beside the captain, while behind him thumped a peg-legged midget. The few that Haru assumed were officers attired themselves as the captain did, in severe-fitting uniforms of blue and gold, but like the rest of the crew they shared nothing else in common, being of every shade and shape. The captain himself was a black-skinned giant, with braided jet hair and long legs that boosted him over the others.

"Cryori!" he called between the vessels. "Is this the ship that carries your Tain? Say so if you understand me!"

He spoke the same tongue as Whistler, a variant of Cryori they themselves had spread across the continent. But though he understood the foreigner's words, Captain Nuara did not reply. Instead, he glanced at Haru.

"Give me the say so; I'll tell him you're not aboard," he said softly.

Haru stepped out from Nuara's shadow and called out, "I am Tain Haru of Nesenor. Why have you stopped us?"

The J'horan captain smiled in delight. "I am pleased to have found you in such a big ocean, Tain Haru. I've come to bring you to J'hora."

His accent was strange, as thick and burly as he was himself.

"It should be obvious that I already have a ship to take me there," Haru called back. The two crafts drifted closer, threatening to collide. The J'horan captain remained calm, though his crew was plainly ruffled.

"Tain Haru, I speak for my master, Reius the Divine. He has commanded me to find you and bring you safely to J'hora for the Guardian Council." He pointed toward the distant landmass. "That's the Horn of Agon. These are J'horan waters. Your ship will not be allowed to come further."

Siva leaned toward Haru and whispered, "An escort? Did Whistler say anything about this?"

Haru shook his head, feeling lost and out of decent options. He glanced at Shadur but the mystic merely frowned, as baffled as the rest of them. The J'horan captain waited for an answer as their ships finally touched, driven together with a thud by the waves and too much sail.

"I can get you aboard safely," promised the captain. "We don't need to anchor. Give the word and I'll throw over lines."

"What's your name? What's your ship?" asked Haru. "I need proof of what you claim. Your master's henchman killed my father. Why should I think you won't do the same to me?"

The J'horan crew sneered at the insult. Once more the ships smashed together.

"My name is Craw," the captain shouted. "This ship is the *Mercy of Taan*. Every word I've told you is the golden truth. I speak for the divine Reius himself. Turn back and go home if you don't believe me, Tain Haru. But the only way you'll reach J'hora is aboard the *Mercy*."

With the two ships slapping together and no time to confer, Haru turned to Siva and whispered, "Do you have everything?"

She nodded imperceptibly.

Haru shouted over the rail, "Throw over your ropes—we'll come aboard!"

Captain Craw gave the order and his crew went to work. As the waists of the vessels aligned, the J'horans quickly tossed over the lines. Nuara reluctantly ordered his men to comply, watching as they wrapped the ropes around the *Gonkin's* stout cleats. Both crews strained to bring the bouncing boats together.

"Captain Nuara, you'll have to sail back to Jinja," said Haru. "Tell Liadin what's happened."

Nuara barely hid his distress. "We're staying right here, Tain Haru. We'll wait."

"You will not. There's nothing you can do for us now, and we've got to get to J'hora." There was no time to confess the truth to Nuara. "Do as I ask. Go back and tell Liadin. He might have other orders for you. If he does, you follow them. Understand?"

"Tain Haru, think a moment—how will you get back?"

"I don't know," admitted Haru, "but we will."

Next to him Valivan nodded. "We will."

"I want you to cut those lines as soon as we're aboard," said Haru. "If it's a trick of any kind you need to get away."

Nuara pointed to the insignia at his breast. "See this? I'm a Captain," he said sarcastically. He held out a hand for Haru. "I expect to see you again, young Tain. Good luck. May you find the peace you're after."

There was no honest way to answer, so Haru merely shook Nuara's offered hand. Captain Craw called over from the *Mercy*.

"We're ready! Come across now."

The two ships were one, with only irregular gaps between their lashed-together hulls. The men on both vessels stared, disturbed by their closeness, eyes wide at the shocking appearance of the others. Captain Craw waved at Haru.

"Come, Tain Haru. We'll help you aboard."

Haru gestured to his robed chorus. "We're all coming aboard," he said. "The five of us."

"I have orders to bring only you, Tain Haru."

"Then you can cut your ropes and sail home to your master. Surely he didn't think I'd come to J'hora without aides. These are my attendants. I go nowhere without them."

The captain of the *Mercy* dithered a moment. With their ships lashed dangerously together Haru had given him no time to decide.

"Bring them," he relented. He looked oddly at Elsifor. "Even that one."

Elsifor leapt across first, vaulting over the side and landing on the *Mercy's* deck. The astonished crew closed around him for a better look. Haru groaned and scrambled over the railing.

"Stupid..."

Craw managed to turn away from the shocking sight of Elsifor, reaching out to help Haru aboard. Haru glared at Elsifor, then watched as Shadur, his hands hidden by gloves, came over next. Valivan, however, let Siva help him over, practically collapsing when he reached the *Mercy*.

"What's wrong with him?" Craw probed.

"The sea—he's not accustomed to it," replied Haru. He put an arm around Valivan, afraid his friend might faint. Val's voice bloomed in his mind.

I'll be alright, Val reassured, but Haru could feel the fragility in his tone. He wondered if it was the newness of all the human minds. Shadur came and helped hold Valivan up as Siva hopped over the gunnel. As soon as she was aboard, Haru turned and waved to Nuara.

"Do it!"

Knives at the ready, the men of the *Gonkin* cut the ropes binding them to their J'horan foes. As the waves beat at their hulls, the two vessels slowly moved apart. Captain Nuara stood at the rail of the *Gonkin* and silently bid Haru farewell. Behind him, the great wing-sails of the *Gonkin* fanned out to catch the wind and speed her home.

Haru looked up into Captain Craw's dark eyes. Valivan managed to straighten beside him, flanked by Shadur and Siva, while Elsifor stared down the human crew.

"Tain Haru," pronounced the captain. "Welcome aboard the *Mercy of Taan*."

Chapter Eleven

ORKORLIS

"**L**ook at those arms! Wipe 'em down good—make him look hard!"

Elsifor had smelled the oil even before the cask was opened. Ten feet up in the rigging, he peered out over the crowd gathered on the main deck. The shirtless, peg-legged midget they called 'Big Baby' pounded his chest, slick with whale oil. His nameless, thin-boned opponent glistened in the moonlight, cracking his gangly knuckles. Captain Craw watched with pleasure from his forecastle, nodding approvingly as his crew and officers wagered on the wrestlers.

It was the third match of the night and Elsifor had watched them all from his ropey perch, fascinated by the show. The night air felt good in his lungs; the sight of men fighting soothed his growing bloodlust. He watched as Big Baby stomped his wooden leg, flexing his surprising muscles as he let out a theatrical howl. The man with the long, thin arms stretched high into the night air, exaggerating his advantage over the midget.

On board the *Mercy of Taan*, Elsifor had everything he needed—except the hunt. So far, he had managed to contain his hunger, but the many days at sea had stoked the urge to kill something. Even the rats in the cargo hold had begun to tempt him.

"Come on, little man," Elsifor rumbled. The one with the elongated torso enticed the crowd, boasting through his broken teeth. The crewmen backed up to widen the circle, while the lone sailor taking bets quieted them with a sneer. If the sailor had a real name, Elsifor had never heard it. Everyone simply called him Worm.

Worm's hand came down like a hatchet to start the fight.

Big Baby lifted his peg-leg, landing the obvious attack between the long man's legs. Just as his opponent bent forward, Baby grabbed his hair, dropped to one knee, and wrenched his rival over like a bag of gangly bones. The thin man looked up, blinking in astonishment as the wooden appendage struck again, slamming into his ribs. An angry hoot went up from his supporters. Worm held them back as the tall one slithered away from the barrage, his oiled skin sliding easily across the deck. He soared up from the deck like a cobra, and with one astonishing blow punched the midget's face.

Big Baby crumbled to the deck.

"Oh!" cried Elsifor.

Crewmen turned to look up at him, the strange animal-man in the rigging. Though they constantly stared, none of them had slurred or insulted Elsifor. Instead, they were proud of their gleaming ship and hearty games, eager to show off what humans had accomplished without their Cryori masters.

In the three days they'd been aboard the *Mercy*, Elsifor and the others had stayed below deck, mostly. Valivan remained sea-sick, his condition worsened by the awful human food, and Siva had been his nursemaid, refusing to let anyone disturb him. Shadur passed the time with small amusements, dealing himself card games and reading the few books Captain Craw could supply. Their quarters were adequate, the food plentiful, and the cabin boys assigned to them polite. With J'hora just days away, Haru did his best to keep his cohorts safe.

Tonight, though, Elsifor just couldn't remain below. The hunger was upon him, driving him up to see the moon. Ignoring the crew-men's stares, he leapt from the rigging, his shoeless feet scratching the deck. The moon-lit sea stretched out forever, strangling him. Without a single tree to climb, with nowhere to shelter himself from his primal desires, madness overtook his mind.

Until he saw the man in white.

He had spotted the odd fellow before, a bald, round human with a gray, pointed beard and white robes that hung in great loops from his arms. They were the robes of a priest, Shadur had explained, which made the stranger one of Taan's deluded devotees. Elsifor caught the man's gaze from across the deck. He stood apart from the other men, watching the wrestling without gambling, his rheumy eyes curious. Elsifor refused to look away, hoping to intimidate the priest. The old man countered with a smile.

Elsifor turned and headed for the back of the ship where the stairs waited to take him below. But when a sudden, darting movement caught his eye, he froze. There were two cats aboard the *Mercy*—Elsifor had smelled them both the moment he'd come aboard. One was an ugly, spotted male, too old and lazy to bother with mousing. The other—the one Elsifor now watched slip across the deck—was a lithe, young female with a coat so black she was nearly invisible at night. The dark feline stalked across the deck, oblivious to Elsifor's piercing stare. Deep inside him, the ancient hunting instinct rose.

Not the cat, he told himself. *They'd miss the cat.*

He could kill a rat, but a filthy rat wasn't enough. Like the long-dead meat he'd been consuming for days, a rodent couldn't quell his hunger. Elsifor took a silent step forward. The cat reached the gate of the cargo hold, disappearing through one of its square gaps. Elsifor padded after it, peering down past the grate. A wooden ladder led into the unlit bay. Elsifor's sharp ears detected the unseen vermin amid the barrels and ballast stored below. Quietly he lifted the grate, slipping through the narrowest of openings and jumping down into the hold. Overhead, the grate slammed shut.

A shaft of moonlight touched him. He scanned the hold, considering the crates and sacks of grain. Black pitch filled the cracks in the planked hull. He had dropped nearly twenty feet, down into the very bowels of the *Mercy*. A low overhead darkened the hold and muffled the noise from the carousing crew. Elsifor moved out of the moonlight, toward the front of the enormous hold. Despite the black cat's efforts, the rats had thrived. He could see them easily in the darkness, scurrying over the barrels and sacks, gnawing at the burlap bags to reach their precious contents.

He crouched low, turning his ears to locate the cat.

"You are quick and you are agile," he whispered. "But I am those things too. It is our nature to hunt."

He listened and heard the cat move amid the cargo.

"Why would you let them take you aboard this foul ship? You are beautiful. You should run. You might escape me."

He wanted to transform, to become the animal-thing he so often did when prowling the forests around Jinja. He wanted to burst from the bay, grim and monstrous, and feast on the gaming humans above.

"You must give your life for them," Elsifor told the hidden cat. Veins swelled within his neck. His hands shook as his fingernails extended. "Because if you don't..." His breathing quickened. "I might kill them all."

Then he sprang, bounding across the cargo hold to the sacks where he knew the cat was hiding. His claw-like hands extended and his body elongated, his garment snapping as he flew. He collided with the grain sacks, squeezing out the frightened cat, sending it screaming into the air. Elsifor rolled and reached up, snatching the creature mid-leap. Slowly he stood up, his hands coiled around the cat's hind legs, the terrified creature spitting wildly. Elsifor put his face as close to the cat as he could, desperate to kill the thing yet somehow dreading it too. His lips drew back hungrily.

"Wait!"

Elsifor dropped back in shock. Across the hold, a man quickly descended the ladder.

"I know you're down here!" called the man. "Whatever you're doing, stop now!"

Elsifor kept hold of the wailing cat, angered by the intrusion. The priest in white stepped off the ladder, waiting in the moonlight below the grate. He looked fearless, fat, and incredibly foolish.

"Get back on deck!" hissed Elsifor.

The bald man shook his head. "I will not. You have the cat; I can hear it."

"Beware me, priest!"

"I saw you follow it down here. Let it go." The priest stood in the moonlight, unafraid. "No one else saw you, and I swear my own silence." His voice grew gentle. "Come out now."

Angry and embarrassed, Elsifor released the cat. The creature bolted across the hold, past the priest and up the ladder through the metal grate. The man in white smiled at the small victory.

"There," he sighed. "Better, yes? You should thank me—that black beast is Captain Craw's favorite."

Elsifor was breathing hard now, burning to kill something. "You need to go," he told the priest. "I'm dangerous tonight."

The priest remained—as did his infuriating smile. "I'm not afraid of you. You won't harm me."

"I would gladly kill a priest of Taan."

"I can hear your suffering. If you tell me about it, perhaps it will ease."

Elsifor stifled a laugh. "You and your make-believe god offend me."

"I have never seen the like of you before, Elsifor. Truly, you are magnificent. Please—come closer and let me look at you."

"I'm not a pet! I am blessed by Paiax, goddess of the forest and giver of life. You've spoiled my meal—but I'm still hungry."

"In my profession, threats are common," said the priest. "I see all sort of desperation." He moved just beyond the light, grabbing hold of a nearby sack and tipping it over. "Come," he bade. He pulled another sack closer then sat down on the first one. "You have to come this way if you want to get out of here, and I'm not leaving until I see you."

His audacity flabbergasted Elsifor. He measured his breathing, his claws retracting as the transformation subsided. Slowly, he moved closer to the priest.

"You've been watching me," he said. "I've seen you. Why is there a priest aboard?"

"This vessel is the hand of Reius, and Reius does the divine work of Taan," said the priest. "Bringing you and your Tain to J'hora is a holy mission. I am here to help the crew any way I can."

Elsifor slipped closer. "A holy mission?"

"Of course. What's more holy than peace?"

"Why aren't you afraid of me?"

"Because you're a child of Taan."

"I am not," rumbled Elsifor. He emerged into the edge of the moonlight, hovering over the seated priest. "I'm Cryori. I'm a child of the only gods that exist."

The priest looked up, his eyes full of awe as he regarded Elsifor. "My name is Orkorlis. Will you sit with me? There is so much I want to learn about you and your people, and as you can see, I'm no threat at all."

Elsifor thought of heading back up the ladder, but in truth the priest had charmed him. "If you're here to spy for Captain Craw, you'll be disappointed. I merely serve my Tain."

"I should confess something, then—I am here to spy. On *you*, Elsifor. I've been wanting to see you from the moment you came aboard."

Elsifor grimaced. "Because of how I look?"

"Of course. That offends you?"

"It does. But I'm used to it."

"You must be. You don't look like the other Cryori. What...*are* you?"

"Special," said Elsifor.

"Are you a Venerant?" asked Orkorlis. "I've heard the Venerants wear robes such as yours." He touched his own garments. "And mine too!"

"No," said Elsifor. Just as they'd practiced, he added, "I'm an advisor to Tain Haru."

The priest looked puzzled but not suspicious. "The woman too?"

"Yes. Her name is Siva."

"So none of you are Venerants?" Orkorlis frowned. "That's disappointing. I really want to know more about your gods. Almost all the old books about them are gone."

Elsifor's own curiosity made him sit. The grain sack stretched out comfortably for his backside. "Why don't you know about Clionet and the others? They were once your gods too."

"The gods of Nesenor were abandoned the day your people left our shores, praise Taan. But they do interest me. If just once I could see one of those creatures for myself!" Orkorlis regarded Elsifor hopefully. "Will you tell me about Paiax? Have you seen her?"

"Of course. I've seen her, spoken to her—how else could I know her?"

"Ah, you lay traps for me, Elsifor," grinned Orkorlis. "You think because I've never seen Taan I cannot truly know his grace?"

"No one has ever seen Taan," said Elsifor, "because Taan isn't real. Taan is a myth. You call my gods creatures, but at least they're real. We can touch them. When we pray to them, they listen, because they have ears! We can see them."

"Taan can be seen," countered Orkorlis, "but he chooses not to be. Our minds could never comprehend his glory. To look upon him would burn our mortal eyes to cinders. But he does speak to us. He's spoken to Reius."

"Has he ever spoken to you?"

"I'm not a prophet like Reius," said Orkorlis. "But I have heard his voice in my heart. Once, I suffered too. Not from your affliction, of course, but just as deep. Until Taan healed me."

Elsifor leaned closer, completely forgetting their dismal surroundings. "Were you ill?"

"I speak of wounds of the soul, Elsifor." Orkorlis patted his chest. "This bag of flesh is nothing—we are all immortal beings, like your Cryori goddess. Until I understood Taan's plan, I was the unhappiest man in the world. I drank and made J'hora's gutters my home. I fought; I stole." He laughed. "I was a womanizer! Can you believe it?"

Elsifor grinned. "Women are strange."

"Oh, I did love my whores." Orkorlis kissed his palm and held it skyward. "But Taan saw into my heart. All my loathing and hatred, all my fears. You wonder why I'm not afraid of you, Elsifor? Because I wear the armor of Taan. I am invincible! You might kill me, but I would still have his eternal love." He looked into Elsifor's animal eyes. "And his acceptance."

Elsifor smiled. "I was chosen by Paiax," he said softly. "When I was still in my mother's womb. Later, when I was very young, she came to me in the forest. She explained to me that once in a great while a special child is born. A child like me. One who belongs not just to the world of men but to the world of the forest as well. To her world. Look at me, Orkorlis! You said I'm magnificent. I can change my body." Elsifor held up his hand. "Look at my fingers. My mouth, my teeth—I can make them like a jaguar's. No man alive can run faster than me. I've been to the top of the tallest trees. Can you do those things, Orkorlis?"

"And yet you suffer," observed the priest. "With all your gifts, you're still an outcast."

"I am not."

Orkorlis sighed. "I know outcasts, Elsifor. Outcasts are my calling. Just as you can see a cat in the dark, so can I spot an outcast across the deck of a ship. So, I ask you—why did your goddess not take away your misery, as Taan has taken mine?"

He posed his question with a child's innocence. Elsifor struggled with it.

"It's true, my nature gives me pain," he said finally. "But also so many glorious things. I can endure the difficulties."

"Is a gift something to be endured? A gift should make a man happy, as I am happy. You could know true grace, Elsifor. True acceptance. Taan loves all his children. If you knew his adoration, you would not long for the acceptance of others."

His words troubled Elsifor more than they should have. Suddenly, he needed to get away.

"Orkorlis, you're kind to worry about me," he said. He stood up. "Will you keep my secret about the cat?"

"Of course," Orkorlis nodded, looking disappointed at Elsifor's departure. "Will you consider what I've told you?"

"Yes," replied Elsifor honestly.

Like it or not, he knew forgetting the priest's words would be impossible.

"In a few days we'll be in J'hora," said Orkorlis. "When we get there, you will see the true glory and power of Taan."

Chapter Twelve

THE WHITE

The *Mercy of Taan* sailed east for four days. By the time Haru awoke on the fifth morning, they were docked in J'hora. Valivan delivered the news of their arrival like a child. Perched over Haru's bed, his red, wild eyes were the first thing Haru noticed.

"We're here!"

Haru shook off the shroud of sleep, pulled on his boots, and raced for the ladder. The striking shadow of the city engulfed him as he emerged on deck. He paused at the last rung of the ladder, frozen by the sight of J'hora.

"Go, Haru," urged Valivan impatiently, eager to follow his Tain up the ladder. "I want to see!"

Haru stepped slowly onto the deck. There was the capital, like nothing in any of his books or sketches. Tall and enormous, it assaulted Haru, crushing all his mistaken beliefs. He moved unthinkingly toward it, dazzled and afraid, surrounded by crewmen happy to be home and the noise from the hundred other docked ships in the harbor. Valivan stumbled into the sunlight, sharing Haru's dreadful awakening.

J'hora was a city of gold and crimson, with spiraling towers and domes of gleaming stone. Impossible bridges linked the looming structures together, floating above the teeming streets. The dusty ruins of crenellated walls stood in broken patches throughout the city, kneeling in the shadows of gleaming columns and minarets, the new rulers of a reborn capital. Horses and hairy oxen drew carts and carriages through the wide avenues. A sprawling marketplace bustled near the sea-stained docks. Homes with red-tiled roofs covered the hills around the city, and ornate temples rose up from the crowded streets, their gilded spires shining in the golden, morning light.

"It's...*giant,*" said Valivan in disbelief. He staggered past Haru toward the rail where Siva and Shadur waited, his legs wobbly from the voyage. Siva turned and gave Haru a troubled look. Around them the crew of the *Mercy* moved like eager ants, loading and unloading cargo. A gangplank had been lowered, allowing the men to disembark or take up fresh supplies from the dock. Captain Craw conversed with his officers, nodding when he noticed Haru.

Haru said nothing, too stunned by the sight of J'hora to speak. His people had abandoned the continent decades ago, leaving humanity to scavenge in the ruins of their conquest. Now, the scale of their rebirth overwhelmed him as Valivan's soft voice intruded into his mind.

Haru? What do we do?

We go ashore as planned, replied Haru. *We take Reius away from them.*

He went to stand beside Siva and Shadur, leaning on the ship's rail and seeing an ornate carriage waiting near the docks. Six white horses pulled the carriage, draped in gold and silver and looking oddly appropriate among the varied ships. "Is that for us?" Haru wondered out loud.

"It's been there since I came above," replied Siva. She gestured with her chin toward the driver, a man in a long red coat and plumed hat, staring straight ahead. "He hasn't looked this way. Not once."

"Where's Elsifor?" asked Haru.

Shadur grimaced. "Ashore," he said. "With the priest."

"What?"

"They left as soon as we docked," said Siva. "I told him not to go. I'm sorry Haru—I thought he'd be back before you awoke."

"Haru scanned the crowded dock for Elsifor and the priest, not noticing Captain Craw until the big seaman was standing just behind him.

"Tain Haru," said Craw loudly. "Welcome to J'hora!"

The captain grinned at the bemusement of his passengers.

"Where's my advisor?" snapped Haru. "You let him off the ship with your priest?"

"Orkorlis isn't my priest or my property, Tain. We don't have slaves here in J'hora. This isn't Nesenor, after all."

Behind Craw, one of his officers snickered.

"Yes, you've grown up, humans," Haru admitted. "I've never seen a city like this one. The way it erupts from the ground—like a boil."

"That's progress, my lord." Craw swept his arm proudly toward the many ships in the harbor. "They come from across the world to be here for the Council. Truly, we are an Alliance now."

"When do we see Reius?" asked Haru. "And how do we get back when we're done here?"

Captain Craw replied, "I have no idea. I'm a sea captain—I'm told all I need to know. If I'm told to sail you home to Nesenor, I will. But until I get new orders, the *Mercy* will remain here." Craw pointed down to the waiting carriage. "He's your escort now."

"And where will he take us?"

"Don't know. The Palace of Prophecy, I suppose." Craw joined his curious passengers at the ship's rail, directing them toward the center of the city. There, crowded by a trio of looming towers, rose an ornate structure of gold and ruby spires. "My master's home," he said. "And the place where Reius holds his Guardian Council."

Haru squinted for a better look. Like so many of J'hora's structures, the palace looked frightening and beautiful.

"I can't go anywhere without my advisors," he said. "All of them."

I found him, said Valivan suddenly. *He's coming.*

"There he is," Siva said, pointing down the dock, her tone full of obvious relief.

Indeed, it was Elsifor, his hood clamped tightly around his face as he and Orkorlis threaded through the crowds toward the waiting carriage. Noticing Haru at the ship's rail, he raised his hairy hand in greeting.

"Go get him," Haru told the others. "Wait for me by the carriage and make sure he doesn't wander off."

Siva grabbed Valivan's arm, and together with Shadur guided him toward the gangway. Haru composed himself as he watched them leave.

"Your advisors," said Craw. "They're like witches."

They were the words Haru had been waiting to hear, the unspoken reason he'd let the others disembark without him. Craw had held his tongue from the moment they'd come aboard, but his suspicions were evident. Haru didn't nod, but he didn't deny the seaman's claim either. It was just the two of them at the rail.

"We're Cryori," he said. "Aren't we all witches?"

The human studied his face intently. "I don't know what you are, Tain Haru. All I know is that we'll be glad to be rid of you. Look at that city. We built that. From the rubble of what you left behind, we built it. *Humans*. See what we can do when inspired?"

Haru glared at Craw. "I'm a Tain of Nesenor. It takes more than a tall tower to make me swoon."

"It's time for you to get off my ship...*Tain*."

All the feigned politeness fled Craw's dark face. Haru held back an insult before turning and heading for the gangway. As he descended the wooden plank, the utter silence at his back resounded like jeers. He paused near the bottom of the gangway, realizing he was about to step foot on J'horan soil—the home of his father's killer.

A tiny step was all it took. The others gathered by the carriage came to greet him. There were no bodyguards, only the silent driver atop his cab and the round-faced, eager priest. Around them, the people of J'hora stopped to stare, shocked by the Cryori but silenced by the sight of Reius' crest upon the carriage.

"Tain Haru?" said the priest. "I'm Orkorlis. A friend of Elsifor."

Elsifor stood beside him, looking respectfully guilty.

"I know who you are," said Haru, dreading what was coming.

"Wonderful," pronounced Orkorlis cheerily. "I'm to take you to the palace."

Haru sat back in the enormous carriage, his Chorus and their pretense intact. The bulge of Siva's atlatl creased her robes, tucked safely against her waist. Seated across from him in the conveyance, they shared a knowing glance. Up on his cab, the wordless driver moved with authority through the crowds, the crest on his golden carriage parting the throngs. Haru took a conscious breath. A tiny, triumphant smile curled his lips.

They had made it.

Orkorlis spoke quickly as they traveled, pointing out the exotic landmarks through the carriage's window and recounting J'hora's violent past. Valivan shifted anxiously, his face sweaty as he fought to keep his mental walls from crumbling. Next to him, Shadur rubbed his crystal hand. Unperturbed, Elsifor kept his face close to the glass as he listened to Orkorlis' stories.

"...and there's the Tower of Principles," Orkorlis went on. "Where Chancellor Malon presides. You'll meet her at the Council as well."

Shadur shifted for a better view of the cylindrical tower, a structure of white stone with fluted columns erupting from a green courtyard. Men dressed as priests moved in and out of its many arched entryways.

"What is it?" Shadur asked. "A temple?"

"The Tower of Principles is where the laws of Taan are decreed. Every book and scroll about his teachings are kept there."

"Who's Chancellor Malon?" asked Elsifor.

"Malon is First Follower," said Orkorlis. "The first of us ever to devote herself to Reius and his prophecies. She sits in judgment of the Principles."

"Principles?" queried Siva.

"The Principles are the word," said Orkorlis. His tone filled with reverence. "They are the spoken laws of Taan given to the prophets. Reius is a prophet. The last prophet. We are all his followers, but Malon was the first. That's why she was chosen to rule the tower."

To Haru it all sounded like nonsense. He stared through his gleaming window at one of the broken walls he'd seen from the *Mercy*, a crumbling remnant of Cryori rule. The ruin had clearly been left there on purpose. A reminder of their old masters, Haru supposed. Across from him sat Siva, still listening to Orkorlis' mad lessons.

Suddenly, the carriage stopped.

Haru's daydream vanished. Shadur peered through his window, straining to see.

"What's that?"

Together they crowded to the right side of the carriage. Haru, behind them all, caught the glimpse of something in the street blocking their way, a moving mound of something white.

"Are those people?" he asked.

Orkorlis gave an embarrassed groan, sinking back in the plush seat. "Yes," he sighed. "Heretics."

"Open the door," Haru told Shadur. "I want to see."

"Tain Haru, no," urged Orkorlis. "Stay inside."

Haru and Shadur both ignored him, piling out when the door swung open. A crowd had gathered, choking the avenue. Another carriage rolled slowly ahead of them, behind it a chain of naked men and women, a dozen or more of them, each covered in chalky white paint. With their hands tied behind them and their necks linked together, they trudged slowly behind the carriage, a big, white conveyance pulled along by a team of pristine horses. The men and women kept their heads down in humiliation, their terrified eyes blinking through the paint dousing their faces as the crowd hurled jeers.

"Wretched fools," groaned Orkorlis as he hung out of the open carriage. "The word!" he cried at them. "Hear the word!"

Haru couldn't tell if he was trying to save them or condemn them. Elsifor whirled on the old priest.

"Who are they?"

"As I said, heretics," explained Orkorlis. "They refused the word of Taan."

"The word of Taan?" spat Haru. "Or the rule of Reius?"

A few in the crowd noticed them, shocked by the sight of Cryori in their city. Their silent driver stood up on his cab. The murmur stilled.

"Tain Haru, get back in the carriage," Orkorlis begged.

Haru didn't move, nor did any of his cohorts. It was a horrible spectacle, but it wasn't always so to Cryori eyes. One of the painted captives—a long haired woman of questionable age—looked straight at Haru, as shocked as the onlookers by the sight of him. Her haunted eyes pleaded with him hopelessly.

"What will happen to them?" Siva asked.

"We can talk about this in the carriage," said Orkorlis. "Please."

"Tell us," said Haru.

Orkorlis grimaced. "They were given a chance, Tain Haru." He pointed at the prisoners, exasperated. "Every one of them heard the truth and denied it. They refused Taan."

"Why are they painted like that?" asked Haru.

"That's the whiteness of Taan's purity," said Orkorlis. "One way or the other, they will accept the word."

"Disgusting," muttered Shadur. He shook his head as the doomed party trudged past him.

"Orkorlis, what will happen to them?" asked Elsifor.

"They're being taken to the Tower of Principles," replied the priest. His voice grew regretful. "Elsifor, they were given a chance..."

"They'll be killed?" pressed Elsifor. "Because they don't accept Taan?"

The old priest fumbled to answer, then just stopped trying. The white-painted men and women hobbled toward their condemnation. Up ahead loomed the Tower of Principles. Valivan looked ill. His entire, thin body began to shake. Suddenly his voice bloomed in Haru's mind.

We shouldn't have come.

All of them heard Valivan's silent voice.

You're wrong, replied Siva.

We're looking at our past, said Elsifor. *We made them this way.*

We didn't do this, argued Siva.

Our fathers and mothers did it, said Elsifor. *Through slavery and murder.*

We're not that way anymore, said Haru.

Shadur said calmly, *Let's get back in the carriage.*

Yes, said Haru. *But take a good look at them.* He directed his eyes toward the naked captives. *In a year that could be us. Not just the five of us but all of Nesenor! You want to go home? Or do you want to kill the man who's doing this?*

Next to him, Valivan managed to quell his panic. *Kill him.*

Good, snapped Haru. *Remember their faces. Remember why we came here. And guilt? Forget guilt. When you get home, just wash the blood off your hands and be glad for what you did here.*

Chapter Thirteen

SANCTUARY

W hen the *Gonkin* finally reached Cryori waters, Sailing Master
Ariyo opened a keg of wine from Captain Nuara's private
stash and called his crewmates to the quarterdeck. For seven days
they had sailed west against the wind, lashed by choppy waters that
slowed their progress home. They had done as Tain Haru ordered,
leaving him in the hands of their enemies and returning to Nesenor.
Now, as the calm waters of their beloved island welcomed them, a
mood of sad celebration shrouded the beast-ship.

Captain Nuara stood with his crew, raising a toast to Haru and
the Chorus and taking a long pull from his mug. Soon, he'd deliver
the bad news to Arch-Disciple Liadin. The drink, he hoped, would
steel him. His bloodshot eyes scanned the horizon. Though Nesenor
was still not visible, he could feel home in the way the sea moved.
The *Gonkin's* wing-sails opened slightly as the wind shifted. Up
ahead, a flock of sea birds darted from the sky. Nuara spied the birds
curiously over his mug.

"Ariyo," he said with a gesture. "Look there."

Ariyo lowered his drink with a grin. "Eh?"

"Those birds have found something," said Nuara. He handed his
mug to a crewman, bid Ariyo to follow him, and made his way to
the front of the boat. Once he climbed the forecastle, he could
see the prize the birds were after, a great, bloody mass of blubber
bobbing on the waves. Gulls crawled over the blob, picking at it and
screeching as the *Gonkin* approached. Ariyo ordered the beast-ship

to slow, gradually bringing the vessel closer. Nuara leaned out for a better look.

"Whale?"

He had just gotten out the word when an enormous mouth breeched the water. Nuara reared back, startled. The birds burst into the air. And the giant, snapping head of a black serpent seized the floating carcass.

"Heart of the mother! What's *that*?" Ariyo exclaimed.

Mariners rushed up to see. The sinewy body of the monster coiled around the dead whale, rolling it as it feed. Nuara bellowed for the ship to change course, astonished by the grotesque creature. Twenty feet from its feeding head, the serpent's spiked tail emerged from the water, shaking in warning at the coming vessel.

Nuara had spent his life at sea. He'd seen shenenra and squid as large as the *Gonkin*. He'd even seen Clionet once. But never a serpent. Never such an abomination. The creature held greedily to its dead prey, its yellow eyes fixed angrily on the *Gonkin*, its thick body tightening around the carcass.

"Steady ahead," Nuara said. Ariyo quickly echoed the order, then came to stand beside his captain at the rail.

"J'horan, maybe?" Ariyo surmised, studying the creature.

Nuara shook his head. Things from J'horan had been washing up on Cryori shores for years, but surely he would have heard of something like this.

"It just wants its meal," said Nuara. "But damned if I know where it came from."

The sea snake spied them as the *Gonkin* sailed closer. Its spiked tail rose threateningly higher. Nuara held true, eager for a better look. He held his breath as a second finned head appeared.

"Captain..."

"I see it."

The second black beast broke the surface, winding toward its sibling, hungry for whale meat. As big as the first, the newcomer rose up out of the water as it spotted the coming *Gonkin*, its thick, thrashing body propelling it upward. Like a cobra it hovered there, hissing and spitting, warning off the coming ship. When it saw its rival, the first monster let out a piercing screech. The crew of the *Gonkin* scrambled. Nuara tried to hide his confusion.

"Captain?" probed Ariyo.

If the second monster meant to stop them, the *Gonkin* would smash right into it.

"Steady on," said Nuara. "That thing's mouth isn't big enough for a beast-ship."

Before his theory could be tested, yet another creature joined the fray—the fiery fins of a dragon-whale.

"Shenenra!"

A plume of steam jetted over the forecastle. Ahead of the *Gonkin*, a speeding dragon-whale rose up from beneath the ship, ranging for the second serpent. Its enormous mouth opened as it crested the waves, sparking with angry flames, combustible spittle flying from its tongue. Its black prey let out an astonished cry just as the shenenra leapt.

Like a shark taking a seal, the dragon-whale snatched the giant serpent, crashing back into the ocean and dragging down its thrashing foe. The first serpent unspooled from the whale carcass and darted into the fight, disappearing in the tumult. Fins and tails stirred the sea as the big beasts barrel-rolled. Blood boiled in the foam. An angry cry blasted up from the shenenra's blowhole, then down the three combatants went, disappearing into the depths.

"Closer!" ordered Nuara. "Come about!"

The crew hurried the ship around. The *Gonkin* forged toward the melee. Nuara peered down over the forecastle, trying to penetrate the surface and glimpse the battling creatures. A stream of blood bubbled on the surface.

For a long moment no one spoke. Captain Nuara stared hopefully into the sea. Finally, Ariyo, said the dreaded word.

"Gone."

The *Gonkin* circled for an hour, waiting for any sign of the dragon-whale. When none appeared, Nuara reluctantly gave the order to head home.

The *Gonkin* returned to Jinja just past midnight, following the lights from the town and welcomed into the quiet harbor by the squid-shaped beast-ship *Sethnar*, patrolling in the moonlight. Nuara wasted no time going ashore. Still shaken by the sight of the serpents and the evident death of the dragon-whale, he summoned a ferry from the dock, left his Sailing Master in command, and wondered how'd he'd deliver his news to Liadin. The ferryman rowed his boat with deliberate strokes, steam rising from his forehead in the chilly night, his gnarled hands big in his fingerless gloves. His name was Haik, and he had been the ferryman for as long as Nuara could remember. Known for his quiet, he said almost nothing until halfway through their journey.

"Going ashore for something important, Captain Sir?"

Nuara looked at Haik from his seat across from the grizzled ferryman. Behind Haik glowed the lights from Jinja Castle.

"To see Arch-Disciple Liadin."

Nuara's voice, barely more than a whisper, carried over the still water.

Haik grinned. "You don't know, do you?"

"Know what?"

"About Liadin."

"What about him?"

"He's regent now. You don't know because you've been at sea. Tain Haru made him regent before he left."

"What?" Nuara blinked in bafflement. "Of course I've been at sea! I took Tain Haru to sea! Liadin is *regent?*"

"Declared himself so three days ago," said Haik as he nonchalantly rowed. "Don't know more than that. I'm just a ferryman, Captain."

Nuara sat back, stunned. "Regent...?"

He tried to remember his brief talks with Haru, running though them quickly in his mind. He was sure the young ruler hadn't said anything to him about making Liadin regent. They hadn't even spoken of Liadin at all.

"Double time, Haik. I need to get to the castle."

The castle was quiet when Nuara arrived. Torches lit the road up the mountainside and the wall around the keep. The clip-clop of Nuara's horse echoed on the cobbled road. Nuara hurried through the empty avenue, quickly reaching the keep. A Venerant with a sukatai stood guard at the entrance to the main house. He greeted Nuara with surprise, peering through the darkness to make out the lone rider.

"Who's there?" he called.

Nuara dismounted as the horse stopped. "Nuara," he said impatiently, striding up to face the young man. "I need to see the Arch-Disciple. It's about Tain Haru."

The guard lowered his weapon. "Captain Nuara? The Arch-Disciple is still awake, but he's in the sanctuary."

"So?"

The priest scowled. "He's praying, Captain."

"Boy, I don't give a damn if he's making love to Clionet," said Nuara. "Take me to him. Now."

The young man gave Nuara a scandalized look. "This way," he said hesitantly, then turned and led Nuara into the keep.

The sanctuary was a tiny alcove in a quiet corner of Jinja Castle, away from the ceremonial rooms and living quarters, deliberately placed in the least ornate section of the keep. Here, the smooth, wood paneled walls gave way to the exposed rock of the mountain. There were no doors to the place, just an archway of stone guarded by candles that never went out. A thick silence shrouded the granite hall. The young Venerant paused halfway to the entrance, pointing with his sukatai toward the dark sanctuary.

"At least wait until he's done with his prayers," the priest implored.

Nuara stepped past him. "Go back to the gate."

The priest obliged, leaving Nuara in the quiet hall. Nuara peered into the sanctuary. Shadowy candlelight flickered ahead. A mumbling voice rose and fell within the chamber. Nuara inched toward the entrance. He had never been inside the sanctuary, and in fact rarely prayed at all. A statue of Ayorih, the patron of the Venerants, loomed over the kneeling figure of Liadin. A pool of sacred water soaked Liadin's legs and garments, filled by a steady drip upon the statue's head from the miraculous rocks. The Arch-Disciple continued his prayer, oblivious to Nuara's intrusion, submissive in the shadow of his kindly god, shaking and speaking in the old, indecipherable tongue of his Order.

Nuara's urgency suddenly fled. The despondent sight of Liadin and the serene gaze of Ayorih's statue quieted his ire. The candles along the sanctuary's walls trembled in the breeze. The steady drip from the rocky ceiling pattered calmly on Ayorih's scalp. Unlike Nuara's patron, Ama'aga, Ayorih possessed a gentle demeanor, perfectly captured in his stone likeness. It was not a statue of a grown adult, however. Instead it depicted Ayorih as he often appeared when he walked among the Cryori—as a sweet-faced, innocent boy.

Liadin's voice was hoarse as he prayed, brittle from lack of sleep and filled with heartbreak. Nuara slid into the sanctuary, unsure if he should acknowledge Ayorih in some way. He braced himself and cleared his throat.

Liadin paused mid-prayer. Slowly, he turned with a scowl toward the entrance. His irritated eyes stared at Nuara from across the sanctuary. He got to his feet, his robes dripping wet from his devotion, and stepped out of the limpid pool.

"Captain," he said in a measured tone, "no one has broken my prayers since I became a Venerant."

Nuara began to apologize, then noticed Liadin's bandaged left hand. The entire bottom half of the appendage was wrapped. Splotchy blooms of blood stained the bandage.

"Arch-Disciple?" Nuara went to him. "What happened?" He studied the wound, then the old man's wizened, exhausted face. "You look ill. And your hand..."

Liadin turned back to the statue of Ayorih. He stared up at the child-god's face. "A penance," he explained. "A finger."

"You...?" Nuara halted. "You cut off your finger?"

"Just the little one."

"Arch-Disciple, I just got back," said Nuara. "The *Gonkin* anchored less than an hour ago."

"Just tell me why you interrupted me. You have news?"

"Yes, and I've heard news too. I heard you're Regent now. But that must be just a rumor..."

"It's not a rumor, Captain. Tain Haru made me Regent before he left."

"I left Tain Haru just days ago—on a J'horan ship!"

Liadin turned face him. "What?"

"I took the Tain into J'horan waters, Arch-Disciple. We were intercepted by a J'horan ship. They had orders from Reius to stop us."

"Haru went with them?"

"He insisted. Along with his Chorus. That was just a few days ago!"

"And then?" pressed Liadin. "What happened? What happened to Haru?"

Nuara said with difficulty, "We left them. Haru ordered me home—to speak to you. So I did. But he never said anything about making you Regent. Never."

Liadin grimaced. "You were his ferryman, Captain. He didn't tell you about his mission."

"He *did* tell me," argued Nuara. "All about his peace mission."

"Then he didn't tell you everything."

"Then you tell me, please" bade Nuara. "What happened to your hand? What's happening?"

Liadin looked exhausted. "Penance is a private thing," he said. He turned away, walking back toward the statue of Ayorih and rubbing his bandaged hand. He looked up adoringly at the stone face. "Captain?"

Nuara took one step closer. "Yes?"

"Have you ever prayed to Ayorih? I know mariners pray to Ama'aga. I know you all think Ayorih's love and scholarship is a thing to sneer at, but have you ever prayed to him?"

"No, Arch-Disciple."

"You should. It will bring you solace."

Nuara puzzled over the statement. "Arch-Disciple, tell me why you're Regent."

"I've been in here since the morning. I've prayed and prayed. I've given everything to Ayorih. Everything in my life." Liadin kept his eyes on the statue's gentle face. "All I ever wanted was to serve him." He cocked his head in study of the god. "Look how young he is. Look how beautiful..."

The steady drip of water tapped the statue's head. Nuara felt suddenly chilled. He had seen madness before, in men stuck at sea for months at a time. And Liadin was very old. Perhaps senility had captured him at last.

"Sir?" nudged Nuara. "Arch-Disciple?"

Liadin held Ayorih's gaze. "Haru knew he wasn't coming back. He didn't go to make peace with Reius; he went to J'hora to kill Reius. That's why he took the Chorus with him. It's a suicide mission."

Nuara's insides knotted. "Kill Reius?" The notion seemed impossible—until he realized the reason. "You mean for his father. For revenge."

"I'm surprised you didn't see it in him," sighed Liadin. "It's all over his face. He's not a boy anymore." The old man gave a big, sad smile. "He was a boy until his father died. But then he grew up, just like that!" Liadin snapped his fingers. "Oh, but I loved him. I loved him so much."

"He's still alive, Arch-Disciple," said Nuara. He went to stand beside Liadin, to implore his attention. "He wanted me to come back and see you, to tell you he'd gone aboard the seabreaker. He—"

Nuara stopped himself. Liadin's eyes flicked toward him.

"What did he say?"

"He told me to follow your orders," Nuara said, suddenly remembering. His expression flattened. "You're right, then. He knew he wasn't coming back." Nuara frowned as he looked up at Ayorih's face. Not all children were so innocent, he realized. "I feel foolish."

"Do not. You did what was asked of you. You did your solemn duty, Captain. As I have done mine." Liadin held up his hand. "Penance is a private affair," he said again, "but know this—I didn't maim myself just for the things I've done, but for things yet to come. Every able-bodied man must be ready. Even if Haru succeeds and kills Reius, the J'horans will rain their vengeance down on us."

"But the bloodline. The dragon-whales..."

"The bloodline ends with Haru," said Liadin. "I know the charms. I can make the dragon-whales obey me."

Nuara regarded the old man skeptically. "Pardon me, but that's impossible. It's not just the charms that make the shenenra obey. They're loyal to the bloodline. They're loyal to Clionet and her chosen."

"Yes, well, leave Clionet to me," said Liadin. "I am the Arch-Disciple. I have allies of my own." With his unmaimed hand he took Nuara's shoulder. "We will have the shenenra and the beast-ships and the strong will of our people, Nuara. But do I have your loyalty?"

Nuara didn't hesitate. "Always."

Liadin smiled. "Let them come, then. Let them break themselves against our shores. Let the dragon-whales feast on them. Soon the world will wither again at the sight of Cryori."

He squeezed Nuara's shoulder like a grandfather, then headed out of the sanctuary. Nuara watched him go, and when he was sure the Regent of Nesenor was gone, he once more regarded the silent statue.

"Ayorih? They say you are the patron of truth. Did I hear the truth tonight?"

The child-god, wherever he was, refused to answer. Nuara lingered, watching the water ping the statue's head and pool at its naked feet. Perhaps it didn't matter if Liadin had lied to him. Haru was gone. War was coming.

Nuara thought of his own father.

He said goodnight to the likeness of Ayorih and quietly left the sanctuary.

Chapter Fourteen

CHANSOOR MALO'N

The Palace of Prophecy stood in the very center of J'hora, a stone colossus astride a teeming, restless capital. According to Orkorlis, workers had come from across the continent to construct the palace, raising it gloriously high like a beacon to comfort the word's nations. In the fountains and tapestries and vaulted ceilings shone the painstaking work of devoted artisans. In the countless murals gracing its halls, the dark and violent history of the Alliance came to life. There were no torches or bare walls like in Jinja Castle; candlelight and gilding covered every surface.

And it was vast. Unimaginably so to Haru.

It had taken Haru and the others a full day to tour the palace. They learned of the heroic artisans who'd toiled and died to build it and how Reius had blessed his new home—bleeding himself white from a self-inflicted wrist cut. The blood had pooled upon his throne but Reius—the great and holy Reius—never fainted or flagged. Orkorlis glowed as he told the story.

There were few guards in the palace, a fact that astonished Haru, and although Orkorlis guided them everywhere he explained profusely that they were not prisoners. They were Reius' guests, and no part of the palace was restricted to them. Their own chambers were garish and luxurious, far larger than Haru's own back home, with big, sunny windows and breath-taking views of the bewildering city. On the night of their arrival, Haru and the Chorus spent hours gathered on the balcony, staring out over J'hora, unable to sleep or think of anything but the city's odd magnificence. Exhausted from their long days at sea and Orkorlis' endless chatter, they let the enormity of the place sweep them away, lounging in cushioned chairs beneath the moon while a train of servants offered them foods and wine. Haru picked what he liked from the offerings and made no attempt to speak of their plans, not even through Valivan, who used the peaceful night to quiet his thundering mind and prepare for the difficulties ahead.

Besides Orkorlis and the ubiquitous servants, they received only one visitor that night—Count Whistler. He had arrived two days earlier, he explained, greeting them all with his familiar warmth. Haru gave up his chair for the old Count and shooed away the servants. He poured Whistler a glass of some unknown wine, happy to see a recognizable—if human—face. Amazingly, he seemed bored by the astonishing city.

"We talk and we argue and we pray," he said as he sipped his wine. "That's all a Guardian Council is, apparently. And there's still four more days of it!"

Shadur, more than half-drunk on the powerful wine, sighed in sympathy. "Politics is a curse."

Haru put a hand over Shadur's glass. "Enough now, I think," he said easily, afraid the mystic might slip and divulge their plans. Shadur raised an eyebrow but set his drink aside. Suddenly, Valivan's voice popped into Haru's mind.

Don't worry. He won't say anything. I won't let him.

Haru glanced at Valivan, who was seated somewhat apart from the rest of them, and nodded. Val, still looking sick from his voyage, managed a wink.

"Tomorrow, I get my Chain of Office," said Count Whistler. He raised his glass mockingly high. "I'm almost sorry you'll be there to see it."

The next day—their first full day in J'hora—Orkorlis took them to the Guardian Council.

Haru braced himself, nervous about finally confronting so many humans. He dressed in a fine shirt of Cryori silk, the best garment he had brought with him from Nesenor, making sure his hair was parted properly and his fingernails sparkling clean. Siva, Valivan, Shadur and Elsifor all donned their advisor robes again, their expressions changing the moment the hooded vestments covered their backs. They had practiced their roles and rehearsed their lines, and by the time Orkorlis came to escort them they were confident they could fool their human hosts.

They would not be seeing Reius, of course. The famously private leader would only appear at the end of the Council, when he addressed his devotees. Still, the place would be filled with all manner of J'horan nobility—most of whom hated the Cryori. Though he knew he'd be safe, Haru nevertheless felt a knot in his stomach as he let Orkorlis escort him and his Chorus to the ballroom. Amazingly, the halls leading to the wing were empty of visitors, just as they'd been the day before. Only servants and priests passed them as they made their way to the Council. Siva and Elsifor, both noticing the odd quietude, flanked Haru closely. Shadur and Valivan tailed them, just a pace behind. The servants made no eye contact, bowing politely as they went quickly by. Orkorlis made small talk as he escorted them through the echoing hall, gesturing at the frescoed ceiling.

"...more than six years to complete," said the priest. He looked up to admire the ceiling without missing a step. The youthful eyes of painted, winged children stared back at him, darting between the rendered clouds.

"Orkorlis, where is everyone?" interrupted Haru. So far, he'd been polite to the priest, but the silence had his hackles up.

"Wait," said Orkorlis. He turned to smile at Haru, quickening his step as he walked backward to lead them on. "You'll see."

There was no a hint of danger in his voice. Valivan's reassuring presence crept into Haru's mind, like slipping into a warm bath.

It's nothing treacherous, Valivan told them all. *He's hiding something—like a surprise. I could go deeper if you want...*

Haru stopped him quickly. *No. I don't want him feeling you. As long as we're safe, we keep our secrets.*

Agreed, said Siva wordlessly, but kept her eyes sharp on Orkorlis. Her atlatl bulged beneath her robes. Elsifor quietly tensed his feline muscles. Friend or not, he'd promised to gut Orkorlis at the first hint of deception.

They followed the priest to a wide, golden stairway that twisted upward toward another level. Surprised to be heading up, Haru hesitated.

"I thought the ballroom was on this floor," he said.

"It is," said the priest. "But Tain Haru, you have to trust me. Please, just come with me. It'll be grand, I promise."

Orkorlis bounded up the stairs. Haru and the others climbed after him, first one flight then another, and then heard the noise of gathered people up ahead. Elsifor raised his nose and sniffed. His eyes narrowed, but he kept whatever he'd discovered to himself.

"This way," chirped Orkorlis. "Almost there!"

The stairway flattened out, depositing them in another empty chamber, a gallery of sorts that ended in a balcony overlooking a vast chamber on the level below them. As in the hallways, only servants manned the gallery, waiting for them but not looking up. The luxurious chamber reminded Haru of the Lantern Room back home, obviously meant for Reius and the entertainment of visitors, filled with velvet lounging chairs and hung with portraits of severe-looking holy men. A rambling tapestry of a white seabreaker crashing through the ocean covered an entire wall. Below the chamber, the loud noise of a thousand voices carried up and over the balcony. The servants stepped aside as Orkorlis waved Haru toward it.

"Come and see," said Orkorlis excitedly.

He gestured toward the balcony where a dozen theater seats were arranged in the dark, intimate space. Haru went ahead of the others, now curious. The din increased as he entered the balcony, the rush of voices sweeping up like an orchestra. As he approached the ebony railing, the enormous, crowded chamber came into view. He stood there, awed as Siva and the others came up behind him—all but Valivan, who hovered just beyond the balcony. Orkorlis sidled up to Haru and gave a satisfied sigh.

"Look on," he whispered. "If you could hold the Alliance in your palm, this is how it would be."

The whole world in one room—that's what it looked like to Haru. Amassed beneath him was every shade of skin and every walk of life, every people of the continent who had once known the power of Nesenor, a thousand of them or more, dressed in regal fabrics from their homelands, their voices a swarm of dialects. They laughed and chatted, drank and embraced, argued, bowed, danced to music, raised their glasses...

And dazzled Haru.

A large stage with a ceremonial dais dominated the left side of the chamber, crowded with waiting noblemen. The silver head of Count Whistler stuck out from the group. The Count stood tall, looking anxious on the stage but taking no notice of the Cryori on the balcony. The gathered men and women continued their celebrating, oblivious to Haru and his Chorus until Haru gave a single, wide-eyed utterance.

"Ohh..."

The tiny sound projected out from the balcony. One by one, heads turned upward. The sight of the Cryori hovering above them silenced the crowd. A glass slipped from a startled hand, shattering. A woman in a sapphire gown pretended to faint. Up on the dais, Count Whistler looked at Haru and grimaced. A thousand awed faces stared in disbelief. Afraid to move, Haru managed a twisted smile. As if to poke the crowd, Elsifor lowered his hood and a gasp rose from the chamber.

Orkorlis gently took Haru's arm, bidding him to sit. Yet Haru stood, unwilling to back away. Count Whistler quickly cleared his throat.

Haru wondered if he should greet the crowd, but words wouldn't come. Siva tilted toward him.

"Just sit," she whispered.

Her plea soothed him. Haru took the biggest seat, one like a great, velvet throne. Orkorlis stopped the others before they could join him.

"Just Tain Haru for now," he said. "Elsifor, you and the others can come with me. I'll show you the palace library."

"Wait, what?" said Haru.

Elsifor wedged himself between them. "Orkorlis, we're not going anywhere without Haru."

Orkorlis hurried to explain. "Tain Haru, this is Reius' private viewing gallery. He wants you to enjoy this day, to see Count Whistler receive his honor."

"So? The others can stay, can't they?"

"Your Chorus will be fine without you, Tain. There's been an arrangement made, just for you alone."

Valivan jumped on that. *Haru, I could find out—*

No, replied Haru quickly. He kept his composure and said, "Orkorlis, I need them. They have to stay. Those people down there—"

"Those people mean nothing, Tain." The priest shrugged dismissively. "Nothing at all. You are a guest of the master, and that is all they need to know. If you're fearful of them, do not be. If they offend you, they will die for it."

We can't leave him, Shadur insisted.

Orkorlis looked at them, not hearing a word they shared. "Elsifor, you know I wouldn't lie."

"Go," decided Haru. Then, reassuringly, he added, *I'll be fine.*

Afraid to argue, the Chorus agreed, letting Orkorlis lead them back out of the gallery. The crowd in the ballroom calmed as they departed, eventually managing to pull their eyes from the solitary Haru. Count Whistler nodded at him from the distant stage. Haru watched the dull procession of noblemen and the brightly dressed women. He felt imperious in his velvet chair, but he knew he was just a curiosity to the humans now.

A female figure appeared suddenly, rounding the row of seats. Her shadowed face grinned as she took the chair to Haru's right, plopping down with a dramatic sigh, her big, velvet skirt whooshing like a bellows. The crowd took notice with a rippling murmur. Women raised their eyebrows; men struggled not to stare. The figure found Haru's hand and patted it with her own, ringed fingers.

"Is that not a spectacle?" said the stranger. "The Guardian Council always delights me." She turned her unsettling smile on Haru. "And here you are, a Tain of Nesenor!"

She was unlike any woman Haru had seen, a lithe, serpentine creature with white, sun-starved skin and outrageous red hair that bobbed at her shoulders. The collar of her silver jacket twinkled with sapphires, lighting her powdered, pallid face. Black makeup rimmed her bilious eyes, making them pop from their sockets. Big, overgrown teeth stuffed her jaws. In the darkness of the balcony, she seemed otherworldly.

"Who are you?" asked Haru.

The woman put a hand to her glistening lips, kissed her fingers, then touched them to Haru's cheek. "I am Malon."

Her tone ice was musical; the words danced from her tongue.

"Chancellor," realized Haru. "The First Follower."

"The right hand of the prophet. Did you see the Tower of Principles when you arrived? Be my guest there, Tain Haru, I beg you. Do you like art? I have a collection of absurdist paintings you'll adore. After you've concluded your business with the master, of course."

Haru couldn't help but squirm. Nodding politely, he said, "Chancellor Malon—"

"Chansoor," corrected Malon politely. "I'm from Saxoras, Tain Haru. *Chansoor Malo'n*. That is how it is said." She looked expectedly at Haru.

"Chansoor," said Haru.

"Malo'n."

"Chansoor Malo'n."

Malon beamed. "Beautiful. Do all Cryori speak so liltingly? In Saxoras we value refinement. I myself speak seven languages." Malon paused and said, "*Kais shinbo bokan.*"

The ancient Cryori greeting charmed Haru. "*Bokan*," he replied. "That's very good. Chan—*Chansoor*...I'm impressed. Where did you learn that?"

Malon sniffed and pulled at the cuffs of her glittering jacket. "I struggle with it. If I said more, I would embarrass myself." She swept her arm over the chamber. "Take a long look at those people down there. They come from across the continent but share one language now. The language of J'hora."

"The language the Cryori taught them, you mean."

"Taught, borrowed...why quibble? What matters is their devotion. Devotion to Taan, to Reius, to the very idea of the Alliance."

"You sent my Chorus away," said Haru. "Why?"

"To see if you'd agree. To test you. Yes! Forgive me, but your Chorus...what are they precisely?"

"Advisors," replied Haru carefully. "As I've explained."

"Not bodyguards?"

"Why? Is there something they should be protecting me from?"

Malon's eyes flashed with mirth. "You are safer in this palace than in your mother's arms."

Haru sat back. "Then you're here to spy on me. Like that priest of yours, Orkorlis. Your people have been falling over themselves ever since I stepped foot on your ship. It must be irksome."

"You startle us, Tain Haru, that's all. And many in the Alliance still fear you." Malon's grin thinned out. "But I do not. Reius has invited you here, and Reius is unspeakably wise. Still..." She leaned uncomfortably close. "You are remarkable to look upon."

In the chamber below, a steward called the crowd to attention. The noblemen on stage waited as a long-robed chamberlain spoke their names. Haru pretended to listen, unnerved by the way Malon stared. When Count Whistler's name was called, she raised a single brow.

"Count Whistler is a very good man," she said. "Astute enough to know the Alliance cannot be thwarted. He'll get his Chain of Office today."

"A chain indeed," replied Haru.

Malon licked her painted lips and turned her attention toward the dais. "These men understand the march of history; its ebbs and flows. If I may, Tain, it is low tide for the Cryori."

"I've seen human history, Chansoor Malo'n. Lately it's been washing up on our shores."

Malon laughed. "You have a fearless wit, Tain Haru! But take my meaning—the world has changed. You know it has. Otherwise, you would not have come. Ten years ago, would your father have entertained peace with the continent?"

The question forced Haru to shake his head. "No."

"No precisely. Because Nesenor was stronger then. Every year you slip a little more. You are an ancient people, like an old man. The hands start to shake. The gait grows slower." Malon sighed. "As I've said—the march of time. The Alliance is young, vigorous. Like a lioness in her prime! This is our time, Tain."

Haru knew Malon was baiting him. "Orkorlis told me to expect a surprise. He must think a lot of you."

"Disappointed?"

"Honestly, yes. I had hoped to meet Reius."

"You will, Tain. Soon. But for now, let it just be the two of us, yes? Tell me—what will you say to Reius when you meet him?"

"I plan on listening, not talking. He invited *me*, remember?"

"But you bear the grudge of your father's death. I know you do."

"Did Count Whistler tell you that?"

"Count Whistler told you the truth, Tain. J'hora is innocent."

Haru stared down at the crowded ballroom. He wondered where Malon's questions were leading. He wondered if his friends were being murdered somewhere. "Are you worried about me, Chansoor?" he asked.

"I'm afraid you'll disappoint my master."

"Why? What does he want from me?"

"Peace, Tain Haru. My master wants peace."

"You mean conquest," said Haru.

"I don't think there's a distinction," said Malon. She snapped her fingers, instantly summoning a servant from the gallery. The silver tray in the young man's hands held two identical white cups, each filled with a steaming liquid. Malon thanked the servant, took the cups, and handed one to Haru. "This will relax you."

Haru took the cup but didn't drink. Its contents looked like tea but smelled of liquor. The servant remained, his eyes flicking curiously toward Haru.

"What is it?" Haru asked.

"Ro'lan," said Malon. The world rolled off her pink tongue. "It's brewed from canter leaves. Very popular in my country. Drink it down as fast as you can stand it. Like this…"

Malon tipped the steaming cup into her mouth and, amazingly, swallowed the contents whole. She gave a bracing cough, rapidly blinked her watery eyes, and slammed the empty cup onto the silver tray. She smiled wickedly at Haru.

"Now you."

Haru tentatively put the cup to his lips.

"No, no, quickly," prodded Malon. "Just as I did. No sipping. You'll burn yourself if you sip."

Determined, Haru opened his mouth and poured it down. He expected pain, but got a mild, pleasant warmth instead. He coughed reflexively, blinking quickly as his eyes began to water.

"How…" He coughed again, louder this time. "How's it not burn?"

"Remarkable, isn't it? In Saxoras, ro'lan is a drink shared only by friends." She took Haru's cup, placed it on the tray, and dismissed the servant with a grand wave. "See? Now we trust each other…*Haru*."

"It'll take more than a drink—"

"Wait, wait," urged Malon. She gestured toward the chamber. "It's Count Whistler's turn."

Haru listened as the chamberlain announced Whistler's name. The Count of Agon stepped forward, just as the others had done before him…

And knelt.

"Watch closely," Malon whispered.

Whistler bowed his head as the chamberlain spoke the lofty words. He told the Count to rise, then placed the Chain of Office around his neck, proclaiming him a Lord Guardian of J'hora. Whistler gave a wan smile. He lifted the medallion to his lips, kissed it, and rejoined the line of noblemen.

The spectacle sickened Haru.

"Agon resisted," said Malon softly. "They clung to old ways. Old *beliefs*." Her eyes flicked toward Haru. "Remember the tide."

"I live on an island, Chancellor. Tides go out, but they always come back again."

"Comfort yourself with delusions if you wish," replied Malon. She waved at the people below. "The power of the J'horan Alliance is inescapable. You will discover that one day, just like your friend Whistler."

Haru bristled. "Maybe we're more like the painted people."

"Oh, the heretics. Heart-breaking. Some people never accept the truth."

"So you kill them." Haru scoffed. "And that's the love of Taan."

"I do the will of Reius. That is all."

"Because you're First Follower."

Malon's white face gleamed. "Yes. I met Reius in prison. Did you know that? He shined his light on me. He blessed me. And when I returned to Saxoras, I ministered to the people. The ones that had no gods because the Cryori abandoned them. Soon they came by the hundreds to hear the word of Taan! They called me First Follower. And Saxoras is the First Nation—the first of the Alliance."

Malon's cheeks flushed as she recounted the story. She pulled a kerchief from her jacket and dabbed her tearing eyes. "Ah, your pardon, Tain," she choked. "I'm just very proud."

Her emotion startled Haru, as did her tale. "You met Reius in prison? Forgive me, Chancellor, but you don't look...strong enough for prison. What were you? A pickpocket?"

Malon grinned at the insult. "Tain Haru, I wasn't Reius' cellmate," she said. She tucked the kerchief back into her sleeve. "I was his torturer."

Chapter Fifteen

GOLGIN

E lsifor could no longer stand the confinement.

First had been the ship, stinking and stifling, with all its staring humans. Then the city, too immense to grasp, and the suffocating walls of its gilded palace. Grinding down his instincts. Suffocating him.

So Elsifor fled, bolting away from the others, mad for solitude and the outside.

Mad simply for *air*.

They weren't prisoners, Elsifor told himself. He could go where he pleased, and right now all he wanted was to be away–from Haru, from Valivan's probing mind, from every human eye. He stalked quickly through the palace halls, grateful the others hadn't followed, tracking the almost imperceptible scent of flowers. He had traced the faint smell to this echoing corridor. Up ahead loomed a black, unguarded gateway, sunlight streaming through its iron bars. Elated, Elsifor tossed back his hood. The sound of chirping birds reached his twitching ears.

He loped toward the gate, skidding to a stop at what he saw beyond it. Just past the bars sprawled an enormous walled garden, like a miniature forest sealed off from the outside city. Dainty stone paths lined with flowers roamed along the graceful trees. Elsifor pushed gently on the gate, delighted as the unlocked portal swung open. He stepped into the garden, cautious at first, then exploding toward the trees. Off came his cloak, then his shirt, trailing behind him as he bounded for the branches. Up, up he climbed, his instincts taking over, the scent of some nearby creature luring him higher. Out came his talons, springing for the hunt. Sharp teeth sprouted from his gums. Suddenly he was far from the palace, leaping between the tree tops until he saw the frightened lemur.

Elsifor stopped, the branch supporting him swinging like a pendulum. Wide, simian eyes stared back at him. For a long moment neither he nor the lemur moved. Then, with only yards between them, Elsifor jumped.

For a moment he was flying, his spine arrow-straight, his long fingernails unsheathed. The lemur darted for the leaves. Elsifor broke through the cover, snapping branches as he reached his fleeing prey. One sharp finger snagged the lemur's belly. Elsifor caught a tree limb, swinging himself upward with his skewered prize. With one merciful bite he quickly severed the lemur's neck. Hot, living blood sluiced over his tongue.

Under its spell, he wilted.

With the now dead lemur dangling from his jaw, he surveyed the city beyond the walls. The towers of J'hora watched him from the distant streets. He sneered at them as he drank the blood, then slowly descended into the thicker leaves to feed. The warm meat of the lemur clung to his teeth as he ate, slowly sating him. He pulled the creature apart, listening to the bones pop and skinning it with his fingernails. The music of the nearby birds calmed him. His eyes drooped and his tongue darted out to clean his grimy muzzle. Then, the noise of human voices trickled up from the garden.

Elsifor cocked his head to listen. A woman's voice and the scent of children reached his sharpened senses. He stared down through the branches, spotting them as they moved across a winding path, then stopping at a patch of sunlit grass. Curious, Elsifor moved stealthily through the branches, reaching the tree just above the strangers. With the butchered lemur in his teeth, he slithered down the tree trunk to see them clearly. A young woman and a dozen children gathered in a semi-circle upon the grass. The woman—just a girl, really—began to read from an enormous book. Her melodious voice ensorcelled Elsifor. He studied her and the well-dressed children, their round faces shining as the honey-haired woman spoke.

A storybook, Elsifor surmised.

He leaned comfortably against the trunk of the tree, munching on the lemur like an apple and listening to the woman recount the tale of a giant named Golgin who lived in a cave outside a village and slept in an enormous iron bed. All were frightened of Golgin, said the woman, except for one young village boy who brought the giant bread each day that he stole from the kitchen of a baron. The tale delighted Elsifor so much that he forgot the blood dripping from his meal...until a little girl screamed.

"What is it!" cried the child.

Elsifor looked down and saw her frantically wiping the red smear from her lap. The other children leapt to their feet. The woman with the storybook looked up with alarm.

Elsifor froze.

"Up there!" shouted a boy. "Look!"

The woman held the children back as she stared up the tree, startled when she noticed Elsifor. Embarrassed, Elsifor quickly hid his meal amidst the branches.

"I'm sorry!" he called down to them, mortified. "I...I thought I'd be alone here."

"Oh!" The young woman fumbled to keep back the curious children, but her face was delighted. "You're that Cryori," she said. "The beastly one!"

The children, overcome with excitement, circled the tree like hunting dogs, all craning for a better look.

"Will you come down?" asked the woman. She clutched the big book to her chest. "I've never seen a Cryori before! And we've all heard about you!"

Elsifor thought of darting back up the tree, but he'd already been discovered. Quickly he licked the blood from his hands, smoothing down the fur and retracting his talons. He had no shirt, only a blood-splotched chest of hair, but the woman seemed so earnest...

"I'm an advisor to Tain Haru of Nesenor," he called down to her. "The priest, Orkorlis— he told us to explore the palace."

The woman smiled crookedly. "Orkorlis? He's a friend of yours?"

"A friend? I'm not sure I'd say that, but he has taught me things. Why?"

"Orkorlis is a good man, but eccentric. Not everyone trusts him." The girl waved Elsifor down. "My name is Erinna. I'm a teacher. I live here in the city. If you won't come down, will you at least tell us your name?"

Elsifor couldn't resist. He took a breath, then leapt out of the tree. The children screeched as he fell toward them, landing on his booted feet then springing up to face them.

"Elsifor is my name."

The children broke into astonished gasps. Elsifor offered a tiny grin. The young teacher stepped forward, her eyes tracking up and down Elsifor's amazing body. She was less than twenty, Elsifor supposed, though it was hard for him to gauge human years.

"Elsifor." She spoke his name like music. She glanced up at his hiding place in the branches, then back at him. "Why, you are amazing! And unlike the rest of the Cryori, surely."

"Born special," said Elsifor.

"What were you doing up there?" asked a bold little boy.

"You got blood on me," said the little girl. She grimaced down at her stained dress.

"I'm sorry," said Elsifor. "I was eating up there."

"Eating?" probed another boy, this one with astounding orange hair. "Eating what?"

Elsifor felt his face get hot. Before he could answer another one said, "You're like a cat."

"Like a panther!" said a girl.

Erinna hurried to Elsifor's rescue. "Stop," she scolded gently, but she couldn't hold them back. Elsifor was quickly surrounded.

"I was eating a lemur," he told them. He raised his left hand, letting the talons spring forth. "With these."

The girls jumped back with a giggle. The boys just stared. Erinna leaned in for a closer look at his deadly fingers.

"How?" she wondered aloud. "Were you... born this way?"

"Mostly," said Elsifor. "But my goddess Paiax touched me, made me more than what I was born to be."

"Well, you are remarkable, Elsifor," pronounced the teacher. "And we are honored to know you."

Their welcome surprised Elsifor. So did all their shining faces. He smoothed down his fur, wanting to impress them.

"You said you were listening to us," said Erinna. "Why?"

"Oh, to your storybook, yes. About the giant Golgin."

Erinna laughed. "Storybook? Elsifor, this is the Dhakor. The holy book."

"Holy book?"

"The word of Taan," said Erinna. Her eyes narrowed on him. "You do know about Taan, don't you? I know you have different gods..."

"I know Taan," sighed Elsifor. Before he could say more the boy with the orange hair reached out and touched his belly.

"Ooh, it's like a cat!" he exclaimed.

Erinna pulled his hand away. "Arnan, stop that!"

"No," said Elsifor. "It's alright. If they *want* to touch me..."

He bent down for the boy, encouraging him closer. Arnan reached out again, completely unafraid, and let his tiny fingers run through Elsifor's fur. The other children hurried forward. Elsifor dropped to his knees to accommodate them, reveling in the touch of their small hands. The girl with the blood-stained dress pushed past the others, studied Elsifor's animal eyes, and slowly traced her fingers over his cheek. Her smile made Elsifor melt.

"What's your name?" he asked.

"Tiri," said the girl.

"Tiri." Elsifor grinned. "Are you afraid of me, Tiri?"

Tiri shook her head.

"None of us are afraid," said Erinna.

Elsifor looked up at her. "That surprises me. I thought humans hated Cryori."

"That's fear," replied Erinna. "But these children have no fear." She patted her book with confidence. "They have Taan. Words of love. Words of acceptance."

"That's what Orkorlis told me," said Elsifor. He stayed on his knees, letting the children examine him.

"If Orkorlis is teaching you about Taan you're being well served."

"He told me about Taan's love," said Elsifor. "And acceptance."

"It's all true, Elsifor," said Erinna. She kissed her cherished book. "Every word of it."

"Even the story of Golgin?"

"The story about Golgin is about accepting truth." Erinna looked at him sadly. "So many have forgotten the stories in the Dhakor. They were taken from us by time, by ambition. But mostly by the Cryori. Your people made us forget them."

Something about Erinna made Elsifor want to apologize. "Orkorlis told me that Reius brought the stories back to you." He glanced at the book in the girl's arms. "Are there other stories of Golgin?"

"No, just the one," said Erinna. "But there are stories of heroes and broken souls and powerful tales of redemption. True tales."

"Really?" asked Elsifor skeptically. He scrunched his furry face. "I can't believe that."

"*Can't?*" challenged Erinna. "I think you mean you're not allowed to believe it."

Elsifor loved her boldness. "We have our own gods," he told her. "And we can see and touch ours."

Erinna glowed. "Surely they are wondrous. Miraculous! I would love to know all about them."

"You would?"

"Yes. You can tell us if you'd like."

Elsifor looked around. He had fallen out of the tree into a very strange land. "You know, I think I would rather hear you talk," he told the girl.

"Then join us." Erinna plopped down on the grass and laid the holy Dhakor in her lap. "I will read a story about the love and acceptance of Taan. If you open your heart to his spirit, it will work on you—marvelous Elsifor."

She summoned back the children, who once again formed an eager crescent around her. This time, though, they waited for Elsifor to join them. Young Tiri looked back at him, scooting over to make room.

"Alright," agreed Elsifor. Then, like the biggest, oddest child in Erinna's class, he sat down to enjoy her lesson.

Chapter Sixteen

FATHER OF BEES

Curiosity had always been Valivan's undoing. Some young men had a temper. Some were greedy and untrustworthy, and some simply could not control themselves. Valivan was none of those things. He had always been quiet and timid, and he had always wondered about the world. When other children played with toys, little Val was taking his apart.

The rest of the Chorus had scattered after leaving the gallery. Elsifor had bolted off like a wild animal, Siva had gone off to explore the palace, and Shadur returned to the lavish chambers he shared with the rest of them, urging Valivan to accompany him. It was a sound idea, especially for someone like Valivan. Their chambers were quiet and Valivan loved quiet. But like Siva and Elsifor, he simply couldn't resist the lure of the astonishing palace. And now that the place was nearly deserted, with almost all its people stuffed into its enormous ballroom, Val took his one opportunity to roam.

Unlike the others, Val had enjoyed Orkorlis' tales of the palace and its history. He remembered every detail the priest had told them, filing them away in his feverish brain and recalling interesting tidbits as he studied the tapestries and frescoes of the palace's numerous halls. As always, the few J'horans that noticed him left him undisturbed, passing him with a polite nod or sometimes turning around completely so not to face him. Valivan reached out to touch some of their minds, shocked by the emptiness he discovered. He had thought being around so many of them would shatter his mind. Instead, they were merely a manageable noise.

Yet somehow, they had constructed their amazing city. And within
it, an unrivaled palace of wonders. Val puzzled over the contradic-
tion. It consumed him as he walked through aviaries with colorful
birds and sanctuaries with solemn altars, and a cold, silent statuary
filled with lifeless figures of towering stone. These things—all of
them—had sprung from the inscrutable brains of humans. Impossibly, they had surpassed their one-time masters. Val studied the marble faces of the statues. Sunlight streamed into the round chamber
from a glass oculus. The sound of a fountain splashed nearby. He
paused at a statue of a young woman, her hair draped over her naked
shoulders, the bevel from a sculpting tool bringing her stone eyes
to life. On her pedestal was carved a single word in an old J'horan
tongue, an alphabet indecipherable to Val. He reached out to touch
her precious face. As he did, a bumblebee landed on his palm and
stung him.

"Oww!"

He cursed and swatted at the bee. The insect hovered in front of
his nose, staring back at him. Val rubbed his sore palm and looked
into the bee's faceted eyes, gasping with realization. Another bee
appeared, then another and more, buzzing around his head. He
turned to see a swam of them hanging in the sunlight, directly
beneath the oculus.

"Jyx," he whispered.

The bees around him joined the others, and the swarm slowly
moved off, luring Val down a winding path through the statuary.
He followed dutifully, partly fascinated, partly dread-filled. He saw
the fountain ahead, but its gurgling noise wasn't caused by water.
The entire structure was encrusted in honeycomb, teeming with
bees and gushing honey into the fountain's basin. The bees buzzed
furiously as Val approached. The swarm went to them, making a
black, shifting halo around the oozing fountain. Val put his hands
over his ears, maddened by the angry din. The buzzing grew into a
painful crescendo...

Then stopped. And all was silent. And the bees crawled into their
honeycombs.

Val stepped forward and gazed into the basin filled with golden honey. The statues around him turned their heads to stare. Behind him rang laughter—the nameless statue of the girl, come to life.

It was a fine illusion, frightening and marvelous, especially when the statues blinked. Val's mind grew blessedly quiet, no longer burdened by the thoughts of living things. He had only known such sacred peace a few times in his life, and only one being could grant him such serenity.

"It's hard to get you alone these days," said a voice. A bee had peaked out from its honeycomb to speak. Val stared at its tiny, booming mouth.

"I have...been around," stammered Val.

Another single bee fluttered out from its sticky home. It circled Val's head, considering him. "But your curiosity finally brought you back to me. Always your curiosity."

"I want...to see...the palace," said Valivan. "Not you, Jyx."

"And I am hurt by that," said a third bee. "Why do you no longer call on me?"

Val held up his palm. "You..." A long pause this time. "...stung me." He sucked on the wound. "Hurts."

Jyx the Trickster, the god who had made a joke out of giving a curious boy the ability to know anything, often appeared as a swarm of insects. Ancients called him the Father of Bees. Valivan simply called him 'patron.' When he realized Valivan wasn't charmed by his living statues, Jyx killed them with a thought. Like snuffing out a candle, they once again were stone. Val looked down once more at the honey in the basin. This time, the thick, sweet substance moved with life.

"Why do you run from me?" said Jyx. The honey congealed, forming a mouth first, then the rest of a golden, featureless face. "We are one. I am always watching over you, Valivan."

The face tilted upward, forming a dripping head. The image of Jyx rose slightly, just up to his naked shoulders. The first time Val had seen his patron it had been in such a form, rising up from a lake of honey in the woods near his childhood home. It terrified him then. It did still.

"I...had to...come," managed Valivan. Confronting Jyx always made him stutter. Worse, the god who gave him the power to reach into other's minds always made him speak aloud.

"Because you're one of the Chorus! The brave, loyal Chorus. So what have you learned from the humans?"

"About...?"

"About their plans. About Sh'an. About Reius."

"Nnnn...nothing," confessed Val. "Haru—"

"Doesn't want you using your gifts, right? Because the humans might discover them."

Val nodded.

"Haru doesn't want it," mused the honey-god. The golden lips made a disapproving, smacking sound. "Hmm."

"Wh...why..."

"Because I care about you. I wanted to be sure your curiosity wasn't getting you into trouble." Slowly, Jyx rose up out of the basin, using all the honey dripping from the combs to form his lithe body. He sat down on the edge of the fountain, looking absurdly casual. "Don't worry, no one is around to see me," he assured Val. "Which is good, because if they saw me, they'd kill you."

"I...I...don't..."

"You don't believe I'm here to help you?" The honey-mouth curved with a sarcastic smile. "Tell me—how are the others? How is Haru?"

Val braced himself. "Fine."

"Because you followed him here without a thought. Without any questions. At least Shadur had some questions. Not you, though. You blundered into the human world just like that!" Jyx snapped his soft fingers. When they made no sound, he shrugged. "Whoops."

Val worked to control himself as pearls of sweat popped onto his forehead. Of all Clionet's immortal clan, Jyx was the least trust-wor-thy. Val knew his patron didn't love him, certainly not the way Jaiakrin loved Siva or Paiax did Elsifor. Jyx loved only himself. And chaos.

"Remember how you'd follow Haru around when you were younger?" asked Jyx. "Delightful. Like a puppy. And then when you got older, how you wanted to be around Haru because all the girls liked him and none of them liked you? That was sad." The blank, golden eyes looked at Valivan. "Remember that?"

Val nodded.

"Girls like a sweet-talker. A honey tongue, you might say. Shame about the stammer." Jyx leaned on his elbow, balancing on the thin ledge of the fountain. Honey dripped from his smooth body onto the tiled floor. "But you are the most powerful of the Chorus. That's why Haru wants you here. Without you they'd fall apart."

"No."

"It's true! They wouldn't be able to speak without you, or keep all their little secrets from these human monkeys."

"I'm glad he needs me," Val shot back. His anger cleared his stammer. "He's my friend."

"Of course he is! A dear friend. And your Tain, too—let's not forget that! It's your duty to help him. Just be careful."

"Why?"

"No, no, I shouldn't have said anything. It's good to be loyal. Really. It is." Jyx sighed. "I've always been fascinated by loyalty."

"You have none."

"Oooh, little mortal!" Jyx sat up straight again. He stretched his liquid body to hover over Val. "You're more like Haru every day. Mother Clionet puts up with mortal mouthiness." His voice became a hiss. "But I do *not*."

"Jyx..."

The god held up a glossy hand. "No. No apologies. You've ruined my visit. It will be a long time until you see me again, Valivan. I came to help, but I see you don't need me."

"Jyx, what..?"

The trickster fell back into the fountain, his body splashing into honey again. Val hurried to the basin but saw only his reflection in the golden pool.

Jyx was gone, leaving Valivan to wonder about his game—and what the humans would think of the enormous beehive he'd left behind.

Chapter Seventeen

THE SQUARE

When Haru asked Orkorlis to find him a secluded, romantic spot overlooking the city, the priest knew just the place. The roof garden was private and breath-taking, and when she saw it, Siva melted.

"Reius comes here himself to pray and mediate," said Orkorlis. As he spoke the night air chilled his breath to mist. "But tonight, it's yours, Tain Haru. I promise—you won't be interrupted."

The old priest winked at Haru, who grinned back at him secretively. Beside Haru stood Siva, dutifully silent and confused, still dressed in the dowdy robes of a Cryori advisor. The noise of the bustling city clawed its way up from the distant streets. A swollen moon lit the garden perfectly.

"Thank you, Orkorlis," said Haru, eager for him to leave. "We'll be here for some time."

"I understand, Lord Tain." Orkorlis bowed as he backed away. "Please...enjoy."

Haru waited for the priest to descend the tower's staircase. When he was certain they were alone, he turned to study the marvelous garden. Built in tiers across the tower's roof, the garden sprawled with plants and miniature trees. Big, bell-shaped blossoms hung from wooden trellises protecting thorny roses, and creeping green vines struggled to reach the streets below, drooping over the ledges of the roof. Lilacs sweetened the air. A lone hummingbird flitted between the blooms. Haru took a step deeper into the garden, past a small, stone bench suitable for lovers, and listened carefully. Except for the sounds from the surrounding city, the garden was quiet—just as Orkorlis had promised.

"Haru? What are we doing here?" asked Siva. She followed him along the cobblestone pathway. The hummingbird darted away as they approached.

"I wanted a place to be alone with you," said Haru. Smiling, he pushed through draping fronds, making his way to the far side of the roof. "Someplace romantic."

Siva gave a delicious pause. "You...? What?"

Haru turned to face her but couldn't contain his laughter. "Don't worry—it's just an excuse. And it worked. See? I told you I could be a Tain."

"Childish, but alright," remarked Siva. "Now what?"

"I'll be meeting Reius soon," he said softly. "There're only a few days left for the Council."

Siva looked at him oddly. "Did Malon tell you that? About meeting Reius?"

"She did. And...other things."

"What things?"

"Later," whispered Haru.

"Why'd you ask Orkorlis to take me to the garden?" she asked.

"We're not here for the garden," said Haru. He turned and started down the path again. "We're here for the view."

Haru broke past the trees and reached the opposite ledge of the roof. "Look."

Far below lay the west side of the city, dominated by an enormous square. Several palace buildings jutted into it, but mostly the space was deserted, a plaza where people could gather and be close to their prophet, Reius. Numerous other buildings surrounded the commons, and beyond those sprawled the rest of J'hora, all lit by a million candlelit windows.

"It's...." Siva paused and said no more.

"What?"

"Sort of beautiful," said Siva. "I don't want anything the humans make to be beautiful."

"Look closer—being up here is like having a map! We can figure out how to escape."

They studied the buildings and balconies, the distance from the square to the outskirts of the city, the towers of the palace—anything that might prove useful. To their left lapped the ocean and its teeming harbor, filled with J'horan ships.

"That's where the *Gonkin* was supposed to wait," said Haru. "I had hoped she'd be ready to sail, that maybe we could escape somehow, maybe outrun the seabreakers they'd be sending after us. But we're on our own now."

"Doesn't matter. That was a foolish plan anyway. There was never any way out of the city. Now maybe you'll admit it."

"Admit what?"

"I told you—we know what we signed up for, Haru."

"Dying isn't the plan, Siva. I'm going to get us out of here."

"But we still don't know where Reius will be."

"He'll be outside when he speaks to the people. He has to be. It's the only place big enough."

"Probably. So, it might be there..." Siva pointed to a lonely balcony sticking out from one of the palace's towers. "If he's going to address a crowd, that's the perfect spot."

Haru nodded. "I'll ask Orkorlis."

"Don't be obvious."

"Orkorlis will tell me. He loves to talk."

Siva surveyed the landscape below, tracing things with her finger and mumbling to herself as she made calculations. Finally, she frowned and shook her head. "The others should be here. They need to see this for themselves."

"See what?"

"The distance, Haru." She turned and faced him, her expression disbelieving. "We don't have a ship. We don't have any horses. We don't have any allies to hide us. We don't know the city or what's beyond it."

Haru pointed past the edge of the city. "That's mostly countryside. Probably some good roads."

"Haru, even if we kill Reius—"

"We will kill Reius."

"And then?"

Haru looked around. "We'll run. We'll hide. And we'll get to safety. We're the Bloody Chorus."

Siva laughed. "I love your confidence. But run where?"

"To Agon."

"Agon? Haru, no..."

"No, think about it—we do have any ally! We have Count Whistler. He'll be leaving here after the Guardian Council. If we can make it to his country, he can protect us. He can get us back home."

"He won't, Haru! We'll be outlaws. Even if we made it all the way to Agon, he'd turn us in." Siva shook her head. "How can that be your plan? It's ludicrous."

"And your plan? To lay down and die? Is that better?"

"My plan is to fight and take as many of these murdering cows with me as possible."

"But my plan is to save us."

"That's not a plan, Haru—it's an ambition!"

Their argument echoed through the garden. Haru turned, exasperated, and backed away from the ledge. He made his way again to the little stone bench, slumping down on it. A fruit tree shaded him from the moonlight; stars twinkled through the branches. Siva glided toward him. She hovered there in the cold air.

"Siva, I want to go home," Haru told her. "I want to *see* home again. And when I get there I want it to be like it was. When we were kids."

"Me too," said Siva.

He looked up at her. "But I'm not a kid, even though that's how Shadur sees me. And Elsifor. And you too, probably."

"Oh, me definitely," joked Siva.

"I'm trying to figure it out. It's hard, though."

"You know me, Haru. You shouldn't have brought me here if you didn't want me to speak up."

"I want you to help me fight."

"I'll always fight. You know I'll always fight."

Haru nodded. "I know that."

Siva shifted closer, playfully knocking him with her shoulder. "We can try it your way. We can try to make our way to Agon. The worse that happens is we die."

"No, the worst that happens is that we get captured and wind up in Reius' dungeon."

"I won't allow *that*, ever," Siva assured. "I'll slit all our throats first."

"Friendship!" Haru chortled, but he turned serious again quickly. "They built all this because of Reius. Once we take him away, they'll be lost."

"They might. Or they might just want revenge. Like us. That's the gamble you've taken, Haru." Siva pretended to look at the stars. "I'll tell the others. We've got four days until the Council ends. After that, Reius greets his people."

"And that's when we kill him," said Haru darkly. "In front of everyone."

Chapter Eighteen

MOAJE

Haru sat on a plain wooden chair in the courtyard, sipping a warm drink in the cold sun. The hooves of J'horan horses made the earth flutter beneath him. A leather ball the size of a boy's head arced across the field. Riders in bright blue coats and red hats roared and shouted as they thundered over the grass, swinging their bats like swords as they fought for the ball. They paid no attention to their tiny audience—just Haru and Elsifor—as they battled to score. Though the intricacies of the game were lost on him, Haru watched politely, nodding as Elsifor spoke into his ear.

"...to see her again. She invited me, Haru. How can I refuse her?"

"Erinna," said Haru. "Pretty name. But that's not why we're here, Elsifor."

"What do you mean?"

Haru's eyes flicked toward his friend. "They told us to make ourselves at home here. I don't think that meant taking their women."

"Haru," grumbled Elsifor, "that's not why I'm interested in her."

"It's not?" Haru shrugged. "Alright. Why then?"

Elsifor struggled with his answer. "She teaches me things. Like Orkorlis."

"About what?"

"About...Taan."

Haru stayed quiet for a moment. "Taan." He decided to speak carefully. "Can I ask why?"

"Because it intrigues me, Haru." Elsifor pretended to watch the game. "I never knew anything about Taan. His stories—they bring people happiness. Real happiness."

Haru watched the opposite team smash the ball across the field, his eyes tracking it as it sailed through the sky. "Hearing you say that frightens me, Elsifor. Taan is a lie. All those stories are lies. Maybe they're interesting, but they're make believe. You know that, don't you?"

"I do," sighed Elsifor. "But you should hear them. Even if they're make believe, they're very wise stories. When Erinna reads them, they feel real to me."

"But they're not real. Paiax is real. Clionet is real."

"I know," said Elsifor.

"We've all gotten too comfortable here," lamented Haru. "You, Siva, even me. Look—no one's even watching us! They don't even care we're here."

"They trust us," said Elsifor.

"That's irksome."

They had been in J'hora for days, indulging in its excesses and being treated like princes. At first, they'd kept to themselves, but the pull of the palace and its many curiosities had lured and charmed them all, even Valivan, who seemed better in the crowded human city than he ever had back home, and Shadur was spending all his time in the palace's library, a place he claimed had more books and scrolls than all of Nesenor.

Haru watched the game, clapping suddenly at what he supposed was a good shot. "Stay away from that girl Erinna, alright Elsifor? And stay away from Orkorlis."

"Orkorlis? Why?"

Haru shrugged. "Because this place is changing us."

He let the pounding hooves drown their conversation. The two teams of riders galloped across the field. A flash of movement captured Haru's vision. A man approached, one of the palace's ubiquitous servants. Haru tipped his glass to his lips, draining the contents and expecting a refill, but as the man drew close Haru realized he'd never seen him before. Dressed in a mosaic of silk vestments, his long jet hair pulled back in a braided tail, he strode confidently toward them, ignoring the galloping horses and deadly-quick ball. Elsifor sniffed the air.

"He smells like smoke."

Haru rose to greet the man; Elsifor quietly parroted the move. The riders took no notice as the stranger fell to one knee before the startled Cryori, bowing his head so his hair tickled the ground. He was darker than most of the humans, not black like the seamen on the *Mercy*, but not pinkish either, and certainly not like the milk-colored Malon.

"I am Aryak, Tain Haru," said the man. "The holy prophet begs to see you."

Haru nearly dropped his glass. "Reius?"

"Yes, Tain."

"Now?"

The man kept his eyes down. "If it is convenient."

"Yes," said Haru. "It's...yes..." He glanced at Elsifor, feeling un-ready, and absently handing him the empty glass. He had expected more warning, more formality. He wasn't even armed. He looked down at his shabby clothes, dusty from the field. "Just me?" he asked the man. "What of my advisors?"

"You alone, please," replied Aryak.

Haru glanced around. "Where is he? Is it far?"

"Not far, Tain." Aryak continued kneeling. "I will escort you."

Haru was only nervous for a moment. He straightened, standing over the servant. "Take me to him," he pronounced. "Now, please."

He said nothing to Elsifor, not even good-bye, following Aryak as the servant rose and led him back the way he'd come, toward a small building with square, wavy windows bordering the courtyard. The structure was plain but charming, made of the same granite blocks as the rest of the palace but decorated with intricately patterned chips of multi-colored tiles. Odd, golden lettering ringed by a rope of stone hung over the arched doorway. Haru remembered seeing the crest before in books he'd read back home. He studied the crest as he neared the building—the Seal of Taan.

"He's in there?" Haru asked, startled.

"As I said, not far," replied Aryak.

Haru had spent most of the morning in the courtyard—just yards away from Reius. He braced himself, surprised by the modesty of Reius'...what? Home? The whole palace was Reius' home, he supposed. He followed Aryak to the open entrance, where the servant paused and stood aside.

"The Prophet awaits you," said Aryak, inclining his head to indicate he'd go no further.

Haru peered inside. The smell of burning coal filled his nostrils. A small hall led from the doorway to a larger chamber beyond with flickering shadows. Haru went ahead, instantly swallowed by the hallway as the noise from the field faded behind him. When he reached the chamber, he paused at the threshold. A single room spread out before him, colorful and cluttered, strewn with pillows and thick with sweet-smelling smoke. A single, miserly window admitted a narrow shaft of sunlight. Light smoke rose up from a coal-filled brazier, intensely warming the air. A bed with four golden posts and a canopy of gossamer fabric stood against a wall. Pillows and stubby chairs littered the center of the room.

And there were papers, hundreds of them, left in crooked stacks along the floor and jammed into shelves on the wall and strewn across a vast desk at the far end of the chamber, nearly hidden by a staggering collection of teetering books. Haru squinted to see past them, then noticed a figure seated at the desk. Hunched over, his back turned toward Haru, the man worked feverishly, the pen in his hand audibly scratching parchment. Haru inched closer, peeking around the tower of books.

The man wore no shirt. His bald head gleamed with sweat. Colorful swirls and patches blotched his skin; tattoos, Haru realized. The strange illustrations rolled along his big arms and shoulders, spreading across his muscular back and reaching up his neck to his illustrated head. The man slapped his pen loudly on the desk, pushing back from his work with a sigh.

Haru inched closer. "I'm here," he pronounced.

The man turned to face him. Like his tattooed back, his bared chest was equally inked. He rose purposely to his feet, towering over the stacks of books and revealing his enormity. Wide and stoutly muscled, his skin had the look of worked leather, his eyes the flint of exhaustion.

"You're coming here lifts a giant burden from me," he said. "For that I owe you thanks."

"Are you Reius?" asked Haru.

The giant nodded. "I am Reius."

Haru had rehearsed this meeting a hundred times. Now, he groped for words. "Burden? What do you mean?"

"The horrors you've spared me," said Reius. "I have never murdered a race before."

His terrible words hung in the air. Haru steadied himself.

"Maybe not a whole race," said Haru. "But there is one Cryori you've murdered."

Reius said intensely, "Have you come to find your father's slayer?"

"I came because I had to see you. Because I could not believe your audacity. Because I'm Tain of Nesenor."

"You came for peace," said Reius. "Tell me you came for peace."

"I'm not afraid of you, Reius. My country isn't afraid."

"I didn't kill your father." Reius gestured to one of the chamber's short, cushion-covered chairs. "Sit."

The offer relieved Haru. He sat down in the chair, his backside disappearing in the silk pillows, and watched Reius go to a basin of water fixed against a wall of the chamber. He filled a pitcher from the basin, retrieved a large, alabaster bowl and towel from a shelf, and returned to where Haru was seated. Then, to Haru's shock, Reius dropped to his knees before him. He set down the bowl and pitcher, looking squarely into Haru's eyes.

"Let me give you ease," he said. He reached out for Haru's foot, taking it in his enormous hands. Haru jerked it away.

"What are you doing?"

Reius leaned back on his heels. "We may all be J'horans now, but I was born in Kalmiir," he said. "The dry lands. This is called *Moaje*—the washing of feet. It's how we care for travelers. And you have travelled far, Tain Haru." He put out his hands again. "Will you allow me?"

Haru hesitated. The thought of a ruler washing someone's feet mystified him. He looked at Reius a moment, at his bald head and earnest eyes, then slowly lifted his foot. "Fine."

Reius removed the boot from Haru's right foot, then requested the left. He set the boots aside, gently cradled Haru's foot over the bowl, and lifted the pitcher. The warm water smelled like roses, threading soothingly through Haru's toes. Reius worked without speaking, careful with the ritual.

"You humble yourself like this for strangers?" Haru asked.

Without looking up, Reius replied, "We honor Taan when we care for others."

Coming from Reius, that concept sounded insane. Haru could see the man's many tattoos clearer now, intrigued by the images of battle and women and devotion, like a story told in pictures on his skin. Slowly, he began to relax. Reius, sensing Haru's growing ease, began to smile.

"By the time you leave here, you will believe me," he said.

"About my father?"

"About everything. I do not lie. Not ever. Nor do those who serve me. You trust Count Whistler, yes?"

Haru nodded. "He is a friend."

"Did he tell you I was innocent?"

"He did. I believe *he* believes it."

"But you don't believe me."

"Like I said, Whistler is a friend."

Reius set the pitcher down, then began to dry Haru's feet with the towel. "This is how it must have been for decades," he said. "A human on his knees before a Cryori. But now you've seen how we've changed. How we've grown. You're still a child, Tain. Yet we cannot help but see you as a father. And it galls us that we want your approval."

Haru pulled back his foot. "Cryori don't threaten their parents. We don't plot to kill them."

"We are your offspring, Tain Haru. Born from decades of misrule. But we have found the light now and are no longer children." Reius handed Haru his boots. "Will you talk peace with me?"

"I..." Haru took his boots. "I have questions."

"I have time."

Reius rose and put away the bowl and pitcher. He glanced at his desk, then fell into a pool of pillows near the glowing brazier. He spread his arms wide along the cushions, the muscles of his back stretching like the wings of an eagle. Haru realized he'd been offered no refreshments, an unthinkable oversight in Nesenor. Rather than clean feet, he'd have preferred a cup of tea. But they were alone, without servants or advisors to overhear them, and that was clearly Reius' plan.

"You have a bed here," Haru observed. "Is this your chamber?"

"I spend most of my time here. Working. Writing."

"Writing? You mean all these scrolls?"

"Taan speaks often. I'm called to be his voice."

"But there are hundreds of papers here." Haru remembered the library Shadur had told him about. "These are all your writings?"

"They're the holy words of Taan," said Reius. "Sometimes his voice is like a plague in my mind. It never ceases." He pinched his forehead between his thumb and forefinger. "But Taan gives me strength."

"Why here, though? Why not someplace..." Haru shrugged. "Better?"

"I live here as I lived as a child. As I lived before."

"Before what?"

Reius smiled. "How much do you know of me?"

"We have scholars in Nesenor," said Haru. "They've educated me."

"They've failed you, then. You expected none of this—not our greatness, not our power, nothing. Yet you try to hide it from me. If we are to trust each other—"

"We will never trust each other."

"We will. We *will*. There is no peace without trust. And I want peace, Tain Haru. I want to be spared the awful things of war. I spent my life in war. Look..." He glanced around his cluttered chamber. "These things around me? Memories of war. Helmets, spears..." He pointed to them, laying unceremoniously against a wall, battered and unloved. "Trophies I took when I cared about such things. Things that mattered before I was saved." He held up his big hands. "If you could see the blood on me, you would weep for all the dead.

If you do not trust me, Tain, if we do not make peace, the blood of all Cryori will drown me."

"You want peace but all you do is threaten," said Haru, leaning forward. "Let me tell you what I told your Chancellor—Nesenor will never fall to humans. We are the same people who collared this continent like a dog. We're not afraid of war, Reius. Some of us even welcome it."

"Then I pity them," said Reius. He got up from his seat and went to his cluttered desk. There, propped up against the big wooden furniture, was a stout tree branch, like a club, worn out and stained with what Haru supposed was blood. Reius hefted the weapon, a memory paining his expression. "I was fourteen winters when I became a soldier for the old king. I marched with his legions far from Kalmiir, my home, into the lands of Faa and Ulgur, in the wars with the Sand Barons. I wasn't born to be a warrior. It took me time to learn how to fight, but I survived, and when you survive you get better. Much better."

Haru sat quietly. Reius rubbed the length of the club as he continued.

"I made this myself," he said. "I saw the branch laying in the road one night on a march. We were on a way to a town in Upper Ulgur where Baron Jelian was waiting with his army." Reius flicked his eyes toward Haru. "Ever hear of Jelian?"

Haru shook his head. "No."

"Odious man. He deserved what we did to him. I spent the night trimming this branch, peeling the bark and skin, making it into a weapon because I'd broken my sword two days before. We fought with anything we had, anything we could get our hands on. Because if we didn't fight, we died. Or we ended up in a prison somewhere."

"You were in prison. Chancellor Malon told me you were."

"We'll get to that," said Reius. He went closer to Haru, tapping the club on the ground and standing before him. "The next morning, we fell on that town like wolves. Jelian made his men fight to the death. I don't know why—that town was a hole. Took us two days to just break through the city wall, but when we did, we made Jelian's men pay for it."

Haru watched as Reius' eyes went glassy.

"I had no sword—I told you that. Just this." Reius rested the club on his shoulder. "I don't know how I got cut off from the rest of my legion, but I was alone near the east wall. It was quiet, I remember. I remember thinking it was over. For me it was over, and I was alive! And then he discovered me."

Haru hovered on the edge of his cushion. "Who?"

"A soldier. He thought it was over too. But we saw each other. And we both knew one of us had to die." Reius lifted the club over his head. "He came at me and I swung and I hit him. His mouth exploded. His jaw flew off his face and hit the wall. And I went at him with my club, again and again, and I pounded this club into his skull until his brains stained the dirt!"

Reius screamed as he told his story, acting it out, spittle flying from his lips.

"And then..." Reius dropped his club. "I heard him."

"Who?" Haru nudged.

"Taan," said Reius. He tilted back his head and closed his eyes, reliving the moment. "The first time he ever spoke to me. Clear he was, like my mother's voice. Beautiful." Reius raised his hands in the air. "He saved me. He told me his plans for all humanity. He told me he was back and that he had never forgotten us." Reius opened his eyes and looked at Haru. "He told me he loved me."

"Love?" Haru was careful with his question. "After what you'd done?"

Reius kicked away the club. "There was never a man more wretched than me, Haru. But he chose me. He stuck his finger down from heaven and touched me."

Reius slumped back down in his pillows, looking even more exhausted now. He rubbed his bloodshot eyes and said, "The continent was different then. Full of false gods. No one to rule it. Taan was just a memory until I started reminding people about him. I deserted my legion, started travelling, spreading the word. I was imprisoned many times, in many places."

"Malon told me she was your torturer."

"She was peerless at making men suffer. But she never broke me. She listened to my screams *and* my prayers, and then one day asked me how I could possibly have withstood her tortures for so long. When I told her of my faith, something in her broke."

"She does seem...broken," said Haru.

"No one is beyond the reach of Taan. Not a murdering soldier or a mindless whore. Malon got me out of prison. She became my follower. And together we started changing the world."

"You mean conquering the world, don't you?"

"No, I do not." Reius looked intensely at Haru. "I mean saving it from itself, from the belief in petty gods and poison magic. From war with itself. From hatred of itself. With Taan's help we've brought peace and order. Did the Cryori ever bring us these things?"

"Look at me," said Haru, "and know that I'm serious. We're not humans. We're Cryori. We'll fight you to the death, just like the people in that town."

"Unless you make peace with me. You and I, Haru—we are the only ones who can do it."

"No! You're the only one who can do it, Reius. You're the one making threats. Leave us alone and there won't be a war! Just—"

Haru stopped himself. This wasn't working. He looked around, feeling frustrated. A tattoo on Reius' left breast snagged his attention. He studied the image, a picture of two young boys with identical faces.

"What's that?" asked Haru, pointing at it.

Reius said cagily, "A tattoo."

"Of who? Who are they?"

"My tattoos tell my history."

The half-answer intrigued Haru. He looked over the rest of Reius' tattoos, suddenly remembering the pictures Skorthoros had drawn weeks before. They'd been images of a history, too, of battles and memories unknown to Haru—until now.

"Your tattoos interest me," he said.

Reius frowned. "We can talk about them. We have time. If you'll stay, we can discuss many things."

"Stay? I don't belong here. I only came to hear your offer."

"You shouldn't leave until you make your decision."

"About what? War?"

"About peace."

"We can play this game all day," sighed Haru. "Your offer, please. You must have one. You must have called me here for something."

"Tain Haru, I called you here to save me the agony of destroying Nesenor." Reius got up from his chair, but instead of towering over Haru he dropped to one knee before him. "Listen to me—I beg you," he pleaded. "Those creatures that you call gods brought ruin to our world. They've enslaved the Cryori, but you can break free of them just as we have. You want my offer? Here it is—life everlasting. Truth. And unrelenting love. It's all yours, Haru. All you have to do is accept it."

"What?" Haru was incredulous. "You mean renounce our gods? Accept *Taan?*"

"It's his will that I should ask you this, that I should humble myself and beg you," said Reius. "For years I have prepared for war with you. For years I dreaded the day I'd set fire to Nesenor, burn out the poison of your heresy. But Taan spoke to me! He offers you this one last chance. Do you not see how benevolent he is?"

"Reius...no, I do not," said Haru haltingly. "Are you asking us to be part of the Alliance?"

"You would be a Lord Guardian, Haru," said Reius. "You would have the honor of spreading the word of Taan through your people, of *saving* them."

"Your tattoos—"

"Oh, damn my tattoos!" Reius sprang to his feet. "They tell my story! Here, this one is Kalmiir, where I was born. And this is the face of the man I clubbed." Angrily he pointed out the images. "I will tell you all about them, no secrets—but not now. Now we speak of life and death!"

Haru very calmly rose to leave. "I have to go."

"Wait!"

Haru paused halfway to the door.

"Wait. Please." Reius composed himself. "Let me show you something," he said, and lifted up his left arm. Beneath his armpit was a patch of untouched skin. "There is one more story left to tell. One more tattoo. I have saved this spot for it."

"For what?"

"This is where I will tattoo the fall of Nesenor. Or its salvation."
Reius lowered his arm. "It's up to you, Haru. Taan has put this in
your hands now."

Haru wanted desperately to be gone. He was halfway to the door,
yet something held him there, something real in Reius' eyes. Past
the madness, there was honesty.

"Someone killed my father, Reius," he said. "I loved my father.
Someone murdered him and I think it's you."

"Let me prove my innocence," said Reius. "Remain in J'hora, until
the end of the Council at least. I will answer all your questions. All
I ask is that you grant my words an honest hearing."

Without knowing why, Haru agreed. "Five days," he said. "Until
the end of the Council. Then I go home."

"Taan made the world in seven days," said Reius. "In five, he will
make you believe."

Chapter Nineteen

BORN TO KILL

"They were twins! Just like the ones Skorthoros showed me. Right there on his chest."

Haru spooned himself another helping of fish stew from the steaming tureen. He'd done most of the talking so far, his odd, mismatched family listening intently around the table. Finally, they were all in one room again, engrossed in the tale of Haru's encounter. An elaborate evening meal sat before them, a puzzle of nameless J'horan dishes and confusing cutlery. This time, however, there were no servants to disturb them; Haru had ordered them away.

"I'm telling you, he's lying," said Haru. Standing, he refilled his companions' glasses from a crystal wine decanter. Elsifor reached across the table, eager for more of the ruby liquor.

"It's a tattoo," said Siva. Seated to Haru's left, she'd been waiting for him when he arrived back at their chamber. "Maybe that's all it is."

"You weren't there, you didn't see for yourself," said Haru. He sat down again, waving his fork as he spoke. "He got angry when I asked about the twins. He was hiding something."

Shadur passed a platter of what they guessed was pheasant to Valivan, who passed it on to Elsifor without taking any himself. Elsifor noisily took a handful of the tiny, spitted birds, piling them on his plate. Siva gave a surprising burp.

"Sorry," she said, embarrassed when Valivan laughed.

"Tell me about the other tattoos," said Shadur. "What were they? Try to be exact."

"One was a face—that one I remember clearly," said Haru. "The man he killed when he first heard Taan."

Shadur hovered over his bowl, blowing on his soup and scoffing. "Taan! What else?"

Haru tried to remember, surprised at how difficult it was to recall them all. Mostly he remembered Reius' freakish height—and those flinty, bottomless eyes.

"It was like the things I saw in your house that night," said Haru. "Battles, people, places. I don't know—things. Reius' life. That's what Skorthoros was showing me."

"Maybe," said Shadur, slurping from his spoon. "Or maybe not."

"Why not?"

Shadur lowered his utensil. The others around the table looked at him expectantly.

"Maybe," relented Shadur. "Probably. But none of you know Skorthoros the way I do, and I hardly know him at all. He doesn't speak. He has no real voice. But when he does communicate it's always a mystery."

"It was a mystery," Haru corrected. "Not anymore."

"It's never that simple," sighed Shadur. "There are no straight lines in Skorthoros' world."

"And you said he's mad," Siva pointed out.

"Do you think he's mad, Haru?" asked Elsifor.

"I saw what I saw."

"We're not defending him," said Shadur calmly. "If anyone deserves to die, it's Reius. And he will die. But he took the time to bring you here. You said yourself he seems to want peace. It doesn't make sense."

"Yes it does," said Siva. "He killed Sh'an because he thinks Haru's young and weak. He knew Sh'an would never make peace."

"That's right," said Haru, wagging his fork at Shadur. "He only wants peace to ease his own sick conscience. And to answer your question, Elsifor—of course he's mad. It's insane to think we'd ever give up our gods for Taan."

They all nodded. Haru went back to eating his stew. The others made small talk, commenting on what Haru had told them and noisily enjoying the food. Shadur mentioned the library and all its hand-written scrolls—work they now knew Reius had performed.

"More madness," said Siva. She glanced at Haru. "He never stops?"

"He says he can't," said Haru. "He says Taan is always speaking to him."

"It must be dreadful to be insane," said Shadur. He tore himself a hunk of bread from a nearby loaf, then offered it to Valivan, who declined.

"Val? How come you're not eating?" Haru gestured to him with his chin. "You sick again?"

Valivan shook his head. "No."

"You look good," said Siva. "Better than I ever remember seeing you. Why is that?"

Val shrugged. "I'm not sure. The human minds don't bother me much."

"That's because they're empty!" joked Shadur.

Haru laughed good-naturedly, then said, "That's not Reius. His mind is full of things. Val? Are you sure you're alright? Something on your mind?"

Val hesitated as if about to reveal something, then pushed the food around his plate with a fork. "Nothing."

Siva put her hand on his shoulder. "It's alright to be afraid, Val."

"I'm n-not," said Valivan. When he saw the others grimace, he insisted, "I'm not!"

"Let it go," said Shadur. He dipped his bread into his soup and stuffed it into his mouth.

Haru sipped his wine then lowered his glass. "We've got five days left. Reius doesn't seem very interested in the Guardian Council. He wants to spend time with me, convince me."

"Good," said Shadur. "Get him to trust you. It'll make killing him easier."

"Killing isn't easy," said Siva without looking at him.

"It won't be a close killing," said Elsifor through a mouthful of food. "He'll be up on that balcony overlooking the square—the one you told us about."

"Will he?" asked Haru. "You know that for certain?"

"How do you know?" asked Siva.

"Orkorlis told me." Elsifor grinned. "I asked him."

Shadur laughed. "He wasn't suspicious?"

"He trusts me," said Elsifor darkly. "I don't like deceiving him."

"Elsifor," said Haru. "You're spending too much time with him. Remember what we talked about?"

Elsifor sat back with a hint of annoyance. "I remember, Haru. It's not disloyal to learn things, is it?"

"Good news about the balcony, though," said Shadur. "Looks like it won't be you doing the killing, Haru. I'm glad for that."

"That balcony is pretty high," mused Haru.

"Siva can do it," said Elsifor. He smiled confidently. "She can hit any target."

"Can you?" Haru asked her. "If you don't think you can..."

"I can do it with the atlatl," said Siva.

"With the atlatl it'll be easy," said Shadur.

"Killing isn't easy," repeated Siva, glaring at Shadur.

Shadur clenched his crystal hand. "That's not what I mean. You can do it, that's all. You were born to kill."

"What?" erupted Siva.

"Like Elsifor," said Shadur. "It's in your blood to kill. It must be. Jaiakrin must have seen it in you."

"Easy," warned Haru. "Stop now..."

Siva stood up, her chair falling backward. "It's different, Shadur. Elsifor's an animal!"

"What?" blurted Elsifor.

"Fine, Siva," snapped Shadur. "Maybe you're the one that's afraid, eh? Tell me something—who have you ever actually killed?"

"Quiet, Shadur!" barked Haru.

"I have killed," seethed Siva.

"Who?"

Siva's eyes flashed. She set down her fork, turned from table, and left the chamber, a stunned silence in her wake. Elsifor finally stopped eating and scowled at Shadur.

"Sorry," the mystic offered. "I'll go after her."

"No you won't," said Haru. "I will." He stood, thought about the hot-headed Siva for a moment, then sat back down. "In a little while."

Half an hour later, Haru found Siva on the roof garden. Staring at the dusky horizon, she cocked her head when she heard him coming.

"Good meal tonight," she quipped. "Good company."

Haru glided toward her, sidling up to the ledge, pretending to watch the sunset. "Shadur talks too much. He'll apologize."

"I don't care about Shadur. I don't want his apology."

"Should I go?"

"Yes," said Siva. She lowered her head. "No. I need to tell you something."

Haru let her collect her thoughts. He saw a star blink to life in the darkening sky. He rubbed his cold hands together.

"I've never known why Jaiakrin chose me," said Siva. Her voice was confessional. "But my biggest fear—the only thing I've ever been afraid of—is that Shadur is right about me."

"He's not right," Haru assured her. "And you know why Jaiakrin chose you. To make you strong when you needed to be strong. Because you prayed to him."

"Lots of people pray to him. He could have ignored me."

"He loves you. You know he does."

"That doesn't explain anything."

"Siva, the gods are strange. Clionet loved my father. *Loved* him. Like a husband almost. I don't know what they see in us but it's something. They need us. Not just to worship them but to make them feel alive. Jaiakrin loves you because he sees something special in you. Honestly, I have no idea what that could be..."

"No," pleaded Siva. "No joking..."

Haru turned to regard her. "Tell me who you killed."

"Oh, Haru...you must know. You must have guessed years ago."

"I think maybe I do," said Haru. "But you never told me. You need to admit it."

"My father."

Siva's face turned to stone. Haru shivered.

"He deserved it, Siva. Jaiakrin knew he deserved it. That's why he helped you."

"I killed my father, Haru."

"You saved your sisters and your mother. You saved yourself. I remember those days. He was an awful man."

Siva's hands began to shake. She bit down on her knuckles. Siva's father had done worse than beat his daughters. And Siva was so young. Only a god could have helped her.

"It was Jaiakrin's will," Haru told her. "Not yours."

"Damn it, Haru, stop seeing the good in me! It was *my* will! I wanted him dead so I killed him. I begged Jaiakrin to let me. *I* did that, Haru. And you know what? I've never been sorry for it. I never prayed for forgiveness or lost a night's sleep."

"It's justice, Siva. Right and wrong. Your father deserved it. You know he did, and you know Reius does too. That's all this is—justice. Don't let Shadur get under your skin. Don't get confused."

"We're different, Haru. When I look in the mirror, I see what I am—a killer. When you look in the mirror you see a kid."

"Not anymore," said Haru. "Not after this."

"Reius will die," sighed Siva.

The resignation in her tone caught Haru. "Oh..."

Siva's eyes grew round and sad.

"You still want to die," said Haru. "That's why you came here. That's why you keep talking about not making it home."

"I loved your father, Haru."

"*I* loved my father!" railed Haru. "I loved him! That's why I'm here!"

Siva turned to leave. Haru grabbed her arm and roughly spun her toward him.

"You're not leaving!"

Siva grabbed his wrist, twisted hard, and slammed him to his knees. "Don't!"

Haru hissed at her. "Let me go!"

She released him, hovering over him as he rubbed his throbbing hand. Wondering if it was broken, Haru rose unsteadily, disgusted by his weakness.

"See? *That's* why you're here!" he said. "Call yourself whatever you want, Siva. You think you're a murderer? Fine. Be a murderer. *Please!* When we get back home you can go to Tojira and stay there the rest of your life. But you are coming home. We all are."

"Haru...."

Haru put up his good hand. "No." He tried to keep the emotion from his voice. "I'm your Tain, like it or not. And I say we all go home." He backed away from Siva. "We've got five days." He turned and walked away. "Good night."

Chapter Twenty

DEAD WATER

F loating.

The current buoyed her toward the sun, her mile-long tentacles radiating from her gelatinous body. A slave of the tide, she drifted toward the shore of a nameless island. Her twelve eyes swayed at the end of their stalks, sensing the light and the colors of the ocean. The warmth of the sun touched her as her bell broke the surface. She surrendered to the gentle waves, aware of her countless stingers fanned out like deadly hair, thoughtlessly trapping unseen prey. A school of minnows, a mass of tiny shrimp—the jolt of their dying reached her consciousness.

She had no brain but could think. She had no heart, no blood to pump. Yet she was alive and serene, her strange, jellied body undulating on the waves, the untamed ocean around her. Clionet could mimic nearly any creature in her domain, yet this form was perhaps her favorite. With no mouth to speak or ears to hear, she was wonderfully alone. She let the tide draw her to the shore, let her tentacles drag along the rocks and her vast bell roll upon the waves. A meal of crustaceans digested in her gut. The heat of the sun pricked her pinkish skin.

Then, in her mind she heard a prayer.

At first, she ignored the disturbance, but the tiny, mortal voice persisted. Clionet thrashed. Her mind filled with the voice, distant but clear, calling to her. Its urgency tugged her from her ecstasy. She focused on it, venom seeping from her thrashing tentacles as she awakened. She knew the voice, though he hadn't prayed to her in ages. His insistence frightened her.

Clionet retracted her tentacles. Down she sank, deep toward the gloom, blue light sparking along her body. The province was far and she needed to be quick. A spray of ink cloaked her transformation. Her twelve eyes became two enormous saucers. Suckers sprouted on her long, powerful arms. With a breath she flooded her mantle and let the water shoot from her siphon, jetting her toward Jinja Castle.

When he saw the tide rush in from the catacombs, Liadin knew his prayer had been answered.

It had taken Clionet hours to reach the castle. And he had waited for her patiently, meditating on his prayer, sending it to her like a beacon. Over the years he had seldom prayed to Clionet. She was the patron of royals—Haru's patron—and he was but a loyal priest. Liadin had never been jealous of the order of things, nor was he jealous now. But the sea goddess had something he desired, and his plan required her submission.

He stood at the edge of the canal in a great, circular chamber honey-combed with jail cells. Torches burned on the curved stone walls. A pool of shallow water lapped at his feet, sloshing over the bricks as the sea goddess approached. Liadin held his ground, holding his sukatai in both fists before him. His loyal Venerants had raised the iron gates to let the goddess enter. The canal of dark water crested as Clionet drew closer. He could sense her now beneath the surface, their minds touching as she searched for him.

"I am here, Sacred Mother," Liadin declared. "Show yourself."

A hollow roar blew through the catacombs, striking his face. The torches on the wall flickered and snapped. A wave rose up, breaching the pool and splashing him. Purple tentacles rose like serpents from the foaming water. Liadin looked down into the circular pool. Below the surface, a body writhed in bursts of fiery light, transforming the monstrous squid into a beautiful, sea-green woman. Clionet's shining eyes blinked at Liadin from beneath the water. As she broke the surface, water sprayed from her ruby lips. Blue, iridescent skin cast its glow on the gloomy walls. Her tentacles churned the water, propelling her upward.

Liadin looked up into Clionet's remarkable face. She was magnificent, and her beauty took his breath away. She saw his pained expression and puzzled over it.

"What has happened?" she asked. Her voice filled the chamber like an orchestra. "Where is Haru?"

"Gone," replied Liadin.

"Dead?"

"Do you feel him, goddess?"

"Answer me!"

Her voice was a thunderclap. Liadin held tight to his sukatai and did not waver.

"Haru has gone from Nesenor, Sacred Mother. He has gone to seek vengeance in J'hora."

Horror changed her skin from blue to scarlet. The seaweed in her hair squirmed. "When?" she demanded.

"Weeks ago. If he's alive or dead I do not know. So, I ask again—do you feel him?"

The link between the royals and Clionet was strong, Liadin knew. If she tried, she could sense him, even from such a great distance. But Clionet did not try. Her eyes tracked Liadin with suspicion. He kept up his pretense as though expecting an answer, moving nonchalantly around the pool, pausing halfway to the gate.

"Haru went to J'hora to keep his promise to you," he went on. "Reius called him to J'hora on a mission of *peace*. Sh'an raised a brave son. You should be proud of him."

He could see his words baffling the goddess. Beneath her, the water in which she floated grew eerily still.

"You should know that I am Regent now," said Liadin. He moved closer to the gate. "With Haru gone, Nesenor needs a leader."

The canal trembled. Liadin could feel the new presence drifting toward them. The baffled Clionet, too pained to notice, stared at the Arch-Disciple.

"Regent? If Haru is alive—"

"I control the beast-ships now," said Liadin. "I will have the loyalty of our navy. They will follow me as my Venerants do, because they know what is best for us all." He hovered just before the gate, one step away. "You've always been with us, Blessed One. Be with us now, I beg you."

She looked at him, confused, the color seeping from her eyes, her breath growing shorter. Her bemusement broke Liadin's heart.

"What of Haru?" she asked desperately. Understanding dawned in her eyes. "What have you done to him?"

Liadin's voice cracked as he answered. "Betrayal."

He took the one last step, moving quickly past the threshold and knocking the chock from the gate wheel with his sukatai. The chain ripped upward as the gate crashed down, splashing into the shallow water. Clionet reared back, incensed.

"Deceiver!" Her furious face smashed against the iron bars, transforming into the hissing visage of a hammerhead. "I am a goddess, you crawling little traitor!" Her devilish laughed filled the dungeon. "You think you can bottle me up like a firefly? I will devour you!"

Liadin peddled quickly backward, far from her raging tentacles. The water of her prison sloshed around her, growing soundless. Clionet's suckered tentacles snaked up the gate, ready to shatter it. She smiled hatefully at Liadin, anticipating his grisly death.

"After you, your cohorts..."

Clionet stopped. She swallowed, gasped, and fell back from the gate. Perplexed, she looked down desperately into the impossibly still and silent water. Her eyes filled with a dreadful understanding.

"It's called dead water," Liadin explained. "You know of it. I can tell you do."

Clionet choked as she tried to speak.

"I can make it easier for you, or I can make it unbearable," said Liadin. "Please, Mother, do not make me harm you."

The pool filled with the dead water, like poison flooding in from the canal. Airless, lifeless, the stuff held none of the sustaining elements of the ocean. No sea creature, especially Clionet, could live in it for long. Her transformation faded, returning her normal, now anguished face. Her tentacles slipped from the gate. She collapsed into the black pool, lifting her head to speak.

"Say nothing," commanded Liadin. "Listen. I betrayed Haru but I am no traitor. I am the only hope. War is coming, Clionet. Sh'an courted it and Haru couldn't stop it. Weakness brought us here, but strength will see us through. Nesenor will be great again. But I need your help to defend this island."

Clionet shook her head, barely able to hold herself erect. "Dead water?" she croaked.

"I am not of the blood. I know the charms but I need your blessing. Tell me how to control the dragon-whales."

The goddess spared the strength to snicker. "Never," she gasped, dragging herself toward the ledge, trying to pull herself up and out of the fouled water.

"The air will kill you even quicker than that pool," said Liadin, pitying her. "Please..."

"How?" she gurgled. Her body slid back into the pool.

"The dead water? Only one of your brood can create something so heinous." Liadin banged his sukatai hard on the stone floor. "Come forth!"

In the canal feeding Clionet's prison, the presence in the water made itself known. Ama'aga, the Holy Serpent, rose from the depths, his crustacean-like armor glistening, his fingers dripping the lifeless, suffocating water. He looked at Clionet in her cage, his eyes loveless.

"Mother," he thundered. "I'm home."

Chapter Twenty-One

MENDING

N uara sat on an over-turned basket, watching the red fishing boats pole across the water as he worked to fix his sister's net. The sun was hot and the work simple but tedious, precisely the kind of mindless diversion that had brought Nuara back home. The sunlight tanned his naked back and the toes of his bare feet kneaded the white sand. His fingers nimbly knotted strands of flax, just as he'd learned at his father's knee. Around him played the familiar music of village life, of old boats creaking on the shore and weather-bitten fishermen hauling baskets, their wives washing clothes or cooking in their shabby little homes. Nearby, water buffaloes cooled themselves in the shallow part of the bay; pelicans and herons stalked the muddy shore. Nuara looked up and saw his nephew Jinjon chasing the birds from their trellis of drying pike.

The day was wonderfully good. Nuara smiled. He had come home to Lomoa a week ago, seeing his family for the first time in years. He'd left the *Gonkin* at anchor in Jinja and made the long journey to the province of his dead father, who like himself had heard the call of the sea to leave village life behind. Nuara still loved Lomoa, though. In Lomoa no one called him "captain" or expected him to do anything more than mend some nets. His homecoming had been warm and the villagers generous, and his mother had cooked his favorite dishes to celebrate his return. As he watched Jinjon shoo away the birds, Nuara wondered why he would ever return to the *Gonkin*.

Times were changing. Tain Haru was gone. Now the Venerants were in charge. Even in Lomoa they had heard of Liadin's rise. Nuara's family and friends had peppered him with questions when he came home, wondering if war was coming soon. In Lomoa, today, war seemed impossibly far away. The village was timeless, like the ocean. Nuara had come home just to see it one more time—just to be sure something unspoiled remained of his world.

He continued his diligent work as his sister Kloai unloaded a catch, stooping under her boat's thatched roof as she handed baskets of fish to the teenage boys on shore. Though she was the younger sibling, Kloai looked older to Nuara now. Years of relentless work had calloused her skin. Worry haunted her eyes. There were less fish in the local waters lately. Kloai had told Nuara she'd never had a season so scarce. And she'd seen strange things in the ocean recently, terrible creatures she'd never encountered before, and she was sure they'd frightened away her catch. Rather than worry his sister, Nuara told her nothing of the black serpents he'd encountered on his voyage from J'hora. Nor did he tell anyone of his journey with Haru. He was ashamed of that mission, ashamed of being duped and ashamed of delivering his Tain to a certain death. Only the constant mending of the fishing nets eased his pain.

"Nuara, come help me!"

Nuara looked up at his sister, waving to him from her boat. He set aside his net and jogged across the beach to reach Kloai. The teen boys put down their baskets, wading into the shallow water. There, trapped in Kloai's trolling net, struggled a small, frantic dolphin.

"I didn't see it until now," Kloai explained as she continued hauling up the net. Along with the dolphin flapped a mixed collection of fish. The boys hefted the net to get it into Kloai's boat. Nuara hopped into the vessel.

"Cut it out of there," said Nuara.

"Help me get it aboard."

"Leave it in the water! Just cut it open."

"It's my net, Nuara!"

"I'll fix it!" snapped Nuara. He pulled his stubby knife from his pants and went to slice the lines. Kloai quickly grabbed his hand.

"Don't!" said Kloai, twisting Nuara's wrist.

"Kloai, it'll *die*."

"Just help me get it aboard!"

The dolphin's frightened cries maddened Nuara. He cursed and helped the boys haul the huge net over the ledge onto the narrow deck. The dolphin trashed in the mesh of flaxen rope.

"Open it!" cried Nuara.

Kloai worked quickly, finding the folds of the net and peeling it back, freeing her catch. Fish spilled out of the net, swamping their feet. The dolphin flailed and twisted, its powerful tail slapping the deck.

"Get hold of it," ordered Kloai. She stooped and wrapped her long arms around the dolphin's head while Nuara struggled to grab its tail. "Come on, clumsy..."

"I got it!" said Nuara. He took hold of the jerking tail, grunting as he lifted the heavy creature. "Clear away," he ordered the boys. "Ready?"

His sister shuffled toward the ledge. "Go."

With one swing they tossed the dolphin overboard. It splashed into the shallow waters, laying there shocked and unmoving.

"Ah, no," groaned Nuara.

"Wait," snorted Kloai.

A moment later, the dolphin found its wits. It gave a final screech, dove its nose into the water, and swam off. The boys laughed and congratulated themselves, going quickly back to their work. Kloai turned on Nuara.

"Are you stupid?"

"Eh?"

"I think your years of ease have made you dumb up here," said Kloai, tapping her skull. "They must have. Or do you like fixing nets all day?"

"Years of ease?" Nuara shoved his knife back into his belt. "That thing was going to die, Kloai."

"So? Do you know how many dolphins die every day? I'm supposed to care about every one of them? I make my living with these nets, Nuara. I care about *us* dying." Kloai stood, staring at her brother in disbelief while fish flapped around her ankles. "Don't you ever cut one of my nets without my permission. This may not be the *Gonkin* but it's my boat, Nuara."

Nuara opened his mouth to argue, then saw young Jinjon out of the corner of his eye. His nephew—Kloai's son—watched the argument anxiously. Kloai turned to the boy with a sigh.

"What is it?"

Jinjon shook his head. "Nothing. The pelicans took one of the pike." He shrugged. "That's all."

"You're supposed to watch them, Jinjon. That's your job."

"I'm sorry."

Nuara held his tongue. "I've got to get back to it," he said, then climbed over the ledge of the boat, giving Jinjon a secret wink. He made his way back up the beach to his over-turned basket and went back to work. Unable to help himself, he lifted his gaze back toward his sister and nephew. They were talking, Kloai lecturing the boy, though not unkindly. Jinjon's eager nodding made Nuara smile. His mother had promised a meal of jeongal today—another of his favorites.

A minute later, Jinjon left his mother's boat and made a beeline toward Nuara.

"My mother told me to help you," he said. He sank to his knees in the warm sand.

"Do you know how to mend a net?"

Jinjon nodded. "I know how to do everything."

"That's more than I know," said Nuara, continuing his knotting. "I have a lot to learn. Been gone so long..." He grimaced. "I missed it here."

"Are you mad at my mother?"

"Nope."

"She's mad at you."

"I don't mind."

"But she's happy you're here."

Nuara stopped knotting. He looked at Jinjon curiously. "She said that?"

"She said you came home because of the war. Because you're afraid you might be killed and not see us again. Is that right?"

"No," lied Nuara with a smile. "And you shouldn't worry about it, Jinjon. No one should worry."

"So, why'd you come back?"

"To see you," said Nuara. "And to see my mother and Kloai."

Jinjon thought about his answer. "Why?"

Nuara laughed. "You are full of questions, nephew!"

"Tell me about the *Gonkin*. You said you would."

"Alright," said Nuara. "What kind of story do you want?"

"Tell me about fighting the seabreakers. Tell me about the J'horans."

"Jinjon!" called out Kloai across the beach. "Are you helping?"

"Yes!" the boy called back. He grabbed a handful of the dried-out net. "Go on, Uncle," he urged quietly.

Nuara shifted on his basket. He'd come back to Lomoa to forget the *Gonkin*, at least for a while. "I will tell you about the time I first saw a seabreaker, alright?"

"Did you fight them?"

"No. Not really. But we see them on patrol. We get close to them sometimes."

"Tell me about a *battle*," said Jinjon.

"You're ten years old. Fighting is for older boys."

"I'm going to fight when I get older," said Jinjon. "I hate being here. Stupid nets, stupid fish...I'm going to leave like you left."

"Oh." Nuara looked over at the distant, hard-working Kloai. "Oh." Suddenly, his sister's anger made some sense. "I love it here, Jinjon," he said softly. "I came back because I had to come back. And I can't explain that to you because you'll never understand it, not till you get older." He lowered his mending. "I'm not going to tell you about fighting, Jinjon."

Jinjon looked disappointed. "Why not?"

"Because I hate it."

His answer perplexed the boy. "You're the captain of a beast-ship."

"Yes, I am. I'm a captain. But I'm not a hero and I don't want to be one. Now, I'll tell you a story, but it'll be about your mother and me, when we were younger..."

That night, Nuara ate his meal of jeongal and played card games with the village men and slept in a hammock outside his sister's house, star-gazing until he fell asleep. His belly full and his mind content, he dreamed of his childhood in Lomoa, awakening in the middle of the night with a smile on his face.

The very next day, another visitor came to Lomoa. This one was from the *Gonkin* too, with orders to bring Nuara back to Jinja Castle. When he saw Sailing Master Ariyo enter the village, Nuara realized his time back home was over. He said goodbye to his family, packed his few belongings, and once again became a captain.

Chapter Twenty-Two

THE FEAST OF AMA'AGA

N uara counted the beast-ships anchored in the harbor. A hornet, a scorpion, a seahorse, a swan...he tallied twenty-five of the miraculous vessels, including his own, the enormous *Gonkin*, bobbing on the waves outside Jinja Castle. Each of the captains had come ashore, seated with Nuara around a long table on the shore, a festive pavilion protecting them from the sun. The chatter around the table was loud and anxious. Servants from the castle attended the confused sea captains, pouring them drinks and refilling their plates with the dangerously significant food.

Three Cryori staples were always served before a battle—kelp, chestnuts, and abalone. It was called the Feast of Ama'aga, and none of the mariners around the table knew why they were eating it.

Except for Nuara.

He ate his meal sparingly, tired from his long journey back from Lomoa and having no appetite at all for the food or the events they heralded. He'd done a fair job of dodging questions so far, pretending to know nothing of their Tain's ill-fated mission. Liadin had asked for his loyalty and Nuara had given it. Now, he supposed, the Arch-Disciple wanted all the captains to declare their fealty. At the head of the table waited a single, vacant chair—no doubt meant for Liadin. But though his Venerants milled near shore, the

Arch-Disciple himself had yet to appear. His absence spurred the agitated conversations.

"Nuara?"

Nuara turned to the man seated on his right. "Eh?"

"I was asking when you got the summons," said Rooks. Only captains were seated around the table; their Masters and Mariners were still at sea or awaiting them back in the castle. Rooks' vessel was the *Krym*, a smaller, well-outfitted beast-ship built to look like a seal. Rooks had spent most of the meal talking with the man to his own right—Lodi, captain of the swan-shaped *Dorsakai*. Now the two of them stared at Nuara, waiting.

"I'm sorry. I wasn't listening." Nuara smiled at the men without answering the question.

"I heard the *Gonkin's* been here a week already," said Lodi. He leaned closer and lowered his voice. "Tell us directly, Nuara—did you meet with Liadin?"

"You heard that somewhere?" parried Nuara.

"What do you know?" pressed Rooks. He was a man about Nuara's own age, with a reputation for honesty.

"The Arch-Disciple called us here," said Nuara. "We'll find out why soon enough."

"This is a war council, Nuara," said Rooks. "If you know something you should tell us."

"No," said Nuara. "If I know something, I should *not* tell you. I should wait and be respectful, as should we all."

Lodi scoffed and rolled his metal goblet in his palms. Around the table the other captains murmured and spied the young Venerants, each of them promoting their own theories about the summit. Medryn of the *Charr*, Linos of the *Reikis*, Isar of the *Makeda*—they'd all come ashore at Liadin's summons, called back from their patrols to share in the feast. When Nuara caught the eye of Captain Ora far across the table, he raised his goblet in greeting. Ora of the lion-like *Hakar*, the only other cat represented in the fleet, nodded politely. He sat apart from the others, speaking to no one, his expression preoccupied.

A man of politics. That's what Nuara had called Ora, speaking to Haru that day on the *Gonkin*. He'd meant it as an insult, but he knew

Ora's loyalty to the Tains was unshakeable. Nuara smiled slightly at his old rival. Their silly grudge suddenly made no sense to him at all. Ora glanced at his plate of kelp and abalone, then back at Nuara, who shrugged before turning back toward the harbor. The sun was bright and the water sparkled like a sea of gemstones.

Then, at last, Liadin arrived. He walked so quietly, so deliberately, that Nuara didn't notice him until he reached the pavilion. The sea captains broke from their conversations. Unattended, his ceremonial sukatai tethered to his back, Liadin cut a regal figure in the sunlight, powerful and healthier looking than when Nuara had met with him in Ayorih's sanctuary. He'd taken the bandage off his hand as well, the stub of his severed finger now plainly visible. The waiting Venerants took their places beneath the pavilion, flanking both sides of the table as the Arch-Disciple neared. The gathered captains rose to greet him.

Liadin pushed aside his chair without sitting down. He looked over the gathering with satisfaction. "Great men of Nesenor," he pronounced. "Welcome."

The captains returned his greeting politely, sitting when Liadin bid them to do so. The old priest himself remained standing. His gaze met Nuara's across the table, pausing in a moment of shared secrecy, then moving on cheerfully to the others. Nuara's stomach pitched.

"This is the Feast of Ama'aga," declared the Arch-Disciple. "For twenty generations our fathers have eaten this meal in times of war, to honor the great god of victory and call upon his holy aid." Liadin eyed the captains gravely. "Nesenor is an island in a stormy sea. We must protect ourselves from the storm. We must withstand it. You have questions? I have answers. If you doubt that, do not. I am the Regent of Nesenor now."

Those last words lingered on the breeze. Ora frowned and Lodi nodded. Captain Jancana looked stricken. And no one said a thing.

"Listen to me now," warned Liadin. "You've had your suspicions and your theories. Now know the burdensome truth. Our beloved Haru is gone."

Gasps and murmurs rippled through the gathering. Nuara clenched his jaw.

"Dead?" asked Medryn.

"Perhaps dead," said Liadin. "At least unlikely to return. He went off to J'hora to kill Reius. His Chorus went with him. Whether or not he succeeds, war is certainly coming to our shores."

"J'hora?" muttered Sago.

"How'd he get there?" wondered Isar.

"I took him," said Nuara. He glared at his fellow captains. "I took him to J'hora to die. Now you can all stop wondering."

"Nuara didn't know," said Liadin loudly, quelling the crowd. "Reius invited Haru to J'hora to talk peace. A trap to kill him as he killed our great Sh'an. Haru agreed, just so he could end the tyrant's life." His voice trembled with emotion. "He was compelled by honor and vengeance. I've never seen anything braver."

The captains fell quiet at the enormity of Liadin's words.

"Haru made me Regent before he left for J'hora," said Liadin. "He sacrificed himself for the small chance of putting an end to Reius' evil. Now how should we honor that legacy? Hmm?" With a snarl, Liadin said, "We avenge him."

"Revenge," echoed Isar. Lodi and Rooks quickly joined him. "Revenge!"

"They will come at us, brothers—make no mistake of it," said Liadin. "Their navy is great; their nature savage. They are the worst kind of heathens—impassioned by a non-existent god. They are *humans*."

Liadin's words stoked the crowd. Beside Nuara, Captain Rooks nodded and banged his hand on the table.

"Let us be warriors again!" cried Rooks.

A handful of captains joined his rally, banging in agreement. Others, like Ora, stayed circumspect.

"Go on, Arch-Disciple," urged Ora calmly. "You have a plan to defeat them? Without Tain Haru..."

Liadin quickly stopped him. "I have better than a plan," he said. "I have a vision." He raised a hand to quiet the noise-making. "Sh'an was a great man. He had a vision, too. A worthy vision of peace and an untroubled island. And we followed that vision, all of us, because we knew his heart was pure and that he loved our homeland. If you doubt that—any of you—you are unworthy of your stations."

"We never doubted his heart," said Sago. His dragonfly beast-ship the *Arikika* bobbed closest to shore, a noticeable conceit. "He was a fine man. A good Tain."

"He was a *great* man," rebuked Liadin. "He was my friend. And the best way to honor him and his son is to lift Nesenor off its knees. Once, humankind trembled at the sight of Cryori! We ruled the waves, as is our birthright. We shall do so again. We will not just defend this island. We will turn their invasion back on them. We will reclaim the seas. And they shall fear us once more."

The captains broke into rowdy applause. Nuara held back his approval, mortified by Liadin's plan. Ora, too, looked unimpressed. Over the din he asked a simple question.

"How?"

Liadin, who still hadn't taken his seat, raised an eyebrow. "What?"

"How?" repeated Ora. "Those glorious days you recall so fondly were not the work of beast-ships and men alone. The humans feared our dragon-whales more than they ever feared our ships. Without Tain Haru, the dragon-whales are useless."

"The shenenra will be with us," Liadin assured him.

"They obey Haru's bloodline," argued Ora. "Clionet has decreed it. The royal blood alone..." He stopped himself, then asked, "Arch-Disciple, what of Clionet? We cannot make war and hope to win without her."

"Clionet has always blessed us, has she not?" countered Liadin.

"She has," said Captain Linos. He looked at the others for support.

"Clionet is always with us," agreed Jancana.

"And you have prayed to her about this, Arch-Disciple?" asked Ora. "She has agreed to this...*vision* of yours? Because without the shenenra..."

"The shenenra will be with us!" snapped Liadin. "I will command them!"

Nuara nearly dropped his goblet. The captains blinked in disbelief.

"You will?" prodded Ora.

"We have not been abandoned, Ora," said Liadin. "And the dragon-whales are not the only great power in the ocean. Come..." Liadin stepped away from the table. "All of you, follow me."

Flanked by his Venerants, the Arch-Disciple left the pavilion and walked toward the shore. Nuara and the other captains shared a perplexed glance before following the old priest toward the tide. When they were all lined up behind him, Liadin stepped into the foaming waters. Nuara heard a quiet, indecipherable prayer dribble from his lips. Captain Ora came up next to Nuara.

"What's he doing?" whispered Ora.

"I'm sure I have no idea," replied Nuara. "No idea at all."

Liadin stopped speaking then stared out into the bright waters. Nuara waited, confused as the tide began to swirl. A flock of seabirds wheeled overhead, and the strangest noise Nuara had ever heard began to fill the air. The sound, like the barking of dogs, grew as the ocean twirled and raked the beach, sucking away the sand around Liadin's feet. Nuara winced, watching in amazement as the sea convulsed, the incoming tide bringing forth an enormous, spiky sea beast. The barking noise rattled Nuara's ears. He drew back, unable to look away as his fellow captains gasped.

Suddenly the din flattened. The ocean ceased its frantic bubbling. And the great crustacean in the waves rose up on two legs, revealing itself. From the tattoo on his arm Nuara knew what he was seeing. Ama'aga, the great god of war, strode through the rippling waters, his grim face riven with scales, his bright armor spiny like a crab. Braids of seaweed looped his dripping hair. Rings of pearl adorned his green hands. He strode like a giant up the beach, the ocean retreating around him. Nuara's mouth dropped open.

The Holy Serpent had returned.

Liadin moved aside as the war-god breached the shoreline. Nuara and the other captains peddled backward up the beach. Nuara could hear Captain Jancana's panicked breathing and Lodi's prayer for mercy. The men on the nearby *Arikika* climbed up the riggings for a better look. Ama'aga's dark eyes scanned the assemblage, pausing for one heart-stopping moment on Nuara. When he noticed Nuara's tattoo, he grinned.

Then, to Nuara's astonishment, the god dropped to one knee in the tide, bowing his head to the men on shore.

"I am Ama'aga," he declared. "First-born of Clionet and the Spear of the Seas. Know me, and you will know glory."

The captains were speechless, their faces stunned and colorless. Ama'aga kept his head bowed.

"I abandoned you, my sons," he continued. "Peace is not in my nature. It drove me far from your shores, deeper into my own misery. I kneel for your forgiveness. I beg it!"

He delivered his plea like a thunderclap. The captains inched toward him, astonished. Liadin beamed, urging them closer. Nuara came forward, staring up into Ama'aga's scaly face. Ama'aga remained kneeling, gathering the men around him like children—except for one.

Captain Ora stood apart from his cohorts, his troubled countenance catching Ama'aga's attention.

"What is your name?" the god asked him.

"I am Ora," said the captain. "My ship is the *Hakar.*"

"The lion," said Ama'aga with pleasure.

"Great Ama'aga, have you come to help us battle?" asked Ora.

"I have come to help you triumph," the god boasted. "That is my promise." He studied Ora a moment. "But I see resentment in your eyes. Will you not forgive me?"

"I forgive you, Ama'aga," said Ora. "I believe you have no longer forsaken us."

"What, then?" asked Liadin sharply.

Ora tamed his fear and replied, "You are our patron, Ama'aga. That has never changed. But we are loyal to the bloodline of Hiaran—the first Cryori blessed by Clionet. There can be no war without her blessing now."

Ama'aga rose from his armored knees, his giant shadow falling over the gathering. "You are beast-ship captains. Your loyalty is to me."

"To you—and to your mother. To your family, Ama'aga." Ora hesitated, then asked the dreaded question. "Where is Clionet?"

Ama'aga's big hand shot forward, grabbing hold of Ora and lifting him off the beach. The war-god's eyes flashed with fury as he closed his fist, bringing Ora close to his face.

"Did you not see me kneel?" he asked. "Did you not hear my begging? Watch me humble myself?"

Ora nodded but couldn't speak, his face turning purple as he struggled in the giant's grasp. Nuara froze.

"Holy Serpent, no," pleaded Liadin.

Ama'aga opened his mouth, stretching it like the jaws of a snake, opening it impossibly wide. The horrified Ora looked into the black maw and finally found the breath to scream. Nuara stumbled backward, falling into the sand as he watched Ora disappear, going headfirst into Ama'aga's mouth, the crunch of bones and spray of blood polluting the beach. Captain Isar cried out in shock. Medryn stooped and retched up his meal. Ama'aga chewed and swallowed Ora down, then folded his arms over his massive chest.

"There is no mercy in me," he declared. "You will never find it in me. Nor will our enemies." He scanned the captains with contempt. "Now it is your turn to kneel."

One by one the captains dropped, falling to their knees before the Holy Serpent. Sago, Lodi, Linos...each man bent to the god. Nuara, the last one standing, chanced a look into Ama'aga's terrible face. A stream of Ora's blood trickled down the war-god's chin.

Nuara made his choice and dropped to the blood-stained sand.

Chapter Twenty-Three

SLAVE HILL

"Tell me something terrible about your father."

Haru stopped chewing and lowered his plate. On the other side of the marble bench, Reius looked over the trays the servants had set out for their breakfast, considering his next mouthful. Morning had dawned but an hour ago. Glorious light flooded the statuary, warming the cold stone and shimmering off the little reflecting pool. Around them, the silent statues listened to Reius do most of the talking. The nearest statue, that of a bare-breasted woman struggling upwards out of the stone, smiled at the climbing sun.

"My father was a great man," replied Haru icily.

"Oh, I know. The Cryori who freed the human slaves. You've told me so. Many times." Reius refilled his plate with fresh meat and fruit, all pre-cut into little cubes by the servants waiting a few yards away. A bee circled his head. Annoyed, he swatted it away. "You've told me endless good things about him. Now tell me something less good."

Haru had spent two hours with Reius the day before, getting to know the man he planned to kill. He had granted Reius five days to convince him of Taan's goodness, and Reius had squandered the first of them on small talk. It had been a strangely fascinating meeting, filled with passionate lessons about J'hora and the remaking of its remarkable capital, yet Haru had ended it before noon-time, overwhelmed by his hatred for Reius.

Now he shared a bench with his enemy, breaking their fast together.

Haru had eaten sparingly so far, picking at the fish and vegetables the servants supposed he would enjoy. Reius, however, ate like a giant, as though he was still a famished soldier with a long march ahead. Occasionally he tossed bits of bread into the pool, smiling as the whiskered fish surfaced for the morsels. Sometimes when he spoke he counted the syllables on his fingers. His odd behaviors baffled Haru.

"Let's talk about something else," Haru suggested. "Like why there are so many bees here," he said, swatting another of the annoying insects. Reius gave a grunting laugh.

"They tell me they found an enormous beehive here just days ago," he said. "Biggest one they'd ever seen." He glanced at one of the three servants attending them. "Where was it Maracus?"

"By the fountain of Symidor, Holy One," said the servant.

Reius sucked the pit out of an olive and pointed toward his left. "It's that way," he told Haru. "Beautiful. I'll show you later."

"The hive?"

"The statue. They burned the hive." Reius turned back to Haru. "Your father?"

"He's dead," said Haru. The bench they shared was large but suddenly felt far too small.

Reius counted the two words on his fingers. "We're supposed to be sharing," he replied.

"It's the first thing you've asked me. Why such a strange question?"

"Yesterday was about J'hora," said Reius. "Today, let it be about you."

"I'm more interested in J'hora."

"You're very guarded," Reius observed. He picked up his wine and a wedge of bread, dunking the bread into his glass. It was the kind of thing children did in Nesenor. "We can make a game of it, alright? You tell me something bad about your father and I'll do the same."

"You first."

Reius thought about it as he sucked the wine from the bread. "Very well." He stuffed the bread into his mouth, considering things as he chewed. "I told you we were desert people. You can't know what that's like. All you ever think about is water. In the desert, there is always thirst." He placed his goblet beside him on the bench and rested his hands on his knees. "How often does it rain in Nesenor?"

"Often," said Haru.

"So, you're never thirsty?"

"No. Never."

"Not just your nobles, I mean. The people who serve you—they all have water? The farmers, the workers—they all have enough?"

"There's plenty of water where I'm from, Reius."

"Where I'm from there's plenty of sand! We don't ever take the water from another house. We may share it, but we may never take it. And in Kalmiir we never ask for anything. Even when children are wasting from thirst." Reius' expression grew contemplative. "Once, when I was a boy, the rains never came. Not that whole season. The water had dried away and all our barrels were empty. I was young but I remember being so thirsty..." He put his hand to his jaw. "My tongue was swollen in my mouth. My sister was dying in our veld."

"Veld?" asked Haru. "Is that a house?"

"Like a tent." Reius grinned when he noticed Haru's frown. "It was a home. My home."

"Sorry," said Haru. "Your sister?"

"My sister was dying from a belly fever," Reius went on. His big voice softened. The servants stared blankly ahead, trying not to hear. "She needed water. We all did. Some had gone to search for it, but my family stayed. And my father..." Reius bit his lip. "My father found a cask of water another family had hidden. They'd buried it one night and he saw them. And he stole it."

Haru sipped his wine, waiting for more. "Go on..."

Reius raised his eyebrows. "He *stole* it."

"To save your sister. Isn't that so?"

"We were Kalmiiri. Kalmiiri take nothing."

"Is that supposed to be a bad story about your father?" asked Haru. "He tried to help his family."

Reius grunted in disgust. "You are truly a Cryori. Cryori think nothing of taking what doesn't belong to them."

Haru groaned. "Why are we doing this? You won't convince me to trust you, Reius. Talking about my father won't bring him back."

"You agreed, did you not? I have shared something private with you. Now it's your turn."

Haru desperately wanted to leave. "I never speak about my father," he said.

Reius nodded. "It is difficult for men. This is how you know you're not a boy anymore. When you were a child, you could speak easily about your father, yes? About your love for him?"

"I suppose," said Haru.

Reius pointed toward the sky. "It is different with our father Taan. He can pry open the most rusted of hearts."

"But why tell you something bad about my father? Why are you wasting time, Reius? There's only three days left before I leave."

"Four days. It's only the morning."

"The whole city is waiting for you to speak to them. Don't you have a speech to write or something?"

Reius shooed the bees away from the food trays. "You are an only child?"

"That's right."

"I am one of six."

"Maybe that's why your father had such a hard time providing for you all. Did you ever think of that?"

"I forgave my father a long time ago for stealing that water," said Reius. Sensing Haru's trepidation, he gestured to the servants, waving them away. Haru watched them go, envying them. "One small thing. That's all I want you to tell me."

"This is our third time meeting, Reius, and you've hardly asked me anything about Nesenor."

"Were you expecting an inquisition? I have others who do such things for me. I think you came here because you're curious. You want to know how strong we are, if you can defeat us in a war. You should be as confident as I am about that—you cannot."

"You're not afraid of us at all?"

"I fear the wails of your women and children. I fear the burden of having to destroy you."

"That's all?"

"Taan gives me courage."

"Our gods give us courage."

"Then why do you look afraid?"

Haru smirked. Reius waited for an answer.

"I want to go." Haru got to his feet, finally at eye level with Reius. "I won't ever trust you, Reius. I won't ever believe you. You should know that and stop wasting time."

"I still have four days," said Reius.

"Three," said Haru, holding up three fingers. "This one's over."

He turned and started to go, but Reius called after him.

"No. Tonight. When it's dark. Let's talk again."

"Why?" asked Haru. "Why when it's dark?"

"Be in your rooms tonight. Aryak will come for you. Be ready."

From Reius' determined look, Haru knew he'd get no answers. He reluctantly agreed, then found his own way out of the statuary, still puzzled by the multitude of bees.

Haru had already fallen asleep by the time Aryak came to get him. The evening meal had long been consumed, the Chorus had gone to their own beds, and Haru awoke to find Reius' dark-skinned servant standing over him, nudging him awake.

"Tain? Will you come now?" whispered Aryak.

Haru had just awoken from a dream, and for a moment forgot his latest rendezvous with Reius. He slipped on his boots, surprised when Aryak offered him a cloak.

"Where are we going?" Haru asked, keeping his voice low. He could hear Shadur snoring in his nearby apartment. "Why do I need a cloak?"

"To keep you warm, of course. Come—my master awaits you."

Too curious to refuse, Haru took the offered garment and followed Aryak into the quiet, deserted hall. "What time is it?" he asked. "It must me nearly midnight."

"Nearly," Aryak agreed. He put a finger to his lips to quiet Haru. "Please, mind your voice. Most are sleeping."

His scolding seemed ridiculous to Haru. "You woke *me*," he griped. But he said no more, letting Aryak lead him through the

palace, down steps and through echoing corridors, and finally to a
pair of tall, oak doors open to a courtyard. A white carriage waited in
the yard, bathed in the light of a monstrous yellow moon. To Haru,
the coach looked like the same one that had taken him and the
others from the dock days ago. The driver appeared the same as
well, dark and brooding atop the cab. Aryak stepped outside and
opened the coach's door, revealing its lone passenger. Despite his
hooded face, Haru knew instantly it was Reius.

"Come," bid Reius, waving Haru forward. "Wear your cloak and
raise the hood."

"Why?" asked Haru as he slid his arms into the garment. "Where
are we going?"

"Trust, remember?" Reius stretched out his long legs, looking uncomfortable inside the carriage. "Were you seen?" he asked Aryak.

"No, master," the servant assured him.

"Quickly, then," Reius insisted, urging Haru into the coach.

Haru looked around uneasily, then got into the coach. Aryak
closed the door silently behind him as he sat down opposite Reius,
leaving room for the giant man's booted feet. The carriage lurched
forward, the clip-clop of the horses resounding on the paving stones
as they departed the courtyard. Haru stared at the preternatural
moon. He wondered if it were an omen.

"Now can you tell me where we're going?"

As they pulled away from the palace, Reius closed his eyes and
gave a secretive sigh. His face transformed beneath his hood, the
muscles loosening, his expression relaxed, even blissful.

"Once a month I escape the palace this way," he confessed. "Not
even Malon knows I do it. No servants or handlers, no advisors, no
politics or prayers." He took a deep breath of night air. "Just me."

"Isn't that dangerous?" Haru asked, peering out the window at the
towering buildings growing around them. "A carriage like this one is
hard to hide."

"There are others like it," said Reius. "The people are accustom
to seeing them. Are you afraid of being robbed?" He laughed at the
notion. "No one would dare."

"Because they'd wind up in your prisons," said Haru with a smirk.

Reius opened a single eye. "I've heard your castle has dungeons that rival my own. Never mind...we'll talk about that."

"Will we?"

Reius put his face to the window. "Look up ahead."

Haru slid across the leather bench, sharing the window with his host. In the moonlight loomed the Tower of Principles, that unforgettable edifice of stone he'd first seen when he'd arrived in J'hora. The structure was quiet now. A lone priest moved across its grounds. A solemn bell sounded in its belfry. The carriage trotted into the circular road surrounding it, giving them a grand view of the place.

"Are you spying on them?" Haru wondered aloud. "On Malon?"

"Pray you ever have a friend you can trust as much as I trust Malon," said Reius.

"Why then?" Haru pressed his cheek against the glass as he stared up at the forbidding monolith. "Reius, I don't understand what we're doing here. Why do you ride around alone like this?"

"To see my city the only way I can," replied Reius. He gazed lovingly at the tower. "The province you come from—Jinja. It is very quiet there, yes?"

"Yes," said Haru. "It's nothing like J'hora."

"They would mob me if I were to walk like you do among your people, Haru. When I address them at the end of the Council, you'll see what I mean. They adore and worship me, and they've made the palace my prison. But at night—even in this ridiculous conveyance—I am unknown."

"That's pitiful," said Haru "You wall yourself away in your chambers. You do nothing but write those silly scriptures all day. That kind of aloneness will madden you. Maybe it has already."

Reius grinned like a shark. "You talk to me as though you have no comprehension of what's about to happen to your country. Think on who you label insane, Tain."

"The first thing I saw when I came to your city was a group of men and women being dragged in chains to that tower," said Haru, pointing out the window. "They were naked and terrified and covered in white paint. And they knew they were going to die."

"Heretics," snorted Reius. "You were right to forget them. They were given a chance at redemption and refused it."

"Are they dead? Did you kill them?"

Reius shrugged. "They're the problem of the priests now. Surely, they've been given a final chance at repentance."

"Are you sure?" pressed Haru. "Do you know that for certain? How can you know what goes on in that tower if you're always hiding in your chambers or skulking around in the dark?"

"Your Chorus—they advise you, yes?"

Haru braced himself. "Yes."

"But do you know everything that goes on in Nesenor?"

"Not everything. I can't—"

"So, you can't know everything that goes on in a tiny country like yours, yet you expect me to know everything that happens in a city like J'hora? Maybe you don't realize just how large a city this is." Reius smiled. "It's good that you're with me tonight." He leaned forward and rapped on the wall of the cab, signaling the driver to move on. Haru groaned and leaned back, seeing his argument lost. The coach finished circling the tower, then headed deeper into the city.

Reius was right about one thing—J'hora was larger than Haru had realized. The carriage drove on and on through the city's varied neighborhoods, past the towers in the heart the capital, out into its dreary outskirts, over its bridges and into its tunnels, and up to its moonlit hilltops where the modest homes of farmers and mill workers slept beneath the quiet stars. The trip was a revelation to Haru, and he began to understand the solace Reius took from his secret, monthly jaunts. They spoke sparingly as they drove, brought to silence by the hypnotic moon and the lateness of the hour.

Eventually, however, Haru tired of the tour, closing his eyes as the carriage climbed its way up the road of a deserted hill. The lights of the city fell away behind them, but the moon still brightened the way, shining on the trees that lined the road. The swaying of the carriage lulled Haru. Just when he reached the brink of sleep, the vehicle creaked to a stop. Haru opened his eyes, surprised as Reius reached for the door handle.

"Where are we now?" Haru asked. He stepped cautiously onto the grass. The hill was far taller than he'd realized and stood apart from the outskirts of the city, with a view of the harbor and a magnificent bridge. Sure no one would see them, Reius lowered his hood.

"Look," he directed.

Haru turned, startled by what he saw. There in the center of the hill stood a sculpture at least fifteen feet tall, depicting the figures of men and women, their clothes tattered, their faces gaunt with fear, their necks rung by stout, stone collars. A sculpted chain linked them together, some of them kneeling, some of them staring toward heaven. Haru counted ten of them, all with the same forsaken expression.

"What is this?" Haru asked. "Who are they?"

"This place is called Slave Hill," said Reius. "They are the damned."

"No, no riddles, Reius. Explain it to me. I don't understand."

"Don't you? These are the people your fathers took with them back to Nesenor. These are the ancestors of your houseboys and maids. They were stolen from their homes. Ripped away from these lands before they ever had a chance to hear the word of Taan."

"No," said Haru sharply. "I didn't do any of this. We don't even have slaves in Nesenor now. My father ended it years ago."

"Look," urged Reius. "Look."

So Haru did. He stopped arguing, quieted himself, and for the sake of the unknown slaves looked into their stone faces. They reminded him of the heretics he'd seen, and he could not understand why Reius refused to acknowledge the similarities.

"No one knows how many were taken," said Reius. "Thousands."

"Not by my father," said Haru. "And not me."

Reius turned to study him. "I have been wondering if you are a good man. I think you might be, but I need to make you see the value of the Alliance. Before Taan came back to us, the lands of J'hora were at war. That's the legacy the Cryori left us. They took our gold and our children, took our food, took our honor. They left us to fend for ourselves like animals."

"And you want credit for ending all that?"

"Not me," said Reius. He pointed skyward again. "Taan."

Haru regarded the memorial, trying not to let it soften him.

"J'hora is filled with memorials like this one," said Reius. "Dedicated to people taken as slaves or killed in raids or orphaned in massacres. It's important to remember." His eyes flicked toward Haru. "Your people were a blood-thirsty lot. Worse than any of the old kings of J'hora. Do they teach your history back home? Do your people know what they were like? Or are they still as cruel as always?"

"Some are," Haru said honestly. "So perhaps you should beware us."

"I blame your gods. They made your people cruel. You do their bidding because you fear them. I've studied them, all of them—Clionet, Ama'aga, Paiax. Their temples still litter this continent. I know what they're like. They may be immortal, but they are not gods."

"No? What are they?" Haru challenged.

"Demons. They are demons."

The driver shifted atop the carriage as his horses munched the grass. There seemed no way to penetrate Reius, no way to convince him of his own mad ideals. Yet he was not at all the man Haru had expected to find in J'hora. He was just a dangerous fool. Haru looked at the horizon, wondering when dawn would come, desperate for the sunlight.

"Do you want to know the worst thing about my father?" he whispered.

Reius smiled as if he'd finally made a breakthrough. "Will you tell me?"

"Yes," sighed Haru. Suddenly it hardly seemed to matter. "The worst thing about my father is that he wasn't a father to me at all. He wasn't there. Those slaves my father freed—they ruined him. The nobles couldn't stand the idea of them being free, so they killed most of them. They drowned them and hung them from trees. Sometimes they just marched them into the ocean. We call it the Massacre of Chains. People who knew my father said that it broke him."

"Massacre of Chains." Reius' face darkened. "A terrible name."

"Some people call it 'Sh'an's Slaughter.' That was probably even worse for my father to hear. I would have liked to have known my father before he changed but I never got the chance. This all happened before I was born. The father I knew wasn't anything like the one I wanted. He thought I wasn't good enough. He was unfaithful to my mother. And he never wanted me to become Tain."

"Maybe to protect you?" suggested Reius.

"No. I'd like that to be true but it isn't. He didn't want me to be Tain because he had no faith in me at all." Haru turned toward Reius and shook his head in disbelief. "All your father ever did was take some water without asking."

Reius stared. Haru could see him struggling to understand.

"So, forgive me if I'm still not convinced," said Haru. "I still don't believe you. It's just that now...I wish I could."

He turned and walked back to the carriage, climbed inside, and waited for Reius to join him.

Chapter Twenty-Four

DOUBTS

Haru arrived back at the palace at dusk, back to his apartments and the promise of a quiet bed. He pulled off his cloak as he entered his darkened rooms, letting the garment fall to the floor behind him. The first tepid rays of sunlight crept through the windows. He reminded himself not to wake his cohorts—then saw them standing mutely in the shadows. Siva, Shadur, Elsifor, and Val—all dressed in their severe-looking robes, waiting like disapproving parents.

Haru stopped, startled by them. "What is this?" He looked at each of them. "What you are doing up?"

They confronted him in a tight semi-circle, Siva standing just inches ahead of the rest, her arms folded as if to scold him. Val stood meekly beside her, looking out of place, the only one of them who refused to look at Haru.

"Haru, it's time to talk," said Siva.

"No, it's time for bed," replied Haru. "I'm tired."

"You must be," said Siva. "You've been out all night."

Her tone made Haru chaff. "I've been with Reius," he said. "Another meeting. Let me sleep a little; we'll talk about it later."

Shadur shook his head, looking more uncanny than usual in the dimness. "Let's talk now. It's important."

"Can I sit at least?" asked Haru irritably. He grabbed one of the cushioned chairs, dragged it around to face his inquisitors, then collapsed into it, exhausted. "Be quick, will you please? I can barely keep my eyes open. And why are you all dressed like that? You going somewhere?"

"With you, Haru, the next time you go see Reius," said Siva.

"We're supposed to protect you," said Elsifor. "Haru, you were gone *all night.*"

"That's not all of it," said Shadur. "You've been keeping things from us, keeping all your talks with Reius to yourself."

"We're worried," said Elsifor. "It's two days until the Guardian Council ends."

They circled Haru's chair, staring down at him, their faces anxious and concerned—even Siva's. Haru groaned, desperate for sleep.

"We have a plan," he told them. "Nothing's changed."

"Yes, *we* have a plan," said Siva. With her thumb she gestured to the others. "We've been the ones talking about it, working it out. You haven't been around."

"What difference does it make?" Haru argued. "The plan hasn't changed."

"Shhh!" scolded Shadur. He looked sharply at Siva and Haru. "Listen Haru, you need to tell us what's going on with Reius. Where were you tonight?"

Haru frowned. "Why?"

Siva was incredulous. "Why? Because we're a team, remember? You're the one who keeps telling us that! We're not supposed to be keeping secrets!"

"Quiet," chided Shadur. He looked toward the door across the room. "Don't let them hear you."

"Hear us?" snapped Siva. "How could they? They're not listening. They don't even care that we're here! They let us roam around the palace, go anywhere we please...they've never even followed us. Not once. Don't you think that's strange, Haru?"

"It's Reius," said Haru. "I told you—he trusts me. And he wants me to trust him, too."

"He knows we're not advisors," said Elsifor. Sick of standing, he lowered himself to the floor by Haru's chair, folding his legs beneath him. "They all know."

"They've separated you from us," said Shadur. "That's dangerous."

"And you let him do it, Haru," said Siva. "Reius calls and you come running."

Haru bristled. "That's not fair. I'm learning from him. I'm getting him to trust me."

"Trust you? We came here to..." Siva calmed herself. "We came here to *kill* him," she whispered. "Or maybe you've forgotten that, eh? You could have killed him a dozen times over by now. That's what you were going to do, remember? Get close to him? Kill him yourself?"

"Haru, we're just worried about you," said Shadur. "We're afraid you're getting too close to Reius. We're afraid you're having doubts."

Elsifor looked up at Haru and nodded. "Right."

"Really?" Haru snorted. "Really?" He looked at Shadur. "Haven't you been enjoying that library you keep telling me about? How many hours a day do you spend there, Shadur? Should we be worried about that?" Haru kicked at Elsifor with his toe. "And what about you? Are you still smitten with that girl you met? And that priest? Are you still spending time with him, letting him teach you about Taan?"

Elsifor nodded. "Yes. But I'm not keeping it secret, Haru. Go on—ask me anything you want."

Instead Haru glared at Valivan, who so far hadn't said a word. "And Val? Look at me."

Val shyly raised his gaze. "Yeah?"

"I'm disappointed you're even here," said Haru. "You're the smartest one of us—you always were. Do you believe this?"

"He believes it, Haru," said Siva.

"Does he?" Haru glared at Valivan. "Really, Val? Because I don't know what to believe about you anymore. Look at you! I've never seen you better. You're not sick, you're not hiding in a dark room under your blankets. But do we hear anything from you? Not a word. I know you, Val. I know how you get all quiet when you're worried about something."

"I'm...not," stuttered Val.

"You are," pressed Haru. "You've got a secret. What don't you tell us all what it is?"

"Haru, stop," warned Siva.

"Stop?" jeered Haru. "Why, Siva? Because you don't have any secrets? Oh, that's right—all you want to do is die!"

Elsifor sprung to his feet. "No more," he hissed, getting between them. "This place has maddened us all!" He went quickly toward to the door to listen, then returned, sighing. "Haru, Shadur's right—you can't keep us out of this. The Council's almost over. We need to know what's going on with you."

Haru leaned back in his chair, trying to sound conciliatory. "He trusts me. He *does*. Last night he took me around the city. He's trying to convince me how great Taan is, and how bad the Cryori are. And our gods."

The Chorus got silent.

"He took me to a place called Slave Hill," Haru told them. "There's a monument there. A memorial to the humans who were taken to J'hora." He rubbed his temples, the image of the stone slaves still powerful in his memory. "It's our history; the bad part of it."

"Y-y-you had nothing to do with that," Val stuttered.

"None of us did," said Haru. He scratched absently at the arm of his chair. "I don't know if he wanted me to apologize or just feel guilty."

"But you do," said Shadur. "I can tell by your face. You do feel guilty."

Haru blanched. "I do," he admitted. "I do! And alright, yes, I have doubts!" He banged his chair with his fist. "But he's nothing like I expected! I know he's insane or...*something*. He counts his fingers when he talks, he hears voices. And yes, he's threatening us. But...I have doubts!"

"He killed Sh'an," said Siva.

"Did he?" Haru threw up his hands. "I'm not even sure about *that* anymore. He says he didn't, and let me tell you—he absolutely believes that." He looked at the stunned Shadur. "You even told me we couldn't be sure. You did say that, don't forget."

"I haven't forgotten," the mystic snorted.

Siva circled them, exasperated. "Doubts," she spat. "It's weakness, and we can't afford it. That's why we're going with you, Haru. When is your next meeting?"

"I don't know," said Haru. "Reius told me he'd send for me. But you're not going with me."

"We are going," said Siva. "We're your Chorus. We should never have ever let you out of our sights."

"Siva, no."

"Why not?"

"Because I forbid it." Haru got out of his chair. "Because I'm Tain."

"Stop," groaned Elsifor. "We have a way to fix this easily. Haru, let Valivan go with you. Let him touch Reius' mind. Let's end all this wondering! If Reius killed your father, Val will know it."

"Right! We should have done that a long time ago," muttered Siva. "The moment we got here."

Shadur shifted his piercing gaze toward the youngest of the Chorus. "Valivan? What do think? Can you do that?"

Val nodded awkwardly. "Yes. I can do that."

"No," said Haru. "He can't. Not without Reius knowing."

"Yes, I can, Haru," said Val with confidence. "I'm c-c-careful. Let me. I can do it."

Siva looked crossly at Haru. "Or maybe Val should poke around your head, find out what's really going on up there."

Her suspicions irked Haru, but in truth he understood them. Reius had stirred something in him. It wasn't just Slave Hill or the cruel history of his people. War was afoot. He'd come to J'hora thinking he would slay an enemy and run home to safety, but there was no haven now. He slumped back into his chair.

"Valivan stays here," he said.

Siva jumped in. "Haru..."

"Siva, listen to me. Just... listen." Haru closed his eyes to think. "If Valivan makes a mistake—any small mistake—they'll suspect us. Right now, they don't."

"They do," said Shadur. "They must."

"No," said Haru. "It's hard to believe, but Reius trusts. And that trust is all we have right now. I have one more day left with him. After that the Guardian Council ends and he makes his address."

"You wanted to kill him in front of all those people," Elsifor reminded him. "But not anymore?"

"I made a promise to Clionet," Haru reminded them. "I'll avenge my father. But killing Reius won't help if he didn't do it."

"Then let Valivan find out," urged Siva.

Haru tossed back his head with a groan. "Don't you see? If we kill Reius, there's a war. And if there's a war..."

He couldn't even bring himself to say it.

"We can't win. Is that it?" asked Elsifor. "Is that what you mean?"

Haru gave a dreadful nod. "When I decided to come here, I knew we'd set off a war. But I thought that killing Reius would be enough. I thought they'd be lost without him, that we'd cut off the head of the dragon and watch it die. But I was wrong. They're too strong for us. I tell Reius everyday that they'll never be able to defeat us, but even I don't believe that any more. I'm trapped! I can't leave here. Not after the Guardian Council. Not until I convince Reius to leave Nesenor alone. I need to make a real peace with him."

Siva dropped to one knee before him. "He killed Sh'an, Haru. He killed our Tain. Your *father*. Don't forget why you came here. Don't forget what you told me on Tojira. You promised us vengeance." She took Haru's hand. "I want my revenge, Haru. Let's just kill him and be done with it!"

"We don't vote on it," said Shadur. "Get up, Siva. It's Haru's decision."

Siva's coral eyes filled with pain. "I've waited long enough. I can't wait any more. He has to die, Haru. For what he did to Sh'an, he has to die!"

"That's why we all came here," Elsifor added. "We're not afraid. And neither is the rest of Nesenor. We're all ready to fight, Haru. We're all ready to die."

"Are you sure Elsifor?" asked Haru. "All that you've heard from Erinna and Orkorlis, all that you've learned. All those stories about love and peace."

"Those stories are for *me*, Haru," Elsifor assured him. "I came here for Nesenor. I came to kill Reius."

The impossible situation made Haru's head spin. He held on to Siva's cool hand, squeezing it, trying to get strength from it.

"I can do it, Haru," Siva promised. She ignored the rest of them completely. "Let me kill him. Let me do what I was born to do."

Haru smiled at her. Her appetite for vengeance was even worse than his own. "You're not a born killer, Siva. And you're not the Tain."

She let her hand slipped out of his grip. She said nothing. Her argument lost, she stood up and backed away.

"One more day, alright?" asked Haru. "That's what I gave Reius. One more day."

"One more day for Reius to live, then," said Siva.

Haru's troubled mind begged for sleep. "Go back to bed," he bid them all, pulling himself out of the chair again. "Tonight, you'll know my answer."

He staggered past them, his eyes blurry, and spied his waiting bed. Suddenly, nothing in the world seemed more important than those silk J'horan sheets.

Chapter Twenty-Five

THE OLD MAGICS

Haru slept, and his sleep was plagued with dreams.

At first, he was a boy again, with his mother still alive. A whiff of brine brought her to life, sweeping her into his slumbering mind. They walked together on a beach, she young and beautiful, him a naked toddler with sand squishing through his toes. Out on the water the gods were playing games, tossing a leather ball over the waves like the one he'd seen the J'horans use. His mother held his tiny hand as they walked, telling him of her impending death. Her voice was serene, the way he always remembered it, but the story frightened him and he began to cry.

He woke, but only for a moment before slipping back again. This time when exhaustion took him, he dreamed of Clionet.

Now it was the goddess on the beach with him. His mother was gone but he remained naked, with Clionet encircling him in her purple arms. They would make love, she explained, and he would be her adored forever, and when he tried to explain that he was just a boy and not yet a Tain, she covered his mouth with a powerful tentacle and smothered him.

Haru awoke with a shout.

Alone, he realized, looking around his empty bed. Blessedly alone. The thick curtains of his chamber blocked the window, and he could not tell if it was still day or if night had yet fallen. He got out of bed, cracked open the curtains, and squinted at the stab of sunlight. The traffic of a typical J'horan afternoon clogged the distant streets.

Good, he thought to himself. *Still time.*

Afraid of more dreams, he abandoned sleep completely, pulling the curtains wide and letting the sunlight rouse him. His stomach rumbled from skipping breakfast, but the thought of another J'horan meal ruined his appetite. Nothing was like home here. Not even the fish tasted the same. He stared out the giant window, noting the harbor in the distance, still choked with vessels. *His* vessel, the one ship that could take them all home, had never made it to harbor. He'd sent it away, dooming them.

"Tain Haru?"

The voice surprised him. He whirled and saw the dark-skinned Aryak across the room.

"Aryak, you startled me. I didn't hear you come in. I was...thinking."

The quiet servant bowed politely. "Are you ready, Tain?"

"Already?" Haru took a breath, still not precisely sure of the time. "I haven't even changed my clothes," he realized aloud, looking at his wrinkled garments. "Or eaten."

Aryak was non-plussed. "There's a bit of time for both, Tain. The carriage will wait."

"Carriage? Again? Where to this time?"

"Tain, you know I can't answer that."

"Of course not," griped Haru.

"Take a few minutes. Put on clean garments. I'll have some food brought to you." Aryak turned to go. "I'll wait for you in the hall."

An hour later, Haru arrived in the same courtyard he had before, occupied this time by a different, darker carriage. The sun was bright but clouds hung on the horizon. People crowded the yard and garlands of flowers had been hung from the trees and balconies. Priests prayed with people and shook their eager hands, politely ignoring Haru when they saw him. The city was preparing for Reius' address, Aryak explained.

"Tomorrow night the whole place will be lit with moon lanterns," said the servant. He looked toward the solitary balcony where Reius would address them. "I'll be up there with him."

The unexpected crowd made Haru uncomfortable. He went quickly to the carriage, opening the door himself.

"Where to now?" he asked as he climbed inside. He expected to find Reius waiting for him. Instead, a different figure greeted him. Haru paused in the threshold. "You?"

Chancellor Malon smiled crookedly, amused at his surprise. She leaned on a jeweled umbrella, her cheeks popping with rouge, her red hair slicked back on her bone-white head. The rings on her fingers clinked as she beckoned Haru closer.

"Good day, Tain," she said cheerily. "Have you seen the sun today? Bright as a copper coin! We should have a fine day tomorrow for the festival."

Haru sat down hesitantly on the opposite bench, forgetting the door. Aryak rectified the oversight, closing him in with the odd Chancellor. "I expected to see Reius," he said carefully.

"And I'm not offended at all by the look on your face. Ha! Be at ease, Tain. You'll see Reius soon."

"He's not in the palace?"

"An excellent supposition." Malon banged the floor twice with her umbrella and the carriage lurched forward. Her odd accent made it hard to know if she was being sarcastic or just ridiculously polite. Haru felt a tinge of panic as they pulled away from the crowded courtyard.

"Chancellor Malon—"

"Uh-uh-uh," scolded Malon, raising a painted finger. "*Chansoor*, yes?"

"Yes, alright. Will you tell me where Reius is?"

"At his house in the countryside," replied Malon. "Not a long trip—just an hour or two."

The answer made Haru curdle. He remained silent for a long, rude moment. Malon reached across and patted his knee.

"Don't fret—we will entertain each other," she said. "You'll be leaving soon, and we're still barely acquainted! The trip will give us time to talk. Just the two of us." She giggled. "Nice and intimate."

Haru glanced out the window, trying to hide his displeasure. Suddenly he wished he'd allowed the others to come along; a long journey with Malon was an unbearable thought. "You should have told me we'd be on the road so long," he said. "Why the countryside? Why couldn't Reius wait to speak to me until he got back?"

Malon's eyebrows shot up. "Because he is Reius. Because we do not question his reasons." She set aside her dazzling umbrella and leaned back on the leather bench, pulling at her frilled cuffs, ignoring the passing city as the carriage rolled through the street. Her manner alarmed Haru. He gestured to Malon's hands with his chin.

"That paint on your fingers. It's very bright. I've never seen such a color."

"Like crushed rubies, yes? They make the pigment in Saxoras, just for me." Malon lifted her hands and admired them. "To be honest, it helps cover the grime I acquire in my work."

"Work?" What would that be?"

Malon smiled secretively. "My vocation."

It took a second for Haru to remember. Before Malon became First Follower, she'd had a different, darker life entirely. Haru blinked, not sure what to say, not sure anymore why he was in the carriage or where they were going. Malon sensed his fear, aroused by it.

"It shouldn't shock you," said Malon. "I was a very good torturer. To be good at it you have to enjoy it. But it's a desire, you see. Like a hunger. It never leaves you."

Haru's blood turned to ice. His hand twitched as he considered reaching for the door.

"Fortunately," sighed Malon, "there are no shortage of enemies of the Alliance. And no shortage of thumbscrews to use on them."

"No?" Haru kept his voice steely.

"You're upset." Malon put her hand over her heart. "Forgive me, Tain." Then she laughed. She reached into her sleeve for a handkerchief, covering her mouth with the square of golden silk. "Pardon me...but your face..." Her delight made her eyes water. "Please...please..." She put up a hand as she reined in her laughter. "I swear you're in no danger, Tain. We *are* going to see Reius."

Haru released the breath he was holding. "Chancellor..."

"I know. I'm a terrible tease." She stuffed away her handkerchief and grinned wickedly. "Did you really think we'd be doing anything but talking? Really, Tain Haru, when will you learn to trust us? You're running out of time!"

"And this trip is supposed to make me feel better? That joke?"

"It wasn't all a joke," said Malon. "I *am* peerless at my work. Sometimes my old skills are called upon." She shrugged. "It can't be helped. Heresy, dissent, sedition—the Alliance faces all manner of threats."

"And you torture people? You yourself? Still?"

"I *inquire*," said Malon. "But you can call it torture if you wish. I'm not embarrassed."

"Obviously not," said Haru with disgust.

"Tain, you judge because you don't understand. Torture is a deeply personal process. It's like love-making."

"What?"

"It's true!" The argument animated Malon. She leaned closer, her eyes full of excitement. "If you were my prisoner, you would understand. You would be helpless. Not like a child is helpless. Not like an animal stuck in a trap. I mean totally, unmercifully helpless. Dependent upon me for everything. Not just your life, but your humanity. And I would peel it away from you, gently at first, earning your trust, sharing your terrors..." Malon shuddered. "Anyone could be taught the art, Tain. Anyone could torture another person if the circumstances were right."

"Not me," said Haru. "Never."

Malon grinned. "Some of the best techniques I know came from Cryori texts."

"That's not us. Not anymore."

"I think you would do it. I really do. To save Nesenor you would do it."

"Inflict pain for sport? Hear another man scream? No."

"People don't scream when they're tortured," said Malon. "They howl."

Haru looked out the window. "How long is this trip?"

Malon took his meaning and stopped talking. But from the corner of his eye Haru could see the strange Chancellor studying him. With his back to the driver, Haru couldn't see where they were going—only where they'd been. He watched the towers of the giant palace disappear. The streets thinned of people as they travelled. Malon was quiet for a very long time, perfectly at ease in the awkwardness while Haru pretended to be fascinated by the view. When the silence grew unbearable, Haru spoke.

"I'm wondering something," he said.

"Good," said Malon pleasantly.

"Does Reius approve of what you do?"

"Specifically?"

"Torturing people. Does Reius approve? I ask because he thinks of himself as a changed man."

"My avocation troubles you?"

"Yes. It should trouble you but it doesn't. That's frightening but that's not my question."

"Don't be troubled—Reius knows everything. Well, everything he needs to know. And we all have secrets, Tain Haru."

"Chancellor, you like games too much," said Haru, frustrated. Malon was baiting him but he didn't know why. "Fine." His gaze flicked out the window again. "It doesn't matter."

"*Secrets*, Tain Haru," crooned Malon.

Haru refused to look at her, afraid of her demented eyes. "What about them?"

"We're all alone," said Malon. "Think of me like a priest. You have priests in Nesenor—your Venerants. You trust them, yes? You can tell them anything that's burdening you."

"I'm not burdened."

"A bad choice of words, perhaps. A man can only feel burdened if he feels guilty. And why should you feel guilty? You're entitled to keep things private between you and your advisors."

Haru felt a stab of panic. "My advisors?"

"They've very odd," said Malon. "They make me curious, and curiosity is a torment for me! I've been asked to turn my mind to other things, but it's been enormously difficult."

"You mean Reius doesn't want you asking questions?" This time it was Haru who smiled. "That's a shame."

Malon steepled her hands together. "You're his guest. He fears offending you. But if you would volunteer to tell me about them it would be a joy. It's such a long trip, after all, and we know still know so little about each other."

"They counsel," said Haru. "Not much to tell."

"You call them your Chorus. Why?"

"It's what they've always been called. Reius has you, Tains have a Chorus."

"About what do they counsel?"

"Whatever I need. Didn't Reius say he didn't want me questioned? I feel like one of your prisoners, Chancellor."

Malon backed off, though only slightly. "I've heard—from people who would know such things—that some in your country have magic. Is that so, Tain? Magic fascinates me."

"Magic." Haru rolled his eyes. "Humans are so ignorant. Isn't it outlawed here even to talk about such things?"

"Oh yes. Magic is very dangerous. It leads to great harm, Tain. Great harm..."

Amazingly, Malon let the conversation trail off. She glanced through the window at the changing scenery. She cocked her head contentedly at the view. And for two whole hours, the First Follower said no more.

They were far, far from the city when Malon finally spoke again, driving through a patch of scrubby farmland. A light fog had settled over the hillsides; rain fell in the distance. Cows stood quietly in the meadows and tiny, cobblestone houses dotted the landscape. Haru felt at ease, reminded of the grain fields back home and glad to be far from the bustling capital. Then, Malon's voice intruded.

"We're almost there," she said. "Look ahead."

Haru leaned forward, trying to see out the carriage's window. The dirt road wound out in front of them. A small farmhouse waited half a mile ahead, its stone chimney puffing white smoke. Chickens scratched at the hardscrabble yard. A trio of people tended chores.

"Reius?" asked Haru.

Malon nodded. "He's waiting there for you."

Haru strained to see as the first raindrops studded the window. "Why so far away?"

"Do you know much about J'horan history, Tain?" Malon sat back with a serious air. "Before the Alliance?"

"I don't," Haru admitted. "Not really."

"Do you know we had gods before we had Taan?"

"You had our gods," said Haru. "Before you turned your back on them."

"Before then, even. We had gods *like* your gods," the Chancellor corrected. "Powerful creatures. Immortal perhaps. You call Clionet and her brood a family. We called them clans, and there were many of them. In my country we worshipped Tinora. Have you ever heard of her?"

"I don't think so," said Haru.

"No? You should have spent more time talking to your human slaves. Oh, pardon me! *Servants.*"

"Go on," said Haru crossly.

"Imagine what the offspring of a woman and a black jackal would look like—that's Tinora. Have you ever heard of Arthesel? Or N'nank?"

"No, I haven't."

"Be glad you haven't then, I suppose. They're demons of the highest ilk. Once, when they were powerful in these lands, they possessed men. They turned people to fornication, to war, to butchery. They demanded sacrifices. They deceived. They were a plague, and humans were too dim-witted or superstitious to throw them off."

"And you compare these creatures to the gods of Nesenor? To *my* gods?"

"I'm talking of the old magics." Malon glanced through the window toward the upcoming house. The usual mirth went out of her eyes. "When you think of Clionet, you think of beautiful things. But these so-called gods—all of them—have darkness in them."

Staring through the rain-streaked window, she seemed genuinely sad. Haru couldn't imagine what could touch a shriveled heart like hers.

"This old magic," broached Haru. "It still exists?"

"Like an echo," said Malon. "It's just a whisper now, but it goes on."

Haru thought at once of his father. "But it's outlawed, yes? All the old gods, not just the Cryori ones, right?"

"Laws don't kill demons," said Malon. She turned from the window, looking at Haru squarely. "I am the Chancellor of the Tower of Principles. I am the First Follower. No one has done more to stomp on those old serpents. Yet they live on."

"Why are you telling me this?" asked Haru.

But Malon had timed their conversation perfectly. She smiled as the carriage came to a stop. "We're here. Just remember what I told you—everyone has secrets."

Chapter Twenty-Six

THE SHADOW BOYS

A chilly drizzle struck Haru's face as he emerged from the carriage. He stood atop the vehicle's single step, surveying the house and the farmland around it. A flock of starlings flew overhead and fog hung like a noose around the distant hills. The scent of burning wood climbed into Haru's nostrils. A pair of men and a single, hard-bitten woman stood in the house's overgrown yard, waiting for him, their utilitarian clothing worn from toil, their expressions tired and unreadable. A stray chicken approached the carriage, then ran off as Haru jumped to the ground. The cows in the meadows around the house ignored the rain; a dog barked in the distance. Haru studied the house, then the other houses around it, all of them at least half a mile away.

"What's this place called?" he asked Malon, who remained in the carriage.

"It has no name," said Malon. "We call it the village."

"But what is it?" Haru looked around, confused by the untended farmland and rusty, scattered tools. "Where are all the people?"

Malon shrugged. "Doing what villagers do, I suppose. There aren't many of them anyway."

Haru turned to look at her. "Aren't you coming?"

"I'll wait here," said Malon with a smile. "Go on. Reius is waiting."

Haru didn't see Reius, though, only the three weather-beaten farmers. He ran his hand through his wet hair uncertainly, then waved at them.

"Hello?"

"Don't ask, just go ahead," urged Malon. "They know who you are. They're expecting you."

Haru hesitated. His trip to J'hora was getting stranger by the moment. But he was too curious to refuse, and the thought of getting back in the carriage with Malon spurred him on. The nearest man set aside his pitchfork, stabbing it into the dirt and greeting Haru with an awkward bow. His companions, the man and the woman, both lowered their eyes.

"Tain Haru," said the first man, "my name is Rucan. If you need anything while you're here just ask for me." He gestured to his companions. "This is Dresus and this is Andra. We're the caretakers here."

From the poor condition of the house, it seemed the three hadn't done a very good job. Haru said politely, "I'm just here to see Reius. May I go inside?"

"The Prophet is in the yard," said Rucan. He pointed around the house. "Just go on back."

"He's outside? In the rain?"

The question drew a blank stare from Rucan. "He's around back..."

Haru smiled. He'd come to expect madness from Reius anyway. "That's fine."

With one last glance at the warm and dry Malon, Haru left the front yard and rounded the cottage. Mud and grass sucked at his boots as he walked, a curious rooster following him. The smell of burning wood grew, and when he rounded the house he saw a big, crackling campfire spitting smoke into the air. Around the fire sat three figures—one, the unmistakable, bare-chested Reius, the other two smaller and bent, dressed in dark garments. All three sat directly on the ground, their backsides firmly in the damp grass, their arms wrapped around their knees as they admired the flames. Reius had his back to Haru, telling a story that Haru couldn't hear. The others—both much younger than Reius—listened intently, their odd faces bearing twisted grins. Haru stopped dead when he saw them.

The twins.

He had caught their eyes too late to turn back. One raised his head as he sighted Haru, nudging the other. Their red eyes burned with interest. Stringy hair fell across their foreheads. Both shared the same bronze skin. Hunched and palsied, their arms swung loosely from their shoulders, their heads lolling. Reius turned, his face freezing with apprehension when he noticed Haru. The big man rose, his naked chest glistening with rainwater.

"Haru," he said. "Come be with us."

The twins rocked excitedly on their backsides. Reius waved them to their feet.

"Get up."

They did so, wobbling on their spindly legs, their backs so humped that they couldn't straighten. Haru joined them around the campfire, his gaze jumping between their faces, unable to tell them apart or even guess their ages. One pulled at his spidery fingers, separating them from the knuckles so they dangled by skin. He popped them back in, his glowing eyes dancing with mirth at the gruesome noise.

Reius went to Haru and touched his shoulder, moving him closer to the twins. From the corner of his eye Haru noted the fateful tattoo on the big man's chest.

"This is Artris and Rann," said Reius. "My sons."

"Your..." Haru caught his breath. "You have sons?"

The twins shuffled closer. One offered out his brittle hand. "Artris," he rasped.

Haru took his hand gently, afraid to break it, feeling the cold touch. Like ice, he thought. Like death. Artris' smile never changed as his head bobbed in greeting. The other twin, Rann, flashed his white teeth. It made no sense to Haru. None of it. He let go of Artris' hand.

"What are they doing out here?" he asked. "What...?"

"What are they?" Reius said. "They're what happens when magic mixes with man. They're also my beloved children."

"You keep them here? You hide them here?" Haru could barely look at the twins, nor could he look away. "Their eyes! They're like animal eyes." He looked into them closely. "They glow..."

Artris chittered at the attention, opening his eyes as wide as he could for Haru to examine.

"Animal eyes, like that one you brought here with you," said Reius.

"Elsifor," whispered Haru. "Reius, I don't understand this. Explain it, please."

"You are Cryori. You understand magic, so you'll understand their story." Reius regarded his children with pity. "I loved their mother but she was a witch. She'd dedicated herself to Nafara. In my land they call Nafara the Queen of Scorpions. She's a demon, like the demons of Nesenor but worse. When these two tore their way out of her womb..." Reius stopped and bit his lip. "This is what happens when demons rule us!"

He was shaking, not from cold but from rage, and his two boys nodded at every word he spoke.

"They called them the Shadow Boys," said Reius. "Can you imagine the ridicule? They came out like *that*. Deformed. Broken, and yet unbreakable. And worse."

"What do you mean?" asked Haru.

"Stand there, boys," Reius ordered. "Don't move."

He went to the side of the house where an old shovel rested upon a tree stump. Returning with it in his gigantic fists, he stood before Rann and cocked back for a blow.

"Reius, no!" Haru cried.

The shovel swung forward, its flat metal smashing into Rann's face. The impact sent Rann spinning from the campfire. His brother let out a shocking laugh. Reius sighed and tossed the shovel aside.

"Watch."

Rann staggered back to them, shaking his head, his jaw dangling crookedly from his face. Amazingly, there was no blood. Rann took the dislocated jaw in his palm and moved it side to side, raising his eyebrows comically at Haru. Then, like it was a puzzle piece, he fitted the bones back together, punching them into place with his fist. The gruesome operation made Haru light-headed.

"Mother goddess!" he gasped. He peddled backward, nearly slipping in the mud. "Is he...*alive?*"

"They're alive. And cursed." Reius went to Rann and put a hand gently on his cheek, patting the face he'd just smashed with a shovel. "They're the offspring of Nafara. They're as much her children as they are mine."

"And their mother? Dead?"

"As I said—they killed her getting out of her. It's a good thing they did, too. I would have had to kill her for her witchery."

"Kill her, Reius? Their mother?"

"My wife," said Reius hotly, "and yes, I would have killed her. *She* brought this on them, not our love-making. She was a witch and I adored her, and for that I'm burdened forever with these poor wretches." He patted both their backs. The boys grinned at him.

"How old are they?" asked Haru. "When did this happen?"

"Years ago," replied Reius. "Sixteen, I think. The same age as you, Haru. Their mother was a Kalmiiri, as I am."

Suddenly Malon's odd conversation made some sense. "This is the old magic, then," whispered Haru.

"Now do you see? Do you understand? Finally? This is the kind of misery your so-called gods bring to the world. This is why they can't be worshipped. Not ever. Not even a tiny bit."

"Those aren't my gods, Reius. My gods would *never* do such a thing."

"A lie. That animal man you brought with you—he worships the goddess Paiax, yes? He told my priest so."

"Yes, but Elsifor's not like *them*," argued Haru, pointing at the twins. "Neither is Paiax. This creature you call Nafara—I've never even heard of her."

"Your man Elsifor—does he hunt?"

Haru didn't want to answer. "Does it matter?"

"Does he crave blood? Because my sons do. They can't survive without it. Not even meat is good enough for them, only living blood from a living creature. You see now why I keep them here? Why they can't be around any but the most loyal and fearless who serve me?"

"I'm sorry," offered Haru. For the first time since meeting Reius, he pitied him. "I'm sorry for these children and for your wife, but if you're blaming Nesenor for this, you are wrong."

Reius' expression remained steely. "Let me show you something else." He twirled a finger at his sons. "Go on. Show him."

"May we hunt now?" asked Artris.

"Yes."

The approval made Rann giddy. He stripped off his shirt, fell to his knees, and reached out for his brother, dragging Artris down beside him. Artris shallowed his breathing and placed his palms down on the wet grass. His body began to shudder. His red eyes burst with internal light. The brothers turned their faces skyward, groaning as the bones roiled beneath their skin, shifting and popping, black curls sprouting on their hairless bodies. Rann grit his teeth, wailing as his just-fixed jaw broke free of his face again, extruding outward in a spittle-dripping snout. Hands became claws. Feet burst from their boots. The twins writhed as their bodies transformed, tearing through the clothing until what was left of them was barely human at all.

Haru watched, awestruck and sickened. He had only seen Elsifor transform once, but it hadn't been like this. The wolf-like brothers ripped at their clothing, shredding it with teeth and claw, freeing themselves from the last of their humanity. Their crimson eyes burned on Haru. Reius stepped in front of him.

"Go!" he roared.

Yelping and howling, the monstrous twins scattered, running through the foggy meadow toward the distant hills.

"Pitiful," whispered Haru. "Terrible."

Reius' eyes tracked his sons across the field. "My children."

His voice was colder than Haru had ever heard it. Afflicted.

"Where will they go?"

"They'll hunt. They'll feed. They have to or die."

"People?"

Reius grimaced. "It has happened."

"And you allow it?"

"Should I kill them? What they are isn't their fault."

The logic stymied Haru. He looked around the yard, unsure where to go or what to say.

"Reius, why did you show me this?"

"Why?" Reius went to stand over the campfire. "To make you trust me. Finally. I showed you your past, I told you of your doomed future, but you go on disbelieving. My boys are my greatest secret, Haru. My greatest shame."

"No one knows they're your sons?"

"Malon knows. The caretakers in the village know. Very few others." Reius turned to him. "And now you know."

"I know you slept with a witch. Don't you kill people for that?"

"I have repented. Every day of my life I repent."

"But you love them. Even as they are. If you can do that, can you not leave Nesenor at peace?"

"I'm trying to save you, Haru. All of you." Reius pointed to the meadow where his cursed sons had gone. "Save you from *that*. Ask your friend Elsifor. Ask him if he'd like to be saved."

"No, don't," warned Haru. "You don't know Elsifor. Elsifor's my friend. He's not ashamed of what he is. He's proud of it. We're the ones who make him feel strange. We're the ones that are afraid of him because he's different. And that's why you're afraid of us—because we're different from you. We're *different*, Reius." Haru lowered his head in resignation. "No more meetings. Tomorrow, after your speech, I'm going home."

Overwhelmed, he turned to leave the yard. leaving Reius at the campfire and glad the human didn't follow. The old magic. Was Clionet magic? Goddess or demon; suddenly he couldn't say. As he rounded the house, Haru saw Malon. The Chancellor had at last emerged from the garish carriage. She leaned on the vehicle, one knee cocked as her foot rested on a wheel, studying her painted nails with bizarre interest. When she noticed Haru, she smiled and gave a garish wave.

In an instant, all the doubt fled Haru's mind.

Chapter Twenty-Seven

PRISONER

L iadin heard Clionet's voice before the light of his torch touched her.

"Finally."

She said it with such relief it broke Liadin's heart. He held his torch out as he walked carefully toward her prison-pool, the dead water sloshing against the walls of the canal. He saw the iron bars up ahead, then glimpsed her gigantic eye pressed up against them, the iris shrinking in the torchlight. She was between forms, a grotesque combination of a woman and a cuttlefish, half her face covered with hair, the other striped like a mollusk. Her single breast floated atop the poisoned water. She had been kept in darkness for days; all the light had dimmed in her miraculous body. She blinked with her cuttlefish eye, pained by the torch but too weak to turn away.

Liadin paused, far enough from the iron gate to keep clear of unseen tentacles. He placed the torch in a nearby holder, studying her as the light bathed her watery prison. His Venerants had done a good job of keeping her alive, letting in enough of Ama'aga's dead water to weaken her without letting her die. Death might have been preferable, he supposed. Her lingering looked like torture. Liadin chanced one step closer, pitying her. She took him in her eye and spoke with her distorted lips.

"Why have you waited?"

Liadin replied, "For you to suffer."

"No measure of suffering will change my mind."

"I can keep you here forever, and forever is a very long time for your kind."

"Then imagine what a release death would be."

She had no strength to threaten him, not even enough to complete her form. Liadin inched toward the bars. At the edge of the pool lapped the dead water.

"Ama'aga is a good son," groaned Clionet. "He visits me every day to poison me."

Liadin bristled at the mention of her son. Clionet sensed this and opened her cuttlefish eye wider.

"So, you have regrets already," she said. She coughed with delight. "I can see it in you. What has he done?"

"Ama'aga has filled the hearts of our mariners with hope," said Liadin. "He's reminded them that they are men."

"Ama'aga is the shame of my existence. He will be a tyrant."

"He follows me," said Liadin.

Clionet slumped against the bars. "For now."

"Goddess, you should know my heart in full. You should know I will not surrender to my love for you, and that you will not leave here until you grant me what I need. In time this prison will madden you. Your suffering will become unbearable, even for a god. Before you lose your wits entirely, see the sense in what I ask. Give me dominion over the shenenra and let me save Nesenor."

"The blood-kin of Hiaran command the shenenra," said Clionet. "No others."

"By your decree. And so, you can change it."

"Why would I?"

"Because Haru is dead. You know he is. Tell me—do you feel him?"

"I can feel nothing in this place. Not even my own existence."

"He is *dead*," Liadin insisted.

"Do you wish that so badly?" Clionet closed her mismatched eyes. "He would have had children, given time. He would have been my beloved for years and years. Murderer..."

"Make me Tain," pleaded Liadin. He got down on his knees before her and opened his arms. "I am an old man. I have no children. I have no ambitions. My reign will end with me. I swear it will be so. Just give me the power to command the dragon-whales!"

The goddess refused to look at him. "Let me die."

"Great Clionet, hear me! Why should Nesenor suffer for your broken heart? Haru died bravely. He died to save Nesenor."

"You don't know he's dead."

Liadin lowered his arms. "He must be. And if he isn't, he will be soon. He can never return here, and he has no means to make it home. Alive or dead, his time as Tain is over. No more peace with the world of men. No more living in fear of them."

"No more tranquility. No more mothers watching their sons grow up."

"Yes, war is coming, and that is as it should be! As it must be! Shall it be a long war, then? Is that what suits you?" Liadin got up from his knees. "Or shall we rise together? Shall we sink the human invaders and feed them to your depths? Shall we spread the glory of your family once again to the human heathens, or shall we let them come and slay us? I cannot believe that is your preference, Goddess."

Clionet was silent for a moment. Then her body began to shake with laughter.

"You are an imbecile, truly!" she chortled. "Go now, please, and save me the agony of your company. You will never have my shenen-ra."

"I do not come to torment you, Goddess. I come to beg your aid."

"Do not come at all!" bellowed Clionet. "For if I should escape this place at any time, I will find you, Liadin. I will squeeze you until your bones snap and your eyes pop like grapes. I shall pull your limbs off like spider legs. And I shall eat you and digest you for a hundred years."

"They will come, Goddess," warned Liadin. The humans will come in their white ships. They'll want revenge for their false prophet."

"Let them come then! And let them slay all those stupid enough to follow you! And my wretched son!" Clionet fell back with exhaustion, splashing down into the black pool. "Go now."

Her stubbornness surprised Liadin. "You are a selfish creature," he told her. "Here you will remain until you see the good I do. You will not be rid of me. Soon, I'll return."

"More torments."

"Until you come to your senses, yes." Liadin turned and retrieved his torch from the wall. "Enjoy the darkness," he said, then walked slowly back the way he'd come, abandoning Clionet to her prison.

Chapter Twenty-Eight

PLAYING WITH FOOD

"Haru, come away from the window and eat."

Shadur called to him through a mouthful of food. Standing alone at the balcony, Haru replied with a nod but didn't turn around. Behind him the conversation had gotten loud again; the others were nervous, he realized. He looked out over the city, spying the crowded courtyard in the distance. All J'hora had come out for the festival, just as Orkorlis had predicted. Vendors and musicians and acrobats flooded the streets, and an army of workers had begun lighting the moon lanterns. The sun was already starting to dip, summoning the fire dancers to delight the throngs of children. Flowers and bunches of grapes decorated shop doors and hung in garlands around the necks of the city's many statues. Haru put his hand to the window glass and felt it tremble with the din.

"I've never seen so many people in my life," he said. "Not even when I was made Tain."

"I remember how they came for that," said Shadur behind him at the supper table. "All of Nesenor."

"Come sit," said Siva. "It's almost time and we need to go over things."

"We've gone over things," said Haru. "A hundred times."

"Sit down. I'm in charge tonight."

Haru lingered at the window, straining to see the courtyard. He could barely make out the balcony where Reius would soon appear—and soon would soon die. Finally, after too many days in J'hora, they were ready. Haru had dismissed the servants after they'd brought in the food, giving them leave to attend the festival with the rest of the humans. Count Whistler had said that even the Lord Guardians would be down in the streets to hear Reius' speech. For one day every other year, all the people of the Alliance were equal, Whistler had explained, but he had smirked when he said it, and knew how stupid it sounded.

A great dream. That's what it sounded like to Haru.

He'd been lied to by Reius, but he had almost believed it. He had almost let the madman live. No matter what happened now—if they were killed or if they were captured—he felt comforted. He could finally fulfill his promise to Clionet. He'd found the man who'd murdered his father.

At last he turned from the window. The meal the humans had prepared was especially elaborate tonight, an extension of the celebration outdoors. Shadur and Elsifor tucked into it with their usual appetites, anxious about the coming events but not letting their nerves govern their stomachs. Siva ate, too, her robes now bulging with her concealed knives and the atlatl she would use to blow Reius off his balcony. She ate like a man but watched her drinking, sipping at her wine, determined to keep her wits straight. Valivan sat away from the others, watching them from a heavy chair but not joining them around the table. He seemed more troubled than usual tonight.

Haru pulled out his chair, loading up his plate before sitting down. There was fish in gravy, meats from indistinguishable animals, cheese—a dish completely unknown to Haru before coming to J'hora—and a plethora of fruits and vegetables. A fitting final dinner, Haru decided. They would eat and they would be together, perhaps for the very last time. He finished loading his plate. His Chorus seemed surprisingly content. Inside, he smiled.

"Val, come sit," he told his friend.

"I've e-eaten enough," said Val.

"He's eaten nothing," quipped Siva.

"It's alright to be afraid," Haru said. "We need to go over things again. Come."

Reluctantly, Valivan got up from his chair and joined the others, plopping down between Siva and Elsifor. Siva took his plate and began heaping food on to it, all to Val's chagrin.

"I can't eat," whined Val. "How can any of you? We're about to k-k-"

"Kill someone? That's right." chirped Siva.

Haru glanced at him, sizing him up. "You've got the important part, Val. Are you ready?"

Val nodded. "Easy."

"I've got the fun part," said Siva. She looked askance at Shadur. "Isn't that right, Shadur?"

"As long as you enjoy your work, Siva," replied the mystic. His gaze hovered upon the table a moment and he grinned. "I've been studying the plan too much! Look at the table—it looks like the courtyard." He stood and moved his goblet to the edge of the table where Haru was seated. "This is Reius' balcony..."

Elsifor groaned. "Can't we just eat?"

"No, no, just imagine," urged Shadur. He picked a kumquat out of a bowl. "This is me," he said. "This is where I'll be, close to the palace gate."

Siva sized up his work. "Yes..." She took her fork and placed it parallel to the edge of the table. "This gate."

Shadur picked up another fruit, a plump, round berry. "This is you, Siva," he said, "and this is the tailor shop."

"I'm the fat one?"

Shadur grinned wickedly. "You're the sweet one." He put the berry atop a butter dish he was using for the tailor shop. The shop had a good view of Reius' balcony and would be closed for the festival. Siva was sure she could manage the distance. Elsifor got into the act and started placing more forks around the edges of the table. The courtyard itself was diamond shaped, with main streets entering at the corners.

"Haru, flip over that tea cup," said Elsifor. "That can be the temple."

Intrigued, Haru moved his empty cup toward the very end of the table, far from where Reius would be addressing the crowd from his 'goblet.' The temple was actually outside of the courtyard, nearly half a mile from it, and had actually been a temple before falling into ruin. In the days of Cryori rule, the place had been dedicated to the goddess Paiax. It had been left to stand as a stark reminder to the humans of darker times. They called it the Temple of Tyrants. To Haru and the Chorus, it would be their rendezvous point—after they'd killed Reius.

"So, what am I?" asked Elsifor. He surveyed the edibles for a suitable stand-in, then saw a fuzz-covered peach. "Oooh, that's definitely me." He placed the peach in the middle of the table. It would be his job to make a path for them if necessary.

"Draw little claws on it," joked Shadur.

They all laughed, except for Valivan. "What about me and Haru?"

"You'll be here," said Shadur. He tapped an area close to the goblet. "That's where the Lord Guardians will be. That's where they'll be expecting to see Haru."

"What do you want to be, Val?" asked Haru. He pulled the fruit bowl closer to him, looking for something suitable. "How about a strawberry?" He plucked one from the bowl. "And I'll be this," he said, choosing something dark and seeded.

"They call it a rapina," said Shadur. "Very nourishing."

Haru placed the strawberry and rapina near the goblet. "We'll be able to hear everything he says from here. He'll be speaking for a few minutes at least, so we'll let him talk for a while." He pointed at the bright, round berry standing in for Siva. "Let the people settle in and get comfortable."

"Reius too," said Shadur. "Let him feel safe."

"When he goes down you make sure you run, Haru. You too, Val. Don't wait to see what's happening. They'll be a second or two while people figure things out. As soon as that lull breaks, both of you head for the temple."

Shadur spun the peach in the center of the table. "They'll be running from me so be careful. Don't get trampled. Weave your way through them. Don't look anyone in the eye and don't speak. Just hurry. They might not even notice you."

"They'll notice *you*, Shadur," said Elsifor. "And the priests will figure out what happened. Once they do they'll start looking for us. I still don't think the temple is the best place for us to go."

"It is," said Haru. He had seen the ruined temple on his tour with Reius, and thought it the perfect place to hide. "We won't be there long, just enough to regroup. We can defend ourselves there if we have to. It'll be dark and it's close to roads. We'll be gone before they make a search."

"What then?" asked Val.

"We disappear," said Haru. "We talked about this, Val. We make it to Agon however we can."

Val looked even more worried than usual. Haru wondered if he was losing his nerve.

"Val, look," said Haru. He picked up one final piece of fruit, a red, oval shaped morsel he knew was filled with juice. "This one's Reius." He placed the fruit on the table, placed his palm atop the fruit, and pressed down. It ruptured instantly, spraying pulp and seeds. "That's what we're going to do."

Val just nodded. Haru wiped his hands with a napkin.

"That's enough," he said. "What's wrong with you?"

"Nothing," Val denied.

"It's our last night here," said Haru. "This isn't just about the mission. You've been acting strange for days, and I mean strange even for you. The rest of us aren't mind-readers, Valivan. You have to tell us."

"Tell us, Val," said Siva. "This is the time."

Val put a hand to his forehead. "Jyx. I saw him."

Shadur dropped his fork. "He came to you?"

"Yes," confessed Val. "Days ago, just after we arrived here."

"Where?" asked Haru. Jyx was a trickster, and his appearances were never good news. "Did he speak to you?"

"Yes," said Valivan. He avoided Haru's eyes, staring down at his untouched plate. "In the s-s-statuary."

"What did he say?" asked Siva.

"He was angry. He wanted to know why I hadn't called upon him." Val fought to get the words out, the way always did when talking about Jyx. "I haven't—I haven't wanted to speak to him. He seemed jealous. Or something."

"Bees!" blurted Haru. "There were bees in the statuary when I met with Reius there. He said they'd found a hive. That must have been Jyx."

Val rubbed his nose. "He stung me."

"Valivan, what did he want?" pressed Shadur.

"And why didn't you tell us?" asked Haru, trying not to sound cross.

Val struggled with his answer. "Don't know," he told Shadur. Then, looking at Haru, he said the same thing, tagging on a sheepish, "Sorry."

"Think, Val," Haru pressed. "Jyx never tells things clearly. What *might* have he been trying to say?"

"Haru I...don't know! He just..asked about you."

"Me? What do you mean?"

Val pushed to get the words out. "He...said you...need me."

Haru looked at Shadur. "Does that make any sense to you?"

"No. But nothing Jyx does makes sense to me." He turned to Valivan and said, "Breathe. No one's angry at you. Is there anything else you can remember?"

"Yes." Valivan swallowed and stretched his jaw to overcome his stammer. "He said I'm c-c-curious."

"Curious?" Shadur smiled. "We all know that. What was it? A warning?"

Val answered with a shrug.

"And you haven't seen him since?" asked Haru.

"N-n-no. He said he wouldn't come again."

"Well, that's a relief," said Haru. "You should be glad, Val. Jyx does nothing but torment you. Always has. Bastard." He was about to start eating again when another thought entered his mind. "He didn't take away your talent, did he?"

"No," said Valivan. "I'm fine."

"I'm not," sighed Shadur. "I'm troubled. Jyx wasn't just toying with you, Val. There's always something more with him. Something hidden."

"Alright," said Siva, "but what?"

"Maybe this," said Elsifor, gesturing to them all. "Look how confused he has us. Maybe he wanted to distract us. He knows what we're doing here. Maybe he wants us to fail."

"Why would he want that? Jyx hates humans," said Siva.

"We're speculating," warned Shadur.

"We are, and we need to stop," said Haru. "Val, are you ready for tonight or not?"

Valivan finally sat up straight. "Y-y-yes."

"What about the rest of you?"

The others affirmed without hesitation, especially Siva.

"When I get home, the first thing I'm going to do is get some proper food," she announced.

"Looks like you've been managing to keep up with Elsifor just fine," said Shadur.

Siva took no offense at the barb, laughing with the rest of them instead.

"Daova," she said. "That's what I want. The way my mother made it, with rice and cockles." She closed her eyes and inhaled the imaginary aroma. "Real food."

"I want to smell the air again," said Elsifor. "It stinks here. I want to run through the forest. I want to hunt."

Their reminiscing lifted Haru's sprits. "What about you, Shadur? Are you looking forward to going back to that hovel you call home?"

"I'll miss the library here, but that's all," said Shadur. He wiggled his crystal fingers. "And I can't wait to take off this damn glove."

"Tonight!" promised Haru. He waited for the chuckling to die away. "Tonight." He looked into the faces of the Chorus. The enormity of their task haunted their eyes. "Tonight, we avenge our dead Tain. Tonight, we send the human world a message."

He pushed his plate aside, hungry only for revenge.

Chapter Twenty-Nine

ASSASSINS

The courtyard was more crowded than Haru expected. He had seen the throngs of people from his window, thinking it manageable, but now with Reius' address just minutes away the crowd had swelled dangerously, making it difficult to move. The music had mostly quieted down, and the acrobats and vendors remained in the streets around the central square, entertaining the stragglers. A thousand moon lanterns illuminated the square, and the rain clouds that had covered the city just yesterday had fled, revealing a clear sky and twinkling stars. Haru and Valivan pushed their way to the place near the balcony where the Lord Guardians had gathered. Like Siva and the others, they covered their heads with the hoods of their robes, but they did not go unnoticed. They ignored the pointing and drunken shouts, confident that Reius' safety guarantee still applied. Valivan kept his face down, looking annoyingly guilty. Haru could tell the press of people was killing him.

"Sorry," he whispered to his friend. He held Val's arm as they inched through the crowd. "It won't be long."

In here, Valivan reminded him. *Talk in your head.*

Right, said Haru quickly. He could see the balcony up ahead, lit by candles and waiting for the holy man, a white curtain drawn to hide the room beyond. An occasional shadow moved across the curtain. *He's in there*, thought Haru.

They had all dispersed after the meal, taking their positions as planned. Or at least Haru hoped they had. He glanced behind him, but seeing the others was impossible now.

Val, can you feel them? he asked.

Valivan shook his head. The bit of his face revealed by his cloak was red and wet with sweat. *There're so many people! I can't sort through it!*

You can. You know you can. Remember? You said it would be easy.

I'm sorry, Haru...

Don't apologize. Concentrate.

Haru pushed vigorously toward the front of the crowd, towing Valivan after him. Val stumbled, fighting to control his galloping nerves. Haru ignored the humans completely. Their stares, their phony bowing—it all sickened him. They harbored more than simple curiosity, he knew. They hated him. They hated all Cryori. He would use that, he determined, and let it steel him.

At last, he caught a glimpse of the Lord Guardians. They had assembled in the best spot in the courtyard, just beneath Reius' balcony, their cool demeanor and opulent dress making them easy to spot. Servants and soldiers had created a ring of empty space around them, a blessed sanctuary from the crowd.

See? said Haru. *Not so bad.*

Let's just get there.

Haru let go of Valivan's arm and pulled back the concealing hood. The Lord Guardians and their painted wives halted their conversations when they noticed him. Then, a single friendly face popped out of the crowd.

"Haru!"

Count Whistler emerged with a smile.

"Where have you been? I've been waiting!" said Whistler cheerfully. "I have a spot for you." He looked at Val with surprise. "Where are the others?"

Haru was ready for the question. "They're not coming. We have to leave J'hora soon; they stayed behind to make ready."

Old Count Whistler seemed to believe the claim. "At least you came. I haven't had any time at all to speak with you!" He took Haru's shoulder in his friendly grip. "Come and forget these other fools. They have the manners of chimps."

The old man was as serene as ever, his silver hair lit by lanterns, his smile glowing and genuine. Haru fell into his role as Tain at once.

Val steadied himself, following a step behind, playing his part as best he could, though in his mind Haru could feel his friend's trembling.

The priests and soldiers parted to make way. Haru recognized Orkorlis as the old priest gave him a courteous nod. Around him stood acolytes in flowing robes, and around them milled a dozen soldiers, bodyguards for the assembled elite, each one sporting the unique uniform of their nation.

All of them standing together, Haru noted. The J'horan Alliance.

Siva had made her way to the top of the tailor shop without being spotted. She crouched down low on the roof, spying the crowd in the courtyard below, relieved that so many of them were too drunk and stupid to notice her. In her cloak and discrete manner, she'd been just another faceless reveler, with even her gender concealed beneath her bulky robes. She wasn't as good a climber as Elsifor, and it had taken some doing to scale the wall, but she had found a space between the back of the shop and its nearest neighbor, a ramshackle bakery with mismatched bricks extending out of the wall that she had used like a ladder. After that, making the leap between the roofs had been easy. Now, she crouched in the darkness like a hunting lioness.

Like many of the shops lining the court, the tailor shop had a crenellated roof. The blocks of stone made the perfect shield for Siva, allowing her to peak over them without being seen. She chanced a look, her eyes focused on the tower and its lighted balcony. Down in the crowd, she could see the Lord Guardians and their soldiers. When she saw Haru and Val arrive, she grinned.

But her mind was free of their voices, and that troubled her. She closed her eyes, concentrating on the feeling, sensing only the slightest presence of Valivan in her brain. She reached for it, fell short, and opened her eyes again.

It didn't matter. Nothing mattered. Nothing would save Reius.

She opened her robe and withdrew the atlatl.

In the light of the moon lanterns, Shadur knew his crystal hand would sparkle. Over the years he had studied his magical appendage in all kinds of light, but the soft glow of a flame at night always made his glass fingers luminous. He could feel the hand inside its glove warming to the coming task, eager for release. Somewhere in another realm, his patron god readied the fire. Skorthoros had been barely perceivable to Shadur since he'd left Nesenor, but the god of the balance was a powerful being, and Shadur knew the deity could span the ocean. Around him jostled the human horde. They would scatter and scream, he supposed, but that was the plan and Shadur knew he shouldn't pity them.

So he waited like the rest of them for the false prophet to arrive on his balcony, pretending to be one of them, his hood drawn tight, his manner that of a patient pilgrim. He had lied a bit to Haru when he said he wouldn't miss the city. More than just its fabulous library, the entire place was a marvel, the kind of thing he doubted the Cryori could ever build.

Small things, he thought to himself. That's what the Cryori were good at now. Soon war would swallow them. Killing Reius might be the last big thing his people ever did.

Elsifor?

Valivan concentrated, shutting out the endless chatter in his mind, reaching for Elsifor's unique brain. Overwhelmed by voices and his own relentless fear, it had taken Val longer than usual to locate his friend, but at last he broke through, feeling the animal-man's presence.

Val, where are you?

The sound was more like a whisper than a voice. Valivan struggled to reply.

With Haru, he said. *With the Lord Guardians.*

Are you safe?

Haru's talking to Count Whistler. Valivan watched the two men speaking. *We're fine. For now.*

And the others?

No, said Val. *I mean, I can't find them. Too many people.*

There was a long, troubled pause.

I can't see them, said Elsifor finally. *Just be ready.*

Valivan shut his eyes tight and began to tremble. *Damn me!*

The Lord Guardians wore their impressive chains of office, even Count Whistler, and all but the Count ignored Haru. Too afraid to engage him, they chatted with their wives and fellow dignitaries, laughing politely at meaningless jokes and looking completely uncomfortable amidst the throngs of commoners. Haru looked them over, fascinated by the women in their colorful gowns. Human women were tall. The way they clung to their husbands reminded Haru of decorations. He listened half-heartedly as Whistler droned on, telling of his long trip to the city, and how he'd ridden to J'hora rather than take a ship. Then, Whistler tilted forward and lowered his voice.

"Haru, tell me what you've decided," he whispered.

Haru smiled at the expected questions. "We're going home, my friend."

"And?"

"And...you were right about Reius. He wants peace."

Whistler beamed. "You see? Didn't I tell you? Look, you're still alive!" He grabbed Haru's shoulder. "No plots here. No plans of murder. And you believe him about your father, don't you?"

"Yes," lied Haru behind his grin. "You were right."

"And you told Reius this, yes?"

"I haven't had the chance yet. But I will before we go."

"When will you leave?"

"Soon. As soon as we've made arrangements. We need a ship." Haru laughed nervously. "Obviously!"

"A seabreaker. Why go, though? You can stay. Make the peace arrangements."

"I...will think on it," said Haru. "And you? When do you leave?"

"Tomorrow, and I cannot wait for it! To be back in a small place again, that's what I want." Whistler swiveled, taking in the grandness. "This city is a monster. I don't belong here. Give me my old chair, my hearth, my dogs..."

"And you're riding home? Horses?"

"Of course horses," laughed Whistler.

"No ship? A ship would be faster, I mean. How long will it take you?"

"Two weeks if I take my time. And I *will* take my time. Plenty of good taverns along the way." The old man winked at Haru. "You could come if you'd like. I see the way you spy these women. Your father liked human girls too, you know."

"Did he? Well. So, it's north from here, yes?"

"What?"

"Agon. You ride north from here?"

Whistler frowned. "Haru, you know it is."

"Yes," grinned Haru. "I was just thinking about your ride. You're not a young man, Count. It's a good road, yes? A safe road?"

"Yes, it's safe, it's good...why the questions?" Whistler looked at him oddly. "If you want to come with me, Haru, I told you you're welcome. If you're not comfortable talking peace from here, I can mediate. Agon isn't so far."

Whistler stared at him, and just for a moment Haru wanted to be honest, and tell the old man of their plans. But the moment passed without confession.

"Thank you," said Haru. "But we'll go home now. I need to speak to Liadin. I'll need his advice."

"Peace," sighed Whistler. "It's unbelievable."

"Yes," said Haru. "It is." He turned toward Valivan, noticing then how sick his friend looked.

Val?

Valivan lifted his wild eyes but didn't reply.

You're panicking, said Haru. *Don't.*

Whistler touched his arm again. "Haru..."

"Yes?"

"You haven't told me about your time with Reius."

Haru's eyes flicked toward the balcony. "Later, I think. We should be quiet now."

"Nonsense," laughed Whistler. All around them the others caroused. "Tell me what happened. None of us ever get to see him, and you've spent so much time with him, more than any Lord Guardian, certainly." The Count pressed closer. "Tell me what he's like."

From the corner of his eye Haru noticed a group of priests watching him. He looked about for Orkorlis, but the old cleric had gone. His young acolytes, however, inched closer.

Val, they're listening to us, warned Haru.

Who?

The priests.

Count Whistler awaited Haru's answer. "Tell me, boy. You know you can trust me."

Before Haru could answer the crowd gushed with applause. The Lord Guardians and their wives pointed toward the balcony. Haru twisted toward it just as the priests rushed in around him. The candles on the balcony stirred as the white curtains were drawn back and the big figure of Reius came into view.

Then came the roar. Like the ocean it rolled over the crowd, a tidal wave of joyous human voices. The priests circled Haru, looking up adoringly at the balcony. The Lord Guardians fell to their knees. The soldiers put their hands to their hearts. Haru felt breathless. He stared up at Reius, swept by the emotions flooding the courtyard. Reius stepped to the edge of the balcony and raised his hand in greeting. He looked serene—and frighteningly powerful. He imbibed the ovation, his face aglow, and when he looked down at his kneeling governors, he lingered for a moment on Haru.

And then, as if Haru was invisible, his gaze moved on.

Get ready, Val, said Haru. His heart began to pound. *It's almost time.*

Reius summoned the Lord Guardians to their feet. He looked giant on his balcony—a nice, big target.

Let him start talking, said Haru. *Val, can you feel Siva yet?*

When he got no answer, Haru turned to find his friend. The press of priests made it difficult to see. Alarmed, he stood on his toes to search.

Val?

No answer.

"Val!"

Haru pushed the priests aside, breaking away from their little gathering. The ring of soldiers stared up at Reius, enthralled as the applause finally began to fade. Haru scanned the sea of people. He tossed himself into them, wanting to scream.

Valivan! Where are you?

Silence.

Haru froze.

Up on his balcony, Reius began to speak. "Great citizens of the Alliance!" His voice boomed over the din. "From the dust, we rise!"

Terror tugged at Haru. His mind tripped as he tried to untangle his thoughts. The priests! He spun to look back at them. They had come from nowhere. They had blocked him. Now they stared up at Reius, their faces full of peace. The memory of Siva burst in Haru's mind.

The square was half a mile wide, and from where he stood Haru couldn't even see the tailor's shop. He ran toward it anyway, diving into the crowd.

Let him talk a few minutes. That's what Haru had told her. So Siva readied herself and listened.

She had given up trying to reach Valivan. She supposed the crowd had been too much for him, and really, she didn't need him anyway. There was no need for the Chorus to speak to each other. Like a complex, beautiful dance, they all knew their moves. In a few minutes she would kill Reius. Shadur would give them cover, and Elsifor would cut a path for them. Panic and mayhem were their allies now. But Siva wasn't panicked, and she wasn't at all afraid. She knelt behind the stone blocks of the roof as Reius' words reached across the courtyard. Atlatl in hand, she thought of Sh'an.

"....of the peace Taan has given us..."

His voice had made her heart swell.

"...the great gift of his bottomless love..."

Such a brave leader. Such a good man.

"...unstoppable when we come together..."

She missed him. As her eyes lingered on the mysterious Reius, the break in her heart widened.

Wait, she told herself. Let the madman speak.

Halfway to the tailor shop, Haru spotted Elsifor.

He had managed to fight his way past the throngs, their attentions too transfixed by Reius' voice to pay him any mind. Frantic and out of breath, he waved his arms to catch Elsifor's eyes. Elsifor's keen gaze caught the movement. Shock seized his face when he realized it was Haru. They quickly shouldered through the crowd to reach each other.

"Val's gone!" gasped Haru.

"Gone?" Elsifor's eyes darted through the crowd. "You lost him?"

"I think they took him," said Haru desperately. "We need to stop Siva. We need to find Val."

"Haru, we can't! It's too late to change plans—"

"Elsifor, I can't leave Valivan here. Forget Reius. Get Siva—stop her!"

For a moment Elsifor hesitated. Only a moment. Then suddenly he was the fastest creature Haru had ever seen, and transformed right before his eyes.

It was the touch of Paiax that truly made Elsifor special. She had told him children were sometimes born like him, ready for her touch, and for that she adored him more than any mortal could. As he changed, he thought of her. His robe fell from his shifting body. He leapt out of the garment, summoning the change, his bones stretching with fiery pain, his muscles thickening like ropes. Out came the claws, springing from his fingers. The world poured into his heightened senses. He felt the teeth burst from his gums, the taste of blood in his mouth.

Human screams reached his twitching ears. Shocked faces froze at the sight of him. Elsifor bounded through them as he spied the distant tailor shop. Somewhere behind him Haru was trying to keep up, but Elsifor knew only he could reach Siva in time.

His voice a growl, he cried out for the humans to make way. Up ahead he saw the tailor shop at last. He spied the roof, caught a glimpse of the crouching Siva, and raced toward her.

Shadur stood in the center of the crowded square, listening to Reius with a secretive smile. The madman was talking about peace. Shadur marveled at the size of him. The so-called holy man wore simple, almost peasant-like clothes, his eyes sparking with zeal. His voice was musical. His words poetic.

Shadur prayed as he listened, summoning the gift of his patron god, and very calmly slipped off his velvet glove.

After nearly four minutes, Siva had heard enough. With Reius' voice rolling over the courtyard, she stood up from behind her crenellated shield. Half a mile away, the man who'd murdered her beloved Sh'an looked small on his candlelit balcony. She held the atlatl just the way she'd practiced, just as Jaiakrin had taught her, and drew back for the blow. Instantly, the summoned power of her patron appeared, scintillating into a glowing spear. Siva steadied herself.

"Jaiakrin, guide my hand," she whispered.

"Siva, no!"

The cry came just as Siva released the spear. A creature bounded into her, knocking her down, misdirecting her bolt. She hit the stone roof hard.

"Motherless whore!"

Elsifor was over her, holding her down, his body convulsing and transforming. He looked with horror toward the balcony.

"Idiot!" cried Siva. "You—"

"Quiet!" growled Elsifor, covering her mouth. A flash lit his hairy face. A rumble shook the roof. Siva didn't need to look. She ripped Elsifor's hand from her mouth.

"Damn you, Elsifor!" she hissed. "Damn you forever!"

Haru had almost reached the tailor shop when he saw the glowing spear streak overhead. Like a fast, flaming bird, it showered the balcony in sparks.

"No," he groaned. "Oh, no."

A sickening knot tied in his stomach. He scanned the balcony for a hint of Reius. A stunned silence gripped the crowd, followed by a mournful wail. Reius was down. Maybe dead. Maybe not.

"Clionet, help me," he gasped. "I need to find Val!"

Then, before he remembered what was happening, a spout of black fire erupted in the courtyard.

Of all the gods the Cryori worshipped, Skorthoros was certainly the oddest. Shadur had known that all his life, yet had devoted himself to the strange deity, making requests of Skorthoros that sometimes were granted and sometimes were not. For this request, Shadur had prayed mightily.

Between life and death was a barrier of fire. Black and terrifying, it was a thing that Shadur had studied for years and still didn't understand. He felt its frigid heat every time he summoned Skorthoros or spoke to the dead or used his gifts to glimpse the future. He had suffered its fury when he'd turned his hand of flesh to glass. But the black fire could be summoned and shaped, and it could be done through Shadur's crystal hand...*if* Skorthoros allowed it.

Shadur had watched Siva's spear fly across the sky. He felt the impact and the flash. He waited curiously for Reius to reappear. When the holy man did not, a wicked smile crossed his face. He took his time counting to ten, then raised his crystal hand and loosed the gloomy flames. It spewed from his fingers like a fireball, astonishing him and blinding him with its black light, blowing out the moon lanterns and darkening the sky. Babies cried and children screamed. Stricken on-lookers covered their dazzled eyes.

When panic finally, fully seized them, the humans ran.

Chapter Thirty

THE TEMPLE OF TYRANTS

R un. That was the only thing Haru had thought to do.

If he'd been a real Tain—if he'd been his father—he might have hatched a better scheme. But he'd run just like the humans, speeding off to the temple ruins as planned, leaving Valivan behind. Now, crouched beneath a forlorn statue of the goddess Paiax, he fought to catch his breath and consider what he'd done. A jagged gash in the roof of the dilapidated temple let moonlight dapple the goddess' face. Dust and filth swirled at her stone feet, blown in through the missing doors. Elsifor stood guard at the broken entrance, hidden in gloom, listening to the commotion of the disoriented city. Siva still had her atlatl in hand. Her open robe revealed a belt of knives. On the other side of the temple, Shadur peeked through a gaping window, the glass shattered long-ago. Paiax looked at them all with half a face, the other half smashed away by human vandals.

Haru could barely straighten. He bent at the waist, panting with his hands on his knees, thinking he might vomit. The night had been a disaster, and he was to blame for it—all of it. He closed his eyes, trying to focus on Valivan, to summon his friend's gentle face and reach his hidden mind, but all he felt was blackness and terror.

"He's gone," he said again. The realization nearly collapsed him. He looked up at Siva. "Gods, Siva, he's gone!"

Siva stooped and put a hand on his shoulder. "Haru, you need to listen to me. We can't stay here. We have to move."

"Not without Val," groaned Haru. "We have to go back for him."

"They'll be looking for us, Haru. They've probably already started." Siva's tone was fearless. "Catch your breath but do it fast."

Shadur moved away from the window. "Nothing." He called across the temple to Elsifor. "Anything?"

"I hear people but they're not getting closer," replied Elsifor. His shirt hung from his torso in rags, shredded by his transformation. A hint of his jaguar form made his voice sound gravelly. "Not soldiers. Just normal people, I think. For now."

"Haru, Siva's right," said Shadur. "We have to go. They'll be looking for whoever killed Reius."

"I *didn't* kill Reius," seethed Siva. "He's alive. I know he is." Her eyes flicked hotly toward Elsifor. "I missed him."

"I saw the blast," said Shadur. "That spear probably killed him."

"Probably?" spat Siva.

"It wasn't Elsifor, it was me," said Haru. He stood and faced Siva. "I tried to call it off. They took Valivan, but I didn't know it." His throat constricted. "They took him."

"But who?" wondered Shadur. "You said Reius trusted you, Haru."

"I don't know," said Haru. "Priests? They circled around me before Reius came out. They separated us."

"Priests," muttered Shadur. "It's Malon. It must be. She sent that old fool Orkorlis to spy on us."

"No." Elsifor's voice came angrily out of the dark. "It wasn't Orkorlis."

"We don't know who it was, so stop guessing," ordered Siva. "It doesn't matter who did it. Valivan's gone. And we've got to go. Now."

"I'm not going without him," said Haru. "I have to go back for him."

Shadur scoffed. Elsifor was quiet.

"Haru, you're not thinking straight," said Siva. "Your eyes—you look like a mad dog."

"I'm the one that left him!"

Siva's hand snapped out and grabbed his collar. She spun him around and smashed him back against the huge statue. "You're not going anywhere near the palace again. You're coming with us.

Stop being an idiot and think!" She banged him against the stone. "Valivan's gone. Probably dead. Now you start living with that, you hear me?"

"I'll trade myself for him," said Haru. "If he's still alive, they'll want me!"

"And what about Nesenor?" raged Siva. "Are we supposed to lose another Tain? We just started a war! We have to get home. We have to get *you* home!"

Haru heard her words as if through a haze. "But I *promised* him. I said we'd all make it back!"

"Well, you were wrong," said Siva mercilessly. She held on to his collar, putting her nose right into his face. "And you were stupid. Stupid to think that you could do this without risk. Stupid to call it off when I could have killed Reius!"

"Wait, quiet!" hissed Elsifor. In the shadow of the open entrance, he cocked his head toward the outside. "They're coming."

Siva released Haru and took two blades from her belt. Shadur quickly stepped up beside her. Haru searched his belt for a weapon, realizing dreadfully he had nothing.

"We should go," he whispered. "Through the window."

"No," said Siva quickly. "Elsifor, hide."

"What?" blurted Haru.

"Shut up and stand there," said Siva. "Let them see us."

Elsifor backed away from the wide entrance, clinging closely to the wall. His razor-like claws extended slowly from his finger tips. The noise of approaching men grew louder suddenly, crunching on the dead leaves outside the temple. The footfalls paused just out of sight. A moment later four burly men appeared in the threshold. Soldiers, Haru realized. Stunned expressions lit their faces when they noticed Haru and his two companions.

They might have been Lumeszians or Ghanans—Haru couldn't tell from their scarlet armor, nor remember one human tribe for another. All four drew their swords. Their leader stepped cautiously forward.

"Cryori," he pronounced, stunned that he and his men had actually found them.

Haru said nothing, following Siva's lead. The soldiers each took another step closer.

"You need to surrender," said the leader. He hefted his weapon. "If you fight us, you'll lose."

Siva twirled her knives in both hands. "Elsifor, don't let them leave."

Out of the shadows came Elsifor, blocking the exit. In the dark he had transformed again. Now, halfway between man and beast, his yellow eyes glowed with bloodlust. Shadur pushed Haru back behind him and Siva. The soldiers positioned themselves to fight.

"The throats, Elsifor," said Siva calmly. "Quick, so they can't scream. Like this..."

Her hands flashed outward, firing her blades. The lead soldier caught them with his neck. He wobbled, eyes widening as his wind-pipe opened, whistling blood. His sword clanged to the floor. As he crumpled Siva sprang, unsheathing another pair of knives and bounding over the fallen man to reach his shocked companions. Elsifor joined her with a growl. His outstretched claws severed an elbow as a soldier bumbled a blow, then spun to rupture his throat. Blood pumped from the soldier's wound, splashing Elsifor's face as Siva's blades found their target, taking off a head with two quick slices. The helmeted head tumbled to the floor. The last, horrified soldier stared at it, his sword trembling. He opened his mouth to shout...

And Elsifor's claw came out of it.

The man dangled like a puppet from Elsifor's gory hand, his face burst open from behind. Elsifor pulled back his appendage and let the soldier fall into the heap at his feet. Animalistic pleasure lit his eyes as he licked the blood from his furry fist. Siva stooped and pulled her knives from the freshly killed soldiers. She wiped them on the scarlet uniforms, replaced them in her belt, and strode back toward Haru.

"I'm in charge now," she told him. "Not you. We're your body-guards and we're going to keep you alive. We're not losing anyone else."

"We're the very Bloody Chorus!" chimed Elsifor.

"We have to go," said Shadur. "They'll be more coming."

"Wait," said Siva. She looked right at Haru. "We can make it if you listen to me," she told him. "I'll get you home. Nesenor needs you. Just do what I say. Will you do as I say?"

All Haru could think about was Valivan. Choked with guilt, he nodded. "I will."

"Good," said Siva. "Now let's strip what we can from these fools and get moving. Grab a weapon."

Haru moved like syrup, confused and unsure what to look for on the corpses. He avoided the decapitated one completely, going to the one Siva had killed first—the leader. Warm blood sluiced from the man's cut throat. Amazingly, he still clung to a fraction of life, his beating heart animating his chest. Haru reached out and closed the man's searching eyes, then rummaged quickly through the pockets of his uniform. He felt something square and hard and pulled it out.

"What's that?" asked Shadur as he quickly searched the others.

"A book," said Haru. He held it up to the moonlight. "A journal, I think."

"Leave it," ordered Siva. "Get his sword."

But Haru couldn't leave the journal behind. His own bloody fingerprints had already marred its leather cover. It was his now. He stuffed it into his pocket, then swept up the man's sword and stood. Shadur and Siva quickly finished fishing through the other soldiers, taking some money and undoing their sword belts. Seeing this, Haru stooped again and undid the belt and sheath from the man he'd just robbed. He fixed it around his waist, placed the weapon in its holder, and looked to Siva.

"Now what?"

"We go."

"What if they see us?"

Siva looked at him as if it was the stupidest question ever. "If they see us, they die. Come on."

She was first to the exit, searching the outside and then stealthily exiting the temple. Elsifor followed close behind her, as did Shadur. Haru gave the dead men a final look, then went after his comrades. The night was surprisingly still, the ruins hidden from the rest of the city by the trees and weeds that had grown untended around the dilapidated temple. Siva gazed around for the best way out, then began stalking toward the single road she knew passed nearby. No one said a word as they picked their way over the grass and dead leaves, sticking as much as they could to the shadows. The city was loud in the distance. The lights from the infinite moon lanterns cast a glow through the trees. This would be the hardest part, Haru knew—escaping the city. Their odds were exceedingly bad.

When they reached the road, Siva stopped. The rest of them froze.

"No," groaned Siva.

Haru hurried up beside her. There in the road sat a beat-up carriage with a square, covered buckboard and two brown, tired-looking horses. A driver sat atop the cab—a bald man with a peculiar smile. Though he'd managed to cover up his priestly robes with a long, dusty coat, they recognized the man at once.

"Orkorlis?" whispered Elsifor.

The priest put a finger to his lips to silence them, then waved at them to hurry.

"It's impossible," said Haru.

"It's Orkorlis!" argued Elsifor.

"Why?" asked Siva. She raised a threatening knife as she approached the wagon. "How did you find us, priest?"

"No, no time," whispered Orkorlis. He looked terrified, but not of Siva. "Get in the wagon now."

"Orkorlis, we can't!" said Elsifor. "We can't trust you!"

"You have to trust me! If I found you this easily so will others. People are leaving the city. We can hide in the panic."

Haru studied Orkorlis' face. He saw no deception, only fear. Though he'd agreed to follow Siva, he made a decision for all of them.

"Get in the wagon," he told the others. "We're going with him."

Chapter Thirty-One

THE VOICE

For a day and a half Malon waited over Reius' bed, praying over her unconscious friend and staring quietly at his wounds. The physicians had managed to stop the bleeding from his shoulder and neck, promising they'd done a "good, clean job" of sawing off his useless right arm. They had pumped him full of medicines as well, mysterious potions they said would help him survive and quiet his pain. But they could not predict when the prophet would awaken again, and so Malon worried, refusing food and rest as she watched over Reius like a grieving mother and imagined her revenge. She had not expected the magical blow, for surely that's what it was. She had seen the lightning bolt herself, appearing from nowhere out of a perfectly clear sky. Had Reius let her be more protective, Malon knew she could have stopped the Cryori plotters. Instead, she had only managed to grab one of them, tragically too late.

Malon herself was half asleep when Reius finally awakened. The room smelled like blood and burnt flesh, and Malon was slumped over in her chair. She heard the rustle of the sheets and a straggled murmuring. The shock of seeing Reius rouse himself awakened Malon at once. She got out of her chair and hovered closely over her friend.

"He's awake!" cried Malon. "Come in here!"

A pair of physicians, the best Malon could find, hurried into the chamber. They had tended to Reius since he'd been dragged back into the palace, and the relief on their faces now was palpable. One put a hand on Reius' damp brow, testing the prophet's fever. The other took his wrist and tapped his palm.

"Holy One?" he probed. "Can you open your eyes?"

Malon held her breath. Very slowly, Reius' eyes fluttered open. The physicians beamed. Eager to be the first one seen, Malon pushed closer and smiled to get Reius' attention.

"I'm here, Reius," she said. "You're in the palace. You're alright now."

Reius' eyes had lost their intensity, but he managed to hold Malon's gaze. His lips moved with effort, the pain of his bandaged throat evident. Finally, he spoke a single, whispered word.

"Haru?"

Malon grimaced, crestfallen. "No. No, it's me. It's Malon. I've been here with you the whole time."

Reius thought for a moment, then nodded.

"Chancellor, he's still feverish," said the first physician. "We should let him rest."

"Yes, we should," agreed Malon. "Leave us."

The men shared a confused glance.

"Go," hissed Malon.

The physicians hesitated, considered arguing, then wisely kept their mouths closed, leaving Malon alone with Reius and the stench of sickness. Malon went to the window and opened the curtain a little more, providing cheery sunlight to the room. She had much to discuss with Reius, much of it bleak. The light would make it more bearable. Outside, hundreds of people were holding a vigil, waiting for word of their beloved Prophet. They noticed Malon in the window at once, cheering when she waved to them.

"Hear that?" asked Malon. She turned back to the bed. "That's for you. The whole city prays for you, my dear one. Their prayers have brought you back to us."

Reius' eyes darted about the room in confusion, then became clearer as his memories coalesced. He cleared his throat and rasped, "Tell me."

Malon went back to the chair, pulling it close to Reius as she sat. She had wondered how she would make her confession, and now that the time had come it seemed no easier. She reached out and stroked the hair above Reius' forehead, gleaning a sad smile from her friend.

"It was Tain Haru," said Malon. "He and his people tried to kill you. Do you remember?"

Reius thought a moment. He struggled to speak. "The balcony."

"That's right. Now just listen to me. Don't talk..."

"My arm," croaked Reius. "Hurts."

"I know," nodded Malon. She tried to keep the sorrow from her face. "They had to take it, Reius. Your arm was burned too badly. It's gone."

Reius turned his head to see. "I feel it."

"I suppose a salamander feels its tail after it's been chopped off. There's a hole in your throat too. Do you feel that?"

Reius nodded.

"You have some cuts in your belly and a broken rib or two," Malon continued. "But your legs are good. You'll have no trouble walking. You need rest, though. You have a crack on your head the physicians are worried about. You'll feel dizzy if you try to rise, so don't."

"I must walk."

"And you will. You are a giant. You will be a giant again," Malon assured him. "Do not be afraid. I will not let anything harm you."

Reius looked away, his eyes welling with emotion. "Haru..."

"He has betrayed you. But we'll find him. We already have one of his cohorts." Malon summoned her courage. "Reius, you trusted him, and look what it brought you. Forgive me but this must be said. I did not do as you asked of me."

A questioning rumble came from Reius' bandaged throat.

"I disobeyed you," Malon confessed. "But it's not my job to trust! It is my job to protect you and the word of Taan. So, I had them watched when I could. It was only that night that I knew they were plotting something. I'm sorry..." Malon squeezed Reius' hand for forgiveness. "I tried to save you. Now I will avenge you."

Reius began to sob. He let go of Malon's hand, searching the stump of his arm and gritting his teeth against the tears. "Peace," he shuddered. "I wanted peace."

"I know! I know you did. You did all you could for it!"

"Taan wishes it! He told me so!"

Malon pushed back her chair and fell to her knees at the beside. "Taan knows you tried! He knows your heart better than anyone. You are his beloved! How many times have I fallen to my knees to him? How many times have I begged him to speak to me? I hear nothing, because you are his chosen. You are his voice."

Reius shook his head as if Malon's praise was unbearable. He took his hand from his severed shoulder and wiped at his tears until Malon produced a silk handkerchief and did it for him.

"Now stop this," said Malon gently. "There are a thousand people in the square that love you. Remember, you are a soldier of Taan! You must be strong for us all." She smiled as she dabbed at Reius' tears. "But while you are unwell, you must let me help you. You tried to make peace, but now you must see the will of Taan in your failure."

Reius tried to speak but Malon stopped him.

"No, you *must*," scolded Malon. "See his hand in this, Reius. The time has come."

"Not yet," burbled Reius. He put up his hand. "No."

Malon sat back and regarded him. "Don't frustrate me, old friend. Let me do what must be done. The White Fleet is ready. I know you are heart-broken, but you must bear it."

Reius turned his head away.

"Then at least let me hunt them down," pleaded Malon. "Take my shackles off! I'll find them and I'll kill them for what they did to you. And when we make war on Nesenor—"

"Wait," rumbled Reius. "You will wait." He closed his eyes. "I must pray."

"Yes," sighed Malon. She rose from her knees. "Rest and pray. And as soon as you are ready, let me know your mind." She smiled despite her disappointment. "Just remember how Tain Haru wronged you. He may be a charming boy, but he showed he is your enemy."

"Go," implored Reius.

His voice was a ghost of what it had been. Malon tried to smile. "Rest," she said. "Rest and trust me."

She bent low and kissed her friend's cheek, then left the chamber, exhausted and glad to be away from the unsettling smells. She needed sleep and she needed food, but there was one more thing to do first. Out in the hall she found the physicians, waiting for her.

With them stood Count Whistler. Haggard and worried, the Count approached Malon quickly.

"Walk with me," Malon commanded. She said to the physicians, "The Prophet must be given ease. Provide it."

Both men gibbered a response, then hurried to check on their patient. Malon strode away with Count Whistler on her heels.

"How is he?" asked Whistler.

"He lives, no thanks to the Cryori."

"I know he's alive, Chancellor. But how is he? How's his mind? Is he strong?"

"He is strong enough to do what must be done. And so am I." Malon stopped and faced Whistler. "He has yet to give the word, so for now we wait. Go back to Agon. Sea-Master Larius will take you aboard the *Witch Breaker*. The rest of the White Fleet will arrive soon after. Prepare."

Whistler's old face was whiter than usual. "Did he say that?"

"I said that," hissed Malon. "You may have a tender spot for that demon-loving Tain, but I do not. And once Reius comes to his wits he won't either. You're a Lord Guardian now, Count. You'll do what the Alliance requires."

"I will," said Whistler. "I have."

"You've done nothing but indulge Reius' fanciful dreams. You brought Tain Haru here, Count." Malon pressed a finger against Whistler's chest. "*You* said he could be trusted."

Whistler grimaced. "Then who killed his father?"

"How should I know? Kings die all the time!" Malon pointed back the way they'd come. "There's one lying there right now! Assassins are always preying on kings. I don't know who killed Sh'an, Count Whistler, but I know who'll kill his son. Me!" The galloping in her head made Malon rub her powdered brow. "I need sleep. You get aboard the *Witch Breaker*. I know how you love sea travel."

"Yes," said Whistler dryly.

Malon turned away, disgusted. "And no more talk of peace. If I ever hear you utter that word again, you'll be my guest in the tower. Like that stuttering idiot Valivan."

Reius slept.

His brief talk with Malon had exhausted him, and the medicines his physicians had forced through his veins had made his eyelids too heavy to open. Ghosts and memories chased him. Nightmares clawed at his mind. He tried to rouse himself a dozen times, falling each time into the abyss of slumber, and he wondered how close to death he was, and if Taan was waiting for him on the other side. Death would be a release, he decided, but not unless Taan willed it. To pray for death would be unholy.

Then, at midnight, Reius awoke. A bell tolled the hour in the square, echoing through the open window of his chamber, reaching into the darkness of his mind. The beautiful plainness of the tolling soothed him. His eyes opened out of a dream. His room was empty; Malon had gone. Reius thought he was alone until he heard the familiar voice inside his head.

"Yes," he whispered with a smile.

He listened. Absently he touched his bandaged shoulder stump. The pain was gone. He cleared his throat, able to speak without rasping.

"Thank you." Taan's love surged through him. "Adored one..."

He lifted his head off the pillow. The stranglehold of sleep had left him. He kicked off the sheets, tossed his legs over the bedside, and got to his feet, realizing Taan would catch him if he stumbled.

"My arm?" he asked hopefully.

The answer disappointed him.

"Of course, you're right," he said. He didn't need an arm. He had the grace of heaven, and that was stronger than anything.

"Your will was peace," he said softly, drifting toward the open window. A breeze stirred the curtains. Reius hid behind the fabric, peeking curiously into the square below. The quiet vigil Malon had told him about continued. Hundreds of people had gathered, all of them silent now so not to disturb their slumbering prophet. The sight of them warmed Reius. He backed away from the window. "You confuse me," he said.

He listened to the reply. No man could comprehend the awesome strangeness of Taan, not even him.

"Yes," he said. "But why all of this?"

Taan silenced him, commanding him to listen. They had tried peace and failed. The Cryori boy had betrayed him. Tried to kill him. And used magic to do so. Reius nodded, trying to unknot Taan's plan. It was the betrayal that pained him more than anything.

"I tried," he lamented. "I tried and he deceived me..."

Forgiveness fell on him like rain. As a soldier he'd been deceived, many times. Deception was the way of war. Reius knew he had not brought this war upon them. He basked in Taan's mercy, letting it cleanse his conscience. Haru had birthed the war. Haru, who he'd taken into his confidence. Haru, who he'd dared to think a friend.

"Attend me!" Reius cried suddenly.

Out in the corridor a servant stirred, roused by the command. He hurried into the chamber, rubbing sleep from his eyes until he saw the prophet standing before him. Astonishment shook the man awake. He fell to his knees at the sight.

"Holy One! You are healed!"

The words sounded strange to Reius through the fog of medicines. "Find Chancellor Malon," he told the man. "Have her bring my boys to me."

Chapter Thirty-Two

THE ROAD TO AGON

O rkorlis had no map, but he knew the landscape of the continent better than any priest should. In his days before hearing the call of Taan his exploits had taken him throughout the countries that now made up the J'horan Alliance, on the run from authorities and angry husbands and working—sometimes begging—for food. They were good days, Orkorlis explained, regaling his captive audience from the cab of the wagon he'd stolen while they huddled unseen in the covered buckboard. Incredibly, the old priest had no regrets. Not even over helping his new Cryori friends escape.

For two days they travelled north, joining the hundreds of other homebound travelers who'd left the city after the festival. Though they mostly avoided contact, Orkorlis had persuaded them not to risk the smaller, poorly maintained roads. They should hide in plain sight, he explained, keeping to themselves while he did all the talking.

And talk he did.

When they'd first left J'hora, he told Haru and the others how Malon had grown suspicious, and how the Chancellor had called a handful of his most trusted priests into secretive meetings. They were to keep an eye on the Cryori, Orkorlis had heard, but at first he had thought the stories mere rumors, because everyone knew that Reius had guaranteed their safety and that Reius' word was all that mattered. It wasn't until that night—that terrible night—that Orkorlis knew what was really going on.

"She never trusted me," Orkorlis told them bitterly, "because she knew I never liked her."

Malon had kept her secrets close, and had likely taken Valivan herself. Orkorlis' warning was chilling.

"If your friend is still alive, he's been taken to the Tower."

The idea of Valivan being in Malon's hands sickened Haru, and he argued again about turning around and giving himself up. Siva, of course, rejected the idea completely, and Orkorlis backed her up with his usual, folksy logic.

"Then Malon will have both of you," he said.

There would be no trade, he told them all, for Malon was not a woman who bargained. She was the iron fist of J'hora, trusted by Reius and feared by all, and if she found Haru she would surely dissect him with a grin on her face and glass of wine in her hand.

"Pray your friend is already dead," urged Orkorlis. "To whatever remarkable creatures you call gods...pray."

But Haru did not pray. Too full of anger, he knew he didn't deserve absolution. He had abandoned Valivan. After lecturing Val to stay focused, he himself had panicked. If he could have traded himself for his friend he would have done so gladly, but now he had to find the logic in Siva's plan. He was still Nesenor's Tain. He still had a war to win.

Shadur, however, prayed mightily. Keeping to himself in a corner of the wooden wagon and speaking in the dead language his patron favored, he strove to contact his strange god. Skorthoros had been silent since that night, and the pain of it made Shadur grim. To Siva, who knew her patron's love was boundless, Skorthoros' silence was confounding. She comforted Shadur with compliments, but her words were unappreciated. As the hours wore on, Shadur shrank from them all, eager to get home to his old, neglected house.

Finally, on the third night of their journey, Elsifor had Orkorlis to himself. They had stopped on the outskirts of an abandoned farm, driving their wagon deep in the brush and using the cover of rain clouds to hide them. Orkorlis, insisting that they take advantage of the rain, left the others in the buckboard and, with a metal bucket in hand, stalked out into an overgrown potato field to catch the drizzle. It was an entirely mad idea, and Elsifor realized—perhaps for the very first time—that the man who'd rescued them was probably insane. Siva snickered and elected Elsifor to follow him, but she needn't have bothered—Elsifor was quick on the old priest's heels.

In the moonless night Elsifor found him, standing in the knee-high weeds, his bucket outstretched, his face turned heavenward and sprinkled with drizzle. The farmhouse stood like a wraith in the distance, sad and dilapidated. Far from the chaos of J'hora, the world seemed easeful; the sky, impossibly big. Elsifor sidled next to Orkorlis. He stuck out his hand.

"Not much rain to catch," he remarked.

Orkorlis kept his bucket out and his eyes on the sky. "It'll come. We need it."

"We have water, Orkorlis."

"I need it, then."

Elsifor chewed on his answer. He looked harder into the sky. "I can see stars behind the clouds."

"Can you?" Orkorlis smiled. "Remarkable."

"What do you see, Orkorlis?"

"I know what you're asking, Elsifor. Alright, yes—I can't see Taan. But I know he's there."

"That's faith," said Elsifor.

"Now you're learning."

Elsifor nodded. "I think I am." He put out his tongue to catch the rain. It tasted sweet to him, better than it should have. He didn't want to break the spell, but he still had questions. "I have to know something, Orkorlis."

"I didn't betray Reius," said the priest.

"No?"

"I can see it in your eyes. In all your eyes, really. It's alright to wonder; I don't mind explaining. I've seen you change, Elsifor. I've been thinking lately that change is never ending. It's the same as getting older. Even if we like the age we are, we can't stay there. That's like change. It just happens."

"So, you're changing?"

"We met for a reason. Taan made that happen. I couldn't let you die."

Elsifor thought for a moment. "I feel better than I did when I came here. Why is that?"

"The answer is up there," said Orkorlis. "But I know you don't believe that yet."

"I don't think I'll ever believe that," said Elsifor. "But maybe it doesn't matter."

"Maybe not."

"Your arm must be tired. Let me hold the bucket for you."

"No, no. The clouds will thicken. You'll see."

Elsifor was content to wait. For Orkorlis, he knew, the waiting was a penance. He didn't want to consider what would happen to Orkorlis now, or what Malon might do to him. He wasn't even sure that Orkorlis cared. The priest just seemed perfectly, stupidly at ease. After a while Elsifor asked him, "What will you do with the water once you catch it?"

Orkorlis turned to him and replied, "It's not the water. It's that the water comes."

Understanding, Elsifor said no more. Together, they waited for the rain.

It was a two-week journey to Agon, and they knew they would not be home soon. Even on the "good road" Count Whistler had told Haru about, they could only make twenty miles a day. A swollen river or a broken wheel might delay them for days, and though Orkorlis pushed their stolen horses hard, he could not risk exhausting the animals or driving them at night, when a woodchuck hole might break their legs. So they settled in for the long trip, listening to Orkorlis' stories and stopping at night under the stars, where they could at last escape the wagon and stretch without being seen. While Elsifor talked to Orkorlis and Shadur prayed, Haru read the blood-stained journal he'd absconded with from J'hora.

The man's name was Joak Sitirus. A Lumeszian. And on his last night alive he'd eaten pheasant for the first time.

Haru had started reading from the back of the journal first. Joak Sitirus was a soldier—a constable he called himself—who filled his book with the most compelling, mundane things. His wife was named Marciane. He'd married her when she was fifteen and her hair was the color of autumn. They had one child, a boy named Treg, who'd just turned four a few days before his father left for J'hora—a father he'd never see again.

Joak. That's what Haru had come to call him. He guarded the journal jealously, harboring the thought that someday—somehow—he might return it to the woman Marciane. He would apologize, he imagined, and maybe bring a gift for the boy. But his plan embarrassed him, and he knew if he shared it with Siva she would laugh and call him a fool.

A fool. He'd been one a lot in his life. Now he needed to change himself.

By their third night on the road, they'd managed to leave behind most of the pilgrims from J'hora, enjoying enough privacy to peek out of the wagon from time to time or relieve themselves by the roadside. The weather had cooperated so far, and the towns they encountered had accommodated them, allowing Orkorlis to buy food for their journey and fill his skins with water. On this particular night, they had left a town called Moon Hollow behind, parking the wagon an hour from the merchant village along the quiet road. Like a father with a load of cranky children, Orkorlis let his brood out to enjoy the air, confident they were far enough from J'hora now to manage the risk.

Elsifor was first out of the wagon. Having heard a bird in a nearby tree, he bolted like a savage from the covered buckboard, leaping into the dark sequoias to hunt. Shadur was next, eager for a private place to pray, and Siva and Haru looked at each other a moment, alone for the first time in days. Haru still had the journal in his hands, Siva a knife. She nodded when Orkorlis urged them to go.

"If you want to stretch, I'll protect you," she told Haru.

"I'll be fine," said Haru. He tucked the journal into his pocket and climbed out of the wagon. "I have my dagger."

"You have no idea how to use it. I'm coming with you."

She jumped out beside him and glanced around. Night had fallen darkly, with only the moon and stars to give them light. Shadur found a spot far enough away were his appeals to Skorthoros couldn't be heard, and Elsifor scrambled through the treetops, unhindered by the gloom. A lantern was out of the question; only a campfire would do, and then only when Orkorlis was around. When she was sure they were safe, Siva pointed toward a fallen tree.

"There," she directed.

"Am I your prisoner?" Haru squawked. "I don't want to sit. I've been sitting all day, remember?"

"Then just walk circles around it," said Siva. "It's dark. I just don't want to lose you."

"I can take care of myself, Siva."

With her knife Siva directed him toward the tree. "That's obviously not true. Go. I want to talk to you."

Haru made his way to the overturned tree, brushing away the fungus sprouting like ears from the dead bark. Orkorlis got down from the wagon and began collecting kindling for the cooking fire. Watching him made Haru hungry. He sat and looked up at Siva, her face framed by the moon just behind her head. "So?"

"We should talk about Valivan."

"I tried to talk about him. You wouldn't let me."

"Because going back for him would have been gigantically stupid. Even suggesting that makes me afraid for you."

"For me? Or for you?"

"I'll forget you said that. I'm not going to tell you that what happened to Valivan isn't your fault. Maybe you want me to, but I won't. I don't know what happened that night. We all blundered, I suppose.

Maybe we're all at fault. I don't care if you blame yourself or not. I just want you to listen to me now."

"You don't think I can be a good Tain. You never thought so."

"You're *not* a good Tain, Haru. Not yet. You're young. Maybe someday."

"You're only two years older than me, Siva."

"They must have been important years, then."

The argument was going the way all their arguments went. Haru wanted to leave, but he knew Siva was right—he did want her comfort. Anything to ease his pain.

"Here," he said, and pulled the journal from his pocket. "Look at this."

Siva frowned. "Why do you read that? Toss it away."

"No, I'm keeping it," said Haru. He held the little book in both hands. "Reading this can help make me a better Tain."

Siva hovered over him without a word. She put her knife back in its sheath. She slipped down beside him on the log. Haru couldn't look at her. He looked only at the journal.

"Joak Sitirus," he whispered. "That was his name. He grew up on a farm. He hated us. He hated all Cryori. He blamed us for the wars we left behind. But he loved the Alliance." He tapped the journal with his fingertip. "It's all in here. All the things Reius told me when I was with him. It's all true. All the things we did."

"We didn't do any of those things, Haru. It was a long time ago."

"But I'm one of them, Siva. I came here to start a war and now all I want is peace."

"You came here to avenge your father."

"And I failed in that too. I fail in everything! But not anymore. I'm going back to Nesenor and I'm going to be a great Tain. Not a good one—a *great* one. I'm going to make us stand for something. We're not going to be cowards but we're not going to be war-mongers either. So people like Joak don't grow up hating us."

"Joak?"

"That's what I call him. He's like a friend or...something."

"He had to die, Haru. He would have killed us."

"So, not a friend, then." Haru smiled sadly. "Valivan was a friend." The pain of it gripped him. "Siva, I don't know what to hope—if I should hope he's alive or hope he's dead. Malon is a beast. She'll torture him and love it. Torture is a treat for her."

"Don't," said Siva. "Just think of him as gone. Think of him the way he used to be. That's what I do. That's how you go on. And we have to go on, Haru. We have to get you home." She nudged him playfully. "You have big plans for us."

Haru held tightly to the journal. "I have to fix things, Siva." He shrugged. "Somehow."

Siva tossed one leg over the log, straddling it to face him. "You should know that I'm going to get you home, Haru. You should know that I'll protect you. I let Sh'an die, but I won't let you die."

"I believe that," said Haru. "You can stop saying it. You have to stop or you'll go mad again. I'm not my father, Siva. I know you cared about him but we're all to blame for what happened."

"Cared about him?" Siva looked at him pitifully. "Haru, are you blind or just stupid? I didn't just care about your father. I loved him!"

Haru nodded, then frowned. "What?"

"We were lovers, Haru!"

The word jolted Haru. "Lovers?"

"While you were chasing all those serving girls, I was with your father. I was in his bed!"

Suddenly, it was as if the sky collapsed. Haru tried to speak, forcing out his words. "My father?"

"I loved him, Haru. You have to know that." Siva clutched her breast. "I would have torn out my throat to save him."

Haru staggered up from the log. "How long?" he stammered. "You were a child!"

Siva sat calmly. "I'm a woman, Haru. I was broken when Sh'an died. Broken in a way you never were."

"*I* was broken," snarled Haru. "I was his son! I did all of this because of him!"

"Hold it down!" said Orkorlis from the wagon.

Elsifor jumped down from the branches. "What's going on?"

Haru threw up his hands. "I can't say it. I can't even think about it!"

Siva opened her mouth to speak, but a wail from the darkness cut her off. From out the shadows came Shadur, holding up his crystal hand, his face a tangle of agony. Siva sprang to her feet. Shadur stumbled forward, turning his hand in the moonlight.

"Shadur?" said Haru. "What's wrong?"

"My hand!" cried Shadur. "It's dark!"

Haru looked closely at the appendage. The light had indeed gone out of it.

"Skorthoros is gone," said Shadur. "I am abandoned!"

Chapter Thirty-Three

SESSIONS

T here were no rats in Malon's prison. Valivan had expected rats for some reason, but the place was as clean and manicured as Malon herself. He had a cell of his own, a wooden bed with no mattress, and a bucket for relieving himself. He had a view of a stone corridor. Food was given sparingly but water was plentiful, yet he had no companionship, not from his guards or fellow prisoners, and each time Valivan spoke he was ignored, his pleas for release unheeded by his jailors. He hadn't been beaten or harmed, but he had lost all track of time in the Tower's windowless dungeon, and he did not know if Haru and the others were alive or dead.

The one thing he never got—the one thing he craved almost as much as freedom—was quiet. His nights and days were punctuated by screams, and he was treated to a parade of victims past his iron bars—naked, white-painted bodies of people who never seemed to return. Hunched in the corner of his cell, he spent his time with his hands over his ears, protecting himself from the incessant howls. Whips cracked and wheels turned, and if he tried very hard Valivan could hear bones snapping—so he never tried again.

For the first time in years, Valivan prayed.

He prayed to Jyx to hear him, to come to him. To save him. But like his troublesome gift, Jyx had left him. He could no longer read the minds of others or hear their voices in his head. His odd abilities had fled the second the priests had seized him, as if Jyx had picked that very moment to abandon him. It puzzled and panicked Valivan. For the first time in his life, he understood the word "alone."

It may have been the second day of his captivity, or the third day or the fourth, when at last someone came to him. Valivan rose from his cot as the grim-faced priest arrived at his cell, staring at him through the bars. Two gray-cloaked guards were with him, carrying chains and manacles. Valivan shuddered. His voice crumbled into stutters.

"W-w-w..."

"No talking," said the priest. The guards opened the gate, and the priest told his men, "Strip him down."

Please help me, Jyx. Please help me. Please help me. Please help me...

With no way to speak, his mouth secured with a metal bar, Valivan used his mind to pray. Over and over, he said the same words, reaching out to his fickle god, hoping his silent words could penetrate the walls of his prison. Naked and freezing, he was immobilized in a chair-like device. Tiny wooden spikes covered the back of the chair and ran along its arm rests. Loops of iron with protruding nails held his wrists in place, and a sharp metal bar pinned his bare legs, pressing against his bloodied shins. An iron collar circled his neck, and another strip of metal pinned his face to the headrest, wedged into his teeth and drawing back his cheeks in a grotesque, drooling grimace. Saliva covered his naked chest and belly, and if he moved his eyeballs down enough, he could see his genitals, resting vulnerably between his legs.

Already, his agony was incomprehensible.

He was no longer in a normal cell, but in a room with proper walls and a door. A wooden table stood against the wall farthest from him, and near that waited a simple chair, turned toward him but empty. A collection of metal tools rested on the table, along with an old leather apron. An oil lamp suspended from the ceiling by a chain supplied the room's only light. When Valivan cried out through his metal gag, the tiny flame inside the lamp flickered.

Hours past. Or perhaps merely minutes. Valivan's cries went unanswered, as did his constant prayers. He struggled to fathom why

Jyx had left him, but he could no longer think or keep his terror checked. His heart galloped in his chest. If luck was with him, it would explode and kill him. He felt the drool slide down his chin, the growing pain of his misshapen face, and he wondered if this was all there'd be to his torment, or just the beginning. Unable to kill himself or coax his heart to stop, Valivan closed his eyes and once again sent his unrequited pleas skyward.

Time slowed, cracking Valivan's mind so that only unconsciousness relieved him, and he slipped into it like a warm bath, hoping never to awaken. Then, the worse disturbance he could imagine happened—the door to the chamber opened. Valivan's eyes widened as he saw Malon enter. The Chancellor, dressed in a snow-white jacket and skirt, closed the door politely, then turned to study her naked subject. She did not smile or frown. Gone were her rings and ornaments. Malon stepped closer, cocking her head like a curious dog. She reached out a finger and broke a thread of drool dripping from Valivan's chin, plucking it like a spider web.

"When we're done you can have a bath," she said. "You would like that, yes?"

Her accent was strange to Valivan, her tone gentle. Valivan replied with a whimper. He forced his tongue around the metal bar, trying to speak, but the gag was worse than any stutter.

"No, no, don't talk," said Malon. "You'll speak when I want to hear what you have to say. First, just listen. We have work to do, you and I." She grinned. "Mysteries to uncover." She turned and made her way to the table. "I love to unravel puzzles, and you are a great puzzle, Valivan." Malon surveyed her instruments. "You are a stutterer. You were born that way? No, don't answer!" She chuckled. "I've known many stammerers in my day, Valivan. Some of them came to me with perfect diction but stammered like morons when I was done with them. It's mostly boy children who stutter, did you know that?" Malon took hold of the little wooden chair and dragged it a bit closer. "They say that terrible events can cause a person to start stammering." She sat down and crossed her legs. "You must tell me what terrible things happened to you."

Valivan looked at her, pleading with his eyes, trying to form words.

"I was schooling your friend Haru about torture the other day," said Malon. "I told him that anyone could become a torturer, given enough motivation. I don't think he believed me. Your Tain is a man of principles. Ah, but he's young! It's easy to be principled and young. Getting old is the difficult part. Let's see where his principles are in twenty years, eh? Oh, but we can't. Tain Haru won't be alive much longer."

Valivan bit down on the bar and struggled against the chair, scraping his naked flesh and wincing in pain.

"You want to speak, I know. You want to save yourself. But we need to get to know each other first. If I took that bar out of your mouth, you'd spill all sorts of lies. I need to be sure that what you tell me is the truth. And how do I do that? By making you fear me."

"Iah du!"

"Of course you do. But I have to go deeper, Valivan. I have to drill inside you." Malon tapped her head. "Don't panic—that's just an expression." Her grin was insane. "I actually saw a drill used on a man's skull once. Ghastly!" She shrugged her slight shoulders. "We experiment. We learn. I'm sure it's the same where you come from. I'm sure you have all sorts of things to teach me! Are you curious like me, Valivan?"

Desperate for sympathy, Valivan managed a tiny nod.

"Excellent. Then we will explore each other. I won't be selfish with the details. You must know about me if you're going to trust me." Malon's gaze fell to Valivan's groin. "Does it embarrass you to be naked? Please don't let it. Soon you won't even notice. And I promise you, I will not harm your manhood. Good? That can be my gift to you. So many torturers go for the gonads. They slice them off and toss them away like sweetbreads, then they expect their subject's confidence. Ridiculous, yes?"

She rose from her chair and went to the table, retrieving the leather apron. She slipped it over her head, letting it cover her torso and drape her white skirt, tying it behind her.

"I'm fascinated by your stutter, Valivan," she said. "It's obviously a source of humiliation for you, so I think the best way to really reach you is through your mouth. I'm going to take the gag off now. Please don't speak. Whatever you tell me in this first session won't have any real meaning, alright? Don't try to impress me—just sit back and let it happen." Malon looked at her implements and quickly made a selection—a pair of gleaming pliers. "Let's get started. Ready?"

Valivan broke quickly. Before the first tooth came loose, he had confessed every detail of their plan to kill Reius, letting it spill out of him as his mouth gushed blood and his tongue fought to hold back Malon's pliers. Malon worked through Valivan's screams, ignoring his confession and telling him stories about growing up in Saxoras and her early days as Reius' torturer. She worked precisely and with pride, pulling two of Valivan's back teeth with the help of a tiny saw. She worked for hours without stopping, not even to clean the gore pooling at her shoes, pausing only when she had both bloody teeth extracted and jingling in her fist like coins. She pocketed the teeth, thanked Valivan for the conversation, and left the chamber. By the time the guards came to return him to his cell, Valivan was unconscious. He awoke on his cot, his mouth full of bandages and his clothes still gone. When he realized he hadn't died, Valivan wept.

The second session came the next day. By then Valivan's mouth had swollen so badly that he could no longer speak, an impediment that seemed not to bother Malon at all. Once again, she told stories as she worked, ignoring Valivan's howls, which had grown hoarse and weaker since the previous session. Two more teeth came out that time, joining the others in Malon's pocket. She would return the teeth to Valivan, she promised.

"I will make a souvenir for you," said Malon. "To remember your time in J'hora."

By the third session Valivan had lost all the teeth that mattered on the bottom of his jaw. Malon took longer than usual on these, working in silence as though plotting something worse for her subject. Valivan lost consciousness only once in those four hours, enduring the torture with ghastly resistance. Malon stripped off her gloves when she was done, sighing and nodding approvingly at Valivan.

"I have enough teeth now," she said. "Thank you."

Valivan looked at her, hoping her demented smile meant freedom was coming.

"Rest tonight. We'll let the swelling go down so you can talk tomorrow."

Valivan formed a grunting question. *"Tawk?"*

"You've done a find job of listening," Malon complimented. "Tomorrow, we chat like old friends."

A great sobbed racked Valivan's body. *"Tawk?"*

"Just talk," said Malon. "I'll have some tea brought in."

Back in his cell, Valivan was given clothing again and the attention of a surgeon who treated his wounded mouth and applied medicines to the holes where his teeth had been. He declined both food and water but gratefully accepted the sedative the surgeon provided, drinking the potion as quickly as his damaged mouth allowed before climbing onto his rigid cot. The screams of his fellow prisoners no longer disturbed him—after hearing his own screams so long and loudly, he was deaf to them now. He had lost all sense of time; there was no daylight in his life, only night. His mind had left him. He desired death, but settled for sleep.

The sedative took him quickly and powerfully, and for a blessed while he was gone completely, without fear or a body to torment him. When at last he awoke the prison was silent. His eyes opened to the crushing realization that he was still alive. He stared a moment at the bare ceiling. The lantern in the corridor passed its oily light through the bars of his cell. About to close his eyes again, he noticed a figure at the foot of his cot. He sat up, staring at the apparition, sure that he was dreaming.

"Jyx."

His swollen mouth barely formed the name. Jyx smiled, amused at the attempt.

"I knew you'd miss me."

Valivan struggled to sit up, then spat a wad of bloody saliva. Jyx wiped it from his golden garments, teasing Valivan with a pained expression.

"I know. You blame me. But you should be quiet," he whispered. "If you anger them they might take you to Malon for another session. You still have a fair number of teeth to pull."

His taunts were unbearable. Valivan swiped at him to leave. In all his hours of torture, he'd begged the god to help him. He'd even screamed his name. Now, Valivan could barely stand the sight of him.

"Look at you," said Jyx pitifully. "Look what they've done to you!" He came around the cot and bent over Valivan's face, touching his swollen jaw with his soft fingertips. "My beautiful boy."

You left me! rasped Valivan.

"Haru left you," sighed Jyx. His finger travelled up Valivan's face, stroking his head like a loving father. "I tried to warn you. Do you remember that?"

Valivan angrily swatted away his hand.

"You remember," purred Jyx. "You do. So loyal! You still won't hear a word against him, will you? Do you know where he is now? He's safe with that whore, Siva. While you're here suffering for his imbecilic plans."

"No!"

"Oh yes. He'll probably make love to her." Jyx knelt down to whisper in Valivan's ear. "Another meaningless conquest. How many times did Haru throw you his scraps? Like that kitchen girl. What was her name?" He pretended to think. "Megana? As ugly as a smacked ass."

Valivan turned away, but Jyx leaned in closer. His breath smelled like flowers.

"It's Haru that brought you to this," he said. "It breaks my heart that you can't see it. You were always chasing after him, wanting to be like him. Your mother saw it, too. And he was so happy to have you around...like a trained monkey."

"You left me!"

Jyx nodded. "Yes, I did. I wanted to prove that you need me." He bit his lip. "I'm so petty sometimes. It's shameful. But you see? You're really no use at all without me. Have you given a good listen to your voice? It was hardly a prize before. Now, well, you sound like a braying jackass."

The insult made Valivan snap. *"Get out!"*

"Careful," crooned Jyx. "You'll wake your playmates."

"Leave!"

"I can give it back to you, Valivan. Your gift."

"I don't want it," hissed Valivan. "I don't want you!"

Jyx stood up. "Just think on my offer. You'll see—it'll be worth it!"

The trickster god winked then faded into the shadows, leaving Valivan alone again. His slumber ruined, Valivan sank his head into his wooden bed, dreading his next session with Malon.

As promised, Malon had tea waiting when Valivan arrived. The Chancellor, seated in her plain wooden chair, had already begun sampling the assortment of tiny pastries she'd arranged, choosing them with her long fingers and placing them on her porcelain plate. She smiled when the guards brought Valivan into the room, fully clothed and unchained. To Valivan's great relief, the torture chair had been removed, replaced by a duplicate of Malon's own seat. The table had been cleared of instruments, covered now with a frilled cloth that hid its many stains. A steaming teapot rested on the table, painted with pink flowers.

"Valivan, you're going to like this," promised Malon. She looked over the pastries proudly. "These are all favorites of mine from Saxoras. I had the cook make them special for you. Not as good as home, of course. But what is, eh?"

Valivan walked stiffly into the room. The guards left without a word, shutting the door behind them. Oddly, Valivan didn't hear the lock tumble this time. He hovered over the table and its absurd collection of treats.

"They're all soft so you can chew them," said Malon. She selected one off her own plate, a dainty roll of white cake stuffed with syrupy fruit. "Here, try it..."

Valivan shook his head.

"Your mouth looks better," Malon observed. "The swelling has gone down. As I said it would, did I not?" She popped the confection into her mouth, smacking in delight. "Delicious. Sit, please. You should have tea."

The room sickened Valivan. Just being in it again unsteadied him. He sat down in the hard chair, trying hard to hide his fears, knowing the torturer would exploit any little weakness. He watched as Malon poured him tea, dropping lumps of sugar into it and stirring it with a tiny silver spoon. She was once again the familiar Malon, dainty and rouged, her velvet dress both ruffled and ridiculous. Seeing her so meticulous put Valivan at some ease. For today at least, torture was off the schedule.

"Here," said Malon, handing him the cup. "You should drink. It will soothe you." Malon studied Valivan's face as he took his seat. "Your eyes look glassy. If you can speak, say something."

Valivan held the warm tea cup in his lap. He blinked at Malon, hating her but afraid to ignore her orders. "I can speak," he said hoarsely.

Malon brightened. "Your stammer seems better. The medicines have calmed you. Good. We can talk as friends now."

"Friends?" croaked Valivan. "Friends don't pull out teeth with pliers."

"Insults!" beamed Malon. "You *are* feeling better. I should tell you that you were remarkably consistent under the strain." She sipped at her tea. "Your story never changed. So often subjects invent things under questioning, then change their stories when the pain becomes unbearable. But not you, Valivan. You didn't even bother lying. You gave up everything before that first tooth came out." Malon put her tea cup on the table, exchanging it for her plate of confections. "We just need to go over some details." She balanced the plate on her thigh. "You don't mind if I eat while we talk, do you? I've been up late the last few evenings. In your attempt to kill Reius you blew off his right arm. He'll be fine eventually, praise Taan, but for now he's resting."

Valivan sniffed at the news, uninterested.

"Your cohorts haven't been found yet, but they will be. Just to be clear, your plan was to make a run for Agon, yes?"

Valivan nodded.

"Hmm, well, that's disappointing. Count Whistler has been a friend to the Cryori for too long. He's a Lord Guardian now, but...well, doubts linger, don't they? I'm sure you'll understand if I have Haru killed before he reaches Agon."

Haru. Hearing his name made Valivan freeze.

"He's your friend, I know," said Malon. "It will be tough for you. But he's the one that left you here, remember. And he tried to kill *my* friend." Malon stuck a finger in a tart and licked it clean. "That cannot go unpunished."

Listen to her, Valivan. She agrees with me!

The voice made Valivan gasp. He glanced around, looking for Jyx, but the god was only in his head.

"Valivan?" Malon set her plate on the table again. "What is it?"

Look at her. Such a freak. Bird-boned, all that powder on her face... I bet she's a molester.

Malon leaned in closer. "Valivan? Are you afraid for Haru? Don't worry—he won't be brought here to the Tower. I can't risk him getting that close to Reius again. But I can't promise you his death will be quick either. And first I have to find him."

You can help her with that, whispered Jyx. *You should help her with that.*

The words puzzled Valivan. *How?*

"You need to understand what's about to happen," Malon went on. "Your country is going to fall. Eventually, all your silly gods will be erased."

She's talking about me!

Malon reached out and took the tea cup from Valivan's hands. "Are you listening?"

"No," said Valivan. "I'm listening to Jyx."

Yes! whooped Jyx. *Shall I show myself?*

"Jyx." Malon grinned. "You mentioned him. I wrote his name in my notes."

"Jyx is my patron. My god. He's a monster. Like you."

Malon's eyes lit with fascination. "Tell me about him."

Tell her I'm right here!

"He's here with me now," said Valivan without stammering. "He says you're right about Haru. That he left me here."

"Can I see Jyx?" asked Malon.

Jyx scoffed. *You couldn't possibly comprehend me, you chalk-faced vulgarian.*

"Jyx hates humans. He's insulting you now."

Malon licked her lips. "I would dearly love to hear him myself."

Demented, pronounced Jyx.

"Jyx abandoned me," said Valivan. "But he's back now."

I'm not just back, Valivan. I can help you. I can give you back your gift. I can make you more powerful than you ever were!

Without a word, Valivan felt his patron's power flow back into his mind. He closed his eyes, jolted by the surge.

You'll be able to find Haru anywhere he tries to hide, said Jyx. *You'll be able to help this deranged bitch kill him for what he did to you. Do you feel it?*

Valivan did feel it. It wasn't the medicines or his enormous contempt, but the supernatural strength of his maniacal god. He opened his eyes and stared at Malon, looking straight into her brain.

"You were going to kill me after our tea," said Valivan.

Malon grinned. "Did Jyx tell you that?"

"I can see your mind. It's a sewer."

"Indeed?"

Valivan concentrated, penetrating Malon's skull with ease. "That make-up you wear—your parents were performers. You look like them. They passed you around for money."

"They did," said Malon coldly. "What else?"

"When they died you tried to be like them to survive, but you had no talent at all. So you sold yourself."

Malon showed no embarrassment. "That's a talent, of a kind."

Though her demeanor didn't show it, Val could feel her self-disgust. "I can see what those men did to you. And you thought Taan would help you but he didn't."

"Taan has his mysteries," said Malon.

What he found next startled Valivan. "You knew what we were doing..."

Malon smiled.

"You knew we came to kill Reius."

"And you are a bunch of incompetents. Very disappointing."

"I'll tell him," Valivan threatened. "I can reach Reius easily now!"

"You won't," said Malon. "Because you're in the Tower of Principles, and in here I'm the god of everything. Not even Taan holds dominion here, Valivan. Here, I say who lives and dies, and I'm never going to be more than a whisper from giving the order to kill you."

Her coolness terrified Valivan. "Why? I thought you loved Reius."

"I do! Oh, my love is deep and genuine, I swear it. Look into my mind—you'll see I'm telling the truth."

Valivan did see it. In her own, twisted way, Malon adored Reius.

"I gave you every opportunity to kill him," sighed Malon. "Reius can be very charming, I know, but I didn't think your Tain would fall for him so hard. Reius is mad, you see. Tain Haru must have noticed that the moment they met. All that counting when he speaks, all that writing—piles of it! A mountain of trash that no one ever reads. It may be the word of Taan but it's quite tedious, I assure you. That's what happens to a man who speaks with Taan. It shatters the mind."

"So, you'll kill him?"

"I've already started. The surgeons that saved him have been dismissed. I've brought my own healers to care for him. Oh, and he's been eating well, too! The poison should start taking hold soon."

"You're as mad as he is."

Malon flashed a terrible grin. "And now you're one of us."

"I won't let you kill me, Chancellor. You're going to let me out of here. You're going to set me free."

"Am I? Do tell me why."

"You'll do it," Valivan assured him. "Because I'm going to help you find Haru."

Chapter Thirty-Four

REVELATIONS

N uara looked across the harbor at the little boat rowing toward the *Gonkin*. His beast-ship had been at anchor in Jinja for weeks now, stranded in the capital while its sisters prowled the waters that guarded Nesenor from the continent. So far, the White Fleet had been quiet. There'd been no skirmishes between the beast-ships and the seabreakers, but Nuara ached to join them anyway, and he had no idea why he'd been ordered to stay behind.

Ariyo had gone ashore himself to fetch Liadin, a gesture Nuara supposed would impress the old priest. Nuara waved to the boat as it approached. Besides Ariyo and Liadin, two young Venerants were aboard, armed with sukatais. Nuara went to the starboard gunnel as the boat rowed closer and crewmen lowered the rope ladder. Liadin had news, certainly, but the content of it vexed Nuara. He watched as Ariyo expertly guided the boat to the *Gonkin's* hull, quickly grabbing the lines the crew had thrown down. He tied the boat to steady it, tested the ladder, then held out his hand for Liadin.

"Arch-Disciple, I can take the weapon up for you when we bring up the boat," said Ariyo.

Liadin refused the offer and stood. He flipped the sukatai over his shoulder with one hand, tying it onto his back as he'd done countless times before. His bodyguards quickly mimicked him.

"Easy," snapped Ariyo. "Get back down or you'll tip us."

Nuara called down to them, "Arch-Disciple, come ahead. You don't need your guards."

Unafraid, Liadin grabbed the rope ladder with his four-fingered hand. Nuara had seen more than one man fall making the climb, but Liadin made his way up the side of the ship without trouble. Nuara grabbed his arm and helped him over the gunnel.

"He's up!" Nuara called to Ariyo. "Bring the others." He looked Liadin over. "You're alright?"

"I'm old," grumbled Liadin. He looked exhausted. "You've been patient. Thank you for that."

"We've all been waiting," Nuara admitted. "Have we orders finally?"

"You got my dispatches?"

"I did," said Nuara, though in truth they were all just meaningless notes. "But I still have questions."

"You won't like the answers."

"I've made my quarters available to you. We can talk privately there."

Liadin regarded the *Gonkin's* curious crew. "You all want to know where we're going? We're going to Tojira."

The mariners gasped; a handful cursed.

"Tojira?" said Nuara. "That's the holy island. Jaiakrin's island."

"If we leave now, we'll be there before sundown." Liadin watched his bodyguards climb aboard, one after the other. The young priests quickly positioned themselves around him. "Captain Nuara, if you'd give the order, please..."

"Arch-Disciple, I don't know how close we can get to the island. If you're planning on going ashore..."

"I'm not going ashore," said Liadin. "But you need to get us close. Don't worry, Nuara—Ama'aga will protect us. We should talk now. Your quarters?"

Nuara felt the questioning eyes of his crew. Down below, his Sailing Master was still in the rowboat. "Get him aboard," said Nuara to his men. "Prepare to sail."

"For Tojira?" asked a crewman.

"Yes." Nuara didn't wait for Ariyo to try to talk him out of it. "Quickly now. Daylight's burning."

The crew hesitated, then went to work. Nuara gestured for Liadin to follow him. With the young Venerants in tow, they made their way to the back of the ship where Nuara's cabin waited. Liadin told the men to wait outside, then followed Nuara into the chamber and closed the little door. He took the sukatai off his back, laid it against Nuara's desk, and fell with a sigh into the solitary chair. Sunlight streamed through the window. The creak of tightening ropes and the rattle of anchor chains reached in from the decks. Nuara went to his liquor cabinet, choosing a bottle of wine he'd brought back from Lomoa and two short, crystal glasses.

"Why the bodyguards?" he asked as he poured them each a drink.

"I'm a suspicious old man," said Liadin. "Take offense if you wish, but none was meant by it."

Nuara offered him a glass. "Wine from Lomoa—my home village."

Liadin sniffed the amber liquid and blinked. "Smells like Ama'aga's feet." He took a huge gulp, emptying his glass with a whoop. "Oh!"

Nuara traded glasses with the priest. "So, it's bad news, then."

"That's all priests ever bring, haven't you ever noticed that?" Liadin drained the second glass only a little more slowly than he had the first. He leaned his head back in the chair and grinned crookedly at Nuara. "Get one for yourself."

Nuara grabbed the bottle again and refilled both glasses. He moved to his berth against the window and sat down.

"Why Tojira?"

Liadin grimaced. "Because Ama'aga wishes it."

"That's his brother's island. He must know the danger."

Liadin leaned over and set his glass on the floor. "You're being trusted with secrets today, Nuara. Not just by me but by Ama'aga himself."

Unnerved, Nuara finally took a drink. He emptied the glass in two gulps, then told Liadin, "Go on."

"You've pledged yourself to Ama'aga," said Liadin. "I need to re-mind you of that before I say more."

"I remember by pledge."

"You're loyal to him?"

Nuara pointed to the tattoo on his sleeveless arm, the depiction of Ama'aga he'd gotten years before. "How's that for devotion?"

"Enough, I hope. It's time for all Cryori to choose sides, and there's no turning back for either of us." Liadin's tone was grim.

"Ama'aga wants you to be Supreme Mariner. You'll be his voice to the other sea captains. The *Gonkin* will be your flagship."

"Me?" Nuara got up off the cot. "Why? Because of my tattoo?"

"Be serious, Nuara. Ama'aga chose you because you were the last to kneel."

"The last to kneel?" Nuara frowned. "Oh. At the feast, you mean." He recalled Ama'aga chomping on Captain Ora. The grotesque sound of it haunted him. "I knelt because I had no choice."

"But you didn't grovel like the rest of them. You made the right decision without being cowardly."

"But Ama'aga already has you—you speak for the people."

"The people, yes," said Liadin. "Not the captains. The Venerants and mariners have always been separate. That's how it's going to stay. I'll rule the land, but you'll be fighting the war at sea. Believe me—it's how Haru would have wanted it."

"Haru...that's where my loyalty lies, Arch-Disciple—with the Tains."

"The Tains are dead," said Liadin. "Until there is another one, there's only you and me. We have to hold this country together, Nuara. It's cracking right beneath our feet."

"Is it? What's that mean?"

"I'm talking about war. Not just with the humans but between the gods as well. That's why we're going to Tojira."

"Liadin, you're frightening me now." Nuara stood over him. "Explain yourself."

"I have Clionet in the dungeon under Jinja Castle." Liadin clasped his hands together. "Is that clear enough?"

Nuara stiffened. He studied Liadin's face and knew the old man wasn't joking.

"You're drunk or your mad," said Nuara. "And unless you had some wine before coming aboard, you can't possibly be drunk yet."

"It's the truth. She's been there nearly two weeks and Ama'aga knows about it. So do the other gods."

"But...Clionet?" sputtered Nuara. "Why?"

"She's alive. I don't think anything could kill her. It had to be this way, Nuara. I'm sorry. I love Clionet but she would never have gone along with our plan."

"What plan? Make sense!"

Liadin was maddeningly calm. "Keep your voice down. Those men out there will cut off your head and throw it overboard if they think you're threatening me. Now listen—Clionet won't be harmed, but she won't be released either. Not unless she sides with us and grants me dominion over the dragon-whales—which she hasn't, damn her."

"Haru knew about this?" asked Nuara. The thought staggered him. "All of it?"

"Haru sacrificed himself. He was the only one who could get close enough to Reius to kill him. Let's hope he succeeded. But he's dead now and we have work to do."

"Like what? You've had me wasting time here in Jinja! I should be out there on patrol."

"You're Supreme Mariner now, Nuara. Patrols are for your under-lings. You're going to win this war, not just fight it. That means you're going to have to be a diplomat."

Nuara's face soured. "That sounds bad."

"You asked me if I'm going ashore when we reach Tojira. I told you I'm not. Would you like to know why?"

"Because I'm going," groaned Nuara.

"That's right."

"Then you are mad, Liadin. You might as well have your priests kill me now, because if I set foot on Tojira I'm a dead man."

"Ama'aga has chosen you," said Liadin. "He'll protect you from Jaiakrin and the others."

"Others?" cried Nuara. "What others?"

"The gods who've sided with Jaiakrin," said Liadin. "Paiax for certain, perhaps Ayorih, perhaps others. Jaiakrin knows I have his mother imprisoned. He's forbidden me to come ashore. You must show him that the mariners stand with Ama'aga and the Venerants. Solidarity, Nuara! Jaiakrin must not doubt our accord."

"Or what?" pressed Nuara. "War with the gods? What's that even mean?"

Liadin stood up and put his hand on Nuara's shoulder. "It's a frightening burden, I know," he said. "We may die in this, Nuara, but it will be for a reason. What we do will make a better Nesenor someday. Stronger, more vital and capable. We're called to this, you and I. Will you falter? Or will you keep that promise you made to me in the sanctuary?"

Nuara took Liadin's hand from his shoulder. "I won't falter," he said. "I know my duty."

Liadin heard the ice in his tone. "Good," he replied. "Then get out there and do it."

Nuara's berth was surprisingly comfortable, and Liadin fell asleep quickly. Exhausted from his long days preparing for war and the guilt of imprisoning his beloved goddess, he let the rocking of the *Gonkin* lull him to sleep as they set sail for Tojira. Liadin already regretted a lot of what he'd done. He'd killed Calix, allowed Haru to go on his misplaced mission, and summoned a war-crazed deity to aid him. Usually, these things plagued him when he slept, but not today. Today he slept with ease, falling into the embrace of Nuara's amber liquor, dreaming tranquil, child-like dreams.

Then, the strong scent of flowers wafted up his nose, rousing him. Perplexed, his eyes opened groggily. A warm, viscous substance covered his hands. He flexed his fingers, bringing both hands up to his face and realizing his mouth, too, was covered with the stuff. He sat up with a sputter, pulling the ooze from his face. With a cry he flung his feet over the berth, then heard the delighted laugh ringing through the chamber.

"What...?"

Sticky ooze dripped into Liadin's eyes. Through a golden film he saw a figure sitting across the room, covered with buzzing insects. Liadin swore as he wiped at the ooze—honey, he realized. The stuff drenched him.

"Jyx!"

He dropped from the berth, spitting and flinging honey from his fingers. He looked to the door but his bodyguards didn't come. The bees moved from Jyx's face, revealing his amused grin. Honey trickled off his body, pooling on the wooden floor. He brushed the swarming insects off one arm, then the other, then squeezed them out of his long hair.

"What are you doing?" Liadin demanded, but speaking made him swoon. He leaned against the cot to steady himself. Something besides Jyx was wrong with the room. "I'm not awake," he realized. "This is a dream."

"Not exactly a dream," said Jyx. "I'm very much here, Arch-Disciple. But you are still asleep. You must be very tired. Is keeping my mother prisoner really that exhausting?"

Liadin fought to rouse his sleeping brain. Almost everything about the room was perfect, but he could no longer feel the ship moving or hear the waves beat its hull. "What do you want?"

"You're not afraid of me," said Jyx. "Maybe it's just stupidity, but I admire it."

"Let me wake up!"

"Why? You're sleeping like a kitten. I won't bother you long, I promise."

"Then tell me why you're here!"

Jyx stood up. His bees drifted to the ceiling, swarming over his head. He floated toward Liadin, and with a single outstretched finger tipped the old priest back onto the bunk. Liadin looked into the god's sparkling eyes.

"Tain Haru is alive," said Jyx.

Even in his dream-state the news shocked Liadin. "How do you know that?"

"Because I'm a god, you silly old fool. I've been watching him."

Liadin stood up again. "Where is he?"

"On his way to Agon to beg Count Whistler's aid." Jyx laughed. "Aren't you elated? We all know how much you loved him."

"I need to wake up," said Liadin. "Please!"

"Just listen." Jyx spun away from the cot and dropped back into the chair. "You'll still have to keep your secrets, Arch-Disciple. What would happen if Haru made it home? What would happen if Nuara and the other captains found out you lied to them? Oh, and your Venerants! Those two right outside that door—what would they say?"

"Are you going to tell them?"

"Surely not! That would spoil the game. But I do love your arrogance, Liadin. Ama'aga's too. It was a very grand plan."

"It *is* a grand plan," said Liadin. "And it will work. You should join us, Jyx. If you cared at all about Nesenor, you would."

"Hmm, maybe, but I'm more of an outcast, really. I prefer to sit back and watch what happens. And this is going to be a good one."

The out-of-body sensation maddened Liadin. He closed his eyes. His body was in the bed.

In the bed...

"Before you go, there's one more thing," he heard Jyx say. "You summoned Ama'aga, but there's another. You think you can manipulate the gods? You've forgotten one."

"Who?" asked Liadin. He tried to open his eyes but couldn't now. "Who, Jyx? You?"

"No, priest, you think too much of me," said Jyx out of the darkness. "I'm just a trickster. I don't have my hands on the scale."

"Who is it?" demanded Liadin. He could feel his body—his real body—start to rouse.

"I'm going now." Jyx's voice faded. "Welcome to Tojira."

Chapter Thirty-Five

AMONG THE GODS

Tojira was as Nuara expected—tranquil and lush and gleaming like a gemstone, surrounded by water too blue to be real and a beach of blinding white sand. Trees with fronds like painted fans swayed in the sweet-smelling breeze. The call of unseen birds and monkeys emerged from the forest. The crew of the *Gonkin* stood on deck, afraid and awestruck. Jaiakrin's home was a fabled place, the kind of island mariners dreamed of when imagining a life at sea.

"I'll row you across," said Ariyo. "You shouldn't go alone."

"And I would welcome your company," replied Nuara. "But no. Just get the launch ready. I'll take myself ashore."

"Don't get the boat ready," came Liadin's voice suddenly. The Arch-Disciple emerged on deck, striding up to the rail. "You won't need it."

Liadin had been below since coming aboard. He looked haggard, even ashen. His young bodyguards stood close behind him.

"Then how am I supposed to get across?" asked Nuara "Swim?"

"No boats," said Liadin.

"This is as close as we can get, Arch-Disciple. The *Gonkin* has a keel. We'll run aground if we get closer."

"I know that, Captain," said Liadin. He leaned over the rail, searching the clear water. After a moment he pointed to a churn of bubbles coming toward them. "There."

Beneath the surface moved an object, dark and enormous, cutting a wake as it coursed toward the *Gonkin*. A head emerged, then the crustacean-like, armored shoulders. Ama'aga crested as he swam into the shallows. He rose up like a mountain, dripping steaming water as he trudged toward the beast-ship, his snake-like tail having given way to a pair of tree-trunk limbs. The crew cried out, falling to their knees as the war-god's shadow fell across the deck. Ariyo, his face panicked, pulled at Nuara's sleeve.

"We should kneel," he urged as he buckled to the deck.

Nuara looked right into the face of the approaching god. If Liadin wouldn't kneel, he decided, neither would he. The *Gonkin* heeled as the wave Ama'aga created crashed against the hull. The god lumbered to the vessel's side and gazed down at Nuara. His hair dripped seawater onto the deck. He stretched out his enormous hand, his fingers unfolding like stairs.

"Come."

Nuara stared at the immense open palm. Liadin nodded, urging Nuara forward.

"Go," said the priest. "You will not be harmed."

Trust—or maybe fear—drove Nuara forward. He climbed into Ama'aga's hand, letting the fingers close around him. A rush of air struck his face as the god lifted him from the ship, then placed him on an armored shoulder. Nuara grabbed hold of the protruding spikes, nestled himself into a crevice in the shell-like suit, and looked back at his astonished crew. The sight brought his men to their feet. A cheer went up, then a round of laughing applause.

"Hold on to me," warned Ama'aga.

The god's legs pumped beneath the water, his face determined as he made his way toward Tojira. A school of fish darted away and pelicans on the beach took flight. The waves broke against the war-god's thighs as the sea bottom rose, lifting him and his astonished passenger. Nuara spied the island, but even from his height he could see nothing of Jaiakrin or the other gods. Both relieved and disappointed, he turned and spoke into Ama'aga's giant ear.

"Where is he?" he asked.

"He waits," said Ama'aga. "He hasn't the decency to greet me on shore."

His pace quickened as they approached the beach, finally coming ashore with a foaming wave. The god paused on the white sand, surveying the island and the blue sky above it. A trace of sadness marked his brutal face.

"How many forevers has it been since I've been here?" he wondered. "And still it hasn't changed. Still, it is paradise."

From his perch atop Ama'aga, Tojira seemed like heaven to Nuara. "Will I die here?"

Ama'aga's eyes shifted toward him. "Are you afraid?"

"Yes," admitted Nuara.

"Do not be. You are my *sukano*. Do you know that word?"

It was the ancient tongue of the Cryori, known mostly to priests. "No," said Nuara. "What's it mean?"

"It means 'chosen.' Like an adopted son. The sukano of Ama'aga have nothing to fear."

Ama'aga plucked Nuara from his shoulder and lowered him to the beach. He opened his fingers, waiting for Nuara to step onto Jaiakrin's island. Nuara waited, enjoying the enormity of the moment, then left the giant's palm and felt the holy sand of Tojira beneath his boots. His defiance should have shaken the ground, but it did not. The island was tranquil, the birds curious and undisturbed. Ama'aga glanced up and down the beach, then looked toward the trees.

"That way," he declared, stretching a finger toward the forest.

"You first."

Ama'aga surprised Nuara by laughing. "We will go together, sukano," he said, and started off toward the trees. Nuara quickly followed, racing to keep up with the giant's strides. "I am an outcast, remember," said Ama'aga. "My siblings will be no happier to see me than you."

"You exiled yourself," Nuara reminded him. "You left all of us. Why?"

The war-god pushed through the trees to make a path for himself. "That is what you Cryori tell yourselves—that I abandoned you," said Ama'aga. "But ask yourself—what is a war-god without a war?"

"I don't know," said Nuara. "At peace?"

"Peace." Ama'aga snorted as he felled another tree. "I am useless in peace. And if my brother had any sense, he would have met me on the beach, instead of making me work my way to him!"

A shower of leaves fell around Nuara as Ama'aga plowed through the forest. He moved without regard to the trees, cursing them and peppering his swears with Jaiakrin's name. Soon they were deep inside the tropical woods, the trees suddenly freakishly large. Vines dropped down from the canopy. Ama'aga paused. Dew and seawater glistened on his armor as he sniffed the air.

"What is it?" Nuara probed. He followed the war-god's stare but saw nothing but trees.

"My sister," said Ama'aga.

Just ahead of them stood a single tree, as plain as all the others except for a thick black and gold vine coiling up its trunk. The vine began to move, pulling away from the bark until Nuara realized it wasn't a vine at all but a stout, glistening serpent. Its head reared up from the back of the tree, its eyes blinking to life. Quickly it unspooled from the tree, shifting as it hit the ground, transforming into a deer the color of obsidian and bolting off into the forest.

"Go!" bellowed Ama'aga. "Go and tell our brother I'm here!"

Nuara watched the deer prance through the trees and disappear. "Was that Paiax?"

"It was she." Ama'aga's tone was flat. "I smelled her."

"So, they know we're here. Why doesn't Jaiakrin come?"

"You fear a trap?" wondered Ama'aga. "Do not. There is no trap of Jaiakrin's that could ever hold me. I am not my stupid mother. Come. I can smell them all. They're not far."

Nuara sniffed the air the way he'd seen his patron do. "All I smell is smoke," he said.

"Not smoke," corrected Ama'aga. "Fire."

Nuara followed Ama'aga deeper into the forest. As the trees thinned out, the ground turned mossy and damp. Nuara's boots sank into the loam, sucking at the wet earth as he struggled to keep up. Ama'aga, seeing Nuara's difficulties, picked him up and once again placed him on his shoulder.

"Look!" said the giant.

The woods opened into a pristine lagoon, fed by a foaming waterfall and surrounded by flowering hills. White birds skimmed the surface of the lagoon, alighting on enormous lily pads while fish and turtles roamed the crystalline water. A beach of gleaming sand ringed the lagoon, leading Nuara's gaze toward the burning figure of Jaiakrin. Dripping flames, his skin ablaze with light, Jaiakrin awaited his brother at the edge of the water, shrouded in the waterfall's mist. Beside him stood the obsidian deer, now partially transformed into a stunning, bare-breasted woman. A boy sat near her, cross-legged in the sand. Though he looked remarkably mortal, Nuara recognized him at once.

"Ayorih," he whispered.

Along with Jaiakrin and Paiax, Nuara knew them all but for the oddest of the group, a creature that looked like a metal man, all bronze and rivets, leaning on the long handle of a hammer buried in the sand. The being had no face, no flesh at all, just a mask of pounded metal and rigid, bolted limbs. As if sensing Nuara's puzzlement, Ama'aga named the stranger.

"Hor'roron."

Nuara leaned out for a closer look. The builder of the beast-ships and son of Paiax, Hor'roron had been unseen for decades. Among sea captains, he was revered. Just being near him enchanted Nuara. Not even Liadin had been so privileged. Or even Haru.

"I must speak to him," said Nuara. "May I?"

"Speak your mind in full," said Ama'aga. "Remember, you are under my protection."

The birds scattered as Ama'aga strode up the beach. Jaiakrin and the other gods watched silently as he approached, gesturing toward his tiny, mortal rider.

"Let me down," Nuara told Ama'aga. "They shouldn't see me ride you like a donkey."

Ama'aga agreed and lifted him once again from his shoulder, depositing him on the sand. He would walk with the war-god, Nuara decided. Right beside him. Jaiakrin stepped forward as they approached. The flames falling from his golden body intensified, blinding Nuara and forcing him to turn away, a show of displeasure Nuara knew was meant for him.

"Tame your fire," thundered Ama'aga. "This Cryori is my sukano now."

Jaiakrin complied, and as his fire died down Nuara chanced a look at him. He was beautiful, like his island, with proud shoulders and gleaming, golden skin. Perhaps eight feet tall, he towered over Nuara, but compared to Ama'aga he was a midget. The size of his gargantuan protector gave Nuara nerve.

"Jaiakrin, you are magnificent," said Nuara. He inclined his head respectfully. "You are all magnificent."

"Is this all?" rumbled Ama'aga. "Are others hiding?"

"We are all who've come brother," said Paiax.

"And Jyx? What of him?"

"He is neither here nor welcome here," said Jaiakrin. "But you are welcome, my brother." He gave a deep, amazing smile. "You are home."

Ama'aga melted just a little. Ayorih, the patron of the Venerants, stood up and put out his tiny boy-hand for his giant brother. "You belong among us, Ama'aga."

Ama'aga looked hopefully at Paiax. "Are you so glad to see me, sister?"

"I welcome the brother you were to me," said Paiax, "not the war you bring us."

Her voice was melodious, her hair a shimmering mane. Looking at her made Nuara's heart ache. She was the goddess of the lust of men, and seeing her stoked Nuara's desire. Sensing his yearning, Paiax gave him a sensuous smile. Nuara plucked an orchid flowering along the shore and offered it to her.

"I am Nuara from Lomoa," he said, twirling the flower between his fingers.

Paiax accepted the token with a slender hand and held it against her breast. "I am being courted!"

Ama'aga laughed at the display. "Nuara, you ass! Control your appetites before you try to mount her."

Nuara flushed at the insult. Paiax rescued him by putting the flower in her glistening hair. "You are a lovely man, Nuara of Lomoa," she said.

"He amuses," said Ayorih. "But why is he here?"

"My ship is the *Gonkin*," said Nuara. He turned to the metal Hor'roron. "Your creation is mine to command now, great one. She's the finest beast-ship afloat, and I have cared for her as if she were my child."

Hor'roron betrayed no emotion behind his metal mask. The silence from him made Nuara wonder if there was anything but air within the magical suit.

"He speaks for the men of the beast-ships," said Ama'aga, "as Liadin speaks for the Venerants. They are with me, all of them, the mariners and the priests."

"Do they know you have imprisoned our mother?" asked Jaiakrin. He looked pointedly at Nuara. "Do you know that?"

Nuara said honestly, "I do. But I do not approve of it, great Jaiakrin."

"Yet you stand with my brother? You toss away your pledge to your Tain so easily?"

"My Tain is dead," said Nuara. "All I can do now is avenge him."

"By forgetting him?" asked Ayorih.

"No, never," said Nuara, looking down at the boy-god. "By following his plan. This was his plan. To make Nesenor great again. Surely you all must see that. You all must want that too."

"If you believe that, then you don't know Tain Haru," argued Ayorih. "A Tain would never betray Clionet."

Nuara felt himself growing more confused by the moment. "Arch-Disciple Liadin told me of Haru's plans," he said. He looked up at Ama'aga. "Was he lying to me?"

Ama'aga ignored the question completely. He said to Jaiakrin, "Our mother lives because I wish her to live. But she is too old and self-concerned. She's forgotten the Cryori and her pact with the Tains. She grieves still for Sh'an, and now adds his son to her miseries. She weeps. While the humans plot our end, Mother Clionet *weeps*!"

Even in the storm of his brother's rage, Jaiakrin stayed calm. "Release her, Ama'aga."

"I will not," said the war-god.

"Release her."

"Never!"

The brothers locked eyes. Nuara froze.

"Then why have you come if not to bargain?" asked Jaiakrin.

"Brother, I bring the dawn with me," said Ama'aga. He lowered himself, speaking to all of them now. "For decades I was lost, gone from here to the darkness of exile. I never knew such despair until I left these waters. I have seen the ice of the northlands and the creatures that swim there and the odd humans who hunt them. I have seen their world and their unspeakable works. I know their hearts, brothers...sister! It is black. And they come."

His words distressed Jaiakrin. The god's light dimmed a little. "We've seen their monsters. On this very island."

"The effluence of the human world," spat Ama'aga. "Their ships carry persecution in their hulls." He knelt in the sand, stooping to face Paiax. "Sister, they will hunt your beloved birds and jaguars. They will skin them and consume them until they are no more." He turned to Ayorih. "And they piss on wisdom. All their old gods have been driven out. They worship a story now. A myth." To the silent Hor'roron he said, "There are too many of them. In ten more years, none of your marvels will be able stand against them, nephew. Not even your beast-ships."

Hor'roron tilted his head with a sad, clanking sound. Ayorih looked unmoved. Paiax moved closer to her brother, Jaiakrin, an obvious show of loyalty that made Ama'aga sigh.

"You will not be safe on Tojira," warned Ama'aga. "When the humans come, they will find this jewel of yours, brother. They will rape your island forever, right before your immortal eyes."

"You've doomed the Cryori to war, Ama'aga," said Jaiakrin. "And usurped the holy order of things. Our mother! I beg you to stay here on Tojira. Do no more harm and change your mind."

"Release her, Ama'aga," pleaded Paiax. "We will protect you from her."

"That is your bargain?" said Ama'aga. "To keep that crone at bay? I came here for allies! Who will stand with me?"

"I will not," said Jaiakrin.

"Nor will I," said Paiax.

"Nor will I," said Ayorih.

Hor'roron, as always, was silent. The metal god regarded Ama'aga, then the flaming Jaiakrin, then lifted up his hammer—and pointed it at Ama'aga.

"The lesser god," snorted Ama'aga. "The only one of you with courage. Come and stand beside me, Hor'roron."

With a rattle from his metal legs, Hor'roron stepped away from the rest of the gods. Paiax, his mother, twitched her fawn-like ears but said nothing. Ama'aga stood up imposingly, staring down at Ayorih.

"Nothing to say, wise-one?" he asked. "War is not all about weapons. I could use your strategy in the bloody days to come."

Ayorih replied, "You already know the wisest path."

"I will not release her, brother. Not until my war is done."

"Then you will never release her."

His logic made Ama'aga grimace. "Such is my nature. I hunger for war. For decades I starved for it, and now I shall feast." He turned at last to Jaiakrin. "You may have your sanctuary here, brother, for as long as it lasts. Call all of our kin to Tojira who are too meek to join me. You may hide here while the Cryori die to protect you, but know this—I will have no opposition."

"We are still brothers, Ama'aga," cautioned Jaiakrin.

"We are brothers until you contest me, Jaiakrin. On that day, we will be enemies."

Sad flames fell from Jaiakrin's body. "You have always thought yourself wronged, Ama'aga. But your exile was your own, and our mother wept for you just as grievously as she does her dead Tain. I've heard your threats—now hear mine. Though you be a giant, you would fall like a rotten tree under my wrath."

"No opposition," Ama'aga warned.

Jaiakrin's body blazed. "Take our nephew and your mortal traitor and do not return to Tojira until you free our mother." He turned to Nuara and said, "One day you will come to your senses. When dead Cryori choke the harbors and the children wail, you will see."

"I'm not a traitor, great Jaiakrin," said Nuara. "Please believe that."

"Go," said Jaiakrin. "Sukano or not, if you are still on my island in an hour, I will kill you."

The threat chilled Nuara. He watched Ama'aga say farewell to his sister and Ayorih, ignoring Jaiakrin completely, then turn and make his way back toward the *Gonkin*. Hor'roron hoisted his hammer over his bronze shoulder and clanked after Ama'aga, and with a squeaking metal finger bid Nuara to follow.

Chapter Thirty-Six

CARCAZEN

Treg was born today.

That was how Joak Sitirus started his journal. Four years ago, in the life-changing frenzy of becoming a father, he put pen to paper and recorded the milestones of his existence, right up until he'd gone to J'hora and died. There were gaps in the journal, of course, months-long periods in which Joak neglected his story-telling, but he had managed to record the most vital of events, locking them away in a book no one was ever to see.

Haru, who had read the journal backwards, stared at the first page as the wagon bumped along a mountain road. It had taken him nearly a week to finish it, savoring it the way one might a rare meal. He had, of course, stolen glances at that tempting first page, but had managed to discipline his reading, continuing to flip backward through the life of a man they'd killed back in J'hora. He was not a friend, though Haru felt he knew him now, and if he'd been alone in the wagon he might have wept when he read about Treg's birth. But Haru was not alone, and so looked at the page and pretended not to care.

For an interminable week they'd been on the road. Cramped together in the stolen wagon, they had managed to entertain themselves with stories and games, but those amusements had long grown tiresome, and without Joak's journal Haru wondered how he'd ever make it to Agon sane. Thankfully, there'd been no attacks. No one even seemed to be following them. Even Orkorlis had grown confident in the last two days, allowing his Cryori passengers to leave the wagon in the daylight when the road was empty and he was sure they wouldn't be sighted.

But not everything had gone so well.

They were abandoned now, at least by Skorthoros, and Shadur's once glorious hand had turned a chalky white, a dead appendage he could neither move nor understand. Disgusted by the sight of it, Shadur had covered his hand again with a glove, falling into a wordless despair where no one could reach him. After days of prayerful begging, Shadur had simply stopped talking, leaving all of them to wonder about the motives of his capricious god.

And of course, there was Siva.

The commotion over Shadur's loss had eclipsed her confession, but though neither she nor Haru had spoken of it again it had erected a wall between them. He had always considered Siva his closest friend. Now, he could barely look at her.

He closed the journal and thought of Joak's boy. Soon Treg would learn about his father's death. He was only four years old, but Haru knew the pain of losing a father. Four years or forty—age hardly mattered.

"Hey," said Elsifor. He woke the others from their stupor. "Do you smell that?"

"What?" asked Siva.

"Water." Elsifor took a deeper sniff. "That's the ocean."

Haru smelled it too. He stuffed the journal in his pocket and scrambled over Shadur to the front of the wagon, opening the tiny door that let him speak to Orkorlis.

"Orkorlis, are we by the ocean?"

The old priest nodded as he drove the horses. "We are."

Sunlight streaming through the portal overwhelmed Haru. "Stop the wagon! I want to see!"

"Not yet. Let's get a few more miles under our belts first."

"Orkorlis, I have to get out of here," said Haru. "Stop the wagon now, please."

The priest grumbled and directed the wagon to the side of the road, but Haru didn't wait for it to stop. He climbed back over Shadur, flung open the wooden doors, and groaned with delight as the fresh air struck his face. Outside their cage was a beautiful day, the best Haru had seen on the continent. The sunlight lured him out of the wagon.

"Orkorlis! You're keeping all this to yourself?"

Orkorlis reined back the horses. "At least quiet down until we know we're alone."

"Alone?" Haru glanced up and down the mountain road. A small bluff led down to the ocean and a rocky, deserted beach. "There's no one around for miles!"

Elsifor popped out of the wagon and took a great inhalation of air. "He's right," he concluded. "I don't smell anyone."

"Look at that water," said Haru dreamily. "Shadur, come out and see this."

Reluctantly Shadur agreed, following Siva into the sunlight. Together they surveyed the ocean crashing against the shore below. There were no ships on the horizon, just the endless movement of whitecaps.

"Where are we?" asked Siva. "Orkorlis, do you know?"

"Carcazen." Orkorlis jumped down from the wagon and pointed west, toward a sprawling forest at the foot of the mountain range. "That way is Lumeszia, on the other side of those woods."

"Lumeszia?" Haru turned curiously toward it. Lumeszia was Joak's home. "And what about Carcazen? Where is everyone?"

"Up ahead, at the bottom of this road," said Orkorlis. "We'll go around the towns if we can. This is rocky land, mostly. Nothing to grow but pine needles."

"I think it's beautiful," said Haru. The ocean reminded him of Nesenor. "It's unspoiled. Unpolluted."

"It looks safe enough if you want to stop here a bit," said Orkorlis. "The horses need a rest anyway."

"Good," said Haru. The pull of the shore was too much for him. "I'm going down there."

"Oh, Haru, just stay," carped Siva.

"You stay, Siva," said Haru. "I'm going."

"Then I'm going with you," said Elsifor.

He stepped toward Haru but Siva took his arm. "No," she told him. "I'll go. You stay and watch the others."

"Yes, stay and protect us, Elsifor," grumbled Shadur. "Obviously I'm no use anymore."

"Shadur, that's not what I meant," said Siva.

Shadur shook his head and walked away.

"I'm going," said Haru. "Siva, stay with the rest of them. I'll be fine."

"Idiot," Siva muttered, and followed Haru as he skidded down the hillside.

After a week cooped up in the wagon, Haru didn't want company. He especially didn't want Siva's. But the perfection of the day made it impossible for him to be angry. He nearly tumbled down the bluff in his anxiousness to reach the shore, sending an avalanche of tiny white stones plummeting down the grade. He righted himself as he staggered onto the beach, spinning back to see Siva expertly riding the slope. The sound of the ocean roared in his ears. A perfect breeze kept the black flies away. A washed-up jellyfish glistened at his feet. Haru looked out over the sea. Somewhere out there, Nesenor waited.

"I thought we should be alone to talk about your father," said Siva.

Instantly, the mood was ruined.

"I can't."

"You must have questions. You have to have questions, Haru."

"I have nothing but questions. They're all rolling around in my head all the time."

Siva stepped closer, right up to him to share the view.

"You're always saying what a fool I am," he said. "I thought it was because I wasn't serious. Because I was always chasing girls or thinking about ships or something. But now I get it."

"We hid it from everyone, Haru. Not just you."

"I can't believe he took you."

"He didn't take me, Haru. He was gentle and good and he was lonely. And so was I."

"Oh, mother goddess, I can't hear this..."

"You *will* hear it," Siva insisted. She stepped in front of him, blocking the exquisite view, forcing him to see her face. "You were my friend and I needed friends. But I needed more, too."

Haru grimaced at her wrenching words. "Stop..."

"Why don't you want to know the truth? You should know what kind of man he was, Haru. He was kind and unselfish and people thought he was weak but he wasn't. I was happy with him. I was *happy*. If you're my friend, be glad for that."

Haru closed his eyes, afraid he'd start crying. He felt Siva's hands on his face. When he looked again, she was the one weeping.

"I let him die," she choked. "I was so in love with him that I forget to protect him. I live with that every day. And it's agony, Haru. It's agony. So please..." She lowered her head. "Don't harbor this. Remember our friendship and don't murder it with anger."

Haru couldn't speak. He put his arms around Siva and held her, and her embrace broke open the dam of his emotions, spilling them in a great, weeping shudder. Wordless, they grieved, not just for Sh'an but for Valivan and friendship and the terror of the future.

"Alright," whispered Haru. "Alright..."

Siva held him, pulling the bitterness out of him like a sponge, weakening his knees. She kissed his cheek, squeezed his hand, then said goodbye without words, turning and making her way back up the bluff, leaving him alone with the vast, vast ocean.

Haru stayed very still. To the Cryori, water was home. He thought of Clionet afloat on the waves, unable to reach him even with all her power. Somewhere in the far-away depths, dragon-whales prowled. He reached out his hand, trying to sense them, wondering if the bond was real between them, his mind listening for their primeval reply...

To his great amazement, something answered...

Calling his name.

Haru's breath caught at the sound. "What?" He turned, expecting to see Siva or one of the others behind him, but they all remained at the top of the bluff. When the voice came again, it was perfectly clear.

Haru, it's me.

"Valivan?" Haru put his hands over his ears to block out the ocean.

Yes.

"Valivan!" shouted Haru, overjoyed. "You're alive!"

Alive. A long pause ensued. Then finally, *Yes.*

"Where are you? Are you alright?" Haru stalked toward the slope.

Don't get the others, said Valivan. *Let it be just us.*

Haru stopped mid-step. "Alright," he said. "Valivan? Tell me where you are."

The humans have a place they call hell, said Valivan. *That's where I am, Haru.*

The voice was Valivan's but...different. Even frightening.

"Val, where?" asked Haru desperately. "Tell me and I'll come get you!"

A demented laugh filled Haru's skull. *Will you? I waited for you to come! I was sure you would! And you never did.*

"Valivan, I'm sorry! I didn't know what happened to you! I thought you were dead!"

I was alive! Valivan screamed. *You left me here. With* her!

"Where Valivan? With Malon?"

She did things to me. Haru, she did things...

Even in his mind Haru could hear Valivan's voice breaking.

"I'm sorry!"

I don't stammer anymore.

"What? Valivan, how are you doing this?"

I'm stronger. I found you.

"Good! Then tell me where you are so I can help you!"

Run. Just run.

"Valivan, please!"

They're coming for you, Haru. I told them where you are.

"Who?"

The twins.

Haru's heart sank. "Valivan, listen to me. You have to stop. Don't help them. Let me try to find you..."

No, Haru, I'll find you. Wherever you run, I'll find you.

"Valivan!"

Good-bye, Haru.

He was gone in an instant, blinking out of existence with the tide. Haru stood on the slope, shaken and confused until the danger of Valivan's warning hit him like a thunderbolt.

"Siva!" he cried, scrambling up the bluff. "Elsifor! Get back in the wagon! We have to get out of here!"

Chapter Thirty-Seven

HOWL

The midnight thunderstorm had crept over the city, extinguishing the candles in the square and silencing the prayers of the pilgrims who'd gathered to bid Reius farewell. The Prophet had faded quickly the last few days, taking a turn his surgeons were calling mortal and once again flooding the streets of J'hora with grief. He'd recovered so quickly from the Cryori attack that those who had seen him had called it a miracle, but the infection and shock were too great even for the giant Reius to battle, and now Taan was calling him home.

There would be an everlasting peace for him. Soon he would cross into the land of flowers. There was no death for the faithful, only a passage and the bright hand of Taan to greet them on the other side.

"Make a river of your tears," Malon had told the mourners that morning from the balcony. "Let them carry the Prophet into heaven's arms."

Malon was grateful for the midnight rain. She had spent the day at Reius' bedside, holding her own private vigil while the endless prayers floated in from the window. The rain had silenced the prayers and the thunderclaps had frightened many of the mourners into the taverns. There were no surgeons or priests in the chamber now, only Malon and Reius and the occasional flash of lightning. A pitcher of untouched water sat on the table near Reius' bed. A bowl of oily figs sat beside the pitcher. These were picked from a tree in a palace garden and were Reius' favorite. And these were not untouched.

There was no danger of the figs sickening anyone else. It was forbidden to eat food meant for Reius, and Malon was sure none of the attendants had broken that rule. She'd used just enough of the poison to go untasted, but the reaction had spread quickly through Reius' body, and Malon felt unprepared for her friend's death. Blaming it on the Cryori had been easy. Living with it, she knew, would be difficult.

Reius laid soundlessly in his bed, corpse-like, his breathing shallow, his head damp with perspiration. Malon blotted away the sweat, tenderly wiping her friend's brow with her own, colorful handkerchief. Reius occasionally opened his eyes, searching Malon's face with a kind of sad acceptance. He'd never been a plotter. Understanding murder was difficult for him. Too weak to speak, all Reius could do was listen.

"I've always kept your secrets," whispered Malon. "And you've kept mine. You always knew what I was. A whore. Thinking back on it is hard. Taan doesn't judge us for doing what we must. But I still feel hands on me. I can never sleep." She dabbed Reius forehead, wishing her friend would awaken. "I'm not like you. I've never been strong. Do you think Taan will strengthen me now? I do it for him. Not for myself. You see that. You must. Tell me you do."

Reius stirred but didn't open his eyes. Malon spoke softly, just loud enough for Reius to hear her over the storm.

"Count Whistler has gone back to Agon," she whispered. "The White Fleet awaits him there. You would have never given the order, my friend, and we *must*. You were the one who taught me the evils of the old religions. When you see Taan, tell him I'm not a murderer. Tell him I'm his servant. He'll forgive me if you ask him to."

Silence. Thunder rumbled over the city. Malon glanced toward the window and smiled, sure the storm was an omen.

"The gates of heaven are swinging wide for you," she said. "Oh, how I wish I could be at that feast! You've done so much good, Reius. All the world will weep for you. Your work will continue, my friend, I promise. The good work—before you became so demented. When you see Taan he'll tell you the truth. It was never Taan who wanted peace. It was all in your poor mind. Just a fever..."

Malon stroked his head. The touch made Reius' eyes open. The dried lips parted, trying to form a sound. Malon bent closer to listen.

"I'm here," she said. "Tell me."

Reius tapped the last of his will. Words dribbled from his mouth. "My...boys."

"They've been sent after Haru," said Malon. "As you wished. They're hungry for revenge. They won't fail you."

"Care...for...them."

"I cannot," said Malon. "They're abominations. Please, I've already killed you! Do not make me bear that weight as well."

"You must." Reius kept his eyes as wide as he could manage, swatting back death. "Must!"

Malon, seeing Reius quickly fading, said, "Tell Taan to forgive me!"

Reius began to shake. A pair of tears squeezed from his reddened eyes. "My boys..."

"Yes," said Malon desperately. "Alright." She fell to her knees at the bedside and took Reius' hand. "I will care for them. They will be my own. Now go. Go and be whole again..."

As though released at last, Reius closed his eyes and let his breathing lapse completely. Malon studied his face, watching the light go out of it, imagining Reius' spirit ascending from the bed and soaring heavenward. She let go of his dead hand, realizing the best friend she'd ever had would never speak to her again.

Then, like a prisoner in one of her torturer cells, Malon howled.

Chapter Thirty-Eight

ADRIFT

It took four days for the *Witch Breaker* to reach Agon, a far quicker trip than Count Whistler had imagined. The sea was calm the whole way through, and only at the end did the sky finally darken with rain. Whistler had plenty of food, a cabin of his own, and all the time he needed to contemplate the gloomy days ahead, yet the journey still sickened him. He was a horseman and always would be, and though Agon stuck out into the ocean like a finger, he had spent his entire life avoiding sea travel. Despite the placid tide and Larius' promise to keep close to shore, Whistler had felt every rise and fall of the vessel in his guts, and nothing, not fresh air or pretend cures or the promise of home could keep the contents of his stomach from going overboard.

Sea Master Larius had spent precious little time with Whistler. Huddled below deck with his officers, the supreme commander of the White Fleet dropped only worrisome hints, referencing the coming war and the need for secrecy. Whistler had betrayed Haru by bringing him to J'hora. He knew that now and regretted it. His wife had always called him a dreamer, but Whistler preferred the title so many of his noble ilk had bestowed on him over the years—peace-maker. Peace was all he'd ever wanted. Peace had driven him to J'hora to take his Chain of Office. Though the trip home sickened him mightily, he took solace in knowing Agon was safe. That, at least, he had managed to accomplish.

On the morning of their arrival in Agon, Count Whistler awoke with dread. Sweat soaked his shirt; Vomit filled his chamber pot.

He realized at once that the ship had stopped moving forward. He lifted himself from the berth and staggered toward the porthole. The *Witch Breaker* had anchored with its port side toward the city, giving him a perfect view of his rain-shrouded home. His eyes, still blurry from sleep, blinked repeatedly at the sight outside his dewy window. Agon's tiny harbor was choked with ships. Big, brawny, white ships. Ships like the *Witch Breaker*.

Warships.

He could see two dozen of them at anchor, their naked masts piercing the drizzle. Busy crews worked their decks, shuttling supplies from the launches rowing across the inlet. Little Agon clung to the hillside, looking cowed by the might in its harbor. And in its winding streets, cloaked in fog and rain, stood horses and carts and banners and soldiers.

Whistler's old heart sank. He had known what he would see, yet somehow seeing was worse than expected. He stared out the window for a moment, trying to comprehend the awesomeness of what he'd done.

"Taryn!" he cried, scrambling to find his clothes.

His bellow brought the cabin boy running. In came Taryn through the narrow door, shirtless and shoeless. His blond hair, dirty from days at sea, drooped over his panicked eyes.

"Count Whistler? You alright?"

"I'm most definitely not alright! Why didn't you tell me we were home?"

"It's not my home, Sir."

Whistler had one leg in his pants. Had he had both, he might have slapped the boy. "Agon! My home! You let me sleep like some drunk?"

"I'm sorry, Sir," said Taryn quickly. He watched Whistler struggle to dress himself. "Can I help?"

"Yes," snapped Whistler. "No! No, go and find Larius. Tell him I want to get ashore. Now!"

Olive-green eyes stared down at a leather-bound notebook, ignoring Count Whistler as the rowboat plowed through the fog. Sea Master Larius had joined Whistler unexpectedly, noting the Count's alarm at the sight of the soldiers and promising to explain it all. So far, though, he'd wasted the brief journey by scribbling madly in his book, pausing occasionally to look pensively skyward and mumble some numbers or meaningless phrase. He was a youngish man with a reputation for brilliance, but Whistler had never met him before stepping aboard the *Witch Breaker*. In his brief time with the Sea Master, Whistler had found him to be calm, meticulous, and frigidly well-mannered. And he never went anywhere without his notebook.

"Just one more moment," said Larius, holding up a finger while he wrote in his book. "Bear with me."

Whistler waited impatiently, eager to get ashore and see his wife and daughters. His Chain of Office swung from his neck like a cowbell. He'd done everything he could to keep soldiers out of his peaceful city. Years of diplomacy and deal-making had let little Agon go unnoticed—until now. Now, in the fog of morning, he could see the soldiers camped out in the winding avenues, their horses tied up outside the occupied homes of Agoni citizens. Guardsmen from J'hora City, the Cohort of Ghan, Brigadiers from Saxoras, even Saphi warriors from Caiba—all had their banners planted in the city.

"Can you go faster?" Whistler prodded the man rowing them ashore.

"No," Larius countermanded. "Stop."

He shut his notebook with a loud clap and raised his green eyes. The boatman stopped rowing at once. Whistler tried to hide his alarm.

"Why are we stopping?"

The boat coasted toward Agon, quickly losing speed and drifting slowly starboard. Behind Whistler, the boatman stowed the oars. He was one of Larius' seaman, a big but quiet man Whistler had seen swabbing the *Witch Breaker's* decks. He spun backwards suddenly, turning away from Whistler and Larius.

"Count Whistler," said Larius, "there's some things we need to talk about before we go ashore."

He had a colorless voice that chilled Whistler. "My family?"

"They're safe, of course. You're a Lord Guardian."

"I'm not really sure what that means anymore."

"It means you get the protection of the J'horan Alliance. You're a family man so you'll understand this—the Alliance is a brotherhood. When we stand together, we're more powerful, naturally. In fact, the Alliance *is* your family now, Count. And you know what matters most in families?"

"Loyalty?"

"Very good, Sir!" Larius set the big notebook down beside him. "Those men you see on shore? Most of them will be leaving Agon soon. We'll be taking them aboard when we sail for Nesenor."

"You mean to invade."

"Of course."

"And what will happen to my city after that?"

"Agon is very important to us. It always has been. It's a perfect location."

"Tell me what that means."

"Don't be thick. You know what it means."

"Tell me!"

Larius rolled his head on his neck with a cracking sound. "You're not a man of war, so I'll be patient with you," he sighed. "It means we'll be here for as long as it takes to subdue Nesenor. Years, maybe. As I said, most of these men will be setting sail with me, but some will stay behind. And then there will be more. Many more."

"Years?"

"Of course. This first wave is just a beachhead. Your Cryori friends are to be destroyed, like all heretics. Unless they accept Taan, of course."

"They'll never do that."

"I certainly don't expect them to," said Larius. "Why should they? They have their own gods. Real gods. Gods they can touch. All we have is a storybook."

His candor shocked Whistler. "Now I see why you want to be alone."

"I'm a military man. If the Cryori want to worship starfish and squids that's their business. My job is to kill them as efficiently as possible. That's going to take some time. As long as it takes, that's how long we'll be here."

"Larius, this is my country," said Whistler. He jangled the Chain of Office to make his point. "Mine."

"Of course it is," smiled Larius. "But Agon has been blessed. You have food and housing and women for our men. You're part of the Alliance now. You have to share these things. Your good roads, your supply routes. And your wonderful location, of course—right in striking distance of Nesenor." Larius paused. "You look pale, Count."

Sweat beaded on Whistler's forehead. More than anything he wanted to get ashore.

"How will you do it?" he asked. "Invade. How?"

"Through Jinja," said Larius. "We'll fight our way through their beast-ships. They don't have enough to stop us. We'll land in Jinja, take the castle and then hold the city. More ships will come with more men. The Alliance has no shortage of men willing to fight just to be fed! And after the city is taken, well, from there it'll get bloody."

"From there?" sputtered Whistler. "Larius, you have no idea how bloody it will get."

"Thank you for being so precise, Count. That's another reason I came aboard with you." Larius peered over Whistler's shoulder, calling out to the boatman. "Fien, throw the anchor. We're drifting too much."

Fien complied at once, tossing the anchor overboard and feeding out the chain until it touched bottom. Larius picked up his notebook and laid it in his lap.

"You're one of the only humans who's ever been to Nesenor," said the Sea Master. He patted his book. "I have notes I need to go over with you. I need you to tell me all you know about Jinja, Count. Everything you can remember. No detail is too small."

"Please," said Whistler. "Let me see my wife. Let me see that she's safe."

"Tain Haru—he has no siblings, is that correct? We'll have to kill whatever is left of their royal family."

"My wife—"

"Is fine!" Sea Master Larius let his dispassionate façade slip a bit. "She'll be fine as long as you do as you're told, Count Whistler. Now..." He opened his book and retrieved his pen and ink. "Let's start with Jinja Castle."

Chapter Thirty-Nine

THE MOUNTAIN

V alivan didn't cry.

That was one thing Haru admired about him. He had always been timid around others, and always been troubled. But he never, ever cried. Not when Haru had tied him to a tree as a boy and left him there to play with others kids. Not when those same kids mimicked his stutter. Not even when his father died. People didn't know this about Valivan, but Haru knew—he was the bravest of the Chorus, because he'd had the most to overcome.

Valivan had gone silent since taunting Haru at the ocean. He'd made his threat and then he'd disappeared, and though Haru had tried repeatedly to reach him, only the void replied.

But Haru knew he was out there.

For a day and a half, he and his comrades had raced north out of Lumeszia, stopping only briefly to rest their horses. They were less than three days away from Agon now. Food was scarce and so was water. Knowing that Valivan was alive—and left behind—had worsened their already black moods. The mountain roads they travelled only seemed to go upward, never down, slowing their progress. Shadur still had no contact with Skorthoros, and the rest of them were too far from home to reach their patrons. Alone and hungry, they swallowed their fears and trudged onward.

Yet blessedly, the Shadow Boys had yet to find them.

"They'll be quicker than us," Elsifor was first to point out. "They won't need horses. They'll change like I do. Maybe they're even faster than me."

It was a dark admission for Elsifor. Haru could see the doubt in his eyes. Elsifor was many things but he was not unbreakable, and a shovel smashed into his face would do more than slow him down.

"If they're alive they can be killed," Shadur assured them. Talk of the dark pair roused him from his sorrows. "Nothing can live without a head." When he said it, he looked at Siva. "Remember that."

Siva had her knives sharpened and a flinty look in her eyes. Her silence reassured them.

And then, nothing. Just the monotony of the road.

Haru was deep in thought when he felt the wagon pull off the road and stop. Siva quickly stood to block the wagon doors; Elsifor blocked Haru. They relaxed when the familiar knock came. Four staccato raps—Orkorlis' signal that all was well. Haru opened the little partition and peered out at the priest. Night was coming quickly.

"Why'd we stop?" asked Haru.

Orkorlis put the reins down on the bench. "The horses can't go anymore tonight. We're gonna kill them if we keep pushing them like this."

Haru had heard the complaints before. "We have to get to Agon, Orkorlis."

"These horses won't be much good to you laying dead at the side of the road. Unless you think you can get to Agon faster by walking?"

"No," said Haru sourly. "But you said we'd rest in Liconda."

"We will, but it'll be dark soon and the horses are spent. We'll make it there in the morning." Orkorlis stepped down from the coach, letting out a loud, unconcerned groan as he stretched. "Let yourselves out," he told Haru. "We'll camp here for the night."

Haru leaned away from the tiny portal, disappointed and dismayed. Orkorlis had done a remarkable job of keeping them all safe. He knew the roads to Agon and Haru trusted him completely now. But they were on a mountain. They were nowhere.

"You heard him," he told the others. "Let's get out."

Siva unlatched the doors and was the first outside. As usual she checked the area, but waited for Elsifor's nose to pronounce it safe. Haru and Shadur emerged together. Twilight was creeping over the pine trees and rocks. The road they were on clung to a cliff. Haru went to the edge, looking down at the fifty-foot drop. On the other side of the road waited yet another forest, quickly darkening in the setting sun.

"We'll need wood for a fire," he said. "Orkorlis, that's us."

Shadur frowned. "I can help."

Shadur had only one hand now—not very useful for carrying branches. "Unhitch the horses," said Haru. "Tie them up—away from the ledge. Then clear a spot for the fire. We'll need some stones. You know what to do."

Shadur was sullen but eager to help. "What about food?"

Haru looked at Siva. "What's left?"

She shook her head. "Not much. Some of the biscuits we picked up in the last town. Some apples."

The last town was days ago. Haru said, "We'll save it for the horses, then. They need it more than us."

"I need to hunt," said Elsifor.

"You have to go off and kill something now?" asked Shadur.

"Not for me, Shadur, for all of us. We need food! I can bring us back meat."

"Do it," said Siva. "But be careful."

Elsifor left without a word, loping over the road and into the forest. Orkorlis didn't wait for Haru.

"I have to take a piss," said the priest. "Meet me over there."

Siva gave a miserable shrug. "Just go with him," she told Haru. "But if we ever find water again the first thing I want is a bath."

An hour later they were sitting around a campfire, waiting for Elsifor to return. The clouds had gone and the mountain air was cold and sweet. Shadur tossed pine cones into the fire to watch the flames dance. Haru leaned back with his head on a flat stone, counting stars and trying not to think of food. Siva lay beside him, sharing his spectacular view while Orkorlis dozed in the firelight. The old priest was exhausted from the journey, but never once complained, explaining that sacrifice was a priest's duty.

"Haru?" whispered Siva.

"Uhm?"

"What will you say when we get to Agon?"

Haru didn't look at her. "You mean to Whistler?"

"Yeah." Siva laid back with her knives on her belly. "I didn't want to say anything because we have nowhere else to go, but I've been wondering about Count Whistler."

Haru lifted his head just enough to see Shadur through the fire. The mystic had stopped throwing pine cones.

"Me too," said Haru, slumping back down.

"He was there when they took Valivan," said Siva. "He was the one that brought you here." She waited before asking, "Do you think he knew?"

It was a terrible accusation—the same one Haru had been considering for days. "Maybe." He rolled over to look at Siva. "Valivan would have known. He would have known everything if I'd let him use his gift. That's my fault, too."

"You were protecting him." Siva smiled up at the stars. "You were always protecting him."

"Not always," said Haru. "Not when it mattered."

"Do you think Whistler will help us?"

"I have to think that. I don't have another plan."

"They say he's a good man." Finally, Siva turned toward Haru. "Your father said that."

"Yeah."

Siva glanced at Orkorlis sleeping by the fire. "He's a good man."

Haru nodded. "Elsifor was right about him. I wonder what else he's right about."

"What's that mean?"

"I don't think we ever made him feel normal. I didn't think it bothered him, but it does."

"Elsifor's not ashamed of what he is, Haru."

"That's what I told Reius. Elsifor's proud of what he is. I think he's prouder than any of us. But he wonders about things. About life and things. About Taan."

Siva smiled. "Then let's agree that he's a good man too." Suddenly she sat up. She turned toward the dark forest. "Elsifor?"

The sound of something in the trees roused them all. Shadur jabbed Orkorlis awake. The priest sputtered a moment, silenced by Shadur's hand over his mouth. Haru peered into the woods. The sound—like the snapping of a branch—had already gone. Haru relaxed...

Then saw the red eyes.

Two of them at first, like a pair of tiny flames floating in the trees. Then, beside them, another pair blinked to life.

"It's them," Haru whispered. His hand went to his sword. "It's them!"

Siva was on her feet in an instant, blades in hand as the Shadow Boys exploded from the trees. Half-wolf and half-man, they transformed even as they attacked, their hands protruding into claws as their canine legs launched them forward. Shadur grabbed Orkorlis by the shirt, lifting him with his one good hand and shoving him backward. He picked a blazing branch out of the campfire and swung it toward the on-coming twins as Haru pulled his sword.

"Get back, Haru!" Siva snapped. "They want you!"

The black pair divided, one leaping for Shadur, the other for Siva. Shadur's crystal hand shot forward, lodging in the man-creature's mouth as the flaming branch swung to smash its head. Siva tossed her blades, whip-like. Both caught her rushing opponent, stabbing his bushy chest like arrows. She crouched, drew too more knives, and screamed, "Elsifor!"

The world became a blur of noise and fire. Shadur was down, pinned with one of the wolf-men atop him. On them both was Orkorlis, pulling and beating at the creature with his fists. The second twin had already recovered from Siva's knives, leaving them in his bloodied chest as he prowled closer.

"Haru, get to the wagon," she ordered, weaving to guard him. "Lock yourself in!"

The Shadow Boy swept in, his claw tearing at the air. Siva rolled like an acrobat, sprang up with a howl, and caught the beast in the fold of her arm, closing it around his neck like a vice. Together they fell backward, Siva stabbing him repeatedly as claws raked her body.

"Haru, go!" cried Shadur. He was out from under his attacker now, bloodied and wobbling on his knees. Haru raced toward him as the Shadow Boy tossed Orkorlis off his back, sending the priest sprawling backward into a tree. As the thing loomed over him, the priest gave a contemptuous sneer.

"Down!" he commanded. He rose and faced the astonished son of Reius. "Abomination! On your knees!"

Haru pulled Shadur toward the wagon. The Shadow Boy stared at Orkorlis, awed by his command. On the other side of the fire, Siva was tumbling with his twin.

"Kill it!" she roared.

Her cry broke the spell. The Shadow Boy growled, drew back its claw, and with one blow tore out Orkorlis' throat. Horrified, Haru released Shadur and ran screaming toward the murderous twin.

"No!"

His sword swung in a clumsy arc, back and forth, pushing the Shadow Boy backward. The thing dodged every blow, changing completely into a wolf and snapping at the swinging blade. Behind him Haru felt Shadur tugging his shirt, trying to pull him to safety. Siva screamed at them both.

"Get into the damn wagon!"

Out the trees burst another beast. Snarling, fangs bared, it dropped like an eagle onto the thing attacking Siva.

"Elsifor!"

He was as Haru had never seen him before, engorged with muscle, saliva flying from his bone-breaking snout. His enormous paws balled into fists, hammering the Shadow Boy, pummeling his face and pounding his head into the dirt. Siva leapt toward Haru, blocking him from the stalking wolf.

"The wagon!" she roared. "Move!"

Haru spied the wagon near the cliff-side. He grabbed hold of Shadur, pulling him along as he hurried to the wagon, crying out to the wolf, "Come on, shovel-face! Come and get me!"

Siva cursed in disbelief. The wolf snapped and pawed at her, its black hair erect with rage. Haru reached the wagon and climbed halfway inside, dangling his legs off the back like fishing worms.

"Hey!" he cried. "I'm here, you dim-witted mutt!"

Shadur had already figured out the plan. He scrambled up to the driver's bench, pulled the break, then dropped down next to the wagon. Haru waved his sword through the open doors. Siva retreated, grasping Haru's mad game, backpedaling toward the wagon and keeping her opponent at bay with her swirling knives. Haru braced himself. Once the thing came, he'd have to slip it fast.

"Come on!" he taunted.

Siva lured the wolf closer, just feet away now. The wagon doors stood wide. The enormous wolf readied to leap. When it was just close enough, Siva gave the opening.

She dropped to her knees as the beast leapt, leaning backwards as it passed over her and reaching out for Haru's ankle. With one powerful yank she ripped him out of the wagon, the musky skin of the wolf's underbelly scraping his face as he passed beneath it. The ground came up quickly, knocking the wind out of him. Already Shadur was shutting the doors.

"Lock it up!" he shouted.

Inside the wagon the wolf howled and beat against the walls. Haru hurried to his feet and slipped his sword through the door handles.

"Now push!" he cried.

Siva and Shadur put their wounded shoulders to the wagon. Haru squeezed between them, grunting as he summoned every sinew. The cliff loomed just yards away. The Shadow Boy boomed inside the wagon. A fist slammed through the wood, grabbing Haru's shirt. He backed away but didn't stop pushing. Faster and faster the wagon rolled. The furry hand held Haru tight.

"Get away!" Shadur cried.

"Just push!" Haru screamed.

Just feet remained. Six, five.... Haru stopped pushing. The beast held on, dragging him along. Four, three... Up came one of Siva's blades. The claw, still holding Haru, came off at the wrist. Two... The trio dropped back.

One...

And over the wagon went.

It careened down the cliff, bouncing against the rocks, shedding bits of shattered wood until it exploded at the bottom. Behind Haru came a horrified wail. He turned as the other twin raced toward the cliff, leaving Elsifor panting in the dirt. Then, to Haru's ghastly amazement, the Shadow Boy dived off the ledge after his brother. Haru hurried to the edge and stared down into the blackness, but the shadows obscured everything, and he heard nothing from the rocky bottom. Siva grabbed him and pulled him back. He turned to see Elsifor, battered and bloodied, staggering to his feet. Near him lay the unmoving, gory form of Orkorlis.

Dead.

Siva sheathed her knife and dropped exhaustedly to her knees. Her clothes were torn, the skin beneath them scratched and bloodied. Shadur looked only slightly better. Elsifor teetered toward them, his transformation slipping back to his normal form as he collapsed down next to Siva.

"Are they dead?" he gasped.

"I don't know," said Haru. "I can't see."

"We can't wait and find out," said Shadur. "We have to go."

Haru agreed. They needed water more than ever now, not just to drink but to clean their wounds. "The horses," he said. "We'll double up on them."

"They won't make it," said Siva. "They're worn out."

"Then they'll die," said Haru. "We'll take them as far as we can as hard as we can. We're going to Liconda."

Shadur held up his crystal hand and studied it in the starlight. The Shadow Boy's teeth had cut deep grooves into the once perfect glass. "Useless," he muttered. "Completely useless." He headed for the horses and said, "Let's get to that town."

Chapter Forty

ASANA

No one knew if the Shadow Boys were alive or dead, and none of them were willing to stay and find out. With no time to bury Orkorlis properly, they covered his body with stones, said a few grim words over the corpse, then piled atop their exhausted horses for the unknown journey north.

Liconda, Orkorlis had claimed, was at the bottom of the mountain where he'd died, in a valley surrounded by hills and quiet enough that they might go unnoticed. That particular part of the plan seemed unlikely now. Of their quartet only Haru was unwounded. The rest of them, including Shadur, needed attention for their injuries, and all of them—like their flagging horses—desperately needed water.

Being the lightest of the group, Haru and Siva rode together on a horse while Shadur rode alone. Elsifor, having transformed himself into a cat again, took point at the front of their column, using his preternatural eyes to scan the dark road for trouble. Occasionally the riders rotated, sparing the horses what exertion they could as they pushed them past any reasonable demands, making unremarkable progress as they waited for the sun to come up and spare them the terror of another night attack. They had lost everything with their wagon, even the last of the money Orkorlis had appropriated. Two of Siva's precious knives were gone as well, left behind in the chest of a Shadow Boy. Haru, who'd managed to keep his sword, spied the way ahead as their horse picked its way over the rocky road, catching little glimpses of Elsifor in the darkness. Despite his thirst he sweated profusely, attracting a swarm of insects that followed him everywhere. Siva, seated behind him, clapped at the bugs as her stomach growled.

"Not much further," he told her and Shadur. "Liconda's just ahead."

"We're moving like turtles," Shadur grumbled. "It only feels close because we've been out here so long."

His horse wobbled beneath him. Shadur gently patted the creature's neck.

"They're spirited," said Siva.

"They are," Shadur agreed. "Orkorlis certainly knew how to steal horses."

They laughed despite their misery. Siva lifted her head. "Haru?" she asked. "What have you decided?"

Shadur glanced at Haru, waiting for his answer. He'd promised them a strategy for dealing with Liconda.

"I have an idea I think will work," he told them. "The three of you need rest. You need someone to clean those wounds. And we all need food and water."

"So?" asked Siva.

"So, we can't hide. We need their help. We can't pay them. We can't steal from them without being seen. We can't even barter."

"That leaves begging," quipped Shadur.

"No," said Haru. "*Asking*. This Liconda is in the middle of nowhere. We've been travelling for days. What kind of news reaches them from J'hora, do you think?"

"None, probably," said Siva.

"That's what I'm thinking," Haru agreed. "So we tell them who we are. They're going to see we're Cryori anyway. We tell them we're travelling north to Agon, that we met with Reius for his peace conference. We tell them he's the one who sent us to Agon."

"That's a big risk," said Shadur. "Look at us! We hardly look like diplomats. More like thieves."

"That's right, because we were attacked," said Haru. "We don't tell them about Reius' sons. We tell them humans did this to us. Highwaymen."

"They'll kill us, Haru," said Siva. "They hate us."

"No, they won't," Haru insisted. "Remember what Count Whistler kept saying? We're under Reius' protection. How many Cryori do you think these people have seen? They'll believe us."

"What if they know we attacked Reius?" asked Shadur. "What if Valivan tells them?"

"Yeah, well..." Haru blanched at that thought. "Then we're dead."

They all had the same thought at once. Then, after a chilling pause, they all reached the same conclusion.

"Haru's right," said Siva.

Shadur nodded. A mad smile crossed his dirty face. "Wait till they see Elsifor."

They expected to ride into Liconda on horseback. Then, just before dawn, Shadur's horse died.

Its death came all at once, collapsing the beast in a heap, spilling Shadur from its back as its withered heart exploded. Shadur laid there silently for a moment, watching the white foam bubble from the horse's mouth, looking utterly defeated as he leaned on his glass hand. Haru and Siva stopped their own mount at once, dropping down from its back. Shadur shook his head sadly as Siva helped him to his feet. The sun was just coming up and Elsifor was loping toward them. When he noticed the dead horse, Elsifor grimaced.

"We're close," said Haru. He looked at each of his wounded, exhausted companions. "We go on."

Their remaining horse blinked its bloodshot eyes. Its ribcage showed through its dehydrated skin.

"I can't get back on that thing," said Siva. "Look at it. It's cruel."

"You're getting on that horse," snapped Haru. "All of you. You'll take turns. Elsifor..." He waved the man-beast closer. "You're first. I'll take the lead."

Elsifor declined "No, Haru."

"Get on that horse, Elsifor," ordered Haru. He shouldered past Elsifor and started off again down the mountain road. For a moment he heard nothing behind him, just the stunned silence of his remaining

Chorus. He went on, walking without regard, letting his order linger over them.

Then, to his great relief, he heard Elsifor mount the horse.

Three hours later, they sighted Liconda.

It was just as Orkorlis had described, nestled in a valley at the bottom of the mountain, surrounded by hills and crowned with an open, blue sky. A stream of fresh water cut across their path, fed by the eastern slopes and forged by a stone bridge poised to take them into the village. Humans were at toil in the town, in the fields and in the one main street. A handful of rugged farms clung to the hillsides. Beasts of burden pulled plows through the loamy earth. The sight of the serene place made each of them wilt.

"Now what?" asked Siva. She'd been riding the horse alone but dismounted now to stand with the others.

"Just like I said," replied Haru. "No more hiding. Follow me."

He lead them forward toward the bridge and the cool, beckoning stream. A single figure sat by the water, cross-legged in the grass with a fishing pole in hand.

"Hello?" Haru called out. "Can you help us?"

The man near the bridge turned casually toward them, dropping his pole in astonishment. He jumped to his feet, staring at the approaching Cryori, looking panicked and fascinated.

"Please," said Haru, "my friends are wounded. We need water. Food too."

He could see the man plainly now, a young human with yellow hair and dirty, peasant clothing. His shirt hung open revealing his hairless chest and a toe peeked through one of his broken shoes. He peered at Haru through the sunlight.

"Who...?" He backed up a step. "What are you?"

Haru stopped a few yards in front of him. "We're Cryori. We came from J'hora," he said, testing his theory. "From the capital."

The young man's eyes widened. "Cryori!" He leaned forward for a better look. "You're really blue!" He looked each of them over with astonishment, gasping when he looked at Elsifor. "You're Cryori too?"

"I am," said Elsifor carefully. "What's your name?"

"My name's Aylin," he offered quickly.

"Aylin, my name's Haru. I'm the Tain of Nesenor."

"Tain?" parroted Aylin. "What's that?"

"A leader," explained Haru. Behind Aylin other villagers were taking notice. A man tending vegetables in a nearby field stopped working. The stranger started toward the bridge, bringing his hoe with him.

"Aylin, we need your help," said Haru quickly. "My friends are hurt. We were attacked on the mountain."

"Robbers," said Elsifor.

"Two of them," said Shadur.

Aylin looked surprised. "Two men did all that to you?"

"Three," corrected Shadur. "Four maybe." He shrugged. "It was dark."

Haru jumped in. "They killed a friend of ours. A priest. He was taking us to Agon. He was the one who told us about this place. This is Liconda, yes?"

"They killed a priest?" asked Aylin. He seemed more curious than suspicious; a good sign, thought Haru. He caught Haru glancing over his shoulder and turned around to see the man coming toward them. "Carik!" he cried, waving to the man. "That's my brother," Aylin told them. "He'll help you."

Carik, obviously the elder brother, hurried over the bridge, as shocked by the sight of Haru and the Chorus as his sibling. He held his hoe like a weapon as he listened to Aylin's explanation.

"They came from J'hora!" said Aylin. "They're Cryori, Carik!"

Haru was careful not to hide his sword as Carik looked them over. If his scheme was to work, they needed to trust him. Slowly Carik lowered his hoe, amazed by the visitors.

"This is Haru," said Aylin, making the odd introduction. "He's the Tain!"

Carik's ruddy face turned a shade paler. "That's like a king, right?"

"Yes," said Haru. "I lead the Cryori. These are my advisors. We came from J'hora City. Reius invited us."

Invoking Reius worked like a spell. Both brothers drew back, almost afraid to speak. In that instant, Haru knew his plan would work.

"You know Reius?" asked Carik. "You saw him?"

"I did," pronounced Haru. "I spent a week with him during the Guardian Council. Reius begged me to come. To talk peace." Haru spoke confidently, growing comfortable with his pretense. "He sent us off to Agon with a priest to guide us. But your highwaymen attacked us."

"Oh, no. Not our highwaymen," Aylin swore.

"Definitely not," agreed Carik. "Great Tain, I promise you—no one from Liconda would rob you!"

"The priest is dead," said Shadur. "He was a servant of Malon herself."

The threat made Carik blanch. "I swear, it wasn't us! We're farmers!" He held up his hoe as if it meant absolution. "No one here would have done such a thing. We love Reius! We love Taan!"

Haru almost pitied them. "Carik, Aylin said you'd help us. We need our wounds tended. And water..." He gestured to his companions to go to the beckoning stream. "Our horse needs rest and food. We need a place to stay and a meal."

Aylin beamed at the chance. "Come to our house," he insisted. "Our sister will cook for you, and I can clean up all those cuts you got." He rolled up a sleeve and showed a ghastly scar running under his arm from shoulder to elbow. "See this? Got that tracking a mountain lion up in the hills. Sewed it up myself right there in the woods."

Siva smiled at the gruesome offer. "Alright..."

Others from the town started to gather, coming toward the bridge. At Haru's order Elsifor and Shadur went to the stream, cupping the fresh water with their hands and gulping it down. Siva, however, remained with Haru.

"Water the horse," he told her. "I'm fine."

She did as he asked, bringing the horse to the stream. Haru waited as the two brothers waved their fellow townsfolk over the bridge.

"Explain it to them," Haru ordered Carik. "Then take us to your house."

Shadur stopped splashing water on his face and turned to Carik. "And a blacksmith. You have one of those?"

"We've got a fine blacksmith," promised Carik. "Name's Ealex. His shop's near the town well."

"Good. You'll take me there," said Shadur. "After I've eaten and rested a while."

His request puzzled Haru but he said nothing about it, preparing to meet the train of gawking humans coming toward the bridge.

Their sister was called Asana, a name that reminded Haru of home. She was the youngest of the siblings, barely older than Haru himself, and when she saw the Cryori enter her home she dropped a bowl of apples she was washing and screamed.

It was the greeting Haru had expected.

But when Asana finally settled down and the crowd outside the little farmhouse ebbed, she went to work at once washing Siva's wounds while her brother Aylin stitched the worst of Elsifor's cuts with fishing line. He was as skilled as Haru imagined, like a drunken surgeon but eager to help, and while he worked his brother Carik poured wine for the wounded, urging them to drink and ease the pain. Shadur, who'd taken a deep gash along his belly, removed his shirt to reveal a surprisingly lean body. Asana, instantly fascinated by his crystal hand, held her questions as she worked, stealing glances at Shadur while Carik told their story. He explained how their parents had died in a fever epidemic four years earlier and how Liconda was really called the Liconda Valley and how not even the princes of Lumeszia ever bothered to send envoys to their little town. The fact that Orkorlis had known about Liconda at all delighted Carik, and he lifted a glass in toast to the priest.

When they were done being treated, Asana hurried food to them, gathering all the best food she could from their eager neighbors and setting the table with the bounty of the valley. It was a bribe, Haru knew, a gift to convince him not to tell Reius or Malon that they'd be robbed by Licondan highwaymen. As they ate, a steady stream of villagers came to the farmhouse, curious to glimpse the Cryori strangers and ask questions about J'hora, Reius, and what it was like to worship demons. Haru answered every query without offense. The people of Liconda were nothing like he expected. Certainly, they were nothing like the royal, jaded folk of J'hora.

They ate and talked for hours, and when Elsifor finally yawned—spreading his mouth wide like a cat—Carik took the hint. He shooed his friends and fellows out of the house, had blankets brought in so his guests could sleep on the wooden floor, and politely excused himself. Despite the bright sun of the afternoon, the Chorus succumbed easily to the soft blankets, closing their eyes and falling asleep in minutes. Haru, seated in one of the house's only chairs, watched them all drift to sleep while Asana closed the curtains and made the room as dark as she could, tiptoeing around her odd guests like they were babies. Even after her brothers left the house, Asana lingered.

Haru relaxed in the chair, his legs covered with a blanket, spying the girl from the corner of his eye. He wondered if Asana was waiting for something.

"Asana?" he whispered.

She looked at him from across the room. Despite her age, her hands were rough from too much labor. Her hair was a color Haru rarely saw in humans, a sunset orange that set her apart from her tow-headed brothers.

"Thank you," Haru said to her softly.

She could have taken it as a request to leave. Instead, she heard an invitation.

"My brothers said not to bother you," she whispered. "Can I stay?"

Her curiosity charmed Haru. "It's your house."

Her skirt rustled as she stooped over the sleeping Siva. She studied Siva's face, reaching out her fingers, stopping short of Siva's blue-toned cheek.

"What's her name?"

She spoke so softly Haru could barely hear the question.

"Siva," he whispered.

"Siva's very striking," said Asana. "Are all Cryori women like her?"

"She's a rare one," grinned Haru.

Asana remained crouched near his chair. "And who's that one?" she asked, pointing at Shadur.

"He's name is Shadur," said Haru, expecting the question that quickly came next.

"His hand is strange. What is it?"

"It's made of glass." Haru bit his lip. "It's difficult to understand. It's still a mystery to me."

"You're all a mystery to me," said Asana brightly. She crept closer to Haru, crouching down beside his chair as it were a throne. "No one here has ever seen a Cryori. I think you're very beautiful."

Haru liked her hazel eyes. "I think you're very beautiful, Asana."

The compliment shocked her and she blushed, but she only looked away for a moment. "My brothers are afraid. Will you tell Reius we killed your priest friend?"

"No," Haru promised her. "You and your brothers have been kind to us. I'll tell Reius that."

His pledge made her face shine. "Is he wonderful?" she asked. "They say he's very tall. They say the ground shakes when he speaks."

"Yes, he is tall," said Haru. "And his voice—I've never heard anything so powerful!" He kept his own voice low as he spoke, bolstering it with inflections. "He's a great man. I'm honored to know him."

The lie made Asana swoon. "And now there's peace?"

Haru hesitated. "Peace. Yes, that's why I came here."

"And now you'll go back on the ocean?"

"Yes," said Haru. "When we get to Agon."

"I've never seen the ocean," said Asana. "My brothers, my parents—none of us have seen the ocean."

"Never?" That astonished Haru. "In Nesenor everyone knows the ocean. We all play in it, fish in it..." He had to stop himself from bragging. "But you could see the ocean too. It's not so far from here."

Asana giggled. "The ocean is days from here! I could never make such a trip. I'm not a noble. I'm—" She shrugged. "I'm nothing."

Her worn-out clothes and rough skin told the whole story. Suddenly Haru felt immensely stupid.

"You are not," he told her softly. "You are kind and curious and I like talking to you. You are not nothing."

This time, Asana didn't blush but rather smiled up contentedly. "I'm glad you're here," she told him. "I'm glad there's peace now."

Haru smiled. "Me too. I'm trying to be a better Tain," he confided. "I thought I wanted war but I don't. I thought humans were all evil, but I was wrong."

Asana, in all her innocence, reached up to the arm of the chair and touched his hand. "Will you stay? Will you tell me more about your friends and the ocean?"

"I want to," said Haru. "But I can't. I have to get to Agon. I have to get home."

"Tell me now then," Asana implored. "Before you fall asleep."

Chapter Forty-One

THE HAMMER AND THE KNIFE

It was nearly midnight when Shadur awoke. He sat up, annoyed with himself for sleeping so long but pleased to see Haru contentedly snoring in his chair. Siva and Elsifor were asleep as well, having fully surrendered to the big meals they'd eaten and the peace of the farmhouse. Shadur stood up quietly, determined not to wake his companions. They would be leaving in the morning, and it would take time for the blacksmith to do his work. He tiptoed out of the main chamber, floating like a phantom toward the attached room where Carik and his brother were asleep. The room was dark but the only window had been left open, letting in a breeze and a gentle glow of moonlight. Carik and Aylin shared a bed, and waking one without the other would be difficult. Shadur bent down by Carik's side of the bed and gave him a nudge.

"Carik," he whispered lightly. "Wake up."

The elder brother stirred with annoyance but didn't open his eyes. Shadur put his lips directly to his ear and said a single, jarring word.

"Reius."

"What?" Carik sputtered awake, first confused, then shocked when he saw Shadur standing over him.

"Get up," said Shadur. "I need your help. Don't wake your brother."

"Me?" asked Carik, squinting.

Shadur hushed him with a finger and waved him out of bed. "Outside," he whispered.

He turned and went back the way he'd come, prowling past his sleeping friends and heading out the house's wooden door. The fresh air and moonlight felt good on his face. He stared up at the moon and took a deep, cleansing breath. Things had changed. He was alone now. Abandoned. What was he without Skorthoros, he wondered? The sleeping village had no answers for him.

A minute later Carik stepped outside, still in his nightshirt, though he had managed to pull on a pair of soiled boots.

"Did you wake the others?" asked Shadur.

Carik quickly shook his head. "No. My lord? What are we doing?"

"The blacksmith. Remember?"

"What? Now?"

"Where is he?"

"Sleeping!"

"Take me to him," ordered Shadur. He softened his tone just a little. "Please."

Carik glanced back at his house, too afraid to refuse. "He lives alone," he mused, scratching his arm. "I suppose he'll want to help you. But your friends..."

"Let them sleep," said Shadur. "I just need the blacksmith." He looked toward the village. "That way?"

Carik ignored the chill and set off toward the village. His farm wasn't large and the walk into town wouldn't take long. Ealex's shop, he explained, stood by itself on the west end of the village. It was near the town well but not much else, a fortunate thing for Shadur who didn't want to attract attention. They walked quickly in the moonlight, Carik avoiding his obvious questions, still eager to please his Cryori guests. Shadur took notice of the little homes along the outskirts of the town. The windows were dark and quiet. An unseen dog barked from a yard. The sound of animals stirred from pens, but no one came out to discover them or even bothered to light a candle. In less than ten minutes, Ealex's shabby shop came into view.

"There," said Carik, pointing at it at the edge of the village.

Shadur slowed as he approached the sooty, gray cabin. The place was ramshackle, made up of old, pitched logs and a peaked roof with missing shingles. A barrel of charcoal was spilled out over the yard, an iron shovel stuck upright in the pile. Hoops of metal and stone wheels littered the dead grass. A broken chimney stuck out atop the place like a cracked tooth. The sorry place reminded Shadur of home. He followed Carik up to the rickety door, urging him to knock.

"Go on."

Carik rapped reluctantly on the door. "Ealex? You in there? It's me, Carik. Wake up. I need you for something."

His effort wasn't nearly good enough for Shadur, who banged on the door with a closed fist. "Blacksmith! Rouse yourself!"

The banging stirred a presence inside the shop. A moment later the door opened, revealing a grizzled middle-aged man with coal-darkened skin and short cropped hair. His eyes blazed with anger at the intrusion—until he saw Shadur.

"Ealex, sorry," offered Carik, rubbing his hands together. "Can we come in?"

"What?" The blacksmith hadn't bothered to come to Carik's farmhouse like the rest of the town, but he'd obviously heard the news of the visitors. "What do you want?"

"My name is Shadur, blacksmith Ealex. I need your skills."

The tone that had worked so well on Carik fell flat on Ealex.

"What for?"

"Let us in and I'll tell you," said Shadur.

"Ealex, he knows Reius," warned Carik. "Chancellor Malon, too. Open up and let us in."

Ealex stepped aside with a frown, holding open the door. "You should come back in the morning," he said as Shadur entered the shop. "I can't work in the dark."

"I'm leaving in the morning. This has to be done tonight." Shadur surveyed the shop. He'd only been to the blacksmith in Jinja a few times in his life, but he recognized most of the tools. An anvil, a furnace, pliers and tongs—all the things a metal worker needed. And, to his great delight, he saw a series of blades hanging on the wall. "Those knives," he said, inspecting them in the dark. "Did you make these?"

"They're blanks," said Ealex. Like Carik, he was still in his night-shirt and just as bemused. "Not sharp yet. I make them for hunting."

Carik found an oil lamp on a cluttered bench. "You have a fire?"

Ealex took a long wooden matchstick and went to the furnace, still warm from his workday. He opened the iron door to reveal a few smoldering coals and set the tip of the stick aflame. He lit the lamp, letting Carik adjust the wick as he shook out the match.

"What's this all about?" asked Ealex.

Shadur looked over each of the knives. They were indeed blanks as Ealex said, dull, unsharpened stamps of good quality steel in various sizes. *Nothing too big*, he thought to himself. He touched every one of them, going back to some of the knives two or three times before settling on the perfect choice.

"This one," he said, taking it down from the wall. "You can grind this and make it sharp for me?"

"Of course, I can." Ealex took the blank from Shadur. "But you gotta tell me why. What do you need it for?"

"For killing things," said Shadur.

They were attacked on the road," Carik explained. "Robbed."

"Alright," Ealex agreed. "You want a handle for this or something?"

"I do indeed," said Shadur. "I need you to make me something unusual."

"Oh?" Ealex finally seemed intrigued. "I can make anything at all—as long as it's metal. Tell me what you need."

Shadur was barely listening. He scanned the shop for a hammer, found a big, heavy one with a flat iron head, and then went to the anvil.

"Don't speak," he told the humans. "Don't scream. Don't do any-thing. Just...be silent."

Carik and Ealex glanced at each other, confused, but didn't say a word. Shadur hefted the hammer. It was good and solid, heavy enough to do the job. It was what needed to be done. Skorthoros had abandoned him. And maddened him. He could feel the differ-ence in his wits, but he still had a mission. He could still be good for something. He laid his crystal hand atop the anvil, feeling its cold deadness. Its cloudy, milky color sickened him now. An object of wasted devotion.

"I don't know why you left me," he whispered, sure that Skorthoros wasn't listening. "But we are done now. Forever."

He lifted the hammer over his shoulder, bringing it down with a furious blow. The noise of breaking glass filled the shop as the hand shattered, spraying jagged, crystal bits. Carik gasped and Ealex swore. Shadur stared down at his severed wrist. What should have been agonizing passed as painlessly as breathing. He held up his wrist and turned it in the light, blowing the glassy dust from the cauterized stump.

"You're out of your mind," exclaimed Ealex. "That thing was your hand!"

"It was as dead as your hammer," replied Shadur, tossing the tool aside. "Now make me a new one." He pointed at the knife Ealex was holding. "Out of that."

"This?" Ealex went pale. "You want a knife for a hand?"

"Make it fit tight. I don't want something that's going to come off. It has to be permanent."

"Permanent? I'll have to drive screws through your wrist! Do you know how painful that'll be?"

Shadur wanted to laugh. "I spent weeks dripping molten glass on my flesh to make that crystal abomination you saw. If I did lose my mind, that's when it happened. Now I don't have a lot of time, blacksmith. By the time the sun comes up, I need a razor-sharp hand."

Chapter Forty-Two

HOR'ROR'ON'S BEAST

The island of Hamu-Hanza was the last in an archipelago the Cryori called the Outer Chain. She was small, mountainous, and so remote that only wildlife inhabited her, a plethora of grandly-colored monkeys and poisonous snakes that swung and slithered through her rainforest. She was also the closest bit of Cryori land to the J'horan continent, and that fact alone made her perfect for Nuara's base. Any invasion of Nesenor would come past Hamu-Hanza, and Nuara—now Supreme Mariner—had no intention of letting the White Fleet pass. Since Tojira, he had worked tirelessly to arrange the blockade, and now a steady stream of ships arrived on the island daily, unloading cargo on the shore to be tendered to the beast-ships patrolling the nearby ocean.

Nuara sat at his table on the beach, hunched over maps and ledgers, reading the dispatches from his captains. Two dozen tents had been erected near the shore, housing the hundred or so staff Nuara had assigned to himself to get the blockade up and running. His own pavilion was only slightly larger than the others, with a bed he seldom slept in and oil lamps that allowed him to work at night. His ship rested at anchor off shore. Most of her crew had joined him on the island. Sailing Master Ariyo, seated just across from Nuara, read off a list of supplies requested by the *Reikis*. Among them was shore leave for her tired crew.

"Denied," said Nuara without looking up.

Despite its remoteness—or perhaps because of it—Hamu-Hanza had a reputation among Cryori, who longed for its sunny sand and palm trees. Nuara, who had a palm tree all to himself near his pavilion, understood the draw of the place.

"Just for a day?" suggested Ariyo.

Nuara shook his head. He was exhausted from the burden Ama'aga had given him as Supreme Mariner, and the thought of a randy crew running around shirtless on the island irritated him.

"Tell Captain Linos that his crew can have their fill of the island," he said sharply, "*after* they've won the war for us. Next?"

"The *Reikis* has another shipment of ore. I gave them permission to bring it ashore."

"How much?"

"Half a hold. Hor'roron should be happy."

Nuara set down his pen and looked toward the other end of the island. Though mostly obscured by a mountain, Hamu-Hanza was too small to hide the plume of smoke rising up from Hor'roron's secretive work. The iron ore the *Reikis* had brought was only the latest of a dozen shipments the metallic god had requested.

"Smell that?" said Nuara. He took a sniff of the sea air, tainted by the smallest hint of metallic ash. He'd recognized it the moment it started, days ago—the odor of smelting.

"Whatever's he's building, it's big," Ariyo surmised. "Maybe bigger than the *Gonkin*, even."

"I should see," thought Nuara out loud. "I should find out what he's doing."

"You should," agreed Ariyo.

Nuara looked down at his cluttered table. "I have so much to do."

"Right." Ariyo lifted a ledger. "Let's get back to it."

"But I should go." Nuara looked at his friend. "Right?"

"You're Supreme Mariner," Ariyo pointed out. "You don't need my permission."

Nuara rubbed his forehead. "The blockade won't hold without more ships. Not without dragon-whales. It won't hold."

"We have Ama'aga, remember," said Ariyo. "He's worth ten shenenra."

"Not ten. Maybe five. Not ten."

"Our ships are faster. Our men are sharper."

"We have too few," lamented Nuara. He put down his pen again and tilted his head back with a groan. Then, he saw a man coming toward them up the beach. "Who's that? Is that Jollen?"

Ariyo turned to look. "It must be," he said, standing to greet the stranger.

The approaching man looked older than Nuara imagined, wearing the black leathers of a Sailing Master but the whiskers of a man who should have been retired. He walked with a confident gait, his hair longer than most mariners, his skin a faded blue.

Jollen, the only survivor of the wreck of the *Reven*, came to attention when he reached Nuara's table. "Supreme Mariner."

Nuara got halfway out of his chair. "Welcome to Hamu-Hanza. Have a seat."

He offered Jollen one of the canvas chairs around the table. Usually, men of Captain's rank shared the table. Jollen had been passed over for that particular promotion many times. He waited for both Nuara and Ariyo to take their seats before sitting down himself. The activity around them continued as Nuara moved his papers aside, giving the lanky mariner his full attention.

"How's the *Reikis*?" Nuara asked.

Jollen looked uncomfortable. "Perhaps you should ask Captain Linos that, my lord."

"Captain Linos wants your men to come ashore. Captain Linos doesn't seem to think the White Fleet is worth bothering with," said Nuara.

"Did you ask me ashore for that?" asked Jollen. "I'll give Captain Linos your message."

"How long have you been a Master?" probed Nuara.

The question struck the old Master like a manta's barb. "Seven years."

"Why's that, do you think?"

"Because a mariner should go down with his ship. Pardon me, my lord, but you know all this already."

"You knew my father."

Jollen nodded. "I did."

"I remember my father. He was unforgettable, you see. He's the reason I became a Mariner. I don't think he would have wanted you to be eaten by a shark, or rot away in a Lumeszian prison."

"Thank you, my lord."

Nuara grinned. "You're a hard one, eh? Tough to get along with? You could have left the sea a long time ago. No one would have thought you're a coward. So I'm thinking you've got something to prove."

Jollen looked straight ahead. "I've proven everything that matters to myself already. I serve to protect Nesenor."

"Uh-huh. Captain Ora was eaten by Ama'aga. The *Hakar* needs a new captain. You're it."

"What?"

"I thought of giving you the *Reikis* after Captain Linos' idiotic request, but the *Hakar* is scheduled to arrive in two days for a supply pickup. She has an acting captain—a man named Gilla. He'll be your First."

"Yes, alright," said Jollen. "But...*why?*"

"Because I'm the Supreme Mariner. Because I finally have some power to do what I want, and one of the things I want is to right some old wrongs. You might think this is all about my father, Jollen. Well, it isn't. Not all of it." Nuara put his hands together. "I was ten years old when my father died. By the time I got to sea, the wars with the humans were over. Tain Sh'an brought peace. I was glad for that. But it also means I don't know the first thing about war, and neither do most of my captains."

Jollen nodded thoughtfully. "I think I understand. But I was on a wreck. I grabbed hold of some floating timbers and managed to survive."

"Were you afraid?" Nuara asked.

"I was terrified," replied Jollen.

"And people died."

"Yes." Jollen's eyes clouded with memories. "Everyone died."

The pain of his recollection proved Nuara's choice.

"That's all I need," he said. "You'll stay ashore and help us here until the *Hakar* arrives. I'll send word to Captain Linos not to expect you back."

Just like that, Jollen was dismissed. He stood, thanked Nuara awkwardly for the promotion, and headed back down the beach. Ariyo watched him go, waiting for him to be out of earshot before turning his grin on Nuara.

"You lied to him," he said.

"I did not."

"You said it wasn't about your father."

"I said it wasn't *all* about my father."

"Uh-huh."

Nuara avoided Ariyo's skeptical gaze. He gathered his maps from the table, forgetting what he'd been doing before Jollen arrived. He sat back with a frustrated sigh.

"My father shouldn't have died on the *Reven*," he said. "None of them should have. They shouldn't have been sent on that mission in the first place. Stupid decisions get men killed."

"Is that why you asked Jollen if he was afraid? Because you're afraid?"

Nuara couldn't bring himself to answer the question. He had too many responsibilities now, and no time for reflection. His gaze drifted toward the other side of Hamu-Hanza, toward the thread of smoke rising up from Hor'roron's worksite. He'd already delivered a mountain of ore to the silent god.

"Take over for me," he told Ariyo, rising from his chair. "It's time to find out what Hor'roron's been up to."

Nuara rode a bare-backed pony, following the beach for nearly an hour. It was good to leave his base behind, to be alone with his thoughts and the rhythm of the tide, far from the endless convoys and the incessant voices. In just a few days they had managed to turn a small piece of Hamu-Hanza into a bustling village, crawling over it like ants and ruining a bit of paradise. Nuara took his time riding, enjoying the spray of the ocean on his face. The strong breeze blew against the acrid smell of Hor'roron's camp, but Nuara could still detect the stink of sulfur, growing ever stronger as he rounded a stand of mangroves. The plume of smoke had dissipated, but now the faint sound of banging reached him on the beach.

Nuara reined in his pony. Over and over, he heard it, the sound of metal on metal.

Hor'roron's hammer.

He dismounted, leading the pony slowly around the mangroves. A bright-billed toucan called out a warning, startling him, but the banging continued, louder and louder as he rounded the bend. The stink of burning metal was overwhelming now, stinging his nose. The pony bucked at the foulness. Curiosity seized Nuara as he pulled the pony onward, peering around the tightly packed trees to a clearing up on the beach...

Nuara stopped. The reins of the pony fell from his grip.

A plain of sand rolled out before him, cleared of trees and polluted with scraps of iron and streams of molten metal. A huge furnace blazed at one end of the clearing, surrounded by stacks of firewood and piles of black ore. Hor'roron worked near the center of the clearing, his back turned to Nuara, hunched over an enormous anvil as his giant hammer beat against an iron beam. Like the rib of some gigantic beast, Nuara could see what it was meant for—the gargantuan thing taking shape on the beach.

Up, up went his gaze, scanning the thing. A metal monster, like a shenenra, surrounded in scaffolding made from axed trees. Shaped at the base like the hull of a ship, the beast bore a dragon's features, with spiked, mechanical claws and iron scales protecting its flanks. A reptilian head rose from its prow, jointed by rivets, its jaw hanging open to reveal a strange, funnel-shaped weapon. In its belly burned a tank of melted ore, feeding the thing's armatures like blood through a web of coiled, silver vessels. The half-done thing seemed to breathe with magical life, its exposed rib cage groaning in the sea breeze.

Nuara looked around at the poisoned landscape. Hor'roron's giant, oily tools were strewn haphazardly among the beams and coal. Hand-cast rivets and bearings the size of coconuts peeked up from the sand. The stench was unbearable. The heat from the furnace seared Nuara's skin. Hor'roron worked with single-minded fury, sparks flying from his hammer as he bent the metal to his will. The clang of his blows rattled Nuara's teeth.

"Hor'roron!"

The hammer stopped mid-strike. Hor'roron turned toward Nuara, his motionless mask somehow registering surprise. He dropped his hammer to the ground, stared at Nuara for a moment, then pointed proudly at his huge creation.

"I see it," said Nuara. He approached the god, stepping over a puddle of fire. "What is it?"

Hor'roron drew his long, shining finger quietly across his throat.

"Death," said Nuara, taking his meaning. "It looks like a drag-on-whale."

The metallic head gave a creaking nod.

"And a ship." Nuara inspected the beastly thing. "Is it a ship? Will it float?"

Another nod.

"A shenenra," mused Nuara. "Because they won't be with us this time. Smart." He gave the god a grateful smile. "This should even the odds for us, Hor'roron...*if* you can get it done on time."

Hor'roron spread his arms to show how hard he'd been working.

"Yes, I see that," said Nuara. "I'm not sure this place will ever be the same. There's more ore coming, too. A shipment just arrived." He let his eyes move over Hor'roron's monstrous design. "I don't see a captain's wheel. How will the crew maneuver it?"

Hor'roron balled up a fist and banged his chest.

"You're the crew? By yourself?"

Hor'roron pointed toward the thing's reptilian head, stretching out his entire arm. Then, to Nuara's dismay, the metal encasing Hor'roron's arm fell away completely, revealing *nothing* underneath. Hor'roron simply stood there, one-armed, staring at the monster's head. Slowly, the head began to move. The hooded eyes sparked with life. The metal-fanged jaw snapped close.

"You're inside it," exclaimed Nuara. He looked down at the parts of Hor'roron's arm, laying inanimately on the sand. "You'll *be* it." Nuara moved closer to him, trying to find anything at all inside his metal suit. He reached out to touch the invisible, missing arm, his hand passing through the air.

"I'd ask how, but I know I wouldn't understand," he sighed.

The monster's head dropped, lifeless again. Hor'roron stooped and began retrieving the parts of his arm, hanging them on the air like tiles until the appendage was rebuilt. When it was done, he used the hand to point Nuara back the way he'd come.

"Alright," Nuara agreed, anxious to be away from the noxious smell. "I'll have that ore shipment left in the usual spot." He started back toward his pony, then paused. "Hor'roron?"

The big god of metal picked up his hammer and hefted it over his shoulder.

"This has to work," said Nuara. "You understand that, don't you? Hamu-Hanza is it."

Hor'roron drew a line in the sand with his foot.

"That's right," said Nuara. "This far. No further."

Chapter Forty-Three

PORCELAIN

S omehow, Artris and Rann had slipped out of their mother's womb at the exact same moment, making them more identical than any twins should be. Their minds were like a single dungeon, a shared catacomb of carnal, bloody memories, and probing their brains was like walking through mud.

The Shadow Boys had survived their fall with bewildering ease. Only Artris, his chest stabbed by Siva's knives, had been truly close to death, weeping air through his punctured lungs, laying broken at the bottom of the canyon while Rann snapped his own body back together like a child's toy. Valivan had experienced it all with them—the battle, the fall, the painful aftermath...and their never-ending bloodlust. It had terrified him at first. Now, he almost pitied them.

"Tell them Reius is dead," urged Malon.

Her voice drifted into Valivan's brain, sounding miles away despite her closeness. Valivan kept his eyes closed, trying to ignore Malon. After a much-needed rest, he had finally located the twins again. Now, they were back on the hunt. So far, he'd managed to tell them that Haru and the others were nearing Agon. He'd forayed into Haru's mind just hours ago.

"Artris lost a hand. It grows back when he is in his wolf form," Valivan explained. He separated himself just a little from the Shadow Boys, just enough to speak with Malon. "They won't reach Haru before he gets to Agon. They're healed but too far now."

"How far?"

Valivan wasn't sure. The twins could run remarkably quickly in their wolfen form. "A day behind, maybe. Maybe less."

"Agon, then," relented the Chancellor. "If they have to kill him in Count Whistler's castle, fine."

Valivan probed deeper again. The one named Artris was day-dreaming, distracted by hunger. His constant urges unnerved Valivan. In Liconda, Artris had seen a woman working in a field. His mind was filled with her image now, her skirt torn, her breasts spilling out of her shirt in way that hadn't really happened. But it wasn't rape Artris dreamt about.

"Tell them about Reius," pressed Malon. "Have you told them?"

Caught between the Chancellor and the Shadow Boys, Valivan chose the twins, sinking further into their thoughts. He mustered a calming, invisible voice, whispering into Artris' brain, luring him back from his brutal fantasy. There was no point in telling Artris the Licondan woman was innocent or that devouring her was wrong. The brothers had no concept of such things. The mission was all that mattered. *Forget the woman,* Valivan told him. *Remember Haru. Remember your father.*

Artris took a breath of loamy air. Like Haru and the others they had left Liconda behind, now in a woodland thick with birch trees. Valivan could see the stark white forest through their canine eyes.

The twins were at least half-mad. Valivan had felt that the moment he'd touched them. A witch and a zealot had brought them into the world under the curse of a demon. Their minds teetered between human and beast. They craved blood and they craved vengeance, but the one sound note in their discordant minds was the love they had for Reius. Sometimes, it felt to Valivan like the love of loyal dogs, but it was real and it was potent, and Valivan knew that informing them of Reius' death would shatter them.

And that seemed too unfair.

He lingered in Artris' consciousness for a while, speaking mildly to him, making sure he understood. Agon, Valivan told him. That's where they'd find Haru.

Hurry now, Valivan whispered. *Before they take a ship.*

Artris' answer reached him across the countless miles. *Father?*

He's well, Valivan lied. *He's recovered. He's proud of you.*

A great bloom of relief spread through Artris' brain. His brother, connected in a way Valivan still couldn't understand, shared the emotion. Together they thanked Valivan, promising to hurry.

They were not alone. They were never alone, and that's what Valivan admired about them. It was why one brother had jumped off a cliff after the other. Valivan said goodbye to the Shadow Boys and closed the link, opening his eyes to the impatient visage of Malon.

"Did you tell them?" she asked.

Valivan shook his head. They were in his cell at the bottom of the Tower of Principles, decorated now with luxuries to make Valivan's stay more bearable, but still patrolled by constant guards. Books had been brought in for Valivan's entertainment. He had his own lamp now and clean sheets for his bed. Malon had even brought him a vase of flowers, having learned that flowers were common in Cryori homes.

"Well?"

"No," said Valivan, "I didn't tell them."

"No?" Malon gripped the arms of her chair. "Why?"

"They can't go any faster."

"Tell them," ordered Malon.

"If I tell them you killed Reius—"

"Ah-ah-ah," warned Malon. She glanced toward the gate of the cell. The guards were stationed yards away, purposely out of earshot. "Haru killed Reius. Remember?"

"I could tell them," countered Valivan. "All of them."

"You know what? I'm tired of your threats, Valivan." Malon leaned back. "Go on—tell them." She rose out of her chair. "Shall I get them for you?"

They stared at each other. Valivan shook his head. With a taunting grin Malon sat back down.

"You *could* tell them, but they wouldn't believe you. No one would. Why should they? You're a Cryori."

Valivan rubbed his jaw. His mouth still hurt constantly, though the swelling had subsided almost completely. The lack of teeth made him drool when he spoke. His speech sounded like an animal's.

"Keep your promise," said Valivan. "Let me go."

"When Haru is dead," Malon reminded him. "When his head is on my dresser and that cat-man's pelt is on my wall. Then you can leave, Valivan. If you want to."

"If?"

Malon looked concerned. "You haven't thought much about this, have you? I know being tortured can madden a person. I had hoped leaving you alone might give you time to consider things."

"Consider what?" slurred Valivan.

"There won't be anywhere for you to go, Valivan. What do you think is happening in Agon? We're staging our invasion there. I've already sent word to Agon to begin."

Invasion. The word iced Valivan.

"You should know we don't plan on converting your people," Malon went on. "That was Reius' stupid idea. Personally, I expect your people to fight to the death. If you go back to Nesenor you'll just be going back to a ruined rock."

"No..."

"Yes, Valivan. It will take time, of course. Years probably. Nesenor won't be a place for a tender boy like yourself."

The terribleness of the words sank into Valivan like fangs. Even now, Malon was a torturer.

"You should have known all this," chided Malon. "I could have told you if you'd asked. Or you could have found out for yourself. I haven't felt you poking around in here..." She touched her head with a painted fingernail. "Not since that first time. Why not?"

The brief time Valivan had spent in Malon's mind was like being trapped in an asylum. "I..."

"Are you afraid? I've sometimes wondered how my mind differs from others. Was it very odd in there?"

"Odd?"

"Unique perhaps. You would do me a great favor by considering what I've told you. You could stay here after Haru's dead. I'll protect you if you do."

"What?"

"We could be friends! Look, I've brought you something..." Malon reached into a pouch she'd been carrying at her belt. When she withdrew her hand, she opened it to reveal a set of gleaming teeth.

"I made this for you," she said proudly. "I used as many of your own teeth as I could. A lot of them were damaged during extraction, so many of these are porcelain." She held the pairs teeth—both uppers and lowers—beneath Valivan's nose. "Beautiful, aren't they?"

Valivan glared at the ghastly gift. "I...I..."

"I'd have to adjust them, of course, but I have the tools for that. We can start tonight. Open your mouth—let me see how they fit."

"D-Don't...!"

"What's wrong?," asked Malon. "You're stammering again."

Valivan looked at the teeth in Malon's dainty hand. "F-friends?"

Malon's smile was thick. "I lost a friend. You're about to lose a friend. We could commiserate together, yes?"

The thought constricted Valivan's voice completely. He choked on the idea, straining even to breathe. Malon set the teeth aside and leaned back, amused.

"Come on," urged Malon. "You can do it. Speak."

But Valivan couldn't speak. When at last he made a sound, all he could do was scream.

Chapter Forty-Four

ALIVE

Clionet floated in the dark void, her body withered from the dead water. Silence reined. Her son Ama'aga had stopped coming to poison her, and the Venerants posted to guard her had gone. Too weak to move, she had posed no threat at all for many days, and so they had locked her away forever in the catacombs, leaving her addled mind to wander and reminisce about her astonishingly long life. She could no longer lift herself out of her shallow prison. She simply floated, unable to shift her form or open her eyes.

Unable, perhaps, to die.

It was a peculiar gift that Clionet could remember every day of her existence. She had been born—if that's what it was called—upon a tide of crystal foam on a day when the sun was hot. She had been the size of a minnow spawn then, but her mind was instantly big. She recalled her days aloft on the waves, a world alive beneath her, the schools of darting firefish and the teeth of barracudas, and the terrible loneliness of her thousand-year youth.

Clionet cocooned herself inside her mind, forgetting the pain. Ama'aga's dead water had somehow not killed her, but the mystery was too great to contemplate; all she could do was linger and hope that one of her family would find her. She thought of the line of Tains she had known and the accord she'd forged with them. She had loved them, even the tyrants among them, but she had loved Sh'an most of all. She had raged when he'd taken Siva to his bed, and she had forgiven him when he pleaded for it. And when he died it had been strangely unbearable.

Clionet tried to speak his name but could not.

For the first time in days, Clionet heard a sound.

She recognized it as the sound drew closer, but could not open her eyes to acknowledge it. Her body, flaccid and embarrassing, languished in the pool, unmoving. The footfalls drew closer, pulling her from her daydream, then stopped. A familiar voice reached through the darkness.

"I am leaving now, Holy Mother. I go to Hamu-Hanza. I go without your blessing or your aid. I go to fight a war you willingly would have us lose."

Clionet made no attempt to respond. Just hearing Liadin's voice pained her.

"You could still save us. Grant me the shenenra and I will release you—right now, without Ama'aga's consent."

The darkness beckoned her.

"You might never die. Have you not realized that? That this might be your fate forever? Help me now and be released!"

He did not understand, she realized. He never could.

"Haru is dead."

The words harpooned her. He was very near now. She could sense his hovering, his searing frustration.

"Dead! And you—you bitter old cuttlefish—will never know that sweetness."

The sound of his threat echoed long after he'd gone. Clionet slipped back into her memories. He had meant to rattle her and failed. The silence embraced her like a lover. She surrendered to it, grateful for its touch until another voice came—a grating, penetrating crowing that instantly shredded her solace.

"He lies to you."

Of all Clionet's children, only Jyx would dare to taunt her. His presence roused her in a way Liadin could never. With one great effort she found the strength to open an eye. There like an imp he perched, his bare feet dangling in the poisoned pool.

"Haru is *alive*."

His venal smile told Clionet he wasn't lying. With no strength to weep, she merely let the air bubble from her body.

"I have seen him," Jyx goaded. "Even now he tries to make his way home. I wonder what he'll think when he sees you like...*this?*"

His words so often hurt her. Even good news from his lips stung. Jyx threaded his feet through the water like a little boy.

"Did you think this was all Liadin's doing? Or Ama'aga's? You should have known my water-brained brother could never hatch a plan like this. And you were stupid too, weren't you? So blind just because your precious Tain died."

Clionet strained to think. Seeing Jyx scraped the barnacles from her mind. The answer flashed in her one, cloudy eye.

"Yes," sighed Jyx. "Skorthoros."

The goddess saw clearly now. Always of the balance was Skorthoros, her darkest offspring. A balance that had tilted far too much in human favor.

"Skorthoros thinks to sit above us," said Jyx. "All of us. Even you, Mother." He stood and flicked the water from his feet. "You may or may not die here," he told her. "Either way, I shall watch it all with pleasure. When the humans come, they will brutalize your people, Mother. Or are they not your people any longer? You show such little interest in them these days it's hard for me to tell. And think on this while you rot here—you could have granted Liadin the shenenra. You could have saved Nesenor. But now he won't be back for you. At least you'll be spared the horror of watching your sons and daughters fight."

A horror for her, perhaps. But Clionet knew Jyx would delight in it.

"I would kiss you good-bye, Mother, but you're far too hideous now to put my lips upon."

Unable to bear him further, Clionet closed her single eye. Jyx said nothing more, and when she was sure he had gone Clionet sank to the bottom of the pool, the still water drowning her like tears.

Haru. Alive!

In time she would be strong enough. In time she would harbor her power and call to him, and he would rescue her like a Tain of old, and she would be free.

And on that day, she would fall on her enemies like a tidal wave.

Chapter Forty-Five

MIDNIGHT MEETING

C ount Whistler had always described Agon as a sleepy harbor. In his imaginings, Haru pictured it like Golo Lake back
home—tiny, quiet, and undisturbed by the larger world. He might
find a few Agoni trawlers nestled there, riggings stowed for the
night, their crews asleep on shore in their cobblestone houses. If
they arrived past dusk, Haru supposed, they might ride right up to
Whistler's castle.

But the White Fleet greeted them instead.

Haru poked his head through the trees, stunned by the armada
choking Agon's harbor. The flotilla of seabreakers stretched off
into the moonlight, quietly menacing. He could see the streets of
Whistler's little city-state, crowded with horses and supply wag-
ons. Handfuls of soldiers walked drunkenly through the town. The
soldiers were everywhere in Agon, and of every stripe imaginable,
pulled from the corners of the Alliance for the only purpose Haru
could imagine.

Invasion.

They had ridden days and nights to reach Agon. They had lost
Orkorlis and had nearly been killed themselves, all because Haru
was confident Count Whistler would help him. Now, with this final,
impregnable barricade before them, all seemed lost.

"Whistler," whispered Siva despondently.

She didn't have to say the rest. He'd betrayed them. Haru knew it surely now. He fell back into the trees. They were about a half a mile from Agon's harbor, far enough not to be spotted. The moonlight had carved a path for them, and the last few hours of their ride had been nearly giddy, suffused with the hope that soon they'd be home. Now, they had nowhere left to run.

"Reius," spat Shadur. "He didn't tell you this when he was showing you around J'hora, did he? All his lies!" He pointed with his gleaming knife-hand toward Agon. "These are what human friends are like."

Haru couldn't speak. Elsifor's probing eyes tracked him, waiting for an answer. Siva stood silently beside him.

"We could steal a ship," he mused. "I could sail it home."

"Ridiculous," scoffed Shadur.

"I could do it, Shadur. I can pilot a ship."

"But how do we steal one? You're being absurd, Haru."

"We need help," said Siva. "We still need Count Whistler."

"He's betrayed us," growled Shadur. "Face it—we were wrong about him."

"Has he betrayed us?" wondered Elsifor. He peered back through the covering trees. "Those soldiers aren't Agoni. I can't believe Count Whistler wants them here. He always hated J'hora."

"A ruse," said Shadur. "Whistler is just a very fine actor."

"No, it wasn't a lie," Elsifor countered. "He never wanted this. It's impossible."

"Does it matter?" asked Siva. "Maybe he betrayed us, maybe he didn't. But he's under J'hora's thumb now. He's just another dog on Reius' leash."

"Whistler was with us in the capital the entire time," argued Elsifor. "He arrived before we did, even. Maybe he didn't know."

"Oh, Elsifor, open your eyes," argued Shadur. "We barely know the man."

"Haru knows him!" said Elsifor. "Right?" He looked at Haru. "You thought well enough of him to bring us here."

"What?" wondered Haru. "Do I think he betrayed us?"

Siva was stone-faced. "It's your decision."

"Yeah," smirked Haru. "I know."

He wandered back toward their horses, the four stout mounts they'd been given in Liconda. Along with food, water, and clean clothing, the horses had been a generous gift. Carik and his family had treated them royally, believing every lie Haru spoke. Lies were everywhere these days.

"Elsifor's right," said Haru finally. "We need help. And I don't know anyone else in the whole Alliance we can trust."

"Haru, we can't trust Count Whistler," warned Shadur.

"Maybe not. But we can't stay out here. We can't keep running. We have to get home."

"We'll move on north," Shadur suggested. "We'll find you a ship. We'll steal one from another village—one that doesn't have a hundred seabreakers ready to chase us!"

"How long will that take? When are those seabreakers setting off for home, Shadur? When they reach Nesenor, I have to be there."

"Tell us what you want to do," pressed Siva.

"Whistler has ships. He's still the ruler here. He can get us a ship and send us home."

"But we can't get to him," said Shadur, exasperated. "We don't even know where he is."

"I could reach his castle," said Elsifor. "I can take the roofs."

"Maybe," said Haru. "But I know someone even quieter than you."

Haru chose a place away from his friends, a secluded spot near the top of a hill where the foliage was thin and he could easily see Agon in the moonlight. Count Whistler's land really was the way he'd described it, Haru realized. Small and charming, it was only the presence of the fleet and the soldiers that spoiled it. He knew Whistler's heart well enough, he decided. There'd been too many years, too many agreements for the old nobleman to simply forget. Bonds weren't like that. Bonds lasted. Friendship was forever.

He had already felt Valivan snooping around in his brain. It had been happening more frequently lately, ever since they'd left Liconda. Val hadn't really made contact, and perhaps he had thought he was hiding himself, but his presence was too strong, as were the memories, and Haru could detect him the way one might a familiar smell. He needed Valivan now. More than ever, he needed his old friend. He closed his eyes and summoned a picture of them together as boys, a time long before the plights of adulthood.

"I'm not good at praying," he said softly. "I'm not sure how to do this. But I know you can hear me, Valivan, so just listen, alright? I'm sorry for what happened to you. I'm sorry for what I did. I'd trade myself right now to have you back here. I'm afraid, Valivan. I don't want the others to hear me say it, but I'm scared."

Haru opened his eyes and looked up at the sky.

"I thought I could do this, but then it all fell apart. I got you captured and I got Orkorlis killed. And if I die here maybe that's what I deserve. But no one else deserves it. Siva and Shadur and Elsifor—this isn't their fault."

The cold moon gazed down at him, silent and empty. Haru listened for that tiny hint, that little tickle in his brain of Val's presence.

"They're going to invade," he went on. "Just consider that, alright? Think about the people. Your mother, even. They'll all die if Reius gets his way. They can't win if I'm not there. They can't win without the shenenra! You can't want that. You can't want Reius to win."

Reius is dead.

The words struck like a thunderbolt, smashing into Haru's skull. Suddenly his head was filled with rage, with hatred. With Valivan. The fullness of him staggered Haru.

"Dead? Valivan?"

He's dead, Haru. Malon killed him and now I'm her puppet.

"Valivan..." Haru took a breath and sank to his knees. "Valivan, just..." He searched for words he didn't have. "I'm sorry."

There was a long, dreadful silence. Somewhere in a cell Valivan was shaking. Haru could feel him sharing his misery, trying to impart its enormity. Determined, Haru opened his mind and let the agony wash over him. The pain drove him down, down, bowing him to the dirt. Valivan let him have it all—the cell, the nakedness, the extracting of teeth. And all that blood. Haru wretched up his supper, collapsing in a heap upon the grass. He put his hands to his sweat-soaked face.

"Valivan…"

Horrible, horrible…

Haru shrieked at the agony.

He had told the others not to come up the hill. No matter what happened, he told them not to come, so they did not. But Valivan remained with him, like a bird on his shoulder, suffering with him while he laid there. Haru grasped to comprehend it all. He had lost so much. Like a chain of fireworks, bits of his life had exploded one by one since his father's death. For the first time—maybe the first time ever in his life—he felt defeated.

He caught his breathe and wiped the spittle from his lips. He blinked up at the cold sky. "I am finished," he gasped. "Let the Shadow Boys have me." Suddenly he didn't care if Valivan helped him or not. He had occasioned so much pain he could barely look it in the eye. "I'm sorry I called you," he told Valivan. "I'm sorry I left you there to die. I'm sorry I can't save you."

No one can, replied Valivan. *I'm here forever.*

For a long time they both wordlessly sobbed. Haru lost himself in the terrible link. He thought about quitting, then about dying. And then, Valivan spoke again.

Haru, you have to get up.

Haru shook his head. "No. I have to lay here."

You have to hurry because the Shadow Boys know where you are.

Surprised, Haru rolled onto his side. "What?"

You can't outrun them. You have to get a ship. I know what you want—I'll help you reach Count Whistler.

Haru clenched his closed eyes. "Will you?" he sobbed. He wiped his runny nose. "Will you help me?"

Valivan was struggling. *You're my friend.*

Haru laughed and choked back his tears. "You're mine, Valivan. You're mine."

Whistler didn't betray you. He didn't know. I'll reach him. Wait for him. I'll bring him.

"How?"

I'll make him come, said Valivan. *But we have to be quick. You have to be gone before Malon finds me.*

Count Whistler had said goodnight to his wife and daughters, but he had not gone to sleep. Sleep was for men whose countries weren't occupied. A golden clock in his study ticked toward midnight. He glanced at the ornament from the chair at his desk, then returned to gazing out his open window. His wife despised the smell of his pipe, but he needed the comfort of tobacco now, and so puffed contemplatively as he spied the warships in his harbor and waved the smoke out the window.

Two days. That's how long Malon's messenger had given them. Two days to make the remaining preparations. Two days until sailing for Nesenor. Whistler took a long drag of smoke and held it in his lungs, letting it dribble slowly from his nostrils. Like Larius, the J'horan messenger was a guest in his castle. His castle was a whorehouse now. What did that make him, he wondered?

"Sleep," he told himself. One day he would sleep and it would all be over. One day he would sleep and never wake up. His eyes grew heavy. The pipe drooped in his lips. He stood up, stretched, and then felt the oddest shock of his life.

Count Whistler, said a voice, clear and powerful in his head. *You know me as Valivan the Cryori. Listen to me very carefully...*

Haru and the others waited at the top of the hill overlooking Agon, just as Valivan had ordered. It might have been a trap, but Haru didn't think so. The Shadow Boys, Valivan explained, were still hours behind them, and when Haru saw the lone rider coming toward them from the town, he knew his trust had been well placed. Count Whistler came alone but with a sword in his hand, driving his gray stallion up the road in the moonlight, his hood and cape staving off the chill and hiding his features. Haru stood his ground without drawing a weapon.

Count Whistler crested the hill and reined back his prancing horse, shaking off his hood. "Haru," he said in disbelief. "Haru...it is you!" The old man sheathed his sword but didn't dismount. He shook his head in a kind of disgust. "Your man Valivan came to me. How?"

Haru offered the only explanation he could. "My Chorus is...gifted."

"He was in my head!" railed Whistler. He looked around the little encampment. "Where is he?"

"He's back in J'hora," said Haru. "In the Tower of Principles. In one of Malon's cells."

"Still?" Whistler looked shocked. "How could he speak to me from there? That's days from Agon!"

"Still?" asked Shadur, stepping forward. "You saw him there?"

"Aye, I knew Malon had captured the boy. Tortured him. And don't you dare look at me like that, any of you! You're fugitives. Assassins! How'd you expect Malon to treat you?"

Elsifor sniffed the air. "He wasn't followed," he reported.

"Of course I wasn't followed," barked Whistler.

"Please," begged Haru, "we need your help."

"We need a ship," said Siva.

Count Whistler spun his horse around. "You killed Reius. He's dead."

"We didn't," said Haru. "We tried to kill him but failed. Malon killed him, Count. Valivan told us so."

"More magic?" spat Whistler. "More betrayals!" He tossed back his head with an agonized groan. "What has happened to the world? It's damned!"

"Malon took your country," Haru pressed. He pointed at the harbor. "And now she means to take mine. We have to get home, Count. If we can get home maybe I can stop them."

"Stop them?" Whistler reached under his cloak and pulled out his Chain of Office. "I'm one of them now! Just talking to you could get me hanged!"

"But you came," said Haru. He approached Whistler's horse, appealing up at the Count. "You're the only one that can help us. We need a ship, fast. We're being chased."

"Chased?" Whistler grimaced. "By who?"

"By Reius' sons," said Haru.

"Reius had no sons!"

"There are two of them," insisted Haru. " And there's a reason he kept them secret, believe me. They attacked us once and killed the priest who helped us."

"Look at my hand," bid Shadur. He held up his new weapon. "Would I have done this to myself otherwise?"

Count Whistler chewed his bottom lip. "Taan above, what can I do? A ship?" He thought for a moment. "I have a ship. But it's not provisioned, especially not for a long journey. And it may not be fast enough to outrun seabreakers."

"Get me a raft and a sheet, then," said Haru. "Get me anything and I'll sail it home. Please! For my father's sake if not mine. Help us."

"I don't understand any of this," Whistler muttered. He looked over his shoulder toward Agon and sighed. "And I can't get a ship ready from here. You'll have to come back with me."

"Where?" asked Haru.

"You want me to trust you? Then trust me!" snapped Whistler.

"But how?" asked Siva. "We'll be noticed."

"Girl, it's late and I'm old," said Whistler. "I can get you safely where we're going if you hide that blue skin of yours. Just put up your hoods and follow me. If anyone stops us, don't say a damn thing." He looked unhappily at Haru. "You did this all for your father? You didn't know him at all then, boy. He would have never blundered into war."

Chapter Forty-Six

THE LAUGHING GOD

As a boy Valivan had been frightened of the dark. Now, night was the only thing that comforted him. At night the Tower was quiet. At night, no one came to torture him. Valivan laid back in his cot, watching the little tongue of light flicker in his oil lamp. The flame helped him concentrate, focusing his mind. His talk with Haru had exhausted him, but he dared not sleep. Like a juggler he had too many balls in the air to risk closing his eyes. Outside the cell, his one guard had succumbed to his own tiredness. The man had been halfway there already—all Valivan had to do was nudge him. He'd done it before, twice in fact. The new strength Jyx had given him was remarkable, and he had yet to truly test its limits. For the first time in weeks, Valivan smiled. He'd made his peace with Haru and that was good. All he had to do now was help his old friend get home.

Valivan let the memories tumble through his mind. One day, maybe, he would see Nesenor again. He'd escape Malon's horror-house and find his way back, and he'd be a hero. His mother would be proud of him. Her tender face floated through Valivan's imagination. She was worried about him—he knew that without reaching for her. He thought of finding her, of touching her across the miles, but stopped himself. She was his mother. Somehow, she would already know what had happened to him.

On the table beside him sat the teeth Malon had made. Val had refused to let the Chancellor fit them into his mouth, a defiance that had shocked and offended Malon. Val sat up and considered the ugly things. He lifted the dentures in his palm, studying them in the dim light. Very few of his own teeth had made it into the set. The others, porcelain all, looked only vaguely real. Valivan still wasn't sure if the teeth were an act of kindness or some unfathomable jest. He brought the dentures close to his face...

...the shouted when they chattered to life.

He flung them away, watching as they clapped along the floor. A hysterical laugh rang through the cell.

"Jyx!"

His patron crawled out from beneath his cot like a shadow, climbing blackly up the wall, his face a crowing silhouette.

"Pranks," slurred Valivan angrily. He ran to the bars to check on the guard, thankful to see him still slumped against the wall, yards away. Val turned and hissed at Jyx, "What do you want?"

Jyx stretched out a shadowy hand and retrieved the set of teeth. His featureless head peeled off the wall. "What an odd gift. I should like to know more about Chancellor Malon." He held them out for Valivan. "Try them on?"

Valivan swatted them out of his hand. "Go away."

"You've been using your new power. I told you it would be useful."

"When I want you, you ignore me. And when I don't, you're always there! Go away, Jyx, please!"

"You're not afraid of me anymore. When you're scared you stutter like a sick sea lion." Jyx stepped completely off the wall, keeping his shadow form as he stood sideways to Valivan, as thin as a sheet of paper. "She'll never let you go, you know," he said, glancing around the cell. He picked up a book, sniffed a dirty dinner plate. "You shouldn't daydream about getting out of here. You can do too much for her." He tossed the plate noisily aside. "That's also thanks to me, incidentally."

"What do you want, Jyx?"

"I came to tell you some honest things," said the god. He sat down on the cot and put his hands on his knees, his face becoming more defined. "You have always intrigued me, Valivan. Have you ever wondered why I chose to be your patron?"

"I know why," said Valivan. "To torment me."

"It seems that way, but no. You remind me of myself. You're an outcast. When you were a boy, you were neglected. Even your beloved Haru couldn't be bothered to befriend you."

"That's not true!"

"He gave you his scraps and you ate them like candy. I know you helped him tonight. Pathetic."

Valivan stood up straight. "I make my own decisions."

"You're in a cage, Valivan."

"Because of *you*!"

"I meddle. I always have." Jyx gave a rueful smile. "I've been considering my nature lately. You and me were both rejected, you see. That's what makes us alike. But you become soft. Eager to please. And I became what I am."

"Yes," said Valivan. "Cruel."

"And petty and vengeful. I delight in taunts. I long to see those who rejected me suffer. Do you take my meaning, Valivan? I've tried to treat you like a son! I should be proud of you. I should love you. And yet I feel no love for you at all."

Valivan had never seen—or heard—Jyx like this. Gone was the laughing god of tricks and taunts. He looked like a boy seated on the edge of the bed, lost in his own shadows.

"My brothers and sisters are all taking sides in this war your friend Haru has launched," Jyx confided. "Not one of them thought of asking my aid, so I'm going to sit back and watch them hurt each other." He looked at Valivan honestly. "If they'd asked me, I might have done things differently. I might have even helped you escape, Valivan."

Jyx lifted his hand and snapped his fingers. For Valivan, it was like taking the air out of the room. The part of his mind that could reach out to others closed down immediately, sealed as tight as his dungeon.

"I can't let you help him," said Jyx. "Well, I could, but don't want to. I want to see your precious Haru get himself out of this. Just like all the rest of them."

"Jyx, no!"

"Don't worry. Your gift will return. After Haru deals with his own problems himself."

"Reius' sons are coming after them," said Valivan. He dropped to his knees. "I'll beg if that's what you want. Give me back the power! Let me help them!"

Jyx's eyes were pitiless. "Some people want the gods to take care of them. But we're not gods, Valivan. We're just what the humans say we are. We're demons."

"No, no, you're a dark and terrible god and I need you!"

Jyx put a finger to his lips. "Don't wake the sentinel. If you do, you'll just make things worse." His body began melting into murky shadows, flowing over the edge of the bed and oozing onto the floor. "Before I go," he said, his head just a bubble now. "There's one more thing I need to tell you..."

Chapter Forty-Seven

ESCAPE FROM AGON

The home of Harbormaster Larajin rested on the south side of the inlet, nestled at the bottom of a tiered hillside just yards away from the dock. It was a small house, weather-beaten and ramshackle, its yard polluted with anchors and fishing nets and other neglected boating bits. A lopsided lighthouse sprouted out of its side, slick with algae and long-abandoned. A narrow boardwalk led to the house, snaking off from the main dock, and a sign that read 'H.M.' hung from a rusty chain over the door. Salt stained the home's windows—big, cloudy panes of glass that gave the home a good view of the crowded harbor. A handful of houses hung above the harbormaster's home, clinging to the hillside, all of them dark and quiet with sleep. The dock echoed with the sound of rocking boats.

Haru and his companions had left their horses behind, stripping them of everything valuable before sending them off into the forest. They had no need of the beasts anymore, and their footfalls on the dock would have only alerted others to their presence. Whistler had even tied off his own horse in the forest, promising the beast he'd return as soon as possible, then leading the party into the sleeping town. With their hoods and their noble guide, they had so far gone unnoticed. Despite the many ships and soldiers, Agon slumbered soundly.

As they approached the harbormaster's house, Count Whistler pointed down the dock. "There," he whispered. "Your ship."

Haru tugged his hood aside, peering down the dock. A collection of vessels bobbed along the pier, most of them beat-up fishing boats and trawlers. A single, white-hulled sloop stood out from the group. "That one?" asked Haru.

"She's called the *Venture*," said Whistler. "I keep her for trips along the shore, mostly to Lumeszia. She's old but she's solid. She'll get you home if you don't hit a storm."

The ship—just a boat, really—was smaller than Haru hoped, a thirty footer with a single mast. "She'll need a triple mainsail to make her faster," he told Whistler. "Does she take a triple?"

Whistler scoffed, "I don't sail her, boy. Save that nonsense for the harbormaster." He hurried through the harbormaster's yard, knocking on the home's faded red door. When his first attempts went unanswered, he tried again more vigorously. When that didn't work, he gave an angry grunt and pounded.

"Larajin, wake up!" he said, struggling to keep his voice low.

More pounding. Haru looked nervously down the dock, then up at the hillside homes. "Just open it," he urged.

"He always locks it," said Whistler, trying anyway. When the door failed to open, he raised his hand for another round of pounding when suddenly a voice called from inside.

"Lord Whistler? My lord, is that you?"

"Larajin, open the door," said Whistler. "It's me."

Haru heard the sound of a chain behind loosened. Larajin opened the door, his face going from mere surprise to outright shock.

"Lord Whistler? Cryori?"

Whistler hurried Haru and the others into the house, shutting the door behind him. The room was completely dark except for the moonlight pouring through the clouded windows. Whistler went to the closest window and peered furtively toward the dock, nodding with satisfaction.

"No one saw us," he concluded. "At least I think not." He went back to the door and lifted the stout chain dangling from the handle. A thick iron padlock hung with it. The harbormaster shrugged at Whistler's questioning look.

"What am I supposed to do? I chain the door ever since those thieves from J'hora arrived. They take everything!"

Larajin was a round hulk of a man, thin of hair but fat in the belly. His voice had the gravel of someone who'd lived too long by the ocean. Haru found his rasp oddly comforting. He'd been Agon's harbormaster for seventeen years, Whistler had told them. If anyone could get a ship ready to sail, it was Larajin. And just as importantly, he lived alone. Larajin took his measure of the Cryori, baffled by them. Haru pulled his hood back all the way and offered him a wan smile.

"My name is Haru," he said. "We're friends of Count Whistler." He introduced the others. "This is Siva and Shadur. And this is Elsifor."

Elsifor raised a hairy hand. "Hello."

The sight of Elsifor made Larajin clutch his chest. "Great Taan!"

"Haru's the one I told you about, Larajin," said Whistler quickly. "The Tain."

"Ah, the son," realized Larajin. His brown eyes got suddenly wide. "You're the ones that killed Reius."

"They didn't, but it doesn't matter," Whistler told him. "They're being chased and they need to get home. They need a ship. Tonight. Right now."

"Chased?" Larajin went ashen. "And you brought them here?"

"We came here ourselves," Haru told him. "From the capital."

"I mean *here*!" said Larajin. "To my house!"

Whistler said calmly, "Larajin, you need to get the *Venture* ready to sail. They need food and water, enough for the four of them. Get her rigged and ready."

"And charts," said Haru. "Whatever you have. Otherwise, we'll just be sailing in circles."

Larajin rolled his eyes at the requests. "My lord, it's past midnight! How am I supposed to find all that, and in the dark no less?"

"Steal it from the J'horans," said Whistler. "They've got barrels lined up for sailing all along the docks. Get it aboard, but rig her up first."

"In the dark?" squawked Larajin. "There are men up and down that dock all night long. What'll I say if they ask me what the blazes I'm doing?"

"You're the harbormaster, Larajin! And you work for me. Tell them I'm getting ready to sail back to J'hora. Tell them I'm a bloody Lord Guardian! Just go! We'll wait here until the *Venture's* ready."

"And how long do I have for this miracle?"

Haru thought about what Valivan had said—the Shadow Boys were coming. "As quick as you can," he told Larajin. "A few hours at the most."

"A few hours? To get all those needs aboard and the rigging sorted out?"

Whistler opened the door. "Go!"

Larajin threw up his hands. He took two steps toward the door and stopped himself. "You know we'll be killed for this. Larius will find out. He finds out everything."

"He won't," promised Whistler. Then, more sanguinely he said, "Maybe. But this is still our country."

The ruddy harbormaster mustered his courage and headed out. Whistler's brow wrinkled as he shut the door behind him. He glanced around the room, found a chair, and dragged it to the window. "Now we wait," he said. The moonlight through the glass gave his silver hair a ghostly glow. He reached into his pocket, pulled out a pipe, and stuffed it between his lips. "So," he puffed. "Looks like I don't know you Cryori as well as I thought I did."

Count Whistler was a magnificent storyteller. Haru remembered that about him as he listened to his confession, recalling the times the old nobleman had come to Nesenor when he was a boy. Back then he held Haru awestruck with his tales of the continent and the strange world of humans. Now, Whistler recounted everything he knew about Reius, how he had agreed to become a Lord Guardian after years of threats, and how surprised he had been to see the White Fleet upon his return. He'd been promised autonomy, but Sea Master Larius had changed all that. Whistler had gone to Nesenor in good faith, he told Haru, believing completely Reius' desire for peace. Even now, with his little country overwhelmed by foreign soldiers, Whistler was sure Reius had been sincere. The fact that Malon had killed him proved that, said Whistler, a claim that even Shadur seemed to believe.

"I loved your father," Whistler told Haru. His eyes crinkled as he spoke. He tapped the ash out of his unlit pipe, emptying it into a tin cup on the windowsill. "And I still don't believe Reius killed him."

"Then it was Malon," said Haru. He looked around at his companions, all of them seated on the floor as he was. "She's the one that's been manipulating us. She's the one who had my father killed."

Count Whistler stole a glance out the window, checking on Larajin's progress. "To start a war? Maybe. But Malon's the true zealot. And you keep saying it was magic that killed Sh'an."

"Old magic," said Haru. "That's what Reius called it. The kind of magic that made his sons."

"Sons," smirked Whistler. "Another secret. All is deception these days. Look at my beautiful Agon. Look what all these lies have done. Even Taan is a lie." He turned away from the window and pulled the Chain of Office from around his neck. "And this is a lie," he said, looking at the dangling medallion. "A slave collar." He flung the chain across the dark room. "Agon is free. It has always been and always shall be. Free of J'hora. Free of Taan."

"Dangerous talk," said Siva. She got up and stretched, then went to the dark corner where Whistler's Chain of Office had slid under an old workbench, retrieving it. "You might not want it but it's yours now." She held it out for the Count. "You should wear it."

Old Count Whistler looked at the thing, his eyes swelling with regret. But he did not reach for it. "I'll melt it down." He smiled at Shadur. "How about a golden hand for you next?"

Shadur shook his head. "This one's not done yet," he said, flashing his knife-hand.

Elsifor got to his feet, careful to stay out of view of the window. "What about the Shadow Boys, Haru? What's Valivan saying?"

"Nothing," admitted Haru darkly. He broke away from the conversation, trying to summon Valivan in his mind. Not even a trace of Val came through. "It's like that night in the courtyard," he said. "I can't feel him at all."

Siva's face went pale. Haru—all of them—understood her dark assumption.

"No," said Haru. "No, Malon wouldn't have killed him. She needs Valivan."

"Unless Malon discovered he helped us," suggested Elsifor.

"Or unless Jyx abandoned him," said Shadur. "The way Skorthoros abandoned me."

"Explain that to me," said Whistler. He tipped back his chair, settling in for a story. "How'd Valivan talk to me?"

Haru didn't know where to begin. Count Whistler was a human and a friend. He knew more than most of his breed about the Cryori and their gods. But no human—not even Whistler—knew about the Chorus or their gifts.

"You already know about the dragon-whales," Haru began. He remained seated on the floor while his Chorus stood around him. "My father—me—all the Tains can control them. Humans call it magic but it's not. It's a gift given to us by the goddess."

"Clionet," said Whistler.

"That's right. And there are other gods. Like Jyx. Sometimes they choose people, the way Clionet chose my family. They bless these people. The Chorus…"

Haru stopped himself. Siva saw his hesitation and explained it for him.

"You probably saw us when you came to Nesenor, but you never really noticed us. That's how it's supposed to be. A Tain's Chorus is meant to protect him," said. "That's what we are—protectors."

Shadur was unflinching. "Siva's being kind. Our laziness got Sh'an killed."

Whistler remained puzzled. "And all of you have your own god? One that looks after you?"

"That's it, mostly," said Haru. "Siva's patron is Jaiakrin."

"Paiax is mine," said Elsifor.

"I know these gods," said Whistler. "And yours?" he asked Shadur.

"Mine was Skorthoros." Shadur dragged his thumb over the flat of his blade-hand. "But no longer. I am abandoned. But I am not useless, sir."

Haru said quickly, "You were never useless, Shadur. You could never be that." They still hadn't really spoken of that night in Liconda, when Shadur had shattered his glass hand. He'd simply returned that morning with a knife on his wrist instead, and a haunted, hard-boiled face.

"Wait," said Elsifor. His fur-tipped ears pivoted toward the window. "I hear something."

Whistler waved them all to sit then peered through the glass. "Oh, no," he groaned.

"What?" pressed Haru.

"Soldiers," said Whistler. "At the *Venture*. Talking to Larajin."

Haru scooted toward the window, keeping his head low. "How many?"

"Just two for now but there'll be more." Whistler squinted. "They look like Saxorans. Probably drunk."

Haru reached the window on his knees, then lifted his eyes to the sill. He could see the *Venture* on the dock and the two caped soldiers. Larajin was gesturing angrily, trying to talk himself out of trouble.

"Haru," said Elsifor. "Get away from the window."

"No, it's fine. They can't see me."

Then, loudly, "Get away!"

Haru saw a shadow—just before the glass exploded.

The shock felled him. Back he went, dragged by something he realized was Elsifor. He heard the commotion, felt the sting of shards on his face. An angry howl rose up as glass rained around him. Siva was shouting. The blurry vision of a wolf flew at him from the shattered pane. He heard his name, saw Elsifor spring over him. Another creature clawed through the window. Haru leapt to his feet, the dark room spinning. Whistler was sitting upright on the floor, stunned and dumbstruck. Shadur had a look of lust on his face.

"Go!" cried the mystic. He shouldered past Siva, his knife raised high. "Get Haru out!"

Elsifor was already slashing, his hand a quintet of razors. The Shadow Boys dodged his swipes, their mouths sprouting into muzzles. Haru pulled his sword, nearly dropping it as blood dripped into his eyes. In his hand stuck a jagged triangle of glass. He shook it out, pulled Whistler to his feet and shoved him toward the door. Siva barreled toward him.

"Out!" she shouted. She grabbed his arm and flew past him, pulling him toward the door.

"It's locked!" Whistler cried.

"Open it!"

Whistler had left the key in the padlock. He fumbled with it, tripping the lock and then wildly pulling the chain free of the handles. Elsifor slammed against the wall, tossed by a Shadow Boy. Siva released Haru and jumped into the melee.

"Haru, run!" she cried, her knives springing to her fingers, her legs spinning out a jaw-breaking kick. A Shadow Boy bounced back against the shattered window. Shadur rolled out from under the other and turned toward the door.

"Elsifor, Siva, protect Haru!"

The door flung open. Whistler grabbed Haru's shirt. "Everybody, come on!"

Elsifor was on his feet again. Siva ran toward them, waving them out. She snagged Haru's wrist and pulled him from the house.

"Shadur," cried Siva. "Come on!"

"Go!" he shouted back.

The Shadow Boys rose up behind him. Shadur raced toward the door. Elsifor jumped forward, blocking Haru's view. Together they sprinted toward the *Venture*.

Shadur reached the door before the Shadow Boys could grab him. When they saw him shut himself inside, they stopped. Shadur quickly pulled the chain through the handles with his one good hand and looped the padlock through the links. With the lock's satisfying click, he turned toward his stunned attackers. They were wolves completely now, their fanged mouths dripping spittle. The hair on their backs stood up like the spines of a sailfish.

"I'm the one who killed your father," Shadur hissed. "Not that whelp. I'm the one who planned it, shot the bolt...*everything*."

He could see the recognition in their glowing eyes.

"You know what you are, *boys*?" he taunted. "Mistakes. Your witch-whore mother and demented father gave birth to freaks!"

The wolfen twins snapped at him, ignoring the open window. Shadur grinned at their stupidity.

"You think you have an easy meal ahead? I'm made of tougher stuff than that. And I guarantee, at least one of you isn't walking out of here."

Shadur opened himself, standing wide to draw the attack. The twins pawed toward him, their eyes identically furious.

Just one, Shadur told himself. Siva and Elsifor could handle the other.

"Come on!"

They sprang together, their mouths widening, their front claws raking the air. Up came the blade, perfectly aimed, fired right into the left one's neck. Shadur let the beast fall on him, wrapping his other arm around the thing, his legs coming up to embrace it. Blood soaked his face as he thrust the knife deeper, his shoulder twisting to power the blow. He took hold of the creature's hairy head and began his bloody surgery. The beast roared, rolling to escape. Shadur clung to it, riding it like a pony, twisting it down again. Its brother bit down on Shadur's arm.

"You will *die*!" swore Shadur, enduring the pain. He wedged himself beneath his prey, sawing through the Shadow Boy's neck with the remarkable blade. The creature pitched and howled, almost throwing Shadur from its back.

And the saw-toothed knife held fast.

Shadur ripped his arm from the other twin's mouth, rending the flesh from his elbow. He screamed, sawing away at the sinewy neck. Blood coursed from a severed artery. The boy shuddered and its transformation slowly slipped. The hair retreated and the mouth and teeth drew back. Red eyes rolled in agony. The thing was dying but Shadur didn't stop cutting—not even when its brother took Shadur's head in its claws and pressed.

Nails dug into the side of Shadur's face. A claw raked his eyeball. He felt his skull collapsing, felt his brain going dark.

"I loved you!" he spat. In his mind he saw Skorthoros. "I loved you and you left me!"

His rage made him unstoppable. The neck became as soft as liver. Shadur's knife passed through it, bursting out the other side. He held up the bloodied head, victorious even on his knees. The surviving brother gave an agonized wail—then crushed Shadur's skull.

Haru stopped running when he heard the gruesome scream. The door to Larajin's house was closed, and Shadur wasn't behind them.

Haru knew it instantly. Only a Shadow Boy could make such a chilling noise.

Count Whistler raced ahead, his sword raised like a vengeful banner. The commotion inside the house had alarmed the soldiers on the dock. Already more were pouring in from town, called by the shouts of their comrades. Harbormaster Larajin stood by the *Venture*, waving frantically at Whistler.

"You wanted to fight, Haru?" said Siva. "Now's your chance!"

She ripped the atlatl from her belt while Elsifor became a snarling cat. There was only one way out now—the *Venture*. Haru gripped his sword in both hands, the way he'd seen his father do, and followed old Count Whistler into battle.

The half-mile of wooden dock shook as soldiers swarmed the pier. Soldiers from Ghan, soldiers on horseback, soldiers so surprised by what they were seeing they lowered their weapons. Count Whistler came at them like a storm, berserk with rage, his sword held like an axe above his head. Elsifor bounded after him, shredding off his confining clothing and giving a hellish ululation. Siva skidded to her knees, cocked the atlatl to summon a glowing spear, and let it fly. The bolt lit the dock as it sliced toward the soldiers, blowing a cavalryman from his horse. Bloody bits of him showered down amid the sparks as Siva called another bolt. A shout went up from the right as a trio of horsemen galloped toward them from the town. Haru watched as one raised a bow, aiming for Siva.

"Siva, move!" warned Haru.

Siva was already rolling, somersaulting out of the way as the arrow twanged against the deck. She took hold of Haru's arm...

Then heard the door of the harbormaster's house burst wide.

In the threshold stood a Shadow Boy, hulking and gore-spattered, holding up his brother's severed head. His red eyes locked on Haru with a bellow. Siva's face curdled at the sight of him.

"Holy mother..."

Ahead of them grew a mob of soldiers. Behind them, a single, insane Shadow Boy. Haru kept hold of Siva's hand and made the decision for them.

"The ship!"

Deep in the fight, Count Whistler worked his sword, cutting a path with Elsifor's merciless aid. The three horseman galloped down from the hill, their mounts bucking when they saw the Shadow Boy.

Haru knew the boy would best them. Without thinking, without even a flicker of fear, he tossed himself into the fight. He could still see Larajin at the *Venture*, tossing supplies into the boat. Count Whistler fought wildly in the moonlight, Elsifor at his back, slashing away. As Siva drew back her atlatl, Haru plunged in. A wall of blue-garbed Ghanans blocked his way. Haru hefted his sword...

And saw the Ghanans blown apart by Siva's spear.

"Go!" she cried after him. "Get to the boat!"

Haru turned back toward Whistler and Elsifor. The noose of soldiers closed around them. He summoned the will to survive and leapt forward. A man with golden armor and a feather on his spear reared back when he saw Haru's face. Through his helm Haru could see the shock in his eyes. That tiny hesitation was all Haru needed. In an instant his blade punctured the gleaming breastplate. The man's fingers sprang open, the feathered spear dropped to the ground. Haru stared into the man's dying eyes, and for the first time felt the horror of killing someone.

"Forward, Haru!" Whistler cried. The old man waved Haru out of his stupor. "Get to the *Venture*!"

More men galloped in from the town. Whistler turned toward them, his face lighting with glee. Agoni! Without armor, some still in their bed clothes, they came with weapons raised, turning the dock into a groaning battlefield. Elsifor leapt through the moonlight and landed on a man in front of Haru, grinding him into the planks.

"Now!" he urged, pointing toward their waiting ship. "We've got to go!"

Whistler wouldn't join them. The old Count and his ridiculously brave countrymen were buying them time. Haru spied the hole they'd cut along the dock, a beckoning to freedom. Before he could decide, Elsifor was dragging him toward it.

Siva watched as the Shadow Boy pulled the last horseman down from his snorting gelding and lifted the man over his head. The surviving twin had made such quick work of his other two attackers that even Siva was startled by his brutality. He took his time with the last one, however, pumping him up and down as a show for Siva, watching her hatefully while the man above him screamed. Siva dropped to a knee and drew back her atlatl.

"Come and get me, monster!"

Another scintillating bolt appeared in the spear-thrower. Enraged, the Shadow Boy tossed his prey into the river and came snarling after her. Siva loosed the spear, watching as it exploded before the man-wolf. The creature leapt out of the sparks, undeterred. Siva fired again, barely grazing the quick-footed beast. She cursed, jumped to her feet, and ran for the *Venture*. Count Whistler, wounded and bloodied, cut his way towards his countrymen. Through the melee Siva glimpsed Haru and Elsifor scrambling toward the ship. She sensed the Shadow Boy behind her, closing fast.

"Run, Haru!" she cried. "Run!"

She pulled her last two knives from her belt, sprang backward, and plunged the blades into the Shadow Boy.

Haru and Elsifor staggered to the *Venture* covered in sweat and blood. Harbormaster Larajin, still at the boat, helped them aboard even as he watched his fellow Agoni fighting for their lives.

"I've rigged the mainsail and three headsails," he said. "I got enough food and water aboard to take you home." He peered back through the fog of fighting men. "Where are the others?"

"One's dead," said Haru. He stood on *Venture's* gunnel, holding on to a line and leaning to locate Siva.

"I'm cutting the lines!" said Elsifor. He'd pulled himself back to his normal form and ran toward the stern.

"Elsifor, no!" said Haru. "We have to wait for Siva!"

With a swipe of a claw Elsifor severed the aft tether. The *Venture* slowly started drifting. "Haru, we're going! She'll follow if you she can."

"But—"

"No!" roared Elsifor. He hurried toward the bow and cut the fore line. "Get to the wheel! You've got to pilot us past the seabreakers."

Haru turned toward the harbor. The warships were all at anchor, and far too large to approach the dock. Sailors began lining the rails of the distant ships, curious about the battle unfolding on shore. Haru went to the wheel, waving at the lone figure of Larajin.

"Thank you!" he cried. "Tell Count Whistler we'll make it home! Tell him we owe him our lives!"

Larajin nodded and waved back at Haru, unable to speak. At least a hundred men were warring on the pier now and around the houses on the hillsides. Through it all Haru still couldn't find the Shadow Boy—or Siva.

"Haru, the sail!" cried Elsifor. He was at the *Venture's* mast, groping with the lines. "Should I pull it up?"

"Not yet," Haru answered. "We wait for Siva!"

"Haru, we're drifting! Siva wanted to get you home! Let me lift the sail!"

"No!" barked Haru. He'd already left Valivan behind. There was no way he was leaving Siva.

"We can't stay here!" Elsifor argued. "Look!"

Fifty yards away, the nearest seabreaker loomed ever larger. Soldiers lined up on its rail, raising crossbows. Haru turned the *Venture* toward them to present the narrowest target. The wind was good enough to take them from the harbor—if they raised the sail. But when the crossbows opened fire, his confidence shriveled. A bolt struck the wheel, wedging between his fingers. He ducked as three more whizzed overhead. Elsifor scrambled to cover him, dragging him down. Then, from the dock, he heard the glorious sound of Siva's curses.

"Go, you idiots!"

Haru crawled out from under Elsifor, watching as Siva dived into the water and began swimming furiously toward them. Behind her was the Shadow Boy, patchy with wounds, one ear hanging from a thread of skin, one arm severed at the elbow. It splashed into the water after Siva.

Haru scrambled to the mast, ignoring the crossbows and yanking the lines, raising the mainsail. The sail swelled with wind. Haru scurried back to the wheel, ruddering toward the harbor's exit as the *Venture* gained speed. Siva paddled madly toward them, her attacker close behind. Elsifor jumped in after her. Siva waved him off, panicked that he'd left the boat, but Elsifor swam right past her. His claw came out of the water like the fin of a shark. The last of the Shadow Boys breached toward him. Their clash sent up a spray of water. When it cleared, they were both beneath the waves.

"No!" gurgled Siva.

She dived down after them. An arrow thudded against the hull. Haru abandoned the wheel and ran toward the side. A moment later Siva surfaced.

"Siva!" cried Haru. He stretched toward her. "Come on!"

She ignored him, her face frozen in dread as she bobbed on the waves. She didn't dive again or swim for the *Venture*. She merely watched the place where Elsifor had gone down. Haru hovered on the rail. Even in the moonlight he could see the blood bubbling on the waves. When a great, hairy figure burst from the depths, he screamed for Siva to swim.

Until he realized it was Elsifor.

Siva let out a joyous whoop, swimming to Elsifor and wrapping her arms around him. Bloodied and exhausted, they swam for Haru's outstretched hand. The wind was catching quickly now, blowing them in a circle. More and more arrows rained around them. Haru pulled up Elsifor first, letting his wounded friend collapse on the deck. Siva sprang up with little help, flinging her body over the side.

"I lost my atlatl," she gasped.

"You killed him!" said Haru, taking the wheel. "He must be dead!" He steered the *Venture* out of the harbor, waving Siva over. "Hold it just like this. Hold it steady," he told her, then went to the mast and began fumbling with the headsails. They needed speed now, and Larajin had given him the three he'd asked for. He swiftly pulled the lines, raising the triangular sails one at a time. The *Venture* quickened. The entrance to the harbor loomed ahead. The armada of ungainly seabreakers stood at anchor, dwarfing them.

"Get below," Haru ordered.

"Haru," said Siva. "Look at Agon."

Hundreds of soldiers swarmed the pier. The noise of battle and screaming voices reached across the water. Up in the hills a fire had started, engulfing the homes. Haru searched the chaos for Whistler. Unable to find the old man, he turned away.

"Siva, go below," he said. "Take Elsifor."

"Haru..."

"You're just targets up here," he told her. He looked ahead at the maze of seabreakers and the beckoning exit of the harbor. "This is mine now."

Siva wiped her wet and bloodied face. She studied the warships and the jeering men on their decks. She didn't say a word to Haru, just nodded confidently and took the wounded Elsifor below.

Alone on deck, Haru felt the *Venture* beneath him, like a living thing. He wasn't good at much, he decided. Not at being a friend, and not at being a Tain. But he was a born mariner, and with the aid of the wind he steered his ship toward home. Arrows flew at him, but they would never catch him. He threaded the Venture past the anchored warships, dodging the bolts and the human jeers.

"Hold on!" he cried down to the last of his Chorus. "We're going home!"

Chapter Forty-Eight

LINBETH

The solarium had always been Count Whistler's favorite room. It was where he kept his books and all his best pipes, where he could sit for hours and overlook the bailey, watching the stable boys groom his horses. In better days he would light a fire in the big stone hearth and listen to his daughters sing while his wife played the harp. He told them stories, delighting in their laughter.

The solarium was Count Whistler's sanctuary, but not today. Today it was his prison. There were no songs from his captive daughters, no fire in the cold hearth. His stable boys, too, had been arrested, and a gallows was going up in the bailey. Whistler heard the hammer and saws, watching his jailors erect the deathtrap from his window. His wife Carida sat shivering on the settee, comforting their daughters. Whistler himself sat in a chair near the window, his arms manacled behind his back—even the broken one. The battle had taken most of his men. Those who'd survived were doomed to the noose. Whistler's face was a patchwork of lacerations. A thigh wound had all but crippled him. Carida had done what she could for his cuts, dabbing them with strips torn from her dress and wrapping his thigh with a frilly swatch. So far, she and their daughters had been untouched, but Setina and Linbeth were young and beautiful, and Whistler feared for them far more than he did for himself.

For four hours they had been imprisoned in the solarium. After the defeat of his makeshift army, Whistler had surrendered to Larius on the one condition that his family be unharmed. And then he'd watched his friends and servants and retainers be rounded up. They would die, eventually, but not before Larius wrote his records and reports, cataloging his captives like grain shipments. Those that didn't swing on the gallows would be sent back to J'hora for trial at the Tower—all because they'd followed a foolish old man.

Still, Whistler had no regrets. After months of crawling on his belly, he had done the only thing a real man could do. He'd stood on his feet again.

"Carida," he called softly.

His wife left the settee and knelt before him. Without a word she laid her head on his lap. Whistler was desperate to stroke her hair. Unable to move his manacled arms, he pursed his lips and blew down on her pale, beautiful cheek. Carida hadn't wept, nor had the girls. Too strong to grant Larius such a gift, they had been stoic in captivity, like their father. Whistler was proud of them.

"You are Agoni women," he told them. "Teach the world what that means."

Linbeth, the younger of the daughters, made a face of defiance. Of the two she was most like her mother. Setina, more genteel, gave her father a tiny nod. At fifteen, she understood well what might happen to her. The dread of it haunted her emerald eyes. They were exhausted now, all of them. The concussion in his skull made Whistler sleepy. He tilted down his head, bringing it as close to Carida's as he could, and very softly said he loved her.

But when the door blew open, their tender moment died.

Sea Master Larius had dressed for the meeting, his perfect uniform gleaming with medals. A ceremonial dagger hung from a hilt at his belt and the polish on his boots reflected the sunlight through the window. Beneath his armpit rested his ubiquitous notebook. Two Saphi warriors from Caiba followed him into the solarium, their bare chests crossed with bandoliers, the curved swords of their sect strapped to their backs. Caibans were stupidly loyal, making them desirable bodyguards. Since coming ashore, Larius rarely moved without them. Lady Carida got quickly to her feet, blocking Larius from her injured husband. But when Linbeth and Setina rose, Whistler protested.

"No!" he grumbled. "Do not rise for this *creature*."

His daughters retreated, sitting back down on the settee. Larius glowered at the Count.

"Lady Carida, if you would join your daughters, please."

Carida hesitated, relenting only when her husband agreed. She sat back between her daughters, putting her arms around them. The silent warriors remained in the threshold. Larius hovered over Whistler's chair.

"Have you looked out the window?" he queried.

"I can barely stand," replied Whistler.

"You've seen it. I know you have. Oh, the hangman will be busy today!" Larius took the notebook from under his arm and patted it. "I've found more than two dozen conspirators. All their names are right here. You're a very well-liked man, Count Whistler. I had thought more of your people would have renounced you, but you know what they say—Agoni people are imbeciles."

"You can kill them," said Whistler. "But word will spread. People will know what happened here."

"They'll know that you embarrassed yourself."

"And you," Whistler retorted.

"You're a traitor, Count Whistler." Larius reached into his pocket. "Look what was found in the harbormaster's house..." He pulled out Whistler's Chain of Office and let it swing from his stubby fingers. "Do you know what else we found there? Bodies. One Cryori and one...well, I have no idea what that other thing was."

Whistler laughed in his face. "Fool! That abomination was Reius' son!"

"Son?" Larius' alarm pleased Whistler. "Reius didn't have a son."

"He had two of them. Ask Malon."

"Count Whistler, there was a head and body. And a dead Cryori lying next to it! Now you will tell me about this mystery. Clearly you don't care about your own life, but there's a reason I brought your wife and lovely daughters here."

"Leave him alone!" cried Setina.

"Setina..." Whistler frowned at his daughter. "An Agoni woman. Remember?"

His order silenced her. He looked up sanguinely at Larius. "Ask your questions. I will answer them—if you'll spare my wife and daughters."

"Then take my promise as a bond. Who were the Cryori you were fighting with?"

"Tain Haru and his advisors," replied Whistler.

Larius' expression cracked. "The assassins."

"I gave them a ship. The *Venture*. She's quick enough to get them back to Nesenor. You've already wasted too much time to catch them."

"The fleet sets sail tomorrow, Count. I don't need to catch those murderers to make a point of them. Their entire country will pay for what they've done."

"They've done nothing, Larius. Nothing! Malon was the one who killed Reius."

Larius looked doubly shocked. "That's impossible."

"If you don't believe me, make inquiries. That's the kind of Alliance you're serving now, Larius. And now that you know the truth, Malon will kill you, too."

Whistler grinned into Larius' ashen face. The Caibans at the door grimaced. The Sea Master tucked his notebook under his arm.

"On your feet, Count Whistler."

Whistler struggled to rise, a searing pain jutting through his wounded leg. When his wife and daughters rose to accompany him, Larius barked at them.

"Remain!" he hissed.

"The gallows isn't done yet," remarked Whistler. "Where are we going?"

"Just move."

Larius directed the warriors aside. Whistler looked at his wife and daughters, struggling not to break. Linbeth's lips quivered in farewell as her father stepped past Larius.

"Keep your promise," said Whistler as he shuffled toward the door. "I'll sign a confession. Just leave my wife and daughters alone."

"Your wife will live," agreed Larius. "Your daughters too. There's just one thing I want to show them before I let them go..." Larius reached up and grabbed Whistler's forehead. The notebook hit the floor, and the jeweled dagger sprung from his belt. "I want them to see you die, you arrogant fucker!"

He plunged the blade into the back of Whistler's head, jamming it through the base of the skull. The jolt crumbled Whistler to his knees. Carida screamed. Setina shrieked. Linbeth ran toward him, arms outstretched...

Her shattered face was the last thing Whistler saw.

Chapter Forty-Nine

THE VIRTUOUS TIGER

F ifteen feet a person—that's how long a boat should be to sail across the world. Haru had heard that advice countless times from the mariners in Jinja. A smaller boat—a blue water boat—simply wouldn't make it.

At just over thirty feet, the *Venture* was at risk with three aboard. Heavy with supplies and facing the swales of the ocean, Haru could feel every groan she made against the waves. For a night and a day he sailed her eastward, divining their direction from the sun and stars. Jinja's mariners had taught him many things, like how to tack in a strong wind and how to trim a luffing sail, but the most important thing Haru had learned was navigation, and to never, ever journey without charts. It was a lesson Harbormaster Larajin surely understood, yet in his rush to get them sea-bound he'd neglected to supply a single map.

So east they sailed, and then some south, Haru feigning confidence as he tried to point the *Venture* home. With Siva and Elsifor for hands, they left the human continent far behind. Shadur's death had shocked them, but they had found the time to toast their friend that first night at sea, cracking open the kegs Larajin had supplied and drowning their anguish in bitter beer. On the longest night of Haru's life, he drank with the two last members of his Chorus until the tears came, and together they wept like children in the moonlight.

"When you're five years old, your father's a giant. And then when you're twelve, and you're a little bigger and a little stronger, he starts looking smaller. And you start seeing all the things he can't do, because he's really not a giant after all."

Haru looked out over the prow of the boat—*his* boat—and saw how giant the sea was.

"I think he wanted to protect me."

Siva smiled wanly at his conclusion. "He did."

They had time now together, something they never seemed to have before, not since they were children. Haru had given Elsifor his turn at the wheel, dispensing the simple advice to keep the ship steady and hold their heading. With little else to do but talk, he had found Siva at the prow, pensive with the sun on her face and a distant look in her tired eyes. Like Elsifor, she had rinsed her numerous wounds in the same beer they'd drank the night before, bandaging the worst of them with strips of an old blanket she'd discovered in the hold. She looked frail and thin, and without her knives, defenseless.

Haru leaned back on the palms of his hands. To his great relief, a clear sky called them eastward. He would steer them east for another day and then tack south. For now, they were in no danger of missing Nesenor, but eventually they might overshoot their homeland, a fear Haru neglected to confess. He no longer thought of avenging his father or proving his manhood. All those things had just distracted him.

"When we get home, I need to be a Tain," he said.

Siva hooded her eyes from the sun. "You are a Tain."

"People don't think so. They want my father but they have me instead. But I'm going to be a good one, Siva. I'm going to change."

Siva was quiet for a moment, then said, "You have changed, Haru. All of us have changed. That's what happens when people we care about die."

They ate a meal of sardines and horse beans that evening, lingering over it and telling stories and watching the waves swallow the sun. While Haru drew his own charts from the constellations, Siva read aloud from Joak Sitirus' journal, entertaining Elsifor with the tale of the dead soldier's life. So far, the urge to hunt had yet to come upon Elsifor, and he was strangely calm upon the tiny ship. He had killed enough in J'hora to satisfy his lusts, he explained, but Haru was sure the loss of Val and Shadur had tempered his spirit. Drunk on beer and lulled by the waves, Elsifor fell asleep listening to Siva's voice, and sometime after midnight she dragged him below to bed, leaving Haru alone on deck.

It was a night so clear that all the stars came out to greet him, and all the constellations battled for his attention. Fang-Bahu roared brightly in the east, guiding Haru's hand on the wheel. The white tiger hung low in the heavens, his tail of twinkling stars pointing down toward Nesenor. Haru studied the constellation, imagining Fang-Bahu's ancient face and powerful stride. The virtuous tiger only prowled Cryori lands in times of peace. Haru knew he would not see Fang-Bahu in Nesenor soon.

He stretched out his mind to touch Clionet, but even now, upon her ocean, the great goddess of the sea was silent. He closed his eyes and imagined his homecoming. He would need Clionet to stop the J'horans. He would need her shenenra.

"Clionet, please hear me. I'm coming home."

When he opened his eyes Fang-Bahu remained before him, hanging like a portrait in the sky.

Haru.

Haru looked behind him, then realized the voice was in his head. "Valivan?" Overjoyed, he looked skyward. "Valivan? I can hear you!"

Valivan's voice was syrupy slow. *I'm tired, Haru.*

"Where are you, Val? Are you alright?"

I have to tell you something...

Haru wanted to turn the boat around. "We're going home, Val. You saved us."

Not Shadur.

"No," said Haru darkly. "But Siva and Elsifor are alive! And we're going home now. We're going to fight the humans. We're going to win!"

Valivan's reply was faint and sleepy. *It's too much for me, Haru. I can't endure.*

Haru put all the love he could into his reply, hoping Valivan could feel it across the miles. "I know, Val. I'm sorry. Malon's a monster."

Not Malon. Jyx.

"Jyx? What's he done to you?"

I have to tell you something, Haru...

His voice was weaker than usual. Haru locked the wheel and went to the rail, looking out over the ocean. "Valivan? What's happening?"

It was Liadin, Haru. He killed Sh'an. It was always Liadin.

The words chilled Haru. "What?"

Jyx told me so. He did it, Haru. We were wrong.

"No!"

He's imprisoned Clionet in the catacombs. He brought back Ama'aga. He did it with Skorthoros.

Haru paced along the deck. "He's lying! Jyx always lies! He's trying to hurt you, Val!"

Liadin did it, Haru. Be careful of him and the Venerants. Save Clionet. Save Nesenor.

It made no sense to Haru, yet he knew it wasn't a jest. "Why?" he called out.

Jyx tells me what Jyx tells me. He tells me what will taunt me. Val's voice began slipping. *I hate him, Haru.*

"Where are you? Are you with Malon?"

I'm going, Haru.

"Val, no!"

Malon's guards left a knife with my supper. Val shared himself fully with Haru, revealing his every pain. The image of his opened veins made Haru's wrists sear. *It won't take long.*

"Valivan!"

Haru's scream brought Siva running from below. In his mind he could see Valivan clearly now, lying in bed; floating in blood.

"Valivan, don't shut your eyes!" Haru cried. "Get someone to help you! Call Malon's guards!"

I want to go, Haru. Don't be angry.

Siva froze, watching Haru as he sank to his knees.

"No, Val, no," broke Haru. "Please..."

Valivan's contented smile drifted across the water. He closed his eyes as the blood drained from his wrists. Haru held on to him as long as he could, the connection, fading, fading...

...then blowing out like a candle.

Unable to rise, Haru stayed on his knees. Siva knelt down beside him and slipped an arm about his shoulders.

"It was Liadin," Haru whispered

"Liadin? What about him?"

"He did it. He killed my father. I can't believe it...but I do."

"Haru, I don't understand," said Siva. "What happened?"

Haru didn't understand either. Not really. His mind raced to put the pieces together. "Valivan's dead," he said. "And Liadin killed my father."

Siva sank back in shock. "How?"

"Skorthoros," said Haru. "Ama'aga too." The realization of what they were up against chilled him.

"Then Liadin's a dead man," promised Siva. "I'll see to it."

Her face grew rigid. The sea seemed infinite. Haru sat speechless. He wasn't just afraid, he realized. Liadin had done the same thing his father had done by dying. He had broken his heart.

Chapter Fifty

NAGANA AND VAUS

L iadin had never really loved the sea, at least not the way most Cryori did. While other boys heard the call of the waves, Liadin had longed for books as a child, leaving the sea to men like Nuara. And though he could contemplate the ocean's greatness or sing about its beauty, he could never quite understand its glamour. Like most Venerants, Liadin preferred dry, safe land, and had only been upon a beast-ship once before in his life. Now, as he looked out over the rear of the *Gonkin,* he remembered that time aboard the *Reikis* with Sh'an, and the crush of decades saddened him.

Sadness had dogged Liadin all the way from Jinja. It had plagued him for months, really, ever since he'd killed Sh'an, and the memory of that day—that awful day of blood and ashes—followed him everywhere. Not even Hamu-Hanza, with all its tropical beauty, had salved him. Liadin knew his life would likely end soon. He was old, too old to go to war and expect to survive, but that didn't matter. His life was a worthy sacrifice. He could bear the pain and guilt.

He regretted nothing.

The frothy wake of the *Gonkin* stretched out behind her, the ocean churning beneath her perplexing keel. Off their starboard the *Hakar* sailed alongside, accompanying the *Gonkin* to the blockade. The two cat-ships had left Hamu-Hanza hours ago. Liadin had remained above deck, waiting for Nuara to emerge from his cabin. He'd had very little contact with Nuara lately, even on the island, and Ama'aga's hand-picked sukano seemed uneasy. Compared to the White Fleet, their blockade was a relative handful. Worse, they had no shenenra to bolster them.

In that, Liadin knew, he had failed.

Unable to convince Clionet to help him, he had left her in Jinja to wither. The foaming wake made his heart ache for her.

"I am a torturer too," he said to himself.

After a lifetime of piety, his sins were quickly mounting. Murder, betrayal, heresy. And usurper, he reminded himself. All in service to Nesenor.

"No regrets."

Like a Venerant of old he was sailing into battle. Regrets could only weaken him. So far, Nuara had no idea Haru was alive. After giving Liadin that shocking news, that damned jester Jyx had yet to return, but that didn't mean he wouldn't. Liadin cracked his knuckles like a worried teenager. If Haru did return—which he sorely doubted—he would explain himself. He would tell Haru that none of it had been for his own glory.

"But no begging," he promised himself. "Not for mercy or forgiveness."

A call from the crow's nest caught his attention.

"Ship! Four points aft of the beam!"

Liadin followed the call, and a tight smiled stretched his face. Even without a spyglass he knew it wasn't a ship.

Nuara took the report of the sighting in his quarters, then remained at his desk for half of an hour. He had no idea how quickly the thing could travel, but the *Gonkin* and *Hakar* were at full sail and he had no intention of slowing down. He shunted his curiosity aside, concentrating on the hard work of planning his defense. His beast-ships were faster and sturdier than anything the White Fleet had floated, but without Liadin's promised dragon-whales his blockade was vastly out-numbered. Even with Ama'aga, Nuara doubted they could hold the J'horans for long.

A timepiece on his desk ticked away the minutes. Nuara had taken very few items from his father's house over the years, but the time-piece was a treasure, and the one vital thing a navigator really need-ed. He thought of Ama'aga, hidden somewhere beneath the waves. The war-god had disappeared a week ago, leaving Hamu-Hanza when Liadin arrived at the island, empty-handed. Without explain-ing why, Ama'aga had simply vanished into the water, promising to return but leaving Nuara with the horrible notion that he'd been abandoned.

"Gods," he grumbled. Already he was tired of them. They were cruel and capricious and had no use for timepieces. Nuara set down his pen and the final seconds swept past. Time was up.

He surrendered to his curiosity and went above. A pack of crew-men were gathered at the rail, pointing at the "ship" the lookout had detected. Amazingly, the thing had already caught up to them, coming between the *Gonkin* and *Hakar* and casting a giant shadow on the waves. Sailing Master Ariyo went quickly to Nuara, a baffled smile on his face.

"Look at it! Is that what Hor'roron was building?"

Nuara walked slowly toward the starboard rail. "That isn't just what he built," he said. "That *is* Hor'roron."

The metal beast was even larger now than it had been on the is-land, a towering creation of scales and unseen clockworks sheathed in iron skin. A horned head coiled up from its riveted neck, eyes aflame, the mouth a spitting nozzle of combustible venom. Two wing-like fins propelled it through the water, guided by a sweeping, hinged tail. Glowing spikes along its back snorted smoke and fire. The thing—the shenenra—was unmistakably alive. Nuara could sense Hor'roron within its armored hide, animating its mechanical limbs. The grace of the creature astounded him—and his dumb-struck crew. Among them stood Liadin.

"Not the shenenra you promised," joked Nuara, putting his hand on the priest's shoulder, "but it'll do."

Liadin, who'd looked glum and sickly for days, seemed invigo-rated. "Behold the work of gods, Nuara," he said. "What human contrivance could possibly stand against that?"

"It's a sight," agreed Nuara. "But I'd feel better if there were more of them."

"Hor'roron built the beast-ships," Liadin reminded him. He gloried in the spray of the beast's wake. "Mere men built the seabreakers. Mere humans."

"You've got more faith than brains, Arch-Disciple. The humans aren't as savage as you think. And their seabreakers aren't rowboats."

Liadin looked adoringly at the fiery monster and predicted, "You'll believe. When you see Hor'roron crack a seabreaker like an egg, you'll believe."

"As long as it keeps up with us," said Nuara. He turned to make his way to the bow. "Ariyo, get the men back to work. Have the—"

A wave from portside rocked the *Gonkin*, sloshing foam over the rail. The blow caught the crew's attention, bringing them larboard to see a familiar swirl on the surface of the waves. Nuara grimaced at the noise as the water hissed and bubbled. In the spew of steam, a helmeted head appeared, crusted with barnacles and seaweed. Nuara stood his ground even as his men backed away. Liadin came hurrying up to stand beside them.

"Ama'aga!" he declared. "You see, Nuara? He returns!"

The sight of the war-god relieved Nuara, but Ama'aga was not alone. With him rose a pair of black, reptilian heads, bobbing on long, serpentine bodies. The creatures coiled around the god, swimming with the swirling current, surrounding him as he approached the *Gonkin*.

"Those serpents!" he pointed. "Ariyo, remember?"

"I remember," snorted Ariyo.

"Liadin, I told you about them," said Nuara. "When we returned from J'hora, remember? We saw them kill a dragon-whale!"

Liadin's gave a guilty grimace. "I know them," he said. "I knew them then. They are Ama'aga's heralds, Nagana and Vaus."

"Heralds?" asked Nuara. "Those monsters?"

Liadin looked disgusted at his ignorance. "Mariners. You claim Ama'aga as your patron but know nothing of his creed. Have you forgotten he's called the Holy Serpent?"

"Liadin, those things killed a dragon-whale."

"Nagana and Vaus are vowed enemies of the shenenra. But how could I tell you that on the night you came home? I had just become Regent."

Nuara studied the black serpents. "He brought them because of you," he told Liadin, suddenly understanding. "Because you failed to bring the dragon-whales."

"He brought them because we need them," said Liadin.

"You've managed to embarrass me," grumbled Nuara. "Again."

He went to the port rail and waited for Ama'aga as the war-god churned toward the ship, his hissing pets wrapping about his armored torso. Ama'aga's time beneath the waves had changed him. He looked refreshed, larger and more vital than Nuara had ever seen him.

"Sukano!" he said, greeting Nuara as he hovered over the *Gonkin*. "I have rested and I have fed. I have returned as promised. Now, let us make war!"

Chapter Fifty-One

OF THE BLOOD

For six days and nights, Haru had carefully marked the passage of time. He had followed the stars and the moon and the sun, making notes of their positions on the charts he'd drawn and summoning every lesson he had ever learned about navigation. The *Venture* had performed magnificently, helped by strong winds and a sky free of storms, and Haru had done his best to keep a steady speed, noting their progress as accurately as he could. At any other time, Haru would have been proud of himself. He'd kept the *Venture* on course and her little crew alive, and with just a bit more luck he would be seeing Nesenor now on the horizon.

But he was not.

The ocean surrounded them, just as it had for days, without a hint of land or even a seabird to tell them they were getting close. Haru had done his best to navigate by the stars, but the stars were very far away. He stood at the wheel of the boat, misplaced in all the ocean's vastness. Out of options, Haru called for help.

"Siva! Elsifor! Come above!"

Siva's sun-burned face appeared first as she climbed out of the hold. The tone of Haru's voice set her jaw with worry.

"Haru?" She stepped to the wheel as Elsifor came up after her. "Something wrong?"

"Take the wheel," Haru told her. "I need to set the anchor."

"We have an anchor?" joked Elsifor.

"Why?" asked Siva. She'd stripped the bandages from her wounds, and now her bare arms looked dark and muscular. She took the wheel with confidence. "What's the matter?"

"We have to stay put a while," said Haru. "Elsifor, pull in the sails."

As Elsifor went to work, Haru went to the bow and heaved the anchor, letting the rusty chain unspool until the anchor hit bottom, catching the drifting boat.

"We're lost," guessed Elsifor, hopping down from the mast.

Siva looked at Haru. "Are we lost, Haru?"

"You can let go of the wheel," Haru directed. "Just lock it down."

Siva waited for an answer. "*Lost?*"

"We're alright," Haru assured. "We've got food and water and a ship in fine shape. We're close to Nesenor. We must be."

"Haru," said Elsifor easily, "we're not angry. Just tell us."

Haru turned his face away from the breeze. "I didn't tell you this because I didn't want to worry you. I thought if I kept a steady course, we'd reach Nesenor. But without charts..." He shrugged. "I know we're close. We could keep going east but if we do we could sail right past it. Same thing if we head south."

"So, what do we do?" Siva wondered.

"I can climb the mast," suggested Elsifor. "I'll be lookout. With my eyes I'm sure I'll see land."

"No," said Haru. "We can't just keep going, not anymore. We need help."

"Help?" frowned Siva. "What kind of help can we get out here?"

"Clionet won't be able to help us, Haru," said Elsifor. "She's trapped in the catacombs. Even if you could speak to her from here..."

"Not Clionet," said Haru. "I've already tried to reach her. If she's still alive she can't hear me or she can't answer."

"So?" pressed Siva. "Who, then? Not Jyx!"

"No, never," spat Haru. "Jyx can rot. He'd never help us anyway. We need a dragon-whale. They know the ocean better than anything. A dragon-whale can guide us home."

"How can you summon a dragon-whale?" asked Siva. "You need to know the Charm." He smirked at Haru. "Do you know the Charm?"

"Not completely," Haru admitted. "My father never really taught me it, but I heard Liadin speak it once. Just after my father died. He was at the temple of Ama'aga, trying to summon a dragon-whale. He told me he was practicing the charm so he could teach it to me. I was so stupid I believed him!"

"Did it work?" asked Elsifor. "Did he bring a dragon-whale?"

"In a way. There was a dragon-whale. But Liadin told me it came because I was there, because it heard the Charm of Summoning and sensed I was with him. If I can remember the Charm, maybe I can do it again. Maybe a shenenra will hear me out here."

"Maybe," sighed Siva. "If we're close enough to Nesenor."

"And if you can remember the Charm," said Elsifor.

Haru paced across the deck. "I've been trying. I remember some of it, but..." He shut his eyes, trying to conjure the memory of that day at the temple. "The old tongue is hard!"

"Haru," said Siva sharply. "Look at me."

Haru opened his eyes and looked straight into her burnt face. "What?"

"You got us this far," said Siva. "Now take us the rest of the way. You *will* summon a dragon-whale. You're our Tain. You're going to get us home."

Charms were like songs, Haru's father once had told him. If you sang them, they were easier to remember. Being a Tain meant knowing the charms, but not for Haru. He had grown up too slowly for his father to entrust them, and Haru hadn't bothered to insist Liadin teach him, believing stupidly in the old priest's fealty. But Liadin had slipped just enough that day at the temple, raising his voice for the whole world to hear.

For two hours Haru sat on the bow of the *Venture*, his feet dangling overboard as he knitted together his fragmented memory. Shirtless, his trousers rolled up his calves, he struggled to unlock his mind. The sun warmed his naked flesh. His closed eyelids danced with colors. The Charm of Summoning was only part of the conjuring, he reminded himself. Liadin knew it and still couldn't summon the shenenra. But Haru could. He knew he could. He was of the blood.

He opened his parched mouth and sang.

The words came in a broken torrent, at first mangled and meaningless. But Haru kept on. Eyes closed, he tilted his face heavenward and let the old tongue take over, chipping at his rusted memories. He let the sun burn his skin, welcoming the pain like a repenting Venerant, stretching his mind into the water, reaching out toward home. Siva and Elsifor fell away behind him. The *Venture* disappeared. Soon he was untethered, drifting through the ocean. His song grew louder. The words of the Charm formed effortlessly on his lips. Haru surrendered to the sensation, letting it carry him away.

"Haru?"

He opened his eyes with great effort. The blurry faces of Siva and Elsifor stared back at him. Above them, stars twinkled.

"Was I sleeping?" Haru murmured

Siva cupped her hand behind his head, lifting him from the deck. Her concerned face frightened him. "You were chanting," she said. "Elsifor..."

Elsifor hurried a wet cloth to her. "You were out here all day," he told Haru. "We let you go on, and then...you just fainted."

The back of Haru's head hurt. He let Siva wipe his brow with the cool cloth. "I remember," he said weakly. "I wasn't here."

"You were here the whole time, Haru," said Siva. "Just sit still..."

"No." Haru sat up, recalling the odd sensation. "I was in the water! There..." He pointed toward the dark waves. "I could see the dragon-whales!"

Siva and Elsifor shared a skeptical glance. "Alright," said Siva, holding him up. She grimaced at the sight of his dry mouth. "You need water. I'm surprised you can even talk. Don't you remember singing?"

"I was singing," nodded Haru, "and then I was in the water." He looked around, baffled at the passage of time. His skin ached and his head swam. "I don't feel good."

Elsifor backed up. "Can you make it to the rail?"

"I think so."

With Elsifor's help Haru hurried to the side, choking up the nausea from his near-empty stomach. Siva quickly fetched him a cup of water, which he drained at once before hovering over the rail, letting the cool air settle him. The night was still and pleasant, the waves lulling. But not a single dragon-whale showed itself.

"Go below, Haru," said Siva. "You need to sleep."

She took his arm and directed him toward the hold, supporting him as he wobbled. Around him the world began to spin. The *Venture* pitched suddenly larboard, spilling Haru across the deck. Elsifor hurried portside.

"Something hit us," he called. "I felt it!"

When it came again, Haru heard it too. The sudden thump lifted the boat. He took hold of Siva's arm and joined Elsifor at the rail, staring down into the dark water, the chop splashing their faces.

"I don't see anything," said Siva. "Elsifor, use those weird eyes of yours—"

An explosion of water blew her backward. Haru held fast to the rail, astonished as a great, dark maw opened below him. The mouth shot up, seizing him at the waist. Before he could panic, he was overboard. He heard Elsifor's cry, saw Siva scramble after him, then felt the cold shock of water. Down he went, dragged far from the *Venture*, held in the creature's enormous mouth. A stream of bubbles screamed past his lips as the thing carried him off. Seawater raced down his throat. The sharp pain of it nearly blacked him out. After what seemed forever, the creature broke the surface and tossed him into the air.

For a moment Haru saw the sky. Then he was falling, crashing into the sea. He bobbed up, searching desperately for the *Venture* and gasped when he saw it in the far distance. The thing coiled in the waves around him. Afraid to scream, Haru held his breath as a huge, finned head crested the waves. The yellow eyes of a colossal dragon-whale stared back at him.

"Mother goddess...!"

Off in the distance Siva and Elsifor were calling his name. Haru paddled to stay afloat. His side ached from the dragon-whale's bite, but he knew the beast hadn't punctured the skin. Had it wanted to, it could have easily cut him in half.

"Easy," he told the creature. "I'm Haru. But you know that, don't you? You know I summoned you."

The shenenra drifted closer. Recognition shone in its glowing eyes. Its flippered tail lifted from the water, revealing its absurd length.

"Oh, you're an old one, aren't you?" said Haru. "You're the biggest one I've ever seen!"

His voice tranquilized the beast. Seeing its serenity, Haru smiled.

"I saw you in my dream," he told the creature. "I saw you coming to me." Exhausted, he struggled to stay afloat. "We're drifting from my boat." He pointed toward the *Venture*. "You see it there? I need it. I can't swim like you."

The dragon-whale brought its snout right up to Haru and gave him a gentle nudge. Taking the gesture as friendly, Haru reached out and touched the creature's wet nose. The contact brought a shock of revelation.

"Oh!"

He held on to beast, digging his fingers gently into its scales, their minds touching.

"You have...a name!"

He could almost see it in his brain. He focused, sounding it out. "Katsurut...Kairuts ..." Haru stilled his galloping thoughts. "Kairuset! That's your name. And you're a female!" He stroked the shenenra's snout. "I need your help, Kairuset. I need you to get me home. To Nesenor. Will you do that for me?"

His question seemed to penetrate the creature's ancient brain.

"You swim alone," said Haru. "Yes, I see that in you. That's what your name means—lonely swimmer. But your goddess is in danger, Kairuset. Clionet. She needs you, too."

Kairuset opened her mouth again, unspooling her long, powerful tongue. She wrapped it gently around Haru, pulling him back into her mouth. Haru surrendered without a struggle, trusting the shenenra as she nestled him like a baby in her teeth. She lifted him out of the water, turning her massive body back toward the *Venture*. As she did, Haru called out for his crewmates.

"Siva, Elsifor, over here!" he cried. "Look what I found!"

Chapter Fifty-Two

INTO THE FIRE

From the quarterdeck of the *Witch Breaker* Larius could see past his line of ships all the way to the approaching enemy. He counted nearly four dozen of the magnificent vessels, a sight that would have put his ancestors into their graves. They were a beautiful fleet, a collection of creatures fierce and exotic, and through his spyglass Larius marveled at their construction. At the head of them churned a walrus-ship, its two gleaming tusks poised like a battering ram as it sailed toward the line. A barracuda followed the walrus, long and slender, and a scorpion followed the barracuda, flanked by a jackal and a dragonfly. With the wind from the north, the strange sails of the beast-ships turned with a peculiar accuracy. The Cryori had the wind advantage, but Larius had expected that. The beast-ships of Nesenor were superior to his seabreakers in every way, and would easily best them in any even match.

Today, however, the match was grossly uneven.

His scout ships had been correct in their reports. Four dozen beast-ships were all the Cryori had mustered. For days Larius had probed their fleet with scout ships, checking the waters for signs of the terrible dragon-whales, but not a single sighting had been reported, and Larius wondered if the stories he'd heard were true—that only the Cryori Tain could control the giant beasts. He supposed the young Haru had never made it home. Yet despite their advantage in numbers, there was one thing through his spyglass that worried Larius.

"What is it?" he wondered aloud, squinting through the glass.

Next to him, First Seaman Gaige stopped shouting orders just long enough to say uselessly, "No idea, Sir."

Larius lowered the spyglass but could still see the metal vessel and the plume of fire it coughed. He had never seen a dragon-whale, but he supposed the metallic beast resembled one. The source of its locomotion puzzled him. If there were men inside it they were well protected. He brought up the spyglass once more. "That is the damndest thing I've ever seen."

"Damndest thing ever, Sir."

It moved like a living creature, its fins propelling it through the waves. The magic of it startled Larius. He kept the glass on it until a black shadow fell across the viewer and a shout went up from the deck. The shrill cry of his crew made the spyglass slip from his fingers.

Twenty yards ahead of the *Witch Breaker*, the long neck of a serpent rose out of the water. Its huge, fanged mouth opened with a hiss, unafraid of the approaching ship. Larius stared, astounded by the size of it—until its twin surfaced off the larboard side. First-Seaman Gaige shouted to the Second, who roared the order to the gundeck.

"Larboard guns—prepare!"

Gaige awaited Larius' order. The bow-chaser—a triple crossbow primed with harpoons—groaned as its crew wound back its firing cable. The big, black sea-snake fanned its spitting gills. With no time to turn and the larboard guns readying their shots, Larius made his choice.

"Ahead."

Ama'aga swam unseen beneath the hulls of the human vessels, amazed at their sheer numbers. They weren't like his nephew's beast-ships, of course, but the seabreakers were large and quicker than he recalled, and far more warlike than the ships that had plied J'horan waters in the good days of plunder. Ama'aga studied the ships through the shimmering water, watching as his heralds emerged from the depths. Nagana and Vaus had panicked the humans; Ama'aga could hear the commotion even beneath the waves.

He surfaced to the sound of long-guns.

A world of battle rushed at him. Human screams filled his ears. Larger and larger he became, announcing himself with a whirlpool. Ahead of him fought his beloved Nagana, plucking a man off the deck of a ship and swallowing him down. A cannonade heaved the vessel as it fired. Ama'aga let his heralds have the ship and chose one of his own, a proud, two-master with the name *Forbearance* blazoned on its side. Ama'aga crested toward it, letting its crew see him plainly.

"Know me, pink ones!" he bellowed. "Ama'aga is my name!"

The humans answered with a face-full of cannon fire.

From two miles away Nuara heard the long-guns and knew the war had begun. When the boom reached them, the beast-ships broke rank at once. All around the *Gonkin* her sisters chose their prey, catching the wind and readying their weapons. The swan-like *Dorsakai* screamed ahead, passing the *Gonkin* on its way to Ama'aga. A wave peeled from the *Hakar* as Captain Jollen tacked starboard, joining the *Serusus* as the walrus-ship ran for the line. The hornet-shaped *Makeda* headed north, and the windguns of the *Arikika* whirred to life.

There were no signals from Nuara, no colorful flags like those flashing from the J'horan flagship. Nuara's men had simple orders—to stop, to sink, to kill. Like a swarm they went to work. With no dragon-whales to help them, Nuara ordered the *Gonkin* forward, speeding away from the protection of Hor'roron toward the nearest seabreaker.

"Ramming blades, Ariyo," ordered Nuara; his Sailing Master echoed the command. Beneath the forecastle, Nuara felt the familiar shudder of armatures as the blades extended from the *Gonkin's* sculpted paws. They spread out wide, like a fan of daggers. The seabreaker ahead of them changed heading, bringing about their larboard guns.

"Five degrees to starboard," ordered Nuara.

Through the ports of the seabreaker's gundeck, he could see the human crew frantically loading the breeches of their bronze weapons. Like all seabreakers, she was a distance fighter. But like a leopard, the *Gonkin* fought close. The cat-ship's sails yawed them starboard, speeding them toward the seabreaker's stern. Ariyo called for the crew to brace themselves. Nuara grabbed a lashing strap and held on tight. Long-guns took time to load; Nuara knew his enemies would never make it.

The larboard ramming blades clawed through the seabreaker's hull as the ships collided. Timbers screamed and cracked apart. The *Gonkin* straightened, dragged larboard by the blow, and disemboweled the enemy's stern. Nuara ran to the rail, amazed at the ease of the blow, watching the seabreaker heave, water rushing into her shattered hull. Her cannons fell instantly silent as crewman spilled across her pitching decks and into the waves.

"Ahead, ahead!" Nuara cried.

For the first time in decades the *Gonkin* tasted blood.

Larius watched as the sea serpent swallowed down his navigator. He had managed to frighten off its twin with a broadside, but attempting to ram the other had only infuriated the quick beast, tempting it to make a meal of his crew. The *Witch Breaker* was firing at will now, her long-guns detonating in concussive waves. The god-thing that had risen up after the sea beasts had punched a hole in the *Forbearance*, and the *Furious* and *Righteous* were circling her, trying to save their listing sister as they peppered the giant with round-shot. To Larius, the man-god looked like a huge crustacean, his armor spiked like a crab, his helmet dripping seaweed.

Up ahead, the walrus-ship was coming toward them, picking up speed as she aimed her tusks at the line. Larius ordered her engaged and the signalmen flashed the message. The *Aspire* and *Wrath of*

Taan replied, changing course. On the deck around him, archers took aim at the stalking sea beasts. Larius strode to the prow where the giant, three-barreled crossbow waited. Five men attended the temperamental weapon, still struggling with the firing cable.

"Arm that weapon, you shit-birds!" bellowed Larius.

A sweating crewman pointed toward the serpent rising again behind the *Witch Breaker.*

"The long-guns, sir! Turn the ship!"

Larius slapped him hard across the face. "The giant, fool! Harpoon him!"

Already his men were cracking.

Hor'roron's new body felt remarkable. He had lived more years than he could remember, but he had never constructed anything as large and powerful as a shenenra to hold his spirit. The fire within the construct's belly would have melted Ama'aga or turned his mother Paiax to ashes, but Hor'roron had given up corporeal forms eons ago, preferring instead to inhabit the things he could make with a hammer and forge. Like all his creations, he had only to think of an action to make it happen, and after days as a shenenra he could easily turn his enormous reptilian head or swim with his fore-flippers or beat his screw-powered tail. Inside his belly burned a pool of molten coal, spewing fire from his nostrils and scalding slag from his mouth. For the first time in his existence, Hor'roron felt every bit as powerful as the greater gods.

The fleet of beast-ships screeched around him, picking targets and leveling their long-dormant armaments. Hor'roron was proud to see them battling again. He had built the beast-ships to shed human blood. With a twist of his jointed tail, he drove himself against the J'horan line, perplexed by the human method of warfare. While the Cryori had already broken their own blockade to attack, the seabreakers sailed mindlessly forward, a trio of them turning in unison to aim their bronze weapons.

Give me your fire! thought Hor'roron. He had no voice so he could not shout, but he did have a mouth and, like a typhoon, he spoke.

Up came the slag from his burning belly, up through his metal throat and exploding through his teeth, jetting out in a blazing stream. A seabreaker ahead of him caught the blow. Through his gem-cut eyes, Hor'roron saw the kaleidoscopic fire. Hot slag spilled across the deck, engulfing it, immolating the crew. Hor'roron turned against the others, obliterating the mainmast of a seabreaker making ready to fire. The third ship, the farthest away, got off its bombardment. The broadside shook Hor'roron's body. The force of the iron shot dented his metal flesh. Hor'roron, who could not feel pain, let astonishment have its moment. Human weapons had grown powerful! Newly respectful, he stalked closer to the offending vessel, pulling himself through the water with strong strokes, then once again called up the fiery contents of his belly and blew the vessel's quarterdeck apart.

Ama'aga submerged himself in the healing waters of his ocean. The relentless cannon fire had burned his face and smashed his armor. Even his formidable heralds were scarred. Down deep he went, to the floor of the ocean where the kelp was thick and the hulls of the seabreakers could be seen high above. With a great intake of breath Ama'aga opened his lungs to the curative brine, feeling its life-giving power. Nagana and Vaus darted through the kelp, coiling around him, their rage feeding his own. He spoke to them wordlessly, stoking their blood-lust and sharing his healing. From the sky above, the sound of warfare called him forth.

He jetted up from the ocean, his ancient serpents with him, breaching the waves with a thunderclap. The big J'horan flagship loomed ahead. Nagana rose up against it. Ama'aga saw a glinting on the flagship's deck, then heard the twang of a weapon. Too late, he called for Nagana to dive.

Like bolts of lightning came three harpoons. Nagana's head exploded instantly. Vaus screeched when he saw what had happened, spinning through the water toward his murdered twin. Ama'aga froze with horror. Upon the flagship, the human crew was already reloading the deadly apparatus. To his right, another ship fired a volley of arrows, the things bouncing harmlessly off Ama'aga's armor. He heard the cannon fire, saw the flash of bronze guns. The pounding staggered him.

Nagana was gone. Vaus, in grief, had gone below with her body. Ama'aga balled his fists and tossed back his head and let the loudest roar he had ever summoned crack the sky.

Aboard the *Witch Breaker*, Larius ordered continuous fire. The bow-chaser had managed to put down one of the sea beasts, but the shot had been meant for the giant and the death of his pet had enraged him. The *Witch Breaker* came about and opened another volley. At the front of the line, the metal dragon-ship had blown apart the *Perilous* and crippled the *Reaver* and *Abyss*. Beast-ships continued to pick apart the first line. Larius' flagship dodged the giant, holding him back with broadsides. The *Harbinger* and *Oblivion* swept in to her rescue, blinding the man-god in crossfire. The crew of the tri-bow signaled their readiness.

"Have second line close on the iron-hide," Larius told his officers. "Starboard long-guns to fire. I want to take off that thing's head."

Gaige relayed the order and the crew made the sails. From the gundeck below, the heavies turned the air to smoke. Larius knew the beast-ships could be bested. The god-thing, too. But the metal ship—the iron-hide—could ruin them. Quickly he tabbed up his options.

"Everything," he said aloud.

Gaige turned his sweaty face toward the Sea Master. "Everything, Sir?"

Larius studied the iron beast, confident in his decision. "We're taking it to him, Gaige," he said. "All of us."

Liadin remained on deck even as the *Gonkin* raced through the battle line and the enemy long-guns opened around her. As a crewman he was useless, but the mariners saw a symbol in his presence, and he refused to flinch or falter, and felt no pity at all for the humans their beast-ship sent to the bottom. He stood away from the heavy activity, holding tight to the shrouds while the *Gonkin* pitched and prowled the waves, dodging the whistling chain-shot. With his sukatai strapped to his back, he longed to board one of the enemy vessels and show what he could do with the weapon, but Cryori crews never boarded the way J'horan ships sometimes did. There were no prisoners to be taken today.

Far ahead of the *Gonkin*, the great, living beast that was Hor'roron continued its fiery advance. A ring of smoke surrounded the god-ship. The hulks of blazing seabreakers faltered behind it. Liadin peered through the madness. A dozen J'horan ships suddenly broke formation. A dozen more quickly followed. Like a flock of birds, they headed toward Hor'roron. Then, with a skull-splitting bombardment, they opened fire.

Chapter Fifty-Three

THE RETURN

For a day and a half, the *Venture* followed Kairuset, struggling to keep pace with the quick-swimming dragon-whale and following the occasional blast from the old beast's blowhole. Haru had indeed overshot their homeland, and so they sailed south and west, trusting in Kairuset's impeccable navigation while the wind blew them home. Kairuset had been far from the mainland when she'd heard Haru's call. Like a nomad she had wandered away from the hunting waters, restlessly exploring the world outside Cryori shores. In all the stories Haru knew of shenenra, he had never known them to roam the way Kairuset did, and he wondered why the "lonely swimmer" had left her kin so far behind, and what amazements she had seen over her many, many years. She had saved them and Haru adored her for that, but he knew also that he would need more from the old girl than a guide back home. When the time came for battle, he would need Kairuset to fight.

With their moods fine and the weather fair, the *Venture's* tiny crew anxiously watched the horizon for home. After more than a week at sea, Haru had managed to turn both Siva and Elsifor into capable hands. And when at last the first Cryori fishing boat appeared ahead, it was Elsifor who confidently sang out.

"Ship ahead!"

Haru ran to the prow and peered out over the sea. Not a ship but a boat, he realized, a gloriously plain and unthreatening fishing trawler. He gave a gleeful shout as Siva joined them. His practiced eye sighted something even Elsifor had missed.

"Look closer," he said.

Elsifor spotted it first. "Land!"

It lay beyond the fishing boat, like the hazy stroke of a paintbrush.

"Is that it?" asked Siva hopefully. "Is that home?"

Haru clapped her sun-burned back. "It is. It's Nesenor." He leaned over the prow and called out to Kairuset, "Thank you, beautiful one! Take us home! Take us home!"

A joyful geyser blew from Kairuset's spout.

"Louder, Kairuset!" cried Haru. "Let them know we're home! Let everyone know the Tain has returned!"

Kairuset led them to land, and from there they followed the coastline south. The fishing trawler they had first met joined them in their homecoming, pulling in other boats as well as they announced Haru's arrival. News spread quickly of his return, and along the coast all manners of vessels came out to greet them. By the time they reached Jinja, a flotilla was following them.

In the harbor and along the shore hundreds of men and women had come out to see Haru and prove the rumors of his return. The sight of Kairuset delighted them all, especially the children, who tossed flowers into the water to greet their Tain and his amazing shenenra. As the *Venture* pulled closer, Haru could see the robed Venerants waiting for him beyond the dock. Nearly two dozen of them had left their cloister, the guilt of what they'd done apparent on their grim faces. Incredibly, they seemed unarmed, their sukatais left behind, an almost unbelievable sacrifice for a Venerant to make.

"Look at them," sneered Siva. She looked past the throngs of well-wishers, her gaze cold upon the priests. When he realized what she was looking at, Elsifor let his smile melt away.

"Haru?" he asked. "What will you do?"

"There's no time for them," said Haru. He went to the mast and started reefing the sails as the *Venture* drifted toward the dock and tow vessels rowed out to meet them. "We have to get to Clionet."

Kairuset came alongside the *Venture*, nudging her forward. The men in the rowboats waved and called out to Haru. An old man with a tear-streaked face tossed a line over the rail.

"Tain Haru!" he cried.

His name was Pijigo, and nobody could tie knots the way he could. His son Hasa was with him, standing stoically behind his father the way he always did.

"Pijigo!" Haru shouted. He cleated the line just the way the old man had taught him. "Bring us in, bring us in!"

Others quickly joined old Pijigo, and with Kairuset's help the *Venture* soon bumped along the dock. The big shenenra was plainly visible now, her back out of the shallow water, her head spying the swelling gathering. A mass of people stormed the dock. Before Haru could jump the rail, Siva was ahead of him. Elsifor sprang out next, as determined as Siva to protect Haru from the mob.

"Let them in!" said Haru, jumping down to join them as the crowed rushed in. They were on him in seconds, shoving Siva and Elsifor aside and drowning him in kisses. Men fell to their knees and children pulled at his weather-beaten clothing. Haru stooped to greet the young ones, letting them touch his bearded face. The shock of being home again overwhelmed him. He looked up past the crowds toward the castle and swallowed the catch in his throat. Not all of them had made it back. In his mind he saw Valivan skipping through the willow trees, young and stuttering and happy. And old Shadur—Haru vowed to visit his ramshackle house.

First, though, there was Clionet.

"Liadin," Haru asked the crowd. "Where is he? Does anyone know?"

"He's gone to the battle," said a man.

"To war with Ama'aga!" said another.

A woman with a baby in a sling reached out for Haru's hand. "You can save us now, Tain!"

"Bring the shenenra!" called another.

They were all shouting it suddenly, crying out for Haru's help, for the magnificent shenenra to save them. Haru pushed past them, leaving the pier and climbing the path toward the castle. The Venerants came down to greet him, blocking his way. The crowd fell in behind Haru with a hush. Siva rushed in to stand between Haru and the priests, but a gentle touch from Haru moved her aside.

"Jharik," said Haru to the man leading the priestly mob. "Free Clionet."

Like many in the mob, Jharik was a young priest and devotee of Liadin himself. He was tall, thin, and at just over twenty, an odd choice to lead a revolt. Jharik had a look of riot in his eyes. But to Haru's great surprise, he dropped to his knees before his returning Tain.

"Tain Haru, we will not obey you."

Behind him, his followers knelt with him.

"Jharik, tell me—which one of you so-called holymen murdered my father?"

Jharik kept his eyes on the cobblestones. "The blood of Tain Sh'an stains us all."

"Tell me his name! Was he a Venerant?"

"It was an old magic," said Jharik. "Liadin learned it to kill your father."

"Who carried it?" Haru was almost shaking. He squatted down and grabbed hold of Jharik's chin. "Tell me!"

"Ren!" said Jharik. "His name was Ren." He pulled free of Haru's grasp, his voice miserable as he confessed. "He came from Sako province just days before the gathering. No one knew him."

"The gathering," simmered Siva. "When all of us were there—you killed Sh'an right in front of us."

"Ren." Haru chewed on the name. So plain. So forgettable. "Did he know?"

Jharik nodded. "He knew, Tain Haru. He was honored to carry the spell. He believed what Liadin told him. Just like the rest of us."

"What? That my father was weak? Is that what Liadin told you?" Haru stood. "Liadin used you. And I bet you don't know this, but Skorthoros used you too. All of you. Even Liadin."

At last, Jharik managed to look up. "What?"

Haru smirked. "That's what I thought."

"Conspirators," spat Siva. "Please, Haru, let me kill this shit-eater!"

"No," said Haru. Part of him pitied Jharik's blindness. "I can't let you kill him."

"Then I will," said Elsifor.

He flashed past Haru and Siva, wrenched back Jharik's head, and extended his slashing claws, tearing open Jharik's windpipe. The gush of blood horrified the crowd. Screams rippled as the dead priest collapsed. Elsifor stood over him without a hint of regret and theatrically licked the blood off his fingers. He glowered at the remaining Venerants.

"Now," he rumbled, "you're going to help us find Clionet."

Liadin's Venerants had done a masterful job of locking Clionet away. Each gate to the dungeon had been lowered and sealed shut with chains, and the massive iron doorway that allowed the sea to feed the catacombs had been closed as well, keeping out the fresh, invigorating ocean and locking in Ama'aga's poisonous, dead water. Every torch had been extinguished and removed; a torturous darkness shrouded the catwalks. It would have taken sledge hammers a day to break through each padlocked chain, but Haru had a key Liadin had never counted on—an enormous, enraged dragon-whale.

In all his life Haru had never been to the catacombs. They had been sealed and forgotten before he was born, and though every child who grew up in Jinja asked about them, the catacombs had become the stuff of chilling bedtime stories. As he stalked along the ledges with Elsifor and Siva, he imagined the countless human prisoners who'd met their ends in the place. The light from his torch touched the empty cells and rusted chains. The putrid smell of fetid water assailed his nostrils. Elsifor strode ahead of them, his bare feet padding quickly along the narrow walkway. The hulk of a long-abandoned ferry boat spilled rats over its side as the torchlight disturbed them.

The rest of the Venerants had succumbed quickly to Elsifor's questions. They had told Haru where Clionet was held and about the gates and chains and how they had believed Liadin's claims that Nesenor's new Tain was too weak to protect them from J'hora. Haru had let them surrender to his gathered loyalists. He still had a thousand questions, but he could already hear Kairuset bursting through the gates, and the thought of saving Clionet sped him through the catacombs.

"The pool!" called Elsifor. He came to a sudden stop ahead. "I've found her."

The rock walls shook as Kairuset approached. The smell of fresh sea water reached them at last as it seeped into the dark canal. Haru handed his torch back to Siva. A shallow pool of rancid water lay at his feet, walled in by slimy bricks and a huge, barred gate. A bloated carcass lay submerged beneath the water, a few flaccid tentacles floating lifelessly on the scummy surface.

"Oh," groaned Siva, squatting down to see. "Clionet."

Haru couldn't—wouldn't—believe it.

"She's a god. She can't die," he insisted.

He reached into the water, a filmy slime ringing his wrist. The water did indeed feel dead to him. Slowly, though, new water from the sea made its way to the pool. Kairuset's pounding increased as the beast drew closer, tearing through the numerous gates. Dust and chunks of stone flecked down from the timbered roof. "Clionet," Haru said. "It's me. It's Haru. I'm back. I'm here to help you." He took hold of one of her tentacles. The appendage felt cold in his hand.

"Haru, I'm sorry," said Elsifor.

"No, it's impossible," said Haru. "The water will save her. The water is alive!"

Without thinking he lowered himself into the pool, pulling himself along Clionet's tentacle as he searched for her face. Siva walked around the pool to light it. The thunderous noise of twisting metal and cracking rock grew ever louder.

"Haru, I don't think we can stay here," warned Elsifor. "That beast is going to bring the roof down on us."

Haru ignored him and swam down into the pool, searching the inky water until he found the sea-goddess' distended head, frozen halfway between formations, her single, saucer-sized eye still open. He looked into it, remembering how he had first encountered Clionet beneath the waves. A sob bubbled from his throat. She had been so beautiful that day. He couldn't believe what Liadin had done to her. He stared into her eye, knowing she was dead behind it. He stared until his lungs burned and the need for air was crushing. If gods could die, there was no hope at all.

He surfaced with a sob, desperate for air. Elsifor helped him to the ledge. He laid there, despairing. His hand dangled over the edge, feeling the cool, incoming water.

"We're too late," he choked.

"Haru?" Elsifor peered down into the pool. "Haru, look..."

Haru barely lifted his head. "What?"

"No," said Elsifor, disappointed. "Nothing. I thought I saw—"

A blast of water blew him backward. The torch blew out as the spray struck their faces, and suddenly in the pitch the once-dead body of Clionet trembled with light. She rose up from the pool, keening with rebirth, her luminous form rifling through colors, her head and tentacles raging like a storm. Haru and the others drew back as the newborn goddess remade herself, grabbing her own face with her suckers and pulling her missing eye out of the folds of her gelatinous body.

Even hideous, she was beautiful to Haru.

"Alive!" he rejoiced. "Clionet lives!"

Clionet struggled to speak. She slipped a weakened tentacle around Haru's waist and gently lifted him from the ledge. He reached for her, stroking her face. She shuddered at his touch.

"I'm sorry, Clionet," spoke Haru softly. "I wasn't here for you."

Clionet opened her mouth. Instead of words, water gushed from her lips. Haru laughed.

"You're alright now!" he told her. "We're going to get you free."

The eyes of the goddess flared as she gargled up a single word. *"Liadin!"*

"We'll get him, Clionet," Haru promised. "He's gone to war with the beast-ships. There are thousands of humans coming."

His words enraged the goddess. She lowered Haru back to the ledge, then turned against the gate holding her in the pool and wrapped her enormous tentacles around the bars.

"Wait!" shouted Haru. "You hear that?" He raised a finger at the sound of Kairuset's approach. "That's a dragon-whale, Clionet. She's broken down the gates. She'll get you out but you need to wait. You're not strong enough yet."

Kairuset's finned head appeared in the dark canal, just beyond Clionet's prison. She paused when she noticed the goddess, rising up in the luminous gloom. For a moment Clionet's grip on the bars slackened. Kairuset was almost too large to come closer, her body wedged in the canal. Like a dutiful dog, she waited for her goddess' command.

"Let her open it, Clionet," bid Haru. "Save your strength. We'll need you for the fight."

Clionet struggled to speak. "Away, child," she told Kairuset. "Summon your sisters and brothers."

Kairuset obeyed, twisting her enormous self around and disappearing back down the canal. Haru watched her go, dismayed.

"Clionet, don't," he pleaded. "Let us free you ourselves."

The healing waters of the sea brightened the goddess' body. "I am alive, little Tain," she declared, and with the tug of four tentacles she ripped down her cage, effortlessly tossing it aside. She turned and looked at Haru fiercely. "Come with me now, Haru. I am starved for vengeance!"

"We have a boat," agreed Haru. "We can follow you."

"A boat?" scoffed the goddess. "You will come with me and I will have us at the battle before the sun is down."

"How?" wondered Haru. "Without a boat?

"I will carry you," said Clionet. "Inside me."

She began to shift again, her body changing from something squid-like into something like a shark or a whale, a being with a huge, soft mouth and a lolling tongue that rolled out for Haru like a carpet.

"Oh..."

"Haru, don't," said Siva, taking his arm. "We'll go in the *Venture*. You can't possibly get inside...*that*."

Haru gently pulled away. "I trust her," he told Siva. "You and Elsifor stay here."

"Stay? No, Haru. We need to protect you!"

"Clionet will protect me now," said Haru. "There's nothing left for you to do. You got me home." He smiled at her. "Stay here. Protect the people now. If the J'horans get through, they're going to need you."

"What about the Venerants?" asked Elsifor.

"What about them? You've already terrified them by what you did to Jharik. Without Liadin they're done. And Liadin isn't coming back."

"Alright," agreed Siva. "But Haru..."

"I'll be safe," Haru assured her. "Don't worry."

He turned back toward Clionet, and with one deep breath walked into the magical mouth of the sea goddess.

Chapter Fifty-Four

ONE MORE MISSION

By the time Siva returned to the shore, Clionet and Haru were already gone. She waited near the dock with the sun on her face, hoping to catch a glimpse of the sea goddess or at least Kairuset, but the dragon-whale, like her immortal mistress, had disappeared. The crowds had swelled since their homecoming, and now the shore was filled with curious onlookers, all rejoicing in Haru's return. Men from the village played music on homemade shinogins, and the women and children danced and tossed flowers into the surf.

Their jubilation made Siva uneasy.

"Siva?" called Elsifor. "We should go now."

"Go? Where?"

"Back to the castle. We should prepare."

"For what?"

Elsifor looked puzzled by the question. "For the J'horans, if they come." He lowered his voice. "You saw all those ships in Agon. What if Haru can't stop them?"

It was the very question she'd been asking herself. "Look at these people. They have no idea what's coming."

"That's why we have to stop them from coming. Come on."

"I never knew, either," mused Siva. She frowned. "How come we knew so little, Elsifor? How come the humans got so strong without us knowing?"

"Because we weren't paying attention," said Elsifor darkly. "That's how they got strong. That's how Liadin killed Sh'an. It's our fault. Come..."

"You go," said Siva. "I'm going to Tojira."

"Tojira?" Elsifor came around to face her. "Why?"

"I'm no use here, Elsifor. I'm going to see Jaiakrin. Haru needs him. We all need him."

"He won't help us, Siva. He never leaves his island. He doesn't care."

"He cares about me," said Siva. "Maybe he'll help if I ask him. Maybe he'll fight. I'll take the *Venture* to get there."

Elsifor groaned at her plan. "You can't pilot a boat, remember?"

"You're right, I can't." Siva pointed to the old man named Pijigo, still on the dock, still looking overjoyed that Haru had returned. "But he can."

Chapter Fifty-Five

RECKONING

N uara watched the launch depart with the last of the wounded, heading toward Hamu-Hanza through the shark-ridden waters. The sun was almost down and he could see the beach from the deck of his beloved *Gonkin*, busy now with activity as the surgeons on-shore worked in torchlight, stitching wounds and sawing bones. The screams from the beach reached across the water. The smell of blood rankled the air. Nuara's little fleet had tossed countless limbs overboard during the retreat, chumming a path to the island for sharks. Around the Gonkin the remaining ships made repairs, swabbing gore from their decks, tending their shot-riddled sails, and pounding nails.

Forty-five beast-ships had gone to battle. Twenty-four had returned to Hamu-Hanza. The *Makeda*, the *Charr*, the *Krym*—all had been lost to J'horan long-guns. Even the *Hakar* was gone, cut in half by crossfire. And this time, Jollen hadn't survived. But the worst loss of all—the one that made Nuara call retreat—was Hor'roron. It had taken dozens of seabreakers to bring the god down. The bombardment had lasted nearly five hours. Nuara's ears still rang with the noise of it. He had watched Hor'roron's metal monster eat a score of seabreakers. Even in the final hour, he had thought the creation unsinkable.

Nuara wondered if he would ever see the god again.

Gods disappear, he told himself as he turned his gaze from the island. *Do they die?*

Like so many of his men, Nuara had taken injuries. Splinters of wood had been blasted into his right leg. A burn he was unsure would heal had singed the hair from the left side of his face. The pain was bearable, and the surgeons—too busy sawing off limbs—had no time to doctor his wounds. Exhausted, Nuara shuffled along the ship's waist, counting the shark fins and searching for Ama'aga. The war-god had disappeared, too. Wounded from countless cannon shots, he had submerged himself after the retreat, promising to return. But more than a day had passed since then, and Nuara wondered if Ama'aga had simply lied to save himself.

It was good that the J'horans hadn't pursued, thought Nuara. It was good that the Cryori had damaged them so badly, but Nuara knew they would soon return. They would come to Hamu-Hanza with all their remaining, considerable might, and Nuara would not—could not—call retreat again.

"Here," said Ariyo, sneaking up behind him. "Eat."

He had taken one of the round bricks of bread and stuffed some salt-meat into it. Seeing it reminded how Nuara how hungry he was. He hadn't eaten in over a day, and now that the blood had been mopped from the decks his appetite was returning. He took the offering and ripped off a huge chunk with his teeth.

"Thanks."

Ariyo remained, and together they looked out over their crippled fleet. The *Serusus* was missing a tusk. Aboard the *Dorsakai* men were swearing as they struggled to repair her windguns. The *Reikis* had fared better than most, and the *Skare* was already prepared to sail again.

"We should call in more ships," suggested Ariyo. He kept his voice low so the other crewmen wouldn't hear. "Fishing boats, keths, anything that will help remake the blockade. We should do it now while there's time."

Nuara swallowed a lump of food and tore off another. "Those seabreakers would go right through them."

"But we could slow them down. People want to fight, Nuara. You should let them."

"People don't know what they're talking about. Let them spend some time on the beach. Let them hack off a couple of legs and then see if they still want to fight."

"Nuara, I'm serious," said Ariyo gravely. "This far, no further—remember? We won't be able to hold them off. Not with this fleet."

"Ama'aga will come back. Hor'roron will come back."

"Hor'roron is gone," said Ariyo sharply. "Maybe Ama'aga too. Maybe—"

"Stop," said Nuara. "Ha! Just stop." He pointed toward an object cresting toward them. "There he is!" He turned and waved at his busy crew. "Ama'aga is back!"

The other ships saw it too, a mass of water breaking toward them. All at once the fleet picked up Nuara's cry. Nuara tossed his food over the rail and waved the war-god forward. Ama'aga looked different then he had before. There was no noise this time, no whirlpool to announce him. And he was quick, far quicker than Nuara remembered, jetting toward them like a shark or a giant...

Squid?

"That's Clionet!" cried Jai, the navigator. "*Clionet!*"

Nor was the sea goddess alone. Atop her rode a man, secured in a pair of her many arms, his face wet with spray and sunburned so badly Nuara hardly recognized him. But it was a day of miracles, and the revelation turned Nuara's legs to rubber.

"Holy mother," he whispered. "That's—"

"The Tain!"

Aboard the *Gonkin* and the *Skare*, the *Trall* and the *Rantuga*, the men of the beast-ships first fell silent—then roared to life. Who else could ride the goddess into battle? Nuara's heart thumped in his ears. Haru—his Tain—was *alive*.

"Liadin!"

He screamed the name so loud that the commotion brought the old priest hurrying across the deck. When he saw the approaching sea goddess—and the Tain he'd claimed was dead—Liadin's face turned to ash.

"Look!" Nuara shouted. "Look who's alive!"

Liadin didn't defend himself or go for his sukatai. He didn't even deny his treachery. He looked so weakened by Haru's reappearance that Nuara didn't even bother calling men to hold him. He drifted wraith-like toward the rail, his eyes filling with emotion as Clionet and Haru approached. A tear slipped down his cheek.

"Liadin, what happened?" Nuara pressed. "What did you do?"

The old priest said grimly, "I will answer for what I've done, but not to you."

"You used me!" Nuara spat. "You said he was dead!"

"Dead." Liadin's smile was demented. "He certainly should be."

The sea goddess slowed as she approached. Upon her back, Haru pointed out the *Gonkin*, directing her. Unable to wait, he pulled free of her arms and stood, balancing upon her broad back. Seawater dripped into his pain-filled face as he cried out.

"Liadin!"

Nuara turned to Liadin, trying to make sense of what was happening. The guilt in the old man's eyes bespoke his many crimes. "You?" Nuara let the bits and pieces knit together in his mind. "You killed Sh'an."

Liadin said nothing, refusing even to look at Nuara. He stood up tall, facing the young Tain as Clionet reached the ship. The sea goddess transformed instantly, her monstrous face changing into the visage of a raging woman. Swiftly she plucked Haru from her back, bringing him over the rail and spilling him onto the *Gonkin's* deck. As he got to his feet, she swiped Liadin up in her suckered arms. With murder in her eyes, she took hold of his arms and legs, splaying him out like a butterfly in mid-air.

"No!" cried Haru, rushing to the rail. "Clionet, don't!"

Merciless, Clionet pulled Liadin apart. His arms and legs popped off like a butchered chicken. His torso erupted, spilling out his entrails. Haru gave an agonized wail, reaching over the rail as Clionet dropped Liadin's quartered body into the sea. All at once, the waiting sharks went to work.

"Liadin..." Haru collapsed.

The sea goddess rose up over the *Gonkin*, her shadow blanketing the deck. Crewmen surrendered to their knees. Clionet bent low, her tentacles framing her like the hood of a cobra.

"Where is my son?" she hissed.

"Wounded," said Nuara. He helped Haru to his feet, then looked up at the sea goddess. "Great mother, Ama'aga battled with us. Hor'roron, too. Ama'aga has gone to heal himself and Hor'roron might be dead."

"We are gods, child," quarreled Clionet. "We do not die, no matter how our children plot to murder us. Where are the J'horans?"

"West of here. Maybe thirty miles."

"That fleet was enormous when I fled Agon," said Haru. "Is it still?"

"We bloodied them. We did," said Nuara. "Mostly Ama'aga and Hor'roron. But there's so many of them. And there are thousands of men aboard. We need to stop them. *Here.* Tain Haru, you can arrest or hang me. Do anything you want to me when this is over, but don't relieve me. Let me fight."

"Oh, you're going to fight, Nuara," Haru assured. "You're going to prove you're loyal to *me*."

"Tain Haru, I swear—I thought you were dead!"

"And me?" rumbled Clionet. "Was I dead to you? Or were you content to entomb me forever?"

"You?" Nuara was fearless suddenly. "I have had my fill of you, goddess. You and your whole cruel family." He went to the rail and shouted, "You hear that, Ama'aga? Deceiver!" He scratched at his tattoo until it was bloody. "I'm not your sukano!"

"Sukano," sneered Clionet. "You hear, Haru? Nuara has been adopted!"

Haru just shook his head. "I loved Liadin, Clionet. Why didn't you let me speak to him? You just ripped him away..."

"Tears now?" jeered Clionet. "For the man who killed your father?"

"He was precious to me," said Haru. He seemed lost, unspeakably alone. "I loved him. I did."

"Oh, Tain or child!" thundered Clionet. "Decide!"

Her threat would have withered other men. Young Haru simply ignored it. "He was my friend, Clionet. No matter what he did. Look around! Men are dead. And you're offended by weeping?"

Clionet's flesh flushed scarlet. "Damn your sweetness. Let us make the humans wail!"

"We can't," said Nuara. "We're not ready to fight. Ama'aga—"

"You have me now," spoke the goddess. "And I am ten times the nature of my offspring."

"Goddess, look at my fleet! We're decimated! We're too few!"

"No, we're not," said Haru wearily.

"Show him," ordered Clionet.

With Nuara and the crew of the *Gonkin* looking on, the young Tain quieted himself and looked out over the waters of Hamu-Han-za. He closed his eyes, raised his hands, and spoke some ancient, powerful nonsense. One by one the shenenra appeared, breaking the waves, their finned backs glistening, burning geysers spouting from their blowholes. Twenty or more of the monsters, all of them enormous, surrounded the fleet. Like it had been in the old days, thought Nuara. Like it had been in his father's days.

"Gather your courage, Nuara," Clionet commanded. "Now you will see what a goddess can do."

Chapter Fifty-Six

SCARS

A ma'aga slept.

Beneath the water, beneath the mud, he had burrowed himself deep in a kelp forest, far off the coast of Hamu-Hanza where the sharks would not disturb him and the sunlight couldn't reach. The human weapons had battered his armor, even cracking it in places, and the sound of their weapons haunted his dreams. They had harmed him, something Ama'aga thought impossible, and they had taken away his beloved heralds, slaughtering them in iron and fire.

Ama'aga grieved.

He was a war-god and would rise again, and so he slumbered in the curative mud, hiding from the world, and when after many hours he finally awakened, he knew what had happened. Inhaling, he tasted it on his tongue—the unmistakable taint of his mother.

Ama'aga lay frozen in the mud, stretching out his senses and knowing she was there. A hot madness seized him. She had gone to Hamu-Hanza and was powerful again. Enraged, he burst from the sea bottom, roaring in the gigantic kelp, his cry scattering the fish and bubbling up like a typhoon. He would never get another chance to trick or trap her. But still, he could hurt her.

Ignoring his pain and scars, the second son of Clionet trudged out of the undersea jungle and headed toward Tojira.

Chapter Fifty-Seven

BROTHERS

The *Venture* reached Tojira just after sundown, approaching from the south just as Siva had done months before, when the grief over Sh'an's death had lured her to the holy island. The last light of the day had turned the beach a welcoming pink, and nothing at all seemed to have changed about the place, as if nothing ever could. The sounds of insects and monkeys called to her across the water. A shy breeze tickled the palms trees. Siva melted at the sight of it. Tojira felt like home to her; Jaiakrin, her father.

"This is as close as we can take you, Siva," said Pijigo as he let the boat drift sideways in the tide. "You'll have to swim it from here."

"I can manage," Siva assured. They were just over two hundred feet from the shore and Siva knew she could swim it easily.

Pijigo and his son Hasa had been eager to help her reach Tojira—as long as they didn't have to step upon the island themselves. It was a fair bargain and Siva appreciated their risk. Most fishermen never got so close to Jaiakrin's forbidden home. Siva stepped to the edge of the boat. Before sailing home with Haru, she couldn't recognize starboard from port. Now she felt like a seasoned hand. She climbed onto the gunnel, holding on to a sail line, and looked back at her 'crew.'

"Thank you, Pijigo. Thank you, Hasa."

Pijigo's rheumy eyes twinkled. "One day I'll tell my grandchildren how I helped save Nesenor," he said, "if *this one* ever manages to father a child."

Hasa, who was a good deal older than Siva, took the jibe well. "If I do ever have one, I'll make sure he becomes a farmer—so he won't have to spend his days on a boat with *you*."

"Set the sail, boy," said Pijigo. "I want to get out of here before Jaiakrin puts us in his soup bowl."

"Go," urged Siva. "I'll be alright."

Weaponless, without even a knife, Siva dove barefoot off the *Venture* into the warm ocean. Like a hunting gull she sliced deep into the water, the sound of the world falling away behind her. She held her breath as long as she could, her long strokes propelling her quickly, and when she surfaced again the *Venture* was sailing away. Siva bobbed in the waves, watching the fishermen disappear in the dusk. For the first time in weeks, she was truly...

"Alone."

She reveled in the solitude, sucking a mouthful of seawater into her cheeks and spouting it out like a child. Just for now—just for a moment—she wanted to forget about the war and death and lost friends.

"Peace," she said, closing her eyes. The way it had been before.

She twisted to face the shore but swam no closer. She was not afraid of Jaiakrin, only that he might refuse her request. Or, he might try to keep her with him, safe and cared for in his paradise. Siva made up her mind to convince him, but as she started toward the beach an undertow tugged her, gently at first, then suddenly violent. Siva struggled to stay above water as the current swirled around her. When something grabbed her legs, she screamed.

"Pijigo!"

Her cried died in the air. Already the *Venture* was too far to hear her. Panicked, she thought a shark had seized her, but the pain was slight and she was being lifted suddenly, up in the grip of giant fingers. As the grim face emerged from the depths, she sputtered his name.

"Ama'aga!"

Together they came out of the water, the war-god dripping seaweed, Siva gripped in his mighty hand. She didn't struggle or scream; she didn't cry out for Jaiakrin. She looked straight into her captor's eyes, refusing to fear him. Ama'aga grinned, inspecting her closer, then laughed with recognition.

"You are my brother's sukano! You must be!"

"Let go of me," Siva demanded. "Or I will call your brother and he will make a meal of you."

"Oh, I am here to have that battle, little one," Ama'aga assured her. "And now I have something precious to entice him."

His grip slackened a little around her waist. Siva took a much-needed breath. "How do you know me?" she asked. "You've never even seen me!"

"You are known to me, girl," said Ama'aga. He leaned all the way back, floating in the water and placing Siva on his armored belly. Siva balanced on him, incensed at being his plaything. "The priest told me about you. You are infamous. You were Sh'an's lover."

"Liadin is a pig and a traitor!"

"And he is in the belly of sharks now."

"Liadin's dead?" The news startled Siva. "How do you know this? What are you even doing here?" She goaded Ama'aga with a grin. "Did your mother defeat you already?"

"You freed her," Ama'aga surmised. "You and that seal-pup, Haru." He let the tide wash over his torso and soak Siva. "That boy is not his father's son. His father was a weakling."

"He was not!" said Siva hotly. She stumbled up toward his breast. "Sh'an was brave and peaceful and had enough sense to shun you, Ama'aga."

"He turned his back on the old ways. Cryori are men of war. Your lover was an aberration."

"You haven't answered my question," said Siva. "Why are you here?"

"To harm my mother," replied the god.

"How? By harming your brother? Because she loves him more than you? Yes, you're not the only one who knows stories, Ama'aga! You're jealous and you're petty and you're nothing like Jaiakrin! Jaiakrin will crush you."

Ama'aga's smile bemused her. "I have already lost what I came back to get," he said.

"Why?" Siva squatted down on his rolling body. "Don't you think we can win?"

"Against the humans? That battle is already won. When Clionet reaches them, the humans will learn terror. You call her 'mother.' You adore her because you haven't seen her cruelty. I pity the humans for what's to befall them. But..." Ama'aga reached out and took her again in his hand. "I have come for my own battle."

"Ama'aga, don't!" hissed Siva. "Leave here!"

The big god righted himself and started trudging toward shore. "With you I can be assured he will come," he said. "Hold your insults and do not offend me, and you will be unharmed."

"I'm not afraid of you!"

Amazingly, he placed her atop his shoulder. "Hold on."

"I can make it on my own. I don't need your help—murderer!"

"Your tongue wags too much for me. Still it or I will pull it out."

Siva hunkered down in his armor. "I can't wait to see Jaiakrin beat you."

To this the war-god said nothing. He pushed through the tide, growing ever larger as they reached the dusky shore. Ama'aga lowered himself to the beach, letting Siva jump off him into the sand. She wrung the water from her long hair and looked up at him.

"Call him," ordered Ama'aga.

"He already knows I'm here. He always knows."

Not satisfied, Ama'aga put his hands to his mouth and bellowed. "Come out, brother! I have your she-pet! Come before I get hungry and devour her!"

"Beast," snorted Siva.

"Do not worry," scoffed Ama'aga. "A boney thing like you would be like eating sticks." He put his hands up again to shout, but Siva stopped him.

"Save your breath," she said. "I told you—he already knows I'm here."

Ama'aga frowned, then sat down on the shore. He looked peculiar with the waves rushing over his legs. The sand shifted around him.

"You should go," said Siva. "You've lost already. You told me so. This is Jaiakrin's island. You'll never beat him here. You should have stayed out in the water." Puzzled, she took a step closer. "Why didn't you? Why didn't you stay out in the water where you're stronger?"

"You talk too much."

"Do you want Jaiakrin to beat you?" pressed Siva. Suddenly it made sense. "You do! Why? For penance?"

"Stop," warned Ama'aga.

"Ama'aga, go," bid Siva. "I have no wish to see this!"

"Do not plead for me when my brother gets here," said Ama'aga. "If you do, I will harm you. I will do what it takes to make him battle me."

"Do what it takes? You won't kill me. I know you won't."

"You irritate me."

"You're so full of honor. All your hurt feelings—we all had to pay for them!"

Ama'aga started to rise. "Beware me, girl!"

Siva stood her ground. "No, Ama'aga, I will not! I am tired of being afraid! Go back. Go back to wherever you were hiding before all this happened. Go before Jaiakrin discovers you."

Ama'aga opened his mouth to answer, stopping when an odd light touched his face. He looked past Siva toward the mangroves, his expression hardening like cement. "Girl...he has already discovered me."

Jaiakrin emerged from the trees, tall and golden, his entire body raging with flames. The sand burned at the touch of his feet, incinerating it and leaving a trail of glass behind him. He moved quickly, his face terrible, his fists aglow with magic, his hair an inferno. At eight feet tall, he was barely a third the size of his brother, yet the weight of him made the surf retreat and the air around him quaver.

"Siva!" he thundered. "Stand clear."

Siva ran toward him. "Jaiakrin, don't! He can't beat you! He knows he can't! He wants you to kill him!"

"Then he shall have his wish!"

Ama'aga balled his spiked hands into fists. "Our mother lives, brother. She is free again."

"And so you have come to harm me. To harm *her*!"

"No!" screamed Siva. "Listen to me!"

Furious, Jaiakrin waved her away. "Get to safe ground! Get to the hills!"

"The hills? What?"

Ama'aga stepped closer. "Where is Paiax? She should see what is about to happen."

"No one should witness what's about to happen to you, brother. No one should see something so bleak."

"Then let her see what's left of us!"

"Siva, I cannot keep you safe here," warned Jaiakrin. The light around him intensified, growing unbearably bright. "Go to safety. Go far!"

His heat burned Siva's flesh. Unable to stand it, she peddled back and looked at Ama'aga. The war-god stood apart from his sea, vulnerable but unafraid. Resentment darkened his face. Caught between them, Siva gave a frustrated cry, cursing them both as she dashed for the forest. The ground shook beneath her as the gods rushed to battle. Siva didn't look back. She hurried desperately, the noise of their clash sweeping up the beach. A flash exploded behind her, blowing her off her feet.

The world turned orange. Blinded, Siva closed her eyes and ran.

Chapter Fifty-Eight

DRIFTING

Far out at sea, much farther than he could have ever survived on his own, Haru laid back on Clionet and studied the moon. He rested in her bosom, safe from the water, her enormous body reclining in the calm sea and her hair splayed out on the waves. The tide undulated beneath her, rocking them, making Haru's eyelids heavy. It had been days since he'd rested properly. Dawn was only hours away. They had sailed through the night, following the *Gonkin* to the place where the White Fleet had anchored to lick its wounds, stopping just within sight of them. The dragon-whales circled Nuara's remaining beast-ships, protecting them, eager for the coming brawl. But Clionet had taken Haru far from it all, sharing him with no one as she drifted in the moonlight.

"Clionet?"

"Yes, Haru?"

"Why are we waiting until the morning to attack? Why don't we do it now?"

"We wait until the morning so they can see me. I want them to see me, Haru."

Her answer was serene, and he was half asleep between her luminous breasts. He wondered if this what it had been like for his father. Was this the lovemaking Clionet had talked about?

"Clionet?"

"Yes?"

"Why didn't you tell me about Siva and my father? You must have known about them."

"I knew," replied the goddess. "What would it have changed if I had told you? It would have only made you suffer."

"But they were lovers. Does that upset you?"

"No."

Haru believed her. He had learned to tell when she was angry or jealous. She seemed too at peace to be either tonight. He should have been cold in the night air, his hair and clothing damp with seawater, but he was not. Tucked upon Clionet, he was warm. And safe. Like a baby.

"Clionet?"

"Yes, Haru?"

"What will you do now with Ama'aga?"

"I will find him when we are done."

"And Jyx? Will you find him too? And Skorthoros? Will you punish them?"

"Do you want them punished?"

"Jyx killed my friend."

"Valivan killed himself. That's what you told me."

"Because of Jyx. Because of his cruelty."

"I did not know how cruel he had been."

Haru considered her answer and the bigness of the moon. "In J'hora they say that Taan knows everything."

"I am not that kind of god."

"In J'hora they say that you and the others are demons."

Clionet took a moment, then replied, "Tomorrow, I will give them reason to say that about me."

"Clionet?"

"Yes?"

"What are you?"

"I am...me."

Haru decided that was enough. He closed his eyes, certain that she would protect him, and fell quickly to sleep.

Chapter Fifty-Nine

LEVIATHAN

The reports had reached Larius even before the sun came up. His fleet had regrouped twenty miles from the outer chain, patrolling rather than following the damaged Cryori. The armada had taken heavy losses—heavier by far than Larius ever intended—but they had managed to send the beast-ships retreating. The man-giant had gone with them. They had even sunk the metal monster. Larius supposed those victories would rally his captains, but they had not. The loss of the *Perilous* and the *Forbearance* and so many other seabreakers had crushed morale, and now the strange sight through his spyglass had the fleet rattled.

For three days Larius had gotten almost no sleep at all. His eyesight was blurry as he looked through his spyglass, but there was no doubt about what he was seeing.

Dragon-whales.

They surrounded the little Cryori fleet, breaking the water with their finned backs, threatening with their spouts of fire. Impossible to know just how many of the creatures had come, Larius counted at least ten of them. Like ants, he supposed that meant there were many more unseen. At the front of the Cryori line rode their flagship, the huge, leopard-like ship that had sunk the *Strangler*. A single, enormous dragon-whale swam beside it like a sworn protector. Larius held his spyglass steady, blinking to clear his vision. The appearance of the dragon-whales meant the Tain had made it home.

"Damn you, Whistler..."

"Sir?"

Larius didn't lower the glass to address his First. "Mmm?"

"Orders, Sir?"

Gaige wasn't a nervous man. He'd been as hard as steel through the battle so far, but now his voice was brittle. Worse, Larius didn't know how to answer him. It should have been easily done. He had a fleet five times larger than his enemy. He had long-guns, powder, and an army ready to invade. All he needed was a beach-head. Just one little island to start.

"Wait," said Larius.

"Wait, Sir?"

"Wait!"

There was something else in the water as well, something as yet unseen but made the tides move with a weird rolling. Larius focused on the spot, looking for a hint of the man-god's return. The thing seemed bigger than him, though, and far too big to simply be a dragon-whale.

"Why don't they attack?" wondered Gaige out loud.

The *Witch Breaker* rolled on the tide, her crew oddly hushed. The signalmen waited for the Sea Master's word. For the first time since the conflict began, Larius considered retreating, but the notion fled quickly. He would die here or he could die on the gallows—Malon would see to that.

Their fleets facing off like in a J'horan war-text, Larius gave the order to attack.

Haru saw the enemy signal flags wave and knew they wouldn't surrender. He hadn't really expected them to—they still had many more ships than his own fleet—but watching the seabreakers break formation made his breakfast sour in his stomach. Captain Nuara saw the signals too. Instantly he called out to his crew, bringing the Gonkin straight toward the J'horan fleet. Wind snapped the sails and the cat's big claws extended from her bows. Around her, her sister ships fanned out for hunting. The shenenra accompanied them, flanking them like dolphins, their heads rising from the water to the ancient call of battle.

Out of place aboard Nuara's ship, Haru went to the rail and looked down at Kairuset. The big shenenra felt the link between them, answering with a spout of steam. Haru had summoned the dragon-whales and set them loose like wild dogs. But not Kairuset. Kairuset would stay and obey. Like Clionet, she would protect him.

Clionet had rested and fed. She had filled her belly with plankton and krill. She had let the undersea tides heal and strengthen her, and she had become again that thing she had been centuries past, when the Tains of Nesenor tossed humans into the sea for her.

She was enormous now, blue-whale big, with the stingers of a jelly and a white shark's appetite. The sea roiled around her, stirred by her rage, rising up in a tide toward her enemies. She rode the current, collecting it, tossing it skyward, bursting up from the depths to reveal herself. Through her crocodile eyes she saw a ship ahead. The men aboard cried out when they saw her.

The first to die, thought Clionet.

Craw had captained the *Mercy of Taan* for over two years. He counted them the best days of his life. And when he saw the wave cresting toward his ship, he knew that life was over.

Inside the wave was something he had never seen before, not in all his days at sea. It wasn't a dragon-whale as he feared. It wasn't a normal whale either, and far too large to be a shark. It was, as seamen put it, a leviathan, with a mouth as big as the *Mercy's* prow and a mass of squirming arms with hooks in their suckers. It appeared through the foam and spray of the storm, darkening the blue sky as it broke toward the ship, stretching out its arms to devour her.

Captain Craw heard the screams of his men and remembered the young Tain he'd delivered to J'hora. He'd never expected the boy to survive, yet somehow he had, and he wondered why humans had forgotten how ruthless Cryori could be, and why they ever thought they could conquer their island. Craw held his breath as the beast and its storm fell upon his ship. The wave hit first, washing him from the deck. Then came the monster, like a mountain from the sky, breaking the *Mercy* apart even as he slid across it. A blue arm seized him, its suckers puncturing his flesh, their hooks gutting him. Still alive, he prayed for drowning as the leviathan's mouth opened wide.

Haru held tight as the *Gonkin* rode Clionet's wave. In less than a minute she had sunk a J'horan ship, cracking it in half and sending the pieces scattering over the waves. The long-guns opened fire from the line, sending chain-shot toward the beast-ships as the dragon-whales swam in, answering with fire of their own. Except for Kairuset, the *Gonkin* was suddenly alone, peeling off from the rest of the beast-ships as each one chose a target. Nuara stood firm on the forecastle, not even ducking as the shots whistled past him. Clionet's tide had rolled the seabreakers, making their weapons fire far overhead.

The *Gonkin* raced toward its prey. Nuara called the warning. Kairuset submerged, sprinting ahead of the ship and ramming the seabreaker, spinning it sideways. A blast from her blow-hole incinerated the stern. Fighting men along the deck held on tight, shooting crossbows into the water and a three-tipped harpoon at the *Gonkin*. The weapon slammed the beast-ship's hull, sticking into it like a fork as the leopard's claws rammed the bow.

Hopeless.

That was the word that kept running through Larius mind.

It had taken the monster half of an hour to sink a dozen of his seabreakers. The dragon-whales had taken out at least that many more. The *Witch Breaker* herself had managed to evade the beasts so far, but slowly the dragon-whales were working their way through the battle line, and Larius knew he could not avoid them forever. His ears bled from the constant concussion of guns. The ocean rolled from the Leviathan's attack, making him seasick and his quarter-deck slick with vomit. He had dropped and broken his spyglass, holding tight to the shrouds as he unsurely surveyed the battle. Five of his ships had already retreated. Without orders, they had swung to the west to abandon the fight. Larius' men looked at him hopefully, desperate for the word.

Through the smoke and steam and fire, Larius saw the Cryori flagship heading toward his own. The biggest damn dragon-whale he'd ever seen swam before them.

"Gaige..."

"Sir!"

"Come about and strike the colors."

"Retreat?"

"Yes!"

"Thank Taan, Sir!"

Haru was on the forecastle with Nuara when he saw the flag go down. He knew what it meant even before Nuara gave the cry.

"Surrender!" shouted the captain joyously. "Ariyo, bring us about!" He turned to Haru and clapped his shoulder. "Call off your dragon-whale! The flagship's struck her colors!"

One by one the bronze guns halted. The *Gonkin* heeled hard to port, a signal to the other ships to stand down. Confused, Haru ran to the rail to find Kairuset. The link came easily, matching up their minds. Kairuset slowed and turned away from her attack, understanding Haru's thoughts.

You did it! Haru told her. *You're beautiful, Kairuset!*

Her answer lumbered back to him. He could feel her discontentment, her unsatisfied urge for blood. Yet she obeyed, like her siblings, turning back to circle the *Gonkin*. Haru slumped over the rail. His head pounded with relief, but the scars of what he'd seen remained. Behind him the crew was cheering Nuara's name. When he heard his own name cheered, Haru waved them away.

"Stop," he told them. "It's not me!"

But no one listened. They rejoiced in their victory, thanking him and holding up his arms as they danced him across the deck and Nuara smiled and looked unspeakably relieved. But when a shadow rose up over them all, no one dared to laugh.

"No!"

Like a thunderclap came the voice, shaking the *Gonkin's* timbers. Haru spun to see Clionet, her face furious as she rose up over the ship. Bits of flesh clung to her hooks. The ocean sloshed up behind her. The crewmen dashed backward as she loomed ever higher. Unafraid, Haru stepped toward her.

"Why do you rage?" he asked. "We've won!"

"*Won?*" Clionet screamed the word back at him. "They're escaping!"

"They're retreating!"

"No," hissed the goddess. She lowered her face toward Haru. "Call back my shenenra! I cannot sink them all by myself!"

Her ire stunned Haru. "Clionet, no! You'll sink no more ships today! It's done!"

"It is not done!"

Her arm whipped out and seized Haru, swiping him off the deck. The blow crushed the air from his lungs. Nuara rushed forward.

"Haru!"

Clionet lifted Haru into the air. The suckers in her arm pulled at his clothing and flesh. But the hooks never came, and gradually her gripped slackened.

"Clionet..."

The goddess shut her eyes. "They did this to me. You see? They've maddened me."

"You're alright, Clionet," said Haru gently. "And I'm alright. Nesenor is saved."

Clionet floated beside the *Gonkin*, holding Haru aloft. He could see the rage inside her ebbing. The sea around her calmed, and she began to tremble.

"We're not done yet," she said. "There's one more thing."

Chapter Sixty

ON THE BEACH

Like a frightened child Siva hid out in a cave past the mangroves, listening to the furious thunder of battle and watching Jaiakrin's fire light the night sky. She had run as hard and as fast as she could from the beach, terrified by the clashing gods, at last finding refuge in a dark mountain fissure where the rage of her patron shook the rocky roof and the war-god's cries made her bones vibrate. She did not sleep at all that night, for no living thing could possibly have slept through such a cataclysm, and when the sun came up that morning the warring continued, and she did not dare to peek outside the cave to see what was happening.

Finally, an hour after sunrise, the calamitous noise ceased. All was silent. No birds made their morning songs. Not even an insect buzzed. Siva chanced a look outside and saw the tops of trees sheered away. Burnt leaves floated in the grotto. She pulled herself out of the narrow cavern, filthy with dust and spider webs and looked up at the clear sky, afraid of a stray lightning bolt or fireball, but nothing came.

"Jaiakrin."

She said his name but got no reply, not even that peculiar tremble she felt when he was near. She pulled the brambles from her hair, then hesitantly started back toward the beach. Each step took her closer to the battlefield, the evidence of the clash growing more apparent as she neared. Toppled trees blocked her way. Her feet crunched over incinerated branches. A blast had turned the hillside to rubble and flattened the mangroves, revealing the beach and the ocean beyond. Dunes of glass stood where sand had been. And there sat Jaiakrin upon the burnt husk of a fallen tree, slumped with exhaustion. The light had gone from his bronze body. Only the tiniest drips of flame fell from his fingers, and the torch of his hair had been extinguished. He wore no shirt now, no golden belt or pearly rings. Stripped to the waist, his back turned toward Siva, he brooded over the broken figure of his brother.

On the scarred beach lay Ama'aga. Just feet from the healing surf. His shattered armor clung in pieces to his battered body. Welts and burns studded his skin. His limbs lay unnaturally on the melted sand, impossibly bent, and the helmet had been blasted half off his head, revealing a charred and hairless scalp. The sight of him drew Siva running toward the beach.

"Get him into the water!" she cried.

Jaiakrin turned his sad face toward her. Seeing her safe brightened him, but only a bit.

"The water!" Siva insisted. "It will heal him!" She ran past her patron and skidded to her knees before Ama'aga. "Is he alive?"

"He lives," replied Jaiakrin.

Siva could barely believe what Jaiakrin—gentle, kind Jaiakrin—had done to his brother. Ama'aga's face was a pulpy mess, his eyes swollen to slits and his lips bruised and big like melons. Yet somehow, he was indeed alive, and when he saw Siva he tried to speak.

"Get to the water," Siva told him. "Crawl. Try!"

Ama'aga shook his head, unable or unwilling to comply.

"Damn you, you'll die here!" railed Siva. "Jaiakrin, help him, please!"

Jaiakrin didn't even rise from his tree stump. "It's his wish," he said. His voice was grim. His power, depleted. "He waits."

"Waits? For what?"

"For our mother to come."

Siva dreaded Clionet's arrival. "What will happen when she gets here? What will she do to him?"

"Whatever she wishes," replied Jaiakrin. He looked at her strangely. "Why do you care for him, daughter? He plotted with Liadin. They killed your lover."

Siva couldn't answer. She glanced around at the devastated surroundings. Nothing made sense to her. She remained on her knees
beside Ama'aga, perched between him and his hated brother, and
waited for their mother to arrive.

Inside Clionet, the world was quiet and safe. The soothing noise of
the rushing ocean penetrated her womb-like mouth. The beat of an
unseen heart thumped through her blue flesh. Her luminescence
gave Haru light enough to see, and he was not afraid inside her. He
knew that if cried out or panicked, even for an instant, she would
surface and free him. She was, he realized, beyond his understanding. Certainly he should have been dead inside her, digested or
suffocated our ground to dust by her. She was—like so many things
he'd seen so far—an interminable mystery.

Time felt meaningless inside the goddess. Her glowing flesh
calmed Haru, linking him to her so that his mind touched something
of her vastness. Though his body was trapped, he floated inside her,
half-asleep yet wildly alert, and when at last she broke the surface
and opened her mouth to free him, Haru cried out. The sunlight and
wind assaulted him. The noise of the world flooded his senses. Her
tongue lolled out, birthing him onto the sand.

"Haru!"

The voice was Siva's—he knew it before his eyes fluttered
opened. He lifted himself onto his palms as Siva raced toward him.
The tide clawed at his hands and knees. Up on the beach lay the
giant form of Ama'aga. Near him, a golden, half-naked man got to
his feet.

"Jaiakrin..."

Siva hurried to him, helping Haru up. "You're alive! What happened?"

Haru let Siva support him as he trudged up the beach. Once
again Clionet transformed herself. No longer was she the leviathan
or the strange conveyance that had taken him across the sea. She
was beautiful again, like the first day he saw her, womanly and

smaller, her hair still flowing as though it was beneath the waves. Her tentacles propelled her over the sand, and when she came to Ama'aga her face glistened with sadness. Haru held on to Siva and went no further.

Clionet bent low over her fallen son, touching him with her hands and tentacles and looking into his battered eyes. Ama'aga raised his head painfully off the sand. Gently his mother peeled off the shattered half of his helmet.

"What happened?" whispered Haru. The beach was scorched, melted in spots, the trees flattened. "They fought?"

Siva nodded silently. Jaiakrin stood apart from his mother and brother, looking as confused as Haru.

"He came to harm me," said Jaiakrin. "As he tried to harm you, mother."

Clionet seemed shaken. "Where is Paiax? Where is Ayorih?"

"Gone," replied Jaiakrin. "They fled when Ama'aga came. Ama'aga came to fight, Mother. He threatened Siva. He wanted this!"

"And you left him here, in the sun. Ten feet away from the water." Clionet brushed away the sand crusting Ama'aga's face. "Just as you left me trapped in Jinja."

Jaiakrin bridled at her accusation. "I stayed here for peace," he said. "To protect Paiax and the others! Mother, you know what Ama'aga did! You saw! If I had fought him anywhere but Tojira he would have beaten me. That would be me lying there now."

"We are family! We are so few! You knew Ama'aga's nature." Clionet's pain colored her whole body. "And now I know your nature."

"Mother!"

Siva let go of Haru. "Holy Clionet, no! Jaiakrin was protecting me!"

"You?" Clionet reared up. "You are a mortal! You are nothing!"

Haru hurried between them. "Clionet, stop! Leave it be. Please..." He clasped his hands together as if in prayer. "Leave it be."

The pain of her captivity blazed in Clionet's giant eyes. Had she been a person, Haru was sure she would be weeping. "I am changed," she groaned. "I will never forget. I will live forever with this!"

Haru reached out and touched her grieving face. "You are Clionet," he said. "You are my goddess. My beloved."

His words softened her. She turned back to Jaiakrin and said, "In my prison I called to you. I begged like a human for you to come to me, always in secret so that wretched Liadin would never hear me. But you never came, Jaiakrin. You were my favorite. I wasted my love on you."

"I had my island to defend," said Jaiakrin. "My brothers and sister..."

"Stay on your island. Do not call upon me or send me gifts." Clionet's voice was colder than Haru had ever heard it. "Forget me—as you forgot me when I needed you."

"No." Jaiakrin fell to his knees. "Mother, please!"

Clionet wrapped her powerful tentacles around Ama'aga. Though he was a giant, she lifted him from the sand. She said nothing more to Haru. Without even a glance she returned to the sea, taking her battered son with her into the healing waters, disappearing in a froth of bubbles.

Chapter Sixty-One

THE ORDINARY DAY

S iva remained on Tojira for three weeks, then finally returned
to Jinja. She explained to Haru how Jaiakrin had needed her,
and how broken he was by the rejection of his mother. Still, she had
been unable to stay away from Jinja, and hugged Haru when she saw
him and renewed her vow to protect him.

Haru had been busy in her absence. Despite Elsifor's objections
he reinstated most of the Venerants, knowing that the people needed priests even more than they needed gods. He had gone to Valivan's mother and given his condolences, telling her that her son
was brave and that he had saved him. Valivan was the best of the
Chorus, he told her; he doubted he would ever find another friend
so fine. In return, Valivan's mother gave Haru a trinket her son had
cherished—a tiny toy boat that her dead husband had once carved
for her now-dead son.

Haru pocketed the boat, and later that night went to Shadur's
house in the keep. The place was filthier than ever, but the mystic's
possessions had been left undisturbed. No one else would want
the house until it was made more livable, a task Haru put on his
ever-growing list. Before he left, he plucked the nub of a candle
from its holder, and this he pocketed too.

Finally, on the afternoon of Siva's arrival, Haru took her and Elsifor to Ama'aga's abandoned temple, the same place he had played
with Val as a boy—the place he had met Liadin and called his first
dragon-whale. They roamed the grounds for an hour, reminiscing
about their dead friends and the horrible adventure they'd endured,

and laid on their backs on the broken slabs of marble and stared up at the sky and wept.

"I remember," said Haru, "leaving Valivan here one day. We told him we were hiding but we just left him here."

"Oh, I remember that too," said Siva. She laid with the sun on her face and her eyes closed and a look of perfect solace.

"You were awful, both of you," said Elsifor. "I don't know why Val cared so much for either of you."

"You didn't know us then," said Haru. "We weren't always mean to each other."

"Elsifor's right," chortled Siva. "We were awful!"

"Now Shadur, he was awful!" crowed Elsifor.

They all agreed and laughed and then fell sad again.

"Brave," sighed Haru. "Both of them."

Siva nodded and echoed his thoughts. "They were."

"Do you think they'll come back?" Elsifor asked.

Haru rolled onto his side. "Who?"

"The J'horans. Maybe Clionet was right. Maybe you shouldn't have let them go."

"Maybe," said Haru. The question made him restless. He got up and stretched and looked toward the water. "Come with me."

Siva and Elsifor rose from the ruins and followed Haru to the edge of the cliff overlooking the ocean. The broken statue of Ama'aga shadowed them, but there were no gods or shenenra in the water today, making them feel wonderfully plain.

"Here," said Haru as he dug into his pockets. "These are for you." He pulled out the trinkets he had gotten from their dead friends' homes. "This was Val's," he said, handing the toy boat to Elsifor. "His mother gave it to me." Then he placed the candle stub in Siva's hand. "And this was in Shadur's house. This was one of the candles he lit that night he summoned Skorthoros."

Siva closed her fist around the candle. "We should talk about Skorthoros, Haru. We haven't yet but we need to."

"Jyx too," said Elsifor. "They're going to trouble us."

"They might," Haru admitted. "But I don't want to talk about them now. I just want to remember Val and Shadur." He looked out over the sea. "When my mother died my father came up here and tossed his betrothal ring into the ocean. That's how he honored her."

Siva and Elsifor understood at once.

"Should I say something?" asked Elsifor.

Haru shrugged. "I think what we're feeling matters more."

Elsifor agreed, then leaned back and tossed the tiny boat far off the cliff. They watched it sail through the air and disappear in the waves. When it was gone, Siva threw the candle stub. For a long moment they stood silent on the cliff-edge, listening to the roar and tumult and tasting the ocean on their lips.

"You'll need a proper Chorus," said Elsifor finally. "Especially if the J'horans come back. You'll need protection, Haru."

Haru grinned. "Why? I have you two."

"A Chorus is always four," Siva added.

"Two more?" mused Haru. "That should be easy. The gods are always meddling." He sat down near the edge of the cliff, flanked and protected by his friends. "I'll start looking," he promised. "Soon."

THE END

WANT TO READ MORE?

Check out these other epic titles by John Marco:

Tyrants and Kings
The Jackal of Nar
The Grand Design
The Saints of the Sword

The Bronze Knight series
The Eyes of God
The Devil's Armor
The Sword of Angels
The Forever Knight

The Skylords
Starfinder

Discover more at John Marco's Amazon author page or visit him on the web at johnmarco.com.

Printed in Great Britain
by Amazon

37853952R10260